## TRAIN TO NOWHERE

Briggs sat down. Hollywood, his life there, his work—such as it was—was over. There'd be no going back after this. He'd either do what was asked of him—and he knew damned well it'd only be a beginning—or he'd have to go on the run again.

"It begins with the Russian dissident. Mikhail Vladimir Popov," Sir Roger started, and Briggs sat back, his drink in hand.

Popov had been arrested a few days earlier, and their sources in Moscow confirmed that he had been sentenced to the Yedanov Rehabilitation Center outside Moscow. Those who were sent to the YRC were brought by train, which any Russian who knew about it was terrified by. They called it the *train to nowhere,* because once on the train, you were literally nowhere . . . gone, vanished, disappeared.

"No one has ever escaped?" Briggs asked.

Sir Roger shook his head. "But, Popov is a very important man. So they'll want to hang on to him."

"What do we want him—" Briggs started to ask, but then it all came clear. "Popov is a double. He's been working for us . . . for you, Sir Roger."

"For the SIS, yes."

"If that ever got out, we'd be embarrassed, but why the Americans?"

"Popov's contact officer in Moscow," Sir Roger said. "Is a double."

"Lovely," Briggs said. He could almost feel the steel jaws of the trap closing around him already.

# DAVID BANNERMAN THE MAGIC MAN

**ZEBRA BOOKS**

**KENSINGTON PUBLISHING CORP.**

ZEBRA BOOKS

are published by

KENSINGTON PUBLISHING CORP.
475 Park Avenue South
New York, N.Y. 10016

Printed in the United States of America

# PROLOGUE

It was morning again. Mikhail Vladimir Popov lay on his back on the narrow cot listening to the sounds of the prison outside his window. It was hot in his cell in Lubyanka, and a spider was crawling up the wall toward its elaborate web in a corner near the ceiling. Watching the spider, and feeling the sweat running down his chest, made his skin crawl.

Today would be the day they would come to transfer him to one of the gulags, Popov thought. He was sure of it. There would be no escaping this time. From the moment he had left the indicator at the drop site near GUM, the department store, it was over. He was being followed, and they had probably understood what he had tried to do.

No mention had been made of his activities at the trail, other than the accusation that he was a dissident. A political activist who agitated for anarchy; for freedom of art.

"A clear case of hooliganism," the state prosecutor had thundered in his operatic voice.

Wisely, Popov had not risen to the challenge. He had offered nothing in his defense, and the wheel of Soviet justice turned around him, but without his help.

There was a jumble in Popov's head. At forty he looked more like a man of sixty; the skin hung slack on his face and neck, his complexion was pale except where broken blood vessels crisscrossed his cheeks and nose (not from vodka, but from too much mental abuse over the years). But he had accomplished nothing with his life. He was burned out now, or nearly so. A derelict of little or no value to anyone, especially to his mentors.

Lydia and the others would be crying, he supposed. Frightened for him, and even more frightened for themselves. They too were dissidents, and subject to arrest at any time. Only they did not understand the real reason he had been picked up, nor did he want them to understand. If they knew they would be too dangerous.

"Why don't you come out?" his control officer had asked him more than three months ago.

"Not without Lydia."

"They'll arrest you sooner or later, you know."

They had met several blocks away from the British embassy. It was very late at night, and a thin drizzle had been falling. Popov was certain he had not been followed but he wasn't entirely sure about Peter Houten, and he said so.

"I'm clean. I slipped out through the tunnel next door. It's the one thing the bloody fools haven't gotten round to finding out about."

Popov nodded, then took Houten's arm, and they began walking down the block. "We've worked together for a long time, Peter."

"Three years."

"Before that it was with Michael. Before that, Barnes-Noble."

"What are you getting at, Mikhail? What are you trying to tell me? Are you ready to give it up?"

Popov didn't say anything for a few moments; when he finally did there was an odd expression on his face, that Houten would later describe as "haunted."

"We've not won any victories here, you know. Of all the people who started with me, there's only three or four of us left. Aleksi, Vsevold, Karl, all of them to the gulags."

"It's inevitable. But you've protected Lydia. You've managed that much."

"I want no more of this. Can you understand that?"

"You can't just jump out of the boat in midstream. It's not possible alone. Let me help."

"We're tired, Peter. God in heaven, we're tired."

It was Houten's turn to be silent, as he watched the range of emotions playing across the Russian's face.

"I've not supplied you people with one scrap of hard information. I've given you nothing."

"That's not quite true, Mikhail. You can't go running yourself and the others down, now. You've all done marvelously well."

"Marvelously well at what?" Popov shouted.

"Maybe they are right. Maybe we *are* out of our minds. All of us."

"Now you listen here," Houten said disengaging his arm from Popov's grip. "We're fighting a war, and you bloody well know it. That doesn't necessarily mean guns and tanks and bombs and all that sort. At least not in this war. But it means getting to the people. Keeping hope alive."

Popov laughed humorlessly. "Hope. You fucking Englishmen. That is very naive, Peter, and I think you know it."

"Without your people we'd have nothing here. No toehold whatsoever. You talk about hard information? We wouldn't get one scrap of it without your people showing that there is an alternative."

Popov smiled sadly. "In one fell swoop you eliminate Sakharov, Amalrik and Solzhenitsyn."

"You know what I'm talking about, damnit."

"Yes I do. But I'm afraid you don't know what I'm saying. Lydia and I . . . we want to get away. I'm quitting the business of helping you. I'm going to help my own people for a change."

"I can get you to England, you know."

"And Lydia?"

"I could try. But there are no guarantees. If you stay, you will be arrested."

"I don't want to leave without her. I'll stay. I am a Russian. I will do what I can for my people as long as it lasts."

They had come around the block, down a very narrow street of ramshackle, unpainted houses that seemed to lean out over the sidewalk.

"If you need anything, Mikhail, anything at all. If

you just want to talk. Or if you want to get out, leave the message in our drop hole."

"The water fountain?"

"That's the one. We'll get to you somehow. We'll talk. We'll do what we can for you."

It had been too late, Popov thought now, lying on the cot in Lubyanka just three blocks from the message drop.

He had been followed, and he wouldn't put it past the KGB to take apart everything he had come in contact with. They might not understand the significance of the red chewing gum beneath the fountain bowl, but they'd suspect something if they found it. They might put a watch on the area, and see who showed up.

Someone was at the door to his cell, and he sat up as it opened with a loud clatter, and two uniformed soldiers came in. They carried rubber truncheons, and Popov's gut tightened. He was getting too old to take the physical abuse.

"On your feet," one of them growled, slapping his palm with his truncheon.

Popov got unsteadily to his feet. He was wearing only prison overalls, no underwear and no shoes or stockings.

The guards took him by his arm and propelled him out of the cell, down a long corridor, and down two flights of stairs.

He couldn't stop them from doing whatever they wanted to do to him, but he could resist passively by not helping; by not walking or talking or complaining. He was a limp rag. They could do with him what they wanted.

Downstairs, he was dragged along another corridor, this one at the rear of the building, and then outside into the warm morning, where a large black automobile was waiting.

He was put in the back seat, a guard on either side of him, the doors were closed, and the driver drove around the corner, across the wide courtyard, and through the gates, turning right toward Yaroslavskoye Road.

This was something different. And Popov was frightened.

The drive was a short one, and within a couple of minutes they had pulled up at a side entrance to the main Moscow Railway Center, where he was dragged around a back corridor, down to the tracks.

When he saw the train, its engine painted gray, its three cars also gray, he suddenly knew what was happening, and his bowels loosened.

"He knows," one of his guards said, and the other laughed.

Popov knew. They called it the train to nowhere. But he had thought it was a fairy tale. Once on the train there was no returning. Not ever. Its destination was only a few short miles to the northeast out of the city, to a place called the Yedanov Rehabilitation Center. But that was a laugh. No one was rehabilitated there. No one returned from the place. Popov knew that he was a dead man. No one, not the entire British empire could get him back.

"Lydia," he said half under his breath, "God help my soul."

# ONE

It was late on a very cold fall afternoon, and the weather all across southern England was absolutely terrible. A desultory rain had fallen most of the week from a leaden, gloomy sky, and only this afternoon (a Wednesday) had the rain let up, although the temperature had dropped sharply.

Sir Roger Hume, member of parliament, a ramrod straight old gentleman, with a thick shock of silver hair, a hawk-like nose, and jutting angular chin, and wide, very deep blue penetrating eyes, stood at the edge of the south paddock of his estate watching his daughter Sylvia work Princess Belle, the new two year old, through her obedience paces. A slight nudge of the heel on the right flank produced a left sidestep. A counter nudge from the left heel, produced a halt, and a continued nudge, a movement to the right.

Sir Roger, was a proud man, and from where he

sat surveying his world, he had ample reason for his pride. He had been born of money, but had managed not only to hold on to what he had inherited, but actually managed to double it in his lifetime. He was sixty-three this year, but he ruled his house with a fair though iron fist, and no one . . . but no one . . . dared mention an age for him a day above fifty-five, and that for the last five years running.

His wife Caroline had died seven years ago when their only child Sylvia was seventeen, and hardly a day went by that he didn't miss her, or thank the heavens that she had lived long enough to raise their daughter through the difficult years.

His only regret, of course, was that they had never had a son . . . though at times Sylvia had provided him with nearly as much excitement as he imagined a son would.

She had stopped the filly near the fence about fifty yards away, and she waved as Sir Roger watched, then dug her heels into the horse's flanks, and the beast leaped forward with a whinny.

Sir Roger had to smile as he watched the animal race around the large field, and he could almost envision his daughter's nostrils flared as well; her heart racing, sweat pouring down her flanks. He sighed deeply, content for the moment with his "near retirement," as he called it.

His had been an active life. Eaton. Oxford. Then the Fusiliers, and World War II as a young man, under Monty. For a time afterwards he had worked for the Secret Service as a civilian, but then when that had become tedious, he had used the excuse that his father was ailing and he was needed to take care of family business.

That had worked until that impetuous Rodney Harcourt had mentioned him for a seat in Parliament. From that moment on . . . it was in the fifties he seemed to recall . . . his life had been far from dull.

He was an organizer admidst chaos. A doer in the middle of lethargy. And a man who accomplished everything he set out to accomplish in an era of failure.

As a result he had been on so many committees that he had had to open his own office in the city with a rather substantial staff to not only see to his obligations, but to research his positions as and when they were expected of him.

"It is an awesome responsibility being a British citizen," Sir Roger had told a group of publishers at a Government Understanding meeting in London six years ago. "One not only has a reputation to maintain, but one is obligated to do whatever is within one's power and abilities. The rich contribute more than the poor. The intelligent more than the feeble. The strong more than the weak."

A horn beeped from a distance, and Sir Roger turned away from the fence where he had been standing watching Sylvia as a long, low-slung Jaguar sedan, painted a very dark colour came up the dirt tract from the E6.

Sylvia had come all the way round the paddock, and she headed Princess Belle over to where her father stood, evidently spotting the approaching automobile as well.

It came up the hill, bouncing on the deeper ruts

and throwing muddy water as it hit the puddles.

Sir Roger had been expecting no one, but he was not terribly surprised. From time to time he had visitors. And from the looks of the car, and the determined way in which it was being driven over such a terrible road, he suspected it was someone from the government.

Although he was semi-retired, he was still active along a number of fronts, the most important of them besides Parliament, his chairmanship of the Secret Service watchdog committee, which called itself the Ministry Council on Foreign Affairs and Operations. If anything big happened, he was consulted beforehand. Ever since the not so halcyon days of Philby and a dozen other scandals at high levels, the committee had been supreme. Under Sir Roger, the service had not been hamstrung; on the contrary, it enjoyed the most autonomy it had ever known. But he was consulted regularly, and so far as he knew, his opinions were held in more than light regard.

Sylvia beat the car to the gate, and she pulled up short, walking the horse the last fifty feet.

She was a good looking girl, slightly flat chested and thin of hip for her father's liking, but definitely modern, with long dark hair, thin, delicate facial features, but very wide, guileless eyes.

"You didn't tell me we were having guests, father," she called out, patting the horse on its broad neck.

Sir Roger smiled, as he glanced up at his daughter. "You had best get back, my dear, and have Willy give her a rubdown before she catches cold."

Sylvia looked up as the car came round the last bend, and headed directly for them. "I see," she said properly. "Don't be late then."

"I'll try not to be."

"Will you be coming to the house."

"Possibly. You might have cook fix a tray. It is tea time in a half hour."

Sylvia looked with some concern at her father (they had argued more than once about his not so *semi* retirement) then wheeled Princess Belle around and raced back toward the barn.

Sir Roger turned to face the Jaguar as it pulled in and came to a stop. There were two men in the car besides the driver. One of them he did not recognize, but the other was Stuart Hope-Turner, which did not bode well at all.

The driver remained by the wheel as the rear door of the long sedan popped open, and Hope-Turner got out. He wasn't smiling.

"Good afternoon, Stuart," Sir Roger said, coming forward.

Hope-Turner was a very tall, very effeminate looking man, who always dressed well. Sir Roger knew that he was not homosexual, just gentle. He hurried around the car, pulling off his dove gray gloves, and he stuck out his hand. "Sir Roger, you're looking well."

"Any compliment is fine, I always say, but what about the bugger in the car? Someone I know?"

Hope-Turner had to smile. Sir Roger had the reputation of being almost American with his penchant for "coming to the point."

"No sir, I don't believe you know him. But he's

worked with us for a few years. Name is Obyedkov. He worked Trade Ministry Liaison with our embassy in Moscow until a couple of months ago. He's been assigned to the trade mission desk with the Soviet Embassy here."

"Isn't it a bit dangerous carting him around the countryside like this?"

"Somewhat."

"How'd we turn him?"

"He came to us."

Sir Roger's right eyebrow rose, a certain sign he was having some difficulty with what he was being told. "I presume he was studied."

"Oh yes, sir, he was studied. We watched him for twenty-seven months, and in fact have been watching him ever since. But he's never given us cause to doubt him."

Sir Roger studied Hope-Turner for several pregnant seconds, and he had to wonder how he would manage some old fool giving him the first degree if he headed the secret service. He decided he wouldn't take it at all. But then Hope-Turner and he were cut from two different cloths. And the watch-dog committee had been the Queen's idea in the first place. One did not argue with the Queen.

"Tea?"

Hope-Turner nodded. "Yes, sir, I'd like that. But this is not a social call, I need your help."

"Help, Stuart, or approval?"

"Help, Sir Roger."

Cook had made some finger sandwiches, and had placed some cookies on the tea tray, and Elliot had

16

laid out the service in the study. Sir Roger saw Sylvia's hand in it, and he meant to remember to thank her. She was turning out to be quite a wonderfully thoughtful daughter.

They had come in through the side door, and now in the warmth and light of the study (a crackling fire had been laid in the grate) Sir Roger could definitely see that Hope-Turner's guest was Slavic. His features were broad, his complexion dark and his manner somewhat rough.

Hope-Turner introduced him. "Anatoli Fedor Obyedkov."

"Pleased to meet you, sir," the Russian said, his accent very thick.

Sir Roger merely inclined his head. Russian, but he accepted tea in a cup, sampled the sandwiches and had the good grace not to discuss business for at least the first few minutes.

"Will you be racing at Ascot this next season?" Hope-Turner asked.

"Princes Belle may be ready, providing I can keep my impetuous daughter away from her. But we've been invited out to Hong Kong. I'll be needing an amateur rider. How about you, Stuart?"

Hope-Turner laughed. "No, sir. I'd probably kill myself and the horse. But if you are really interested in getting help, I may be able to find someone."

Sir Roger inclined his head. "See what you can do, my boy. But just don't make it your life's ambition."

They all laughed. And then it was time.

"You mentioned help, Stuart. What can I do to be of assistance to the service?"

17

"We've something of an emergency, sir," Hope-Turner said. He sat forward and put his cup down on the low table. Obyedkov sat forward as well, as if on cue, and Sir Roger almost felt as if he were surrounded. He took out his pipe and began loading it, although he had no intention of smoking. He had quit, on his doctor's orders, almost a year ago.

"It is Popov. He is gone," the Russian said.

Sir Roger's first urge was to say, so what, but he held himself in check from such an impropriety. He'd listen to whatever it was Hope-Turner had to say, and make his decision later.

"You mentioned an emergency. Is this Popov terribly important to us?"

"No, sir," Hope-Turner said. "But what I'm about to suggest is. Very important. Possibly more important than anything we're doing at this moment."

Sir Roger settled back in his seat. "I suppose you've planned taking your time to present your case, but do get on with it."

"Yes, sir," Hope-Turner said, glancing at the Russian.

Sir Roger suddenly had a thought about Dunkirk. He had been dancing at the officers' club when word had come through about the gigantic debacle developing. They had all thought it was the very end. Down in analysis, Sir Roger had read the teletypes as they came in. At any moment, it was expected, the Germans would unleash their machine and massacre everyone on the beach. It hadn't happened, but at the time none of them knew it wouldn't. At the time, they'd classified that as an *emergency*. He was finding it difficult to make the comparison now.

"First off, sir, you are—familiar with the name Mikail Vladimir Popov?"

"No, I'm not, especially. Is it significant?"

"Only in the broadest sense, sir, and not really until now although some of his stuff has certainly crossed your desk in the monthlies."

"Don't be boring, Stuart, do go on."

"Yes, sir. Well, Popov had, up until a few weeks ago, been fulfilling a dual mission for us. The first was providing us with low grade intelligence, and the second was with fairly high grade internal propaganda."

"Come now, Stuart, I thought we had decided as a matter of national policy, some time ago, to forego such operations. Are you telling me now that we are still in the software business?"

"Not quite, sir. It's the people Popov is . . . or should I say . . . was associated with."

"It's Brezhnev's daughter," Obyedkov blurted.

Sir Roger was understandably startled. "Leonid Brezhnev does not have a daughter," he said, then he looked to Hope-Turner. "Does he?"

"So far as we knew, he did not."

"Knew?"

Hope-Turner seemed uncomfortable. "There is certain . . . how shall I put it . . . evidence to support, ah . . . certain claims."

"Stuart, what in heaven's name are you trying to tell me, man?"

Obyedkov broke in again. "Lydia Savin is Brezhnev's daughter by his mistress."

"That is unconfirmed as yet," Hope-Turner

19

hastened to add.

"But it is worth a closer look?"

"It was, but now it may have a different significance," the secret service chief said. He actually seemed to be sweating.

"You did speak of Popov's association with the girl in the *past* tense."

"Yes, sir," Hope-Turner said. "For the past forty-one months, Popov has been providing us with intelligence. For the past seventeen of those months he's been associated with Lydia Savin, although we've known . . . or should I say . . . suspected, her background for only the past four months."

Obyedkov looked at him, and he continued.

"At any rate, Sir Roger, Popov has been arrested."

"On what charge?"

"Dissident activities. Possession of illegal art. Hooliganism. Parasitism."

"And now this Lydia Savin is out on a limb, is that what you're saying?" Sir Roger asked. He was being deliberately obtuse.

"To a point, sir, but it's more difficult than that."

Again, he and Obyedkov exchanged glances. And the Russian jumped up, with pure nervousness, as if he simply could not sit any longer.

"Mikail Vladi is a very important patriot, kind sir! You must understand. It is because of him that we have much of the new trend in our literature. A significant amount of our new wave poetry, and certainly a lion's share of our pop art. He is simply the master."

"Is he that important?" Sir Roger asked of Hope-

Turner. The other man nodded.

"Now he is gone. He will never be returned, unless we bring him back."

"Also true?" Sir Roger asked. Again Hope-Turner nodded.

Obyedkov took offense. "What is it? Am I no longer trustworthy that my every word is to be doubted?"

"It is not that Anatoli, believe me," Hope-Turner said.

"I do not believe you, Stuart," the Russian said, and again he turned passionately to Sir Roger. "Popov has been sent away. Banished. He will never return unless we arrange to bring him out."

"You say he was arrested. Where has he been taken, the Lubyanka?"

"No, sir, he has been taken to the YRG."

Sir Roger just looked at the man, Everyone, even the dustmen with their CSS, for City Sanitation Service, played the alphabet game.

"The Yedanov Rehabilitation Centre," Hope-Turner volunteered.

Still Sir Roger held his silence.

"It's a sanatorium," Hope-Turner added. "For the criminally insane."

"No telling what they'll do to the poor sod in such a place," Sir Roger said off-handedly. He had not made his decision yet, but he was getting close, and he decided in the end to stop playing dumb. "Given time they'd turn him, of course. Which means they'd find out about our involvement with him."

"Quite right, sir," Hope-Turner said.

"But there's more. Most important has been

Popov's association with Lydia Savin . . . supposedly Brezhnev's daughter.''

"Yes, sir," Hope-Turner said brightly.

Sir Roger looked at the doorway. "If he's turned, then we come out the barbarians for making use of a man's poor daughter."

"Something like that, sir," Hope-Turner said. "Wouldn't do us any good."

"I suppose we'd better get the poor fellow out then, hadn't we?"

"Yes, sir."

# TWO

Sir Roger offered the other two men tea; they declined so he fixed himself a *cuppa,* with lemon, then sat back and stretched his long legs out in front of him, beneath the tea service cart. From the very start of this little gathering, he had taken the role of the Lion of Tunbridge-Wells . . . a role he had always particularly enjoyed playing. Only, this late afternoon, there didn't seem to be as much kick to it as usual.

"We're talking about a young girl here, are we?" he asked.

"Late twenties, I'd say," Hope-Turner replied.

"And Popov?"

"Forty-five," Obyedkov offered.

"Have we got a watcher on the girl?"

"Yes, sir. Peter Houten. He was Popov's control officer."

"With our Embassy?"

"Cultural Affairs attaché," Hope-Turner said. "Actually it was he who made the request to get Popov out."

"When?"

"Three days ago. It's been in analysis since then. Donald Brett, Meg Balfour and his nibs, Howie Blakemore, all worked up the background and justifications. It's growing credentials."

Sir Roger got up suddenly, and went across to the sideboard where he got out a bottle of Asbach-Urhalt, a German cognac. Before he opened the bottle, however, he turned around and looked directly at Obyedkov.

"Would you mind terribly leaving us? Matter of housekeeping routine I'd like to discuss with Stuart."

Obyedkov jumped up as if he had been shot and hurried out of the room, leaving the impression that he had been highly offended by Sir Roger's suggestion.

"Well," Sir Roger said, looking after the Russian. "Well." He turned back, opened the bottle and poured two snifters of the cognac. He brought them back, handed Hope-Turner his, then sat down.

They drank for a bit in silence, until Hope-Turner put his glass down, a sincere expression coming over him. "I didn't come here, Sir Roger, to waste your time. Nor did I come as an alarmist."

"I understand that," Sir Roger said in the warmest of expressions. "You also didn't come out here to ask my permission to rescue another dissident who got himself in a jam."

"No sir."

"What then, Stuart? Out with it, for God's sake, I'm too old for this kind of fun and games."

"Peter Houten is a double. We think."

Sir Roger rolled the snifter between the palms of both hands, slightly warming the liquor. "You mentioned that he was Popov's control officer."

"Houten may have turned him. But it certainly wasn't from him we got the news about Popov's arrest. Obyedkov came to us."

"Why would Houten want to have Popov arrested and then cover it up? I mean, if the Russian was such a low grade source, why would Houten jeopardize his own position? Sounds on the dim side to me."

"Peter is anything but dim, Sir Roger. We think Popov was on the verge of a gold seam."

"You'd better explain that to me," Sir Roger said irritably. He hated the silly specialised terms almost as much as he despised alphabet soup.

"It's simple. Brezhnev is getting old. He's ill, and on the way out. It's only a matter of time before KGB chief Andropov takes over."

"Spare me the civics lesson, and get on with it."

"Well, yes, sir. With Brezhnev's declining abilities, has come, we think, a wish to make final amends. To make up for his past mistakes."

Hope-Turner was speaking delicately, as was his predilection, but Sir Roger understood what he was driving at. "Brezhnev may be thinking that he's dealt his daughter-by-mistress a less than fair deal, so he's getting closer to her?"

"Something like that, sir. And with Popov in the driver's seat with her, so to speak, well . . ."

"For God's sake, don't be so circumspect, Stuart.

Popov is bedding the young girl . . . or was . . . and as long as he was sticking it to her, she'd tell him all."

Hope-Turner reddened, and Sir Roger had to wonder how in hell the man had ever become the operational chief of the secret service. The man was damned near a priss.

"Now that he's gone, we'll not only *not* get the information we'd love to have, but . . ." Sir Roger prompted.

"But once they find out from him certain of our methods, it'll get back to Houten that we're on to him."

Sir Roger had to smile. This was more his cup of tea. He took another, not so delicate sip of his cognac, then he set the glass down, picked up his pipe and sucked on it without lighting it.

"Do we merely want him out of the sanatorium, or do we want him reinstated?"

"Impossible, the last. No sir, the best we could hope for . . . and I mean hope . . . would be his rescue, although I had something else in mind."

For a long moment Sir Roger drew a complete blank. If not reinstatement, or rescue, what then? It hit him suddenly like a ton of bricks. "Good Lord, you want to murder the poor bastard?"

Hope-Turner looked glum. "It's the only way. The sooner the better. We don't have much leeway, here."

Such an action, or course, demanded some kind of an approval. Some sort of disinterested opinion, if, for no other reason than insurance against a most certain popular repercussion should it ever get out, which dirty laundry always seemed to do.

"So, you've come to me for approval. You certainly did not need the permission."

Hope-Turner didn't say a word. He didn't even look up from his unfinished drink, and Sir Roger was nearly beside himself with impatience.

"Have you an operational plan, or are you sitting on the fence waiting for opportunity to strike?"

Hope-Turner looked up, stung by the remark. "We've an operational plan, Sir Roger. It's just that Popov is an innocent man after all, and, well . . ."

"Well what?" Sir Roger said after a suitable hesitation. He wasn't going to mollycoddle the man.

"Well, I was frankly looking for another opinion. I was looking for suggestions. Short of that, I will go ahead."

"Have you a man for the job, if you decide to go ahead with this," Sir Roger asked without letting Hope-Turner off the hook.

"We've a number in mind, but we've picked no one yet. Whoever it'll be, though, will have to know little if anything about us or our methods. Obyedkov has agreed to train him."

"What's his expertise?"

"He's been there. He was the administrator of the Yedanov Rehab Center."

"And he's an ardent Popov supporter from what I gathered."

"Yes, sir. He's been led to believe it's our intention to get Popov out, no matter how impossible it is."

"He thinks he'd be helping our man get Popov out, when in reality he'd only be providing our man

27

with the means of getting in to kill Popov, and then getting free."

"Yes, sir."

All day Sir Roger had been feeling particularly young, but now he felt like a terrible old fool. He got stiffly up from his seat, and went to the French doors where he looked outside, across at the lovely stand of old oaks and elms alongside the main driveway. The grand old trees had been nearly a permanent fixture in his life. He remembered actually climbing the damned things when he was a lad.

He turned back. "I'm not quite clear on Houten."

"Sir?"

"If Houten is a double, as you suspect, I can understand why he might want to turn Popov to keep him from using Brezhnev's daughter. And I can even understand how and why he was selected to be the girl's watchdog . . . sort of a reverse on the wolf in sheep's clothing. But why would he request our help in getting Popov out of the sanatorium."

"We wondered about that ourselves, Sir Roger. The best we can come up with is that Houten is confident that escape would be impossible. If we tried to spring Popov both he and his would be rescuer or rescuers, would be killed in the attempt. Houten would be killing two birds with one stone . . . getting rid of Popov, and convincing us that he was true blue."

"No chance of getting him out of there?"

Hope-Turner smiled wanly. "No sir. We can't go in there in force, naturally."

"Naturally."

"And even if Houten was on our side, we couldn't depend upon him to run such an operation."

"Of course not."

"And whoever we manage to get in, is certainly going to have troubles enough getting out himself, without taking Popov along."

Again Sir Roger looked out the windows. It was starting to get dark, and it looked absolutely terrible out there. The kind of a day when one wished one lived in Greece, or southern Spain or even Florida.

"It's possible to get a man in there?" he asked.

"Yes, sir. Just."

"But to get out with Popov would be impossible?"

"Totally."

"We'd need a very extraordinary man. Someone who could work miracles. A magic man," Sir Roger said, and he again turned back.

"Yes, sir," Hope-Turner said. He stood. "I'm terribly sorry to have to rush you like this, Sir Roger, but I must get back."

"How about Comrade Obyedkov? How long do we have him on tap?"

"Theoretically as long as we need him. He's not come over yet, nor do we believe he's been compromised. He's out seeing the countryside this afternoon. It's one of the reasons I've got to get back to the city. Too long and he'll be missed."

"Of course," Sir Roger said. "And you'll want to take back my decision."

"Yes, sir."

"I'm going to need a little time, Stuart."

"Sir?"

29

"Time, you do understand the English word," Sir Roger snapped, with uncharacteristic sarcasm.

"We may not have it, sir," Hope-Turner said, this time not backing down.

"You want my approval and backing, then you'll have to give me a week."

"Twenty-four hours, sir."

"Five days."

"Two days."

"Seventy-two hours. A compromise," Sir Roger said.

"We simply cannot afford to wait any longer for a decision than that."

Sir Roger came across from the windows and went with Hope-Turner out into the hall, where Sylvia was just coming down from upstairs. She had changed out of her riding togs and was wearing a pleasant print dress now, a light sweater thrown over her shoulders.

"So it was you in the car," she said brightly. "Leaving already?"

"Afraid so, Lady Sylvia," Hope-Turner said. "Business calls, and all that, you know."

"Rot."

"I agree," he said, and he turned back to Sir Roger. "Three days, sir."

"I'll ring you up, Stuart."

"Very good, sir," Hope-Turner said. He nodded again to Sylvia then left.

She came the rest of the way down the stairs. "I don't like the looks of this," she said, coming across to her father.

"Run along and play like a good girl. This isn't

any of your business."

"Nor should it be any of yours. You're retired, remember?"

"Don't be tedious, Sylvia."

Her mood deepened instantly. "What is it, father? Trouble?"

"Of a sort," he said. He turned to go back into his study, but then he stopped a moment and looked back. "I'm not particularly hungry. Have cook fix me just a bowl of soup for dinner."

He turned and went back into his study before Sylvia had a chance to reply, then shut the door firmly behind him and went across to where he left his snifter, and added some more German cognac to it. He took his pipe from his pocket, looked in the bowl at the tobacco he had carefully tamped, and then pulled a book of matches from his jacket pocket. The doctors had told him no more pipes. They had also told him no more brandy. Hell of a way to live, he told himself, lighting his pipe . . . the first in months.

He went to his desk and sat down, then swiveled around so that he could look out the windows down at the small duck pond. The light was fading, and the mercury vapor lamp on the barn was flickering, readying to come on, and he shivered involuntarily. It was cold out there, but it was cold in his soul as well.

He turned back, switched his desk lamp on, the warm circle of yellow light instantly surrounding him. He had been less than honest with Hope-Turner, and with Obyedkov. He had heard of the Yedanov Rehabilitation Center. But he had learned from the war, and then from his years in Parliment, that the less one showed off one's knowledge, the better off one was. In this business even if the other man was your friend, the less he knew the better off you'd be.

A magic man, he told himself. Someone who, first of all, knew nothing about SIS operations, and yet understood the business . . . understood tradecraft. Someone who was quick on his feet, who could use a weapon or weapons, and wasn't afraid to use them. Someone who definitely wasn't squeamish.

He took a sip of his cognac, and puffed gratefully on his pipe. Smoking after having quit for a time, was like coming home to an old familiar house. It had a lot of problems, but it felt good.

This person would not only have to know the Russian language, but he'd have to understand the Russian mentality. On top of all that, he'd either have to be free to go at the drop of a hat, and willingly, or he'd have to be someone on whom they could bring a lever to bear. A little pressure.

Finally, this wizard, this magic man, would have to have a gift of gab, the touch of blarney, the ability to con.

He looked up at the clock on the fireplace mantel; it was a bit before six. Then set his drink down and picked up the telephone, and dialed for the operator. When he had her on the line, he asked to be connected with the overseas operator for a person-to-person call to the United States. He gave the name and the number, then hung up to wait for the call to go through.

He tamped his pipe and re-lit it. Actually he

hadn't ever really thought he'd be making this call. But now he was becoming somewhat excited. A magic man, Hope-Turner was needing, and by God, Sir Roger was going to provide him with one.

The telephone rang and he picked it up. "Roger Hume here."

"I have your party on the line, sir," the operator said. "Please go ahead."

"David?" Sir Roger said, raising his voice. "That you?"

"Sir Roger, it's good to hear from you," David Stansfield the U.S. Secretary of State said. "How is Sylvia?"

"Just fine David, just fine. I'll tell her you asked after her. And your wife, Stephanie. She's in good health?"

"Couldn't be better, Sir Roger," Stansfield said, then he hesitated a moment. "How are things over there these days?"

"I'm calling, David, because, frankly, I need your help."

"Is your line secure?"

"Reasonably so," Sir Roger said. "I'll be coming over tomorrow. Haven't got my flight yet, but I'm sure they'll squeeze me in somewhere."

"Is this official, Sir Roger, or just social?"

"A little of both, David. We've got a rather tough nut to crack here, and you've got just the right man for the job. One of ours, actually."

"You're coming here to Washington?"

"Be there tomorrow. But listen David, I don't want any pomp and circumstance. As far as the official line is concerned I won't be there. Her

33

Majesty's government officially knows nothing about this.''

"Anything I can do in the meantime?" Stansfield asked. They were old friends, and went back a long time together, since before the war.

"Yes, I want you to pick up our chap. Name is O'Meara. Donald. His friends call him Briggs, from what I know. Big chap. Broad shoulders. Blue eyes. Bit of red hair, Irish you know. A young forty."

"Where's he at?"

"Hollywood, last I heard," Sir Roger said. "California."

"I know where it is," Stansfield said dryly. "We'll have him here when you arrive."

"I wouldn't be so sure, David," Sir Roger said, remembering just what kind of a slippery character Briggs could be. "I just wouldn't be so sure."

# THREE

Wednesday had been an absolute bitch of a day. Briggs had drunk too much at Clancy's after the early evening shooting schedule had been botched beyond recognition, and sometime in the morning hours he awoke with a pounding heart and a splitting headache. He had been dreaming he was back in Soho. Young. Maybe fifteen or sixteen, and he had just killed another nameless, nearly faceless KGB grunt. Nothing more than a legman, a low level goon who would have cracked his knuckles in church if he had gone to church, and now there were a half a dozen of his pals out to avenge his death. A *morkie dela,* they call it. A "wet affair."

The last time he had had a dream like this, right out of his past, he had called Charlene who had come out and they had talked. She had mostly listened, but she wasn't too bright, she was a starlet out of Indiana or Nebraska or some other cracker place like that, and it was not likely that she could find her ass with both hands in a well lit room. But then he was getting bitter, he supposed.

He sat up in the bed and swung his legs around to the floor, burying his face in his hand for a long time. He wanted to die. It'd probably be for the best, for everyone's benefit all the way around. Yet he knew he was merely conning himself, just as he coned everyone around him.

The tape he had put on earlier was still playing softly. Luciano Pavarotti was singing *Vesti la guibba,* with very great feeling.

After a time, Briggs looked up, the telephone on the table staring him in the face, and he actually reached for it, but then could not. He just could not bring himself to call Charlene out here. She had a great body, and all, but he could not face her mindless, big breasted bullshit this night.

Sometimes he thought about his past like an old drunk's nose, with broken blood vessels in red and blue. There'd been false starts and dead ends all over the place. And now, by God, he was nowhere. Exactly nowhere.

He got up from the bed, and padded nude into the living room where he poured himself an Irish whiskey, neat, and went out onto the deck where he leaned against the high rail cap, and looked out across the ocean, lit by a wide yellow streak from the full moon. The moon seemed so large and bright, so terribly close, that Briggs almost felt he was being watched. He had the almost overwhelming nostalgia for a father; an older man, someone he could look up to. Someone, more importantly, he could trust implicitly.

"Christ on the cross," Briggs swore softly, taking a sip of his drink. It burned all the way down, and hammered his stomach. He shuddered. He'd never been able to take straight whiskey with a straight face.

Soho seemed like such a terribly long time ago, and he couldn't really remember Ireland and County Cork, where he was born. Once, however, he had gone to the public library and got some books and magazine articles about Ireland. He had been surprised and disappointed with what he had learned.

Provincial, was the word that had first come to his mind. They were still fighting over who was Catholic and who was Protestant. The only fight that even seemed fun was the struggle against the British. Briggs had nothing against the British, at least not particularly, but a fight was a fight.

He took another drink, the liquor warming his insides, straightening out what he called his "hobgoblins," as he stared out to sea.

Yesterday had been his fortieth birthday, he thought morosely. He hadn't had the heart to tell anyone down at the studio for fear that they might have congratulated him. If they had he'd probably have smashed someone in the face. Forty. Christ.

He took another drink, this time the liquor was nearly tasteless, his mind was so far away. He had no parents. No brothers or sisters. No aunts, and all his uncles had been killed in the war. There was no one, in fact, on this earth who gave a good goddamn about him, except perhaps a couple of the old Russians and Albanians back in Soho. His surrogate parents. An entire district of toothless, but well meaning emigrés, who had taken him under their collective wing when his mother died.

He ran a hand across his eyes. In the darkness he could see some of the same scenes that had been plaguing his dreams lately. Soho, with its twisted, dirtly little streets, and its amalgam of oddly dressed and oftentimes mentally aberrant crowds. Picadilly Circus with its sex shops . . . much like New York's Times Square. But even more importantly was Hyde Park a few blocks to the west, the natural point for ambush. Damn. It was all coming back to him. Every bit of what he had fought so hard to escape and forget, was coming back. The little, but well trafficked free library above the Indian herbal shop where Vatra dispensed his prognostications for an independent Rumania. Where his wife, Romaine (whom Briggs was convinced was a genuine gypsy) drank tea and sucked on sugar cubes day and night. Down the block, behind the coal merchant, was Oumi from Volgograd, who would argue for hours with anyone who'd listen about the red tide moving from the east. They spoke in the sidewalk cafes of revolution, of repatriation, of movements, and border shifts, of the old days, even as far back for some of them as the Czar and Czarina. He wanted to forget it, but the heritage was too rich in his life. They had been his mentors, his teachers, his parents, his controllers when the games began for real. They had taught him the Russian language, so that his speech would be indistinguishable from a native's. They taught him the Russian mentality of fatalism, but with the deep love for poetry and art and music.

They had taught him the Russian custom . . . the rich patina of mores that mixed royal custom with peasant outlook. And they had taught him what was called *Cheka-craft:* codes, letter drops, blind tails, safe houses and rendezvous points . . . and how to kill; silently, efficiently, and with dispatch.

He tossed back the last of the drink, and leaving the glass on the railing padded back into the house where he pulled on a pair of slacks, a light, pullover and deckshoes. He grabbed his wallet and car keys, and singing along with Pavarotti still playing, went out the door.

His car was a Porsche Targa, low slung, and very fast. It had a T-roof which he never put on except in the rainy season, and now as he drove, the clean air seemed to clear his head of some of the cobwebs, making him see certain things very clearly.

It was time either to move on, and try something completely different than directing low budget B-grade movies, or admit that this was where he'd draw the line. Admit that this place of flim-flam, of absolutely uncaring bullshit, was the end of the road for him; his place of last refuge. Home. If he did that, he might be able to make something of it, and of himself in the process. He hoped.

He understood himself well enough to know that staying here would entail the risk of stagnation. There might come the time . . . a morning, or a night like this . . . when he'd wake up and realize that not only was Hollywood nothing but flim-flam and crap, but so was he. At that point he'd probably blow his brains out. He'd have to stay one step ahead of that.

On the other hand, if he did run, if he left his life

here in California, there'd be no stopping for him. Not ever. He could envision himself ending up like Vladimir Piotosky, or Marta Rheinmeister, or the Stepanovich brothers. Derelicts. Men and women without a country, without a place, without any kind of hope other than the dreary day-to-day proclamation: "When the time is ripe, by all the Gods, we will go home!"

Never mind the Red Army, the Warsaw Pact, nuclear weapons, tanks in Hungry, starvation in Poland. By God, they were going home. No longer would they have to be content with their status as emigrés, playing emigré roles and emigré games . . . deadly sport, but games nevertheless.

Briggs shook his head, and glanced at himself in the rearview mirror. Normally he was light and happy. He was well liked in Hollywood. He had carved out his own little niche here. Yet he was not happy now.

He skirted Santa Monica, arriving at the studio gates in West Hollywood a few minutes after four. The sleepy gate guard, an old man with thinning white hair, jumped up from where he had been watching television and came outside. There was a stern look on his face that changed to a sudden smile when he saw who it was.

"Oh, it's you Mr. O'Meara. You gave me a fright, there, I can tell you that," the old man said.

"Top o' the morning to ya Clancy, me lad," Briggs lilted, forcing a lightness to his voice.

The old man whose name was George Johnston, laughed and shook his head at the tomfoolery, as he swung open the barrier. He waved as Briggs went through. Briggs waved back.

This place felt almost like home; the studio staff, almost like family. He had been here eight or ten years now. He hadn't been any place that long before in his life, unless London's Soho district counted as one location, although he had bounced around from family to family there as a young man. Learning a skill from each place he stayed.

The tall sound stages were dark at this time of the morning, except for the small blinking red aircraft warning lights on the corners of the roofs. They were hulking giants, on the outside, while inside magic occurred.

Almost like me, Briggs thought as he drove slowly toward the west side of the lot. Big, dark and hulking on the outside. Only now the magic inside was beginning to fade at the edges with age.

He parked his car in front of his office contained in one of the small bungalows. In the old days the small buildings had been used as the contract stars' private dressing rooms and apartments. A home away from home while at the studio. Now they were used as offices for a number of independent producer-directors . . . such as Briggs.

Inside, he kicked the door shut with his heel, and not bothering to turn on the lights, poured himself a drink, then sat down at his desk, piled high with scripts he was being offered. Most of them were bad . . . terrible. Every now and then, however, one would come along that combined just the right mix of intelligence, yet simple, inexpensive to shoot, scenes. He had to wade through a lot of scripts to find any that came close.

The telephone rang, but Briggs just looked at it. Who the hell knew he was here? Years of being on the run, of lying, of deception, had honed his senses to a fine degree. The phone rang again. Although he had been here in this town longer than anywhere else (except for Soho) . . . longer than Missoula where he had worked as a ranch foreman; longer than Denver where he had managed to foist the deception that he was a drilling engineer; longer than Toledo where he worked as a paramedic for six months until the credentials committee caught up with him; more than a dozen other places, a dozen other jobs and careers he had lied his way into . . . although he had been here the longest, he was still jumpy.

The phone rang a third time, his message recorder kicked off, and with it came a strong premonition that something had gone wrong, or was about to go wrong. He didn't know what it was, but he just felt something in his gut. An unsettled feeling, as if something was sitting bad with him.

He got up, went across to the locked file cabinet, and dialed the combination. The tape was moving, someone was talking to him. Charlene? For some reason he doubted it.

In the bottom drawer he pulled out a thick package in a padded envelope which he brought back to the desk. The thick red wax seal was still intact. Silly, the precaution, but it had saved his life once, years ago in London.

The tape stopped. Briggs looked at the machine for a long moment, then rewound the message and punched the playback button.

He sat down as his own voice came over the

42

speaker: "You've reached O'Meara Productions, my friend, and you're speaking with the head man. My friends call me Briggs." There was a theatrical pause, and Briggs winced with the corniness, as he did every time he heard it. "You say you have a message for me? Well, at the tone, spit it out."

A moment later the beep came. Then there was nothing but very faint music in the background for several seconds. Briggs strained to listen to it, but then a man spoke.

"This is Howard O'Dette, Mr. O'Meara . . . coincidence about our last names." The man sounded east coast. New York, maybe New Jersey. It was hard for Briggs, a foreigner, to tell. "I'm chief of public relations for Microdyne Off-Shore Explorations, and I'd like to speak with you about doing a film for us. I've tried to reach you this evening, but you were out. I'm calling your office early in the hopes you'll get the message first thing in the morning. I'll be there with my associate at eight sharp. Hope to see you then. Oh yes, I want you to know from the start, that we're talking about big bucks here. Top dollars."

The connection was broken, and Briggs just stared at the machine. He was conscious of his heart beating. Bullshit, he told himself. He had done promo films before for other large firms . . . firms that had public image problems, so he knew what their P.R. people were like. But there was a lot wrong here. In the first place these guys never brought "business associates" with them. In the second place, they never, but never, mentioned money in the beginning. And when they finally did, they always played it down. And finally, business people tended to be conservative by comparison with the insanity that went on in this town. An actor or actress might call someone's answering machine at four in the morning. A business type would not.

There was something else bothering him too. In the tape. He rewound it, played it back, beginning with his message, and then the brief silence afterward. There *was* music in the background.

He rewound the tape again, this time he turned the volume way up, as he played it back. It was Pavarotti. *His* Pavarotti albums on tape at the house. They were calling from his house.

If not the business type, and not an actor, (he knew damned near all of them in this city) then who else? The cops? Maybe the FBI? Maybe someone from Soho?

But it had been so many years since Nikolai Kazin and the Red Square Journal business. They had had it coming. One of the old MI6 networks had been deactivated, brought home to roost. They were old men, mostly. Patriots from the last war. Weary by then, and they had taken up their lives in and around Soho with the other emigrés.

The Komitet had sent its people over within six months . . . a trade mission specialist with the embassy, a couple of correspondents, and a pretty airline hostess . . . and the heat had been put on. Briggs had picked them out, and one by one, eliminated them. Nikolai Fedor Kazin had gotten away, however. He had led the affair, and in the end he had simply walked into Scotland Yard, said: "I'm a Russian spy, arrest me," and he was saved. But he promised he'd come back. He promised he'd finish what he had begun.

But that had been in the sixties. There had been other operations before and after, but never one in which Briggs had been pegged so solidly by the opposition. Were they here now after him? Had Kazin risen high enough in the KGB hierarchy after these years, so that he had the power to chase a personal vendetta?

He picked up the telephone and dialed the front gate, intending to ask old George to let him know if anyone strange showed up, but the phone kept ringing. There was no one there.

Briggs' stomach was beginning to do strange things as he jumped up and went to the front window. He could see down one of the long avenues between sound stages. There was nothing but darkness. Nothing was moving out there. Briggs was feeling it though. His skin crawled; someone was closing in on him.

Back at his desk, he quickly tore the package open, and from inside pulled out a fat envelope with five thousand in small bills, and an assortment of passports, driver's licenses, birth certificates, work cards, credit cards and the like for seven different people from three different countries, all bearing his photograph. This was his survival kit. Open in case of fire. His last ditch get away materials.

He tipped the large envelope upside down, and his stiletto slid out. Its highly polished high carbon Swedish steel blade was nine inches long, and razor sharp along both edges. The handle was wrapped with waxed whipping cord, and it was stained. The weapon was sheathed in a scuffed, leather case. Hand stitched, but very plain. Utilitarian. Not a pretty looking weapon, he thought. Not fancy. But efficient, deadly, silent, and very well used.

For a moment or two, as he stared at the blade, half out of its sheath, a host of memories — none of them very good — flooded back to him. Including memories of the old Albanian who had first befriended him, and who had given him this weapon, and who had taught him how to use it, with passion.

"The sword of justice," the old man, Lushnje his name was, after the town, had croaked. In his mind's eye was a vision of freedom for the Balkan states. "For our friends, against our enemies."

Briggs stuffed the money and the papers in his pockets, and the stiletto in his belt beneath his pullover at the small of his back.

He slipped out the back way, and eased around the side of the bungalow so that he could see his Porsche parked out front, and the building across the street. Someone was there, in the shadows of the sound stage. At least one man. Briggs had caught a glimpse of bare white flesh about head high.

He turned, went around back, then raced down the block around behind the next sound stage over, circling finally to a spot just around the corner from where he knew the man was standing, waiting. Watching.

He reached back and slipped the stiletto out of his waist band. It felt comfortable in his hand, like an old friend. Too comfortable. It frightened him. He could turn around and walk away from this right now. He had his money, his papers. He could run.

There was nothing stopping him.

Just around the corner he could see the man, crouched low now, watching the bungalow. Unless there was just one pair, this one and the one back at the house, there'd be someone else.

Something hard and cold touched the back of his neck. "Don't move, Mr. O'Meara . . ." a man started to say.

Briggs never let him finish, instead he dropped suddenly, as he swiveled sharply to the right, then came back up, knocking the gun aside with his left hand, and bringing the point of the razor-sharp stiletto to the man's neck with the other.

"Don't struggle," Briggs said softly, but with urgency.

The man's eyes were very wide. Spittle drooled from the corner of his mouth.

"Who are you?" Briggs asked, taking the gun from him. A Beretta, not a weapon much favored by the Komitet.

"Byers," the man croaked.

"Who sent you?" Briggs asked. He kept one ear cocked for the other man, still watching the bungalow.

"The State Department. Sir Roger Hume sent us."

The name rocked Briggs. It was right out of his past. It was happening all over again.

"He wants to talk to you," Byers said.

# FOUR

Sir Roger had been the one who had closed down most of the old Balkan networks. He had been responsible for putting a clamp on the emigré operations emanating from Soho, and ultimately he was the man responsible for Briggs leaving the U.K. He had sent a message filtering down through all the old contact routes, that there would be no more killing.

"No more blood . . . Soviet or otherwise . . . shall be shed on British soil, no matter what the justification," the message, or words to that effect, had come down.

And Briggs had been targeted for special recognition, special handling, because of his active role . . . one which he had played with deadly accuracy since he was fifteen.

So now what did Sir Roger want? To bring him back to Queen's Bench for prosecution? For murder?

"Who else have you got with you?" Briggs asked the man.

"No one," Byers stammered. "Just Dick around the corner, I mean. We were told to get you to Washington. We're just following orders."

"How about my beach house? How many there?"

"Two."

"Anyone else?"

Byers shook his head very carefully, painfully aware of the proximity of the stiletto to his neck.

Briggs glanced around the corner at the other man. "Get him over here, no tricks. I really don't want to hurt you."

"I . . ." the agent stammered.

"Now," Briggs said softly, smiling.

"Dick," the agent called out.

There was silence.

"Dick. Around the corner. Quick!"

Briggs moved away from the edge of the building, and raised the Beretta. Seconds later the other agent came around the corner, and pulled up short, the barrel of the automatic jammed into his cheek.

"You'll be obliged to drop your weapon, Dicky boy," Briggs said.

The agent looked at the stiletto held to his partner's neck, and he started to back away from the Beretta.

"I'll kill one of you gentlemen, surely. And what's the use of that?"

"For God's sake, Dick, put your fucking gun down!" Byers shouted.

The man complied.

"Now step back a bit," Briggs said. When the

second agent had moved back, Briggs stepped quickly away from them both. He pocketed the Beretta, and shook his head. "Unlovely things, guns, you know."

Byers made to dive for his partner's weapon lying on the pavement, when Briggs stepped smoothly in front of him and sent it skidding a few feet away from the building with his toe. He danced after it, and scooped it up, before either man could react.

"Played a bit of a soccer when I was a boy, you know. Comes in handy from time to time," Briggs said. He was smiling, the two State Department agents were not.

"Let's go into my office, why don't we,' Briggs said. "I believe I'd like to speak with Sir Roger. I'm sure the old boy won't mind a telephone call at this hour of the morning. Besides, it is after seven back east."

The agents hesitated, and Briggs motioned with the gun. Glaring at each other, they went across the street, around Briggs' Porsche, and into his office where Briggs turned on a light.

He sheathed his stiletto, and laid the gun on the desk, motioning for the two men to have a seat.

"Call him."

"We can't," Byers said. "We were never told where he's staying. It's somewhere outside the city. But we don't know where."

"Then your're Russians, and I'm going to have to kill you."

"God . . . no," the other man, whose name was Dick White, said.

"Then telephone whoever sent you."

50

The two looked at each other.

"Now, gentlemen. Before I lose my patience."

Byers finally picked up the telephone and dialed a number. After a few seconds it was answered. "He wants to talk to you, sir," he said. "Yes, sir, we're at his office on the studio grounds." After a moment he handed the phone across the desk. Briggs took it then sat back.

"This is Donald O'Meara. Who might I be talking to?"

"That doesn't matter for the moment, Mr. O'Meara," a man answered. He sounded older. A cultured voice, but not British. "What do you want?"

Briggs had to laugh. "What do I want? You sent your gorillas after me. What do you want?"

"A countryman of yours would like very much to speak with you."

"Yes, I suppose he would, and I'd very much like to speak with him. On the telephone. This moment."

"Impossible."

Briggs smiled. "In that case, old top, how'd you like your two people back . . . in a rubber sack?"

The man gave him a telephone number with a 703 area code, and without another word Briggs hung up and dialed it. There was no answer until the eighth ring, and then a young woman's voice was on the line.

"Yes, who is it?" she asked, sleepily.

"I'd like very much to chat with Sir Roger, if I may," Briggs said.

"Impossible," the young woman snapped. "Who is this?"

"I'm certain the old goat is up by now. Just tear him away from his kippers like a good girl, and tell him Briggs is on the line."

"Oh . . . my," the young woman said. She sounded lovely and Briggs found himself wondering if she was still in her nightclothes.

"Come on now, love, haven't got all morning," Briggs prompted after a second or two.

"Just a moment," the woman said.

Briggs held the phone in the crook of his neck, and while he waited for Sir Roger to come to the phone he took the other Beretta out of his pocket, removed the clip, and levered the round out of the firing chamber. He tossed the weapon back to Byers. Next he unloaded the automatic, laying on the desk, and tossed it back to White. He shoved the clips and the shells into a desk drawer.

"Hello, Donald," Sir Roger's smoothly modulated, richly cultured British voice came over the line. Although he had not identified himself at the time, they had met in Soho some years ago. Hearing him now, brought that all back into sharp focus for Briggs.

"What brings you to America, Sir Roger, and who was the lovely lady on the phone just then?"

"Sylvia, my daughter. Don't believe you two have met."

"Hardly," Briggs said, mimicking the British upper crust accent with the very long, soft "a".

"Don't be an ass, Donald. I've come to ask for your help, actually."

Briggs had to laugh, but he could feel his blood pressure rising. "Help? For fifteen years I've been on the bloody run because of you and your super snoops. Just because I was doing your job for you. And now you've come for my help?''

"Calm yourself,'' the elder man said placatingly. "We could hardly have allowed civilians running around taking potshots at foreign dignitaries.''

"My uncle's ass. They were KGB. Third Department people from the Victor Directorate.''

"It may come as something of a shock to you, my boy, but your Balkan friends were not always infallible.''

Sir Roger had touched on one of Briggs' worries. It was something he had thought about almost constantly for years. Of the men he had dispatched, how many were guilty of nothing more than being Russian?

"We have a job for you, Donald.''

"You want to take me back to England to stand trial for murder?''

"Heavens no.''

"Then no mistakes were made!''

"I honestly do not know. Besides, that was a terribly long while ago. This is now. You are not wanted for anything in Great Britain . . . although the Americans here would like to speak with you on a number of matters.''

"I won't come to you until I know what you want.''

"I can't discuss it over the telephone. You should understand that.''

"Your word of honor, that if I do come in, peacefully, I will be allowed to leave the same way if and when I desire?''

"Have you hurt those chaps who came to fetch you?"

"Not yet."

"Don't, and I can guarantee your safe passage."

"I won't, Sir Roger unless they've harmed our gate man out here."

Byers and White were both shaking their heads.

"I don't know what you're talking about, Donald, but I'm sure those men would not harm any innocent people."

"Tell me where you are. I'll come to you."

"Can't do that either, Donald. You'll be met."

"Your word of honor, Sir Roger?"

"On my word of honor," the elder man said. "I'll be there at the airport."

"See you then," Briggs said, and he hung up. He dug the clips and shells out of the drawer, and returned them to the two agents, then switched on his tape recorder.

"Mary, I'm going to be gone for a day or two, maybe longer, on this Microdyne Off-Shore thing. Have Peter bring my car home for me, and tell Howie and the others I'm sorry I couldn't make the finish of shooting, but they know what to do. I'll call tomorrow."

He flicked the tape off and got up. "Shall we?"

White had loaded his automatic, and he jumped up. He was angry.

Briggs smiled. "I wouldn't if I were you, sport."

"Dick?" Byers said.

But White's anger was building. It was obvious he wanted to raise his weapon. "Outside," he hissed.

"Please?" Briggs said, goading him. He felt loose,

54

every muscle almost like liquid in a hydraulic ram, ready to do whatever he wanted.

White's gun hand started to come up, but Byers stepped in the way and shoved him back.

"You stupid fuck! You read the report. He'll kill you faster than you can blink an eye!"

Briggs stepped lightly around the desk, past the two men and outside, where he lit a cigarette. He'd be damned if he was going to let people like White get to him. There were men on both sides like him, and they didn't mean a thing.

Byers and White, their weapons holstered, came out a moment later and the three of them went around behind the sound stage across the street, where a rental Chevrolet was parked. Briggs got in the back, White in the front and Byers behind the wheel.

"How about George, the gate guard?"

Byers turned around. "He's all right. We came in the back way."

"He didn't answer his phone."

"Maybe he was taking a piss," White snapped.

"We'll go out the front way," Briggs said. White started to object, but Byers started the car and headed toward the front of the lot.

Briggs hunched down as they drove off the lot, and peering over the edge of the back seat, he saw George come out of the guard shack, and scratch his head. He'd wonder where the hell this car had come from, but it didn't matter. He had not been harmed.

They headed up Santa Monica Boulevard, then picked up the Hollywood Freeway south.

White lifted a walkie talkie to his lips. "Unit two,

unit two, this is Dick at one. You copy?"

"We copy. He hasn't shown up here yet," the radio blared.

"We have him. We have him. We're on the way to the base."

"Good work. Head out immediately. We'll catch up."

"Roger and out," White said and he laid the walkie talkie down.


It was a two hour drive out to a small Air Force base in the desert beyond Apple Valley. The two State Department agents left Briggs to his thoughts. As much as London had begun to get hot for him just before he had left, and as much as he had always despised Sir Roger Hume, and men of his ilk, he actually found himself looking forward to the meeting with someone from home.

All these years Briggs had been a loner. There were people around him, of course, friends at least on the surface. But there had never been a single person here in America to whom he could bare his soul; with whom he could be totally honest.

Most of the people he had encountered, were self-serving, in any event, more concerned with their own petty little problems, their own day-to-day worries, than the process of meeting someone halfway . . . actually meeting another human being at a visceral level.

In fact, he took his thoughts a bit further, there wasn't anyone on this earth who knew or gave a damn about his story. Many of his emigré friends were dead by now . . . at least he assumed they were.

Many of them had been in their late sixties or early seventies when he had left. And that had been fifteen years ago. So there was no one who knew everything about him. Sir Roger probably knew a lot. But even he could not know everything; all the intimate, little dirty details. All the back alley meets, the park rendezvous at night in which a man or men would die. But they had not been people. They had been targets. Right? Operations. Counter-affairs—meaning an affair counter to a *mokrie dela,* which was a Russian euphemism for assassination.

They were waved through the gate onto the base by an alert looking Air Policeman, and Byers drove immediately to the airfield where he pulled up across from a KC 135 jet transport that a ground crew was making ready.

White jumped out first and pulled out his automatic as Briggs slid out.

"All right, hot shot, I want that pig sticker of yours."

"For Christ's sake, Dick, knock it off," Byers shouted.

White's eyes never left Briggs'. "What's it going to be, Limey? You going to hand over your toy, or am I going to have to take it from you?"

Sir Roger said these two were not to be hurt, but Lord, a man could take just so much, Briggs thought.

Byers was coming around the car, as Briggs turned right as if he was ignoring the order, and was going to try to run.

"You sonofabitch . . ." White started to say. He stepped forward at the same moment he brought his automatic up.

It was exactly what Briggs thought the agent might do. He swiveled into the oncoming man, placing all his weight on his left foot, and kicking out and up with his knee, connecting solidly with White's groin.

The air went out of the agent. As he doubled up, and sank to the pavement, Briggs took his weapon, and stepped back.

Byers pulled up short, his hand halfway to his shoulder holster. Briggs tossed him his partner's gun.

"Don't let's give it back to the poor sod until after we get to Washington, what?"

Byers looked from Briggs down to the nearly immobile White, shook his head and laughed. He pocketed the weapon.

"The poor bastard is going to be sore for a week," he said. He stepped forward to help Briggs pull White to his feet.

"I hope so," Briggs said cheerfully. "I hope so."

# FIVE

Briggs was tired and cranky by the time they touched down at Andrews Air Force Base just outside Washington. He had managed to sleep for a couple of hours, and he had been fed, but he felt tacky, as if he hadn't bathed in weeks.

It was late afternoon, and the sun was down on the western horizon when Briggs stepped off the KC 135, shaded his eyes momentarily with his hand, then went down to the tarmac, and strode across the ramp to the waiting Continental Mark IV.

White had remained forward, out of sight for the entire trip, but Byers had turned out to be a pleasant, personable man, who lived right in Arlington, with his wife and three children. He promised that a few of Briggs' things were coming on the next plane, and would be sent out to wherever Sir Roger was staying. Briggs got the impression, after all, that Byers knew where Sir Roger was staying, but he didn't press it.

The driver got out of the sleek black limousine and opened the rear door with a click of his heels. "Mr. O'Meara," he said respectfully.

Briggs nodded, then climbed in, coming face-to-face with Sir Roger, who smelled distinctly of brandy . . . good brandy, Briggs supposed.

"Donald."

"Sir Roger," Briggs said, sliding the rest of the way in. The driver firmly closed the door.

"Good of you to come," Sir Roger said. They shook hands.

The driver got in, and within minutes they were heading north toward Fairfax along the Potomac, the traffic very heavy. Sir Roger, dressed in a casual jacket, tweed trousers and jodphurs, seemed very much at home, although it was all too obvious that he was a foreigner. He was too much a sightseer as they skirted the capital city. Briggs wondered just how much Sir Roger really did know about him, but then decided it really didn't matter a damn. Sir Roger had wanted to speak to him, and here he was. They had been driving for ten minutes in silence, and Briggs looked over his shoulder, out the rear window.

"We're quite on our own for the moment," Sir Roger said. "Relax."

"It's been a while since I've been under the gun like this."

"You have found something in California at which you can be accepted?"

"Yes, I have," Briggs said defensively, and immediately he got angry because he felt he *had* to be defensive about his life.

60

Sir Roger anticipated him, however, and he patted him on the knee. "I wouldn't have come out here, you know, if we didn't need you."

"Hell," Briggs said, turning away. For some reason he felt betrayed. He didn't think this was going to turn out well.

"We are countrymen."

"My countrymen were never there for me when it counted. Why now?"

"You were a criminal."

"Yes. A murderer," Briggs said, facing the one man in the world he feared as well as respected. "How about the Storbach network. Your precious MI 6 and then the SIS left them totally out in the cold. Six men and two women shot to death in Prague. What does that make you, Sir Roger?"

"An accomplice to murder, no less than a general in war."

"Balls on the brass monkey. I can name a dozen other networks that fell. I was repayin' a debt."

"Not yours to repay."

"My adopted guardians' debts were mine."

"Wrongly so. They accepted a job, they did it, and they were brought out. What they were doing in the West End was not legal."

"Moral . . ."

"No, Donald, not even moral. Governments wage war, not individuals. It's a lesson your bloody IRA cousins have yet to learn."

Briggs had to laugh. "Gor guvner, your low test is showin' now."

Sir Roger laughed as well. "You're a rascal, Donald O'Meara. But you're going to stay long enough to listen to me, aren't you?"

"Only if you introduce me to Sylvia."

A strange look passed Sir Roger's features, but he nodded, and they drove the rest of the way in silence.

The house was large, almost Victorian in its pretension, with gables and dormers and fireplace chimneys. They pulled up in front and the driver rushed to open the door for Sir Roger. Briggs let himself out on the opposite side.

The fall air was crisp and quite cold in comparison to Los Angeles, but clean and breathable. Briggs took a deep breath, let it out slowly and looked around. The property was situated back from a rather high bluff overlooking the river and the Maryland shoreline to the northeast. The scene was almost old British with its traditionalism; Briggs expected to hear hounds on the hunt at any moment, and see stallions charging up, their nostrils flecked with foam. It was an image he liked to conjure up from time to time, although he had been no closer to the real thing in England than he had here in America.

"A nice place."

"It belongs to a friend of a friend. You will be meeting him, of course," said Sir Roger starting up the walk. Briggs followed him.

Just inside they passed through a narrow vestibule that opened onto a huge foyer, a living room to the right, a formal dining room to the left, and other doors toward the rear. The house was very old, and it appeared that it was being restored bit by bit. Portions of the woodwork had been scraped and varnished, while chipped paint still covered other sections.

An older, very pleasant looking woman came from one of the rooms at the back of the house. She was wearing an apron, a large smile on her face.

"Sir Roger, you're back so soon?" she asked.

"The plane was early," Sir Roger said. "Permit me. Marta, this is Donald O'Meara. Donald, Marta Howard, our hostess."

"We've heard a great deal about you," she said.

Her cheeks, like the rest of her body, were round and soft, laugh wrinkles at her eyes. She was some-one's vision of a mother; warm and soft and comforting.

"I'm at the disadvantage then, ma'am," Briggs said. He couldn't help himself, but at just that moment he felt like a little boy. He wanted to sit on her knee and have her tell him that it was all right.

"I'm sure Sir Roger and my husband will rectify that," she said. She turned to Sir Roger. "He'll be here within the hour if you wanted to get started before dinner."

"We'd better, Marta, thank you."

Briggs looked up as a young, very attractive woman started down the stairs. Their eyes met, and Briggs smiled. She did not.

"Ah, Sylvia," Sir Roger said looking up. "This is Donald O'Meara."

"I know who he is," she said, reaching the bottom.

"My friends call me Briggs," he said.

He stuck out his hand, but she slapped him in the face, the blow stinging, and rocking him back on his heels. "My father's not an 'old goat' nor am I your 'love,' Mr. O'Meara," she said.

Briggs' hand went to his cheek, and he smiled. She was very good looking, and even more interesting, even though she was an upper crust bitch. "Sorry lass, no offense meant."

Sylvia ignored him. She pecked her father on the cheek, then turned to Marta Howard. "I'm going for a walk, Mrs. Howard. I'll be back in plenty of time to help with the dinner arrangements."

"No need, my child," the elder woman said, bemused.

Sylvia turned on her heel, and went out the front door.

"You've apparently made quite a hit with my daughter," Sir Roger said.

Briggs laughed. "Evidently," he said. He was intrigued.


Briggs was shown to his room on the third floor where he cleaned up, then went back downstairs to the study. Sir Roger was just pouring them a drink. It was a terrible, closed-in, stuffy room, filled with old newspapers and newspaper clippings. There were plain gray metal file cabinets off to one side, and a large library table to the other, where newspapers were evidently read and clipped. It looked like an editor's office. Venetian blinds, closed now, covered the windows, and a small light was lit on the table.

"Not a particularly pleasant room," Briggs said, accepting his drink and sitting down in one of the easy chairs.

"No. It's a work room," Sir Roger said, perching

64

in another chair. A third was pushed up against the desk, facing them.

"Why don't we get right to it, Sir Roger, so I can make my decision, and return to California if that's the way it is."

"You've learned directness in America."

"Not in America, on the streets of London."

"We want you to go to the Soviet Union, and bring out a Russian dissident presently being held in a sanatorium a few miles outside Moscow," Sir Roger said. "Is that sufficiently succinct?"

The suddenness took Briggs' breath away. "Why put it to me here?" he asked to cover his momentary loss for a proper reply.

"This is the home of Rudyard Howard, head of intelligence for the U.S. State Department. He and the Secretary of State are old friends. They've agreed to handle it for us, since you're here now in America."

Something was wrong. "First of all the State Department has no intelligence division, as you say, and secondly if this is a British problem—which your presence here suggests it is—and I am still a British subject, then why bring the Americans into it?"

"An astute question, Sir Roger," someone said from the doorway.

Briggs looked around as a short, extremely stocky man with no hair on his head, came in from the hall. He was in his late fifties, early sixties, Briggs guessed, and looked like a bulldog. His neck was massive, his hands like paws, and his arms very powerful. This was one man, Briggs decided, he would not want to confront in a dark alley.

"Rudyard, we didn't hear you come in," Sir Roger said, starting to rise. Howard waved him back, then poured himself a drink, and came back to the circle of chairs, looked at Briggs for a moment, then sat down.

"So this is your boy, Sir Roger."

"Yes. We were just getting started before you arrived," Sir Roger said, and he introduced them.

"Has he agreed?"

"No I haven't," Briggs said. He felt uncomfortable around Howard. He had the feeling that the man had X-ray vision and could see right through anyone he wanted to.

"You haven't told him everything, have you?"

"Just scratched the surface, actually," Sir Roger said.

"Nor do I want to hear the rest," Briggs broke in. "In any event I will not go to the Soviet Union. My face is too well known. I'd be arrested and executed within twenty-four hours of setting foot there."

"If you are speaking of your connection with Nikolai Kazin, the man is dead," Howard said softly.

Briggs was stunned. Just how much did Sir Roger know about him, and how much had he told Howard?

"Besides, Donald, Kazin never knew who you were, from what we could determine," Sir Roger said.

That simply could not be true, Briggs told himself with a sinking feeling. If it was, it would mean that he had lived in fear of a Soviet reprisal for nothing. Kazin had not known him. The KGB then, did not know his face. Christ. He could not accept that his work in London for the emigrés had gone unnoticed. The Russians were not that stupid, certainly not that lax. "Someone in the Soviet Union must have a dossier on me. I was active in London."

"Years ago," Sir Roger said.

"You've not been active in this country, I presume," Howard said, his gaze hard.

Briggs shook his head. "No."

"Whatever I've done has been to protect myself," Briggs flared. He didn't like any of this, yet in a way he was intrigued. He hated the Russian government, hated the Komitet and what it stood for. Deeply ingrained in him was a hatred carefully nurtured by his emigré mentors. To strike a blow against the KGB was tempting. At the same time it was frightening. The KGB . . . the faceless, nameless horde of agents and assassins . . . was his bogey man, his personal thing that went "bump" in the night. "You haven't explained why the Americans have been called into this," he asked Sir Roger, who glanced at Howard.

"At this point it's still your cricket match, Sir Roger," Howard said.

"What the hell does that mean?" snapped Briggs, sitting forward.

"That means if you decide to accept this job you'd be working for Howard."

"He'd be my control?"

"That's correct."

This was getting sour. "I don't like you," Briggs said to Howard. "I don't think we could work together."

"I don't like you either," Howard growled. "But if you don't accept, we'll just ship your ass back to the U.K. After you get out of prison, that is."

Briggs jumped up. There was no way in hell he was going to get himself trapped here. Not like this. If they were going to take him, it'd be after a fight. A very long fight.

"Don't be tedious, Donald. Do sit down," Sir Roger ordered.

Briggs looked from him to Howard.

"Sir Roger has given his word that you will not be detained, and of course I intend to honor his word. So long as you are here, in my home, listening to what is being presented to you. Step out of the door, off my property, and you will be a fugitive."

"I quite agree," Sir Roger said. "So do sit down and at least have a listen."

Briggs sat down. Hollywood, his life there, his work—such as it was—was over. There'd be no going back after this. He'd either do what was asked of him (and he knew damned well it'd only be a beginning. After this assignment would come others) or he'd have to go on the run again. Christ. He was tired of that.

"It begins with the Russian dissident. Mikhail Vladimir Popov," Sir Roger started, and Briggs sat back, his drink in hand, eyeing Howard, who had a slight smile on his lips.

Popov had been arrested a few days earlier, and their sources in Moscow confirmed that he had been sentenced to the Yedanov Rehabilitation Center outside Moscow. It was a one-way street. The center accepted people—patients they called them—but never discharged anyone.

Those who were sent to the YRC were brought by train, which any Russian who knew about it was terrified by. They called it the *train to nowhere,* because once on the train, you were literally nowhere . . . gone, vanished, disappeared.

"No one has ever escaped?" Briggs asked.

Sir Roger shook his head.

"How do we know about the place then?"

"A former administrator, a man named Obyedkov, is currently stationed in London. He's come over, and has agreed to help."

Briggs nodded. But there was more to it. Much more, he could feel it thick in the air.

"If that was the entire problem, it would be easy. You could get in, snatch Popov and get him out. Or, we could just leave him there. It wouldn't be important."

"But?"

"But, Popov is a very important man. He is a lover to Leonid Brezhnev's illegitimate daughter."

Briggs stifled a laugh. It was like an American television soap opera. "The Soviet authorities know this?"

"We would assume they did."

"So they'll want to hang on to him. What do we want him . . ." Briggs started to ask, but then it all came clear. "Popov is a double. He's been working for us . . . for you, Sir Roger."

"For the SIS, yes."

"If that ever got out, we'd be embarrassed."

"It's worse than that."

Briggs nodded, and looked at Howard. "Why

69

the Americans?''

"Popov's contact officer in Moscow," Sir Roger said. "Is a double."

"Lovely," Briggs said. He could almost feel the steel jaws of the trap closing around him already.

# SIX

It seemed, to Briggs, that the day would never end. He had been without rest now for so long he was beginning to float. He'd say something, and an instant later have absolutely no recollection of what he had just said. Or, he would be walking and he'd suddenly wake up to find himself several feet away without having any conscious understanding of how he got there. He knew he was vulnerable like this, but there wasn't much for it.

"Howard is the best there is in this business," Sir Roger was saying.

They were outside after dinner. The moon wasn't up yet, and it was dark and on the cool side. Howard's wife had loaned Briggs a sweater, the collar of which he hunched up as they walked.

"The best at what, Sir Roger, intimidation?"

Sir Roger stopped. "I understand your difficulties, Donald . . ."

"Save me all that," Briggs cut in. He faced the man and in the dim light spilling out from the lights on the house fifty feet away he tried to gauge the real measure of Sir Roger's concern. But he could not, of course. He could only guess. "Who gives a damn about a bastard from Ireland?"

"Your parentage . . ."

"Is meaningless. My upbringing isn't. I'm just a street urchin grown up, Sir Roger. Christ, I have no home. I have no background. No school. No credentials, not a single friend. Still I'm not crying the blues. I'm not even asking for help. I just want to be left alone."

They were at the start of the path that led around the house, and eventually meandered a mile away, through the trees, to the bluffs overlooking the river.

"I can't give you a past, Donald, as much as I would like to."

"No."

"But I can give you a direction."

"I'm tired of the killing, can't you understand?" Briggs cried. He felt as if he were a mechanical man whose heart was breaking, but the machinery kept on functioning despite the hurt it was causing.

Sir Roger looked away for a long moment. "What I ask is important," he said. "I wouldn't be here otherwise."

"Important to whom?"

"Her Majesty's government."

"I don't want that kind of direction," Briggs said. "Can't you understand, Sir Roger? I'm a bloody freak. A man without a past to carry him through the difficult spots. A misfit."

"You are the man for this assignment, Donald. There is no one as uniquely qualified as you. And Popov is important, but turning Houten—the double—is perhaps even more important."

"I want some aunts and uncles, some grandparents, a mum and dad, a wife and kiddies, don't you see, Sir Roger? I have to have a background. A life."

"You've been trained, and trained well in tradecraft, Donald. You can speak Russian and a number of Balkan languages with fluency. You know the mentality of the European Russian. You understand their rationale. You understand how they live and how they think. You could be dropped into the middle of Moscow tomorrow, and fit right in."

"Can't you hear me? Or are you so self-serving, Sir Roger, so blinded by what you term 'duty' that you can't understand another man's needs?"

Sir Roger was an old soldier. Duty and honor, and all that, had been and still were important factors in his life. They were concepts, or ideals, that he did not merely pay lip service to . . . he honestly believed in them. As much as he felt badly about Briggs, he did have his duty. He too could see where this was leading. Yet he had to look at the larger picture, at the risk of swallowing the individual.

"You are right for the job."

"I don't want the job, Sir Roger. I want to go home, put my feet up and live."

"You don't have a home, as you've said. We could give you one, however."

The coldness of the remark hurt deeply. It made Briggs feel very small, very insignificant at the moment. He looked up at the star flung sky.

"Those old people down there in Soho, were hard, you know," he said, mostly to himself. "It had been a long time for most of them since they had kids of their own. And they had gone through the war, and the horrors from the east. They had been used in the networks, they had lied, cheated, stole; they had been shot at, chased after, hunted. By the time I came along they didn't have much warmth left in them . . . not a whole lot left over for some snot nosed kid whose family was all gone."

Briggs looked at Sir Roger. They were walking again.

"I'm talking about the other side of the tracks, now. I don't even think you can comprehend what I'm saying to you. But I was nothing more than a mechanic for them. They trained me and sent me out to do their dirty work. I was their bionic man, just like on the telly."

"We all have our crosses to bear," Sir Roger said with some difficulty.

"Christ," Briggs swore. "You can do better than that. You come over here, have me picked up by a couple of amateurs and then tell me I'm going to be dropped in Moscow for a little job of work. If I don't do it, I'll be sent to jail. Christ."

"It's terribly important, Donald."

"So am I, Sir Roger!"

"Will you help?"

Briggs could not believe the man. "No," he blurted, but then he was confused. "I mean, I don't know. In any event I wouldn't work with Howard."

"This has to be an American operation. If Houten

74

got word that we were sending someone over there, there'd be no hope for that person. In addition Popov would be killed."

"How about the CIA?"

"I'd rather work through the State Department."

"I'd have to fight not only the Russians, but I'd have to watch out for my own people. I don't suppose I'd have the help or even the security of the British embassy."

"The Americans there could offer some help, but they could not become too deeply involved, in case . . ."

"In case what? What? In case I didn't make it? In case they took me? Covering all our bets now, are we?"

"It's not their fight. They would be doing this as a favor to us. Service-to-service."

"It's not my fight either."

"You're a British citizen."

"A citizen you were happy to see leave England," Briggs shouted in frustration. "You watched me all along, and you've been watching me even over here. Why? For just this kind of a project? What have we got here, a regular suicide mission? Send O'Meara, he's expendable."

Sir Roger was not accustomed to being spoken to this way, and it showed that he was having some difficulty in accepting it without lashing back. But he was a gentleman of the old school; control was everything.

They had come around an old rock-lined fish pond where the trees were the thickest away from the house. Sir Roger looked up one of the paths that led back. There were two stone benches on one side of the pond, and a falling-down picnic table on the other in a small clearing. An old wooden rowboat was pulled up on shore. It was filled with weeds.

"I'm returning to the house," Sir Roger said. "We'd like your answer in the morning. There'd be some training you would have to complete before we sent you over. But it would have to go very fast. Hope-Turner, he's our new chief of SIS, is concerned about time."

"I don't see the problem, Sir Roger," Briggs said. "If Houten is a double, then the Russians must know that Popov is sleeping with Brezhnev's daughter. So what's the rush to get Popov out of there?"

"The Soviets will be preparing Popov to go public with what kind of people we British are . . . that we'd use a man's daughter to spy on them. It would hurt us badly."

"Weren't we doing just that?"

"By morning," Sir Roger said. "Your training would begin immediately."

Alone, the darkness seemed oppressive to Briggs as he tried to sort out not only what Sir Roger had told him, but his own varied reactions to the offer. One perverse side of him was intrigued, while the other, more practical side of his nature was clanging on the alarm bells. The chance for success would be very low, he suspected. If Popov was being psychologically prepared as a propaganda tool against the British government, and was sleeping with Brezhnev's daughter (or had been) the Russians would spare no expense or trouble to keep him. At even the slightest hint of trouble, they'd start shooting. A great deal of the chances for success or failure, of course, would depend upon the planners and upon the reliability of their information.

Sir Roger was a bright, if old, hand at this business. His judgment would be impeccable. There wasn't an emigre among the lot in Soho who had a bad word to say about Sir Roger. Even when he was flushing them all down the toilet.

Hope-Turner, on the other hand, was a relative unknown to Briggs, as was Rudyard Howard. Before he made any decision he'd have to find out more about them. Hope-Turner was a fairy, as far as he had heard. And he did not like Howard. Not an auspicious start to a difficult project.

He turned to go back to the house on the same path he and Sir Roger had walked out on, and came face to face with Sylvia, who stood less than twenty feet away. She was wearing the same lovely print dress she had worn at dinner, only she had thrown a jacket over her shoulders. She looked almost like a ghost in the starlight.

"Are you following me?" Briggs asked. She had not said a word to him at dinner.

"I didn't mean to," she replied in a small voice. "But I heard you and my father talking."

"Did you hear it all?"

"Enough," she said. "Are you going to accept the assignment?"

"What do you think?"

"That you shouldn't. That it would be a foolish mistake. And I simply cannot understand my father.

77

Hope-Turner, yes. My father, no."

"Sir Roger is merely doing his job. He's always been very good at it."

"Not like this. It's horrible."

Briggs had to smile at her naivete. "Don't be so hard on your father."

Sylvia seemed taken aback.

"Or surprised that I'd defend him. I have a very high regard for him."

"He is a hard man."

Briggs smiled again. "And Hope-Turner, do you know him?"

"Totally immoral," Sylvia flared.

"Me, or Hope-Turner?"

"Hope-Turner, of course," Sylvia said seriously. "But I have a feeling you are not too far behind." She stared at him for a moment. "You've murdered a man?"

"You're very pretty, do you know that?"

She stamped her foot in frustration. "I may be young, I may even be naive, but I am not stupid, Mr. O'Meara."

"My friends call me Briggs," he said, moving closer to her.

She stepped back and half-heartedly looked over her shoulder. "I'll scream if you touch me."

Briggs laughed out loud, and lunged at her. She jumped back but he caught her easily, raised his knee, forced her over it, and swatted her backside twice, before he let her go.

"That's for being a naughty little girl and eavesdropping," he said.

She clenched and unclenched her fists. "You

bastard!" she cried. "You bloody bastard."

He made as if to grab her again, and she jumped back with a screech.

"I don't think your father would look kindly on your spying on him."

"Leave me alone!"

Briggs stood, hands on hips, looking at her. She was lovely. "I won't leave you here," he said after a bit. "I'll walk you back."

"You'll walk me nowhere, you homeless bastard . . ." she blurted, and then she swallowed her next words.

Briggs was stung for the second time this evening. Under ordinary circumstances the references to his lack of background would not have bothered him in the least. Lately though, he had been feeling down, and he was particularly vulnerable now.

"Like father, like daughter," he said crossly, and he stepped around her, and headed toward the house.

"I'm sorry," Sylvia called out after him, but he continued walking. "Briggs . . . I'm sorry . . ." she called.

She was a silly little girl, he told himself as he strode up the path. She had been born with the proverbial "silver spoon" in her mouth, and she, like her father, had no conception of what any existence other than her own, was like.

She shouted something else after him, but he could not quite catch the words, and then he could see the lights of the house through the trees, and he quickened his step.

Howard was on the back patio-deck, one foot up on a wooden box. He was smoking a cigarette. There was a glass of beer next to him on the railing.

"There he is," he said, as Briggs came around the corner and started up the steps.

Briggs hadn't noticed him, and he stopped, startled for just a moment, but then came the rest of the way up on the deck, which did double duty as a back porch for the rambling house.

"What'd you expect?"

"I figured you'd be long gone by now."

"Thought maybe you'd send White after me again?"

Howard laughed. "That was cute, I'll have to admit. But you've made an enemy there."

Briggs nodded. He felt loose again. "I wondered why I didn't like you. Now I know."

"Oh yes? Why's that?"

"Because you have assholes like White working for you."

Howard stepped down and turned toward Briggs. "I've read your jacket, and I'm not particularly impressed. We have dozens just the same in any Bronx neighborhood. The Barrio is filled with guys like you. Slick talkers. Handle a knife, maybe a chain or a baseball bat. Big men until it comes to some real field work."

Briggs was getting tired of this. It seemed, at the moment, as if the entire world was out to dump on him. And about now he was having his fill of it.

"Another Harvard graduate with a government sinecure who talks big. Wonder how much time you've spent with your back against the wall?"

Howard stiffened. "I hope you turn us down. I even hope you run. It'd be a pleasure to send my people after you."

Briggs laughed. "You'd better send the best, and a lot of them, because I won't be as charitable with them as I was with White."

"You and I are going to go round-and-round, O'Meara."

"Is that a dance?"

"Yeah," Howard said. "But to a different sort of tune than you're used to."

Briggs shook his head, then went into the house. He hung up the sweater in the front hall, and went upstairs to his room. Someone had brought two of his suitcases and set them beside his bed.

He put them up, and opened both of them. They contained a fair selection of his clothes plus his toiletry gear. Whoever had packed them knew what they were doing.

He pulled out his things, laying aside several items he felt he'd need, as he kept one ear cocked for the sounds of the house.

## SEVEN

Briggs was one of those rare people born with an internal alarm clock. No matter how tired he was, he could lie down to sleep with the intention of waking at a certain time; and he would come awake within a few minutes one way or the other of that time.

He woke up now, but did not move a muscle for several long moments as he listened to, and catalogued, the sounds of the house. There was a clock somewhere downstairs . . . he seemed to remember seeing it when he had come in. And there was some sort of a motor running near the back. A water pump? Perhaps a refrigerator or freezer? Ordinary sounds; night sounds. The house was sleeping.

He raised his left arm in front of his face, so that he could see the luminous dial of his watch. It was shortly after 2:00 a.m. A soft yellow glow came in his window from the rising full moon. He got up, and went to the window, where standing to one side, he looked out. At first he could see nothing other than the driveway, a section of the lawn, the woods across from it, and to the right, the large garage. A slight mist curled through the treetops, and an owl or some other night bird flew to the northeast toward the river.

After a moment, though, he spotted what he knew would be there. Across the driveway, in the trees, a pinpoint of light moved upwards in a very short arc, glowed brightly for just a second, then was lowered. Someone was out there, watching the house, smoking a cigarette. If there was one, there'd probably be others.

He shifted his attention toward the right, and within minutes he saw a man peer out around the corner of the garage, then wave at the one across the driveway in the trees.

The front door and the garage. Most likely there'd be one out back as well.

Briggs put on his shoes, and taking the smaller of his two suitcases which he had repacked with a few things he'd need on the run, slipped out into the corridor, and quietly made his way downstairs. He went across the hall and slipped into the study. He put his suitcase down, and went to the window where he parted a couple of slats of the Venetian blinds.

The study window faced the area between the house and the garage, about twenty or thirty feet away. A narrow sidewalk went from front to back, separating a small section of lawn. One window in the side of the garage faced the house. As far as Briggs could tell there was no one out there. One guard was on the other side of the garage, and there was the one out front, and possibly one out back.

He carefully raised the venetian blinds halfway, then unlatched the window and raised it. The aluminum screen stuck on its tracks for a moment, but then came free and he reached outside and let it fall into the bushes.

Back out in the foyer, he went to the front door, unlocked it, and pulled it open.

Next, he raced to the back door, unlocked it, and yanked it open.

Back in the study, he tossed his suitcase out the window and climbed out after it. Outside he reached back inside and lowered the venetian blinds, lowered the window, and forced the screen back on its tracks.

All that had taken less than two minutes. Briggs hunched down in the bushes and listened. Moments later he heard the squelch-hiss of a portable radio from the back of the house. Someone in the front swore, and the guard from the other side of the garage raced up the driveway, his gun drawn.

As soon as the man had passed, Briggs crawled out of the bushes and, keeping low, raced to the rear of the garage, and slipped in the back door.

There were four cars, including the Lincoln that Sir Roger had met him with at the airport. There was a smaller Ford, with government plates, an old Edsel that someone was working on, and an MG sportscar.

Briggs stepped around the Edsel, and looked in the Lincoln's open window, when a man wearing a dark windbreaker stepped out of the shadows on the other side.

"Nice try, buddy," the man said.

Briggs was startled. He jumped back, banging his head on the windowframe. "Damn," he swore, rubbing his head. "Where the hell did you come from?"

The guard was holding an automatic. He laughed, and started around the Lincoln, when Briggs suddenly ducked down out of sight.

"What the hell . . ."

Briggs scooted behind the Lincoln, but instead of going toward the guard, he circled the other way, around the Edsel, and to the front.

"Get up you sonofabitch," the agent swore. He was nervous, Briggs could hear it in his voice.

Briggs looked under the cars, and could see the man's ankles and feet on the other side of the Lincoln. He hadn't moved yet.

A large drop cloth had been laid down and several of the engine parts from the Edsel were spread out on it. Briggs picked up the heavy alternator, and carrying it in one hand scooted around the front of the Edsel and the Lincoln.

He peered around the fender. The agent stood, facing the other way. Briggs stood up, and in one smooth motion hurled the heavy alternator like a shotput. It hit the man in the back, just below the right shoulder blade, and he went down hard, banging against the side of the government car.

Briggs was on him as he tried to scramble up, and clipped him neatly on the jaw. His eyes rolled up, and he folded.

Briggs took the man's gun away, and slid it under the cars, then rolled the agent over. He went through his pockets coming up with his wallet, and a set of

Ford car keys. He rolled the man aside, then checked the keys in the Ford's ignition. They fit. Howard wasn't going to be very happy about his escape, and the State Department Intelligence chief would be even unhappier with how it had been done.

Briggs started the car, then opened the garage door. The house lights were all coming on, when he roared out of the garage, turned up the driveway, and raced past the bewildered agents gathered on the front porch, and then he was careening toward the highway and freedom.

It would only take them a couple of minutes to start after him, and if the police were brought into it he could easily be trapped on these unfamiliar roads. He was going to have to buy himself some time.

He turned west on the highway, without switching on his headlights, and after a few hundred yards, he slowed down as he scanned the trees and undergrowth at both sides of the road.

Within a half a mile, he found what he was looking for. Glancing first in his rearview mirror to make sure he was still alone, he turned the car off the highway, to the right, and managed to drive it deep into the thick underbrush, before it bottomed out and he could go no farther.

Immediately he jumped out and raced back up to the highway, where he checked to make sure the car was not visible from the road. It was not.

Two sets of headlights came around the bend from the east, as Briggs hurried away from the road, losing himself in the shadows of the woods. Both cars passed moments later, going very fast. Smiling, he turned and started through the woods back toward the house, after first retrieving his suitcase from the car.

Sir Roger and his people had evidently kept close tabs on Briggs and the old Balkan networks. And when Briggs had come to the United States, the old man had evidently asked Rudyard Howard to do the same over here.

They had watched him, but they had not arrested him although over the years there had been a number of close calls. Briggs wondered now if Sir Roger, in London, and Howard here in America, had allowed the police to close in on him from time to time . . . just to shake him up. Or if they had directed the police to his doorstep whenever they thought he was becoming too comfortable . . . like in Montana.

That had been years ago, but whenever he thought about Marilyn Page, he had a sharp twinge of nostalgia for what might have been.

He had come up from Denver (rather he had been on the run from Denver) where he had worked for a couple of years as a tunnel engineer for the county's new water tunnels through the mountains. One of the bright boys in administration had a friend of a friend who had gone to the School of Mines Briggs had claimed was his alma mater. It came out then, that he had faked his credentials, and although his work was excellent, outstanding and innovative in most areas, they had fired him, and had called in the police.

Montana was such a contrast to Denver. There wasn't the press of people, or the pollution, or the traffic. Wide open spaces, friendly people and sparklingly clean air.

Briggs spent two weeks at a dude ranch in the eastern part of the state, learning how to ride a horse, rope and brand calves and a host of cowboy lore. The group he was with even participated in a local rodeo. By night, Briggs studied books and government manuals on ranch operations and management.

At the end of the two weeks, he was offered a job, which he turned down, moving to the western part of the state, near Cut Bank, where within a week he had signed on as foreman at a medium-sized spread north of town.

That began what Briggs always thought of as his *blissful* period. He claimed an old back injury kept him from doing too much riding, until his second month there, when some of the hands began to get suspicious. It came to a showdown on a Saturday afternoon, when in front of everyone, Briggs got on a horse, did a little fancy footwork, roped a couple of calves, and finally did a running dismount-mount.

He limped back to where the owner and his daughter, Marilyn were grinning, and tipped his hat.

"Hurts the hell out of my back, so I hope I won't have to do that much any more," he said.

Don Page, the ranch owner, shook his hand and said for the benefit of the ranch hands: "Hired you for your brains, not for your riding skills."

Life for Briggs, after that, had settled into a comfortable routine. Don liked and trusted him. His wife, JoAnn, tried constantly to fatten him up. The hands came to respect him . . . especially his good judgment. And in the end, Marilyn fell in love with him.

It was the marriage license, he supposed, that tipped the authorities. Within a few days after they had applied at the courthouse, the two FBI agents had shown up in their government car.

Briggs had been working in the office, and he happened to look out the window as the two agents came up the walk with Don Page. They seemed to be arguing, and Briggs knew damned well who they were and what they were after.

He skipped out the back door, back to his room, where he grabbed his survival kit (money, passports and stiletto) and took off overland with one of the jeeps.

Within an hour he had made it over to the Interstate, where he had ditched the jeep, and hitched a ride with an eighteen-wheeler heading out to California.

He often wondered what happened to Marilyn. He hoped she had gotten married, and was raising children now. A family that had almost been his.

He came into the clearing with the pond behind Howard's house, and he pulled up short for a moment. Everyone would be gone. He could probably hot wire the MG and drive down to Washington. From there he could take the early morning shuttle up to New York where he could lose himself.

And then what, he asked himself. Another occupation? Another lonely existence? More lies? More deceit? Until one day they showed up for him again.

Christ, he was getting tired of it.

He looked across the pond toward the path where

Sylvia, Sir Roger's daughter, had been standing. *A homeless bastard.* Those had been her exact words. Trouble was, she was right. He *had* no home, unless Soho counted. And he had no family, unless a group of nearly toothless, hairless emigres counted.

Briggs shook his head in sadness. He had always wanted to love them. He had always wanted their love in return. But as he had told Sir Roger, they were a burned out lot. Beyond caring about little street urchins. He had been a tool, and nothing more. They had been too old to run around setting up Soviet KGB agents, stationed in Britain, for the fall, and certainly too old to actually pull the trigger. So they had poured their expertise, their experience and wisdom, and most of all their hate, into Briggs. He became a first class operative, and only by some genetic quirk, some fate of his Irish heritage, did he keep his sanity, and his sense of humor. He remained sane in the midst of insanity. Rational despite the irrational acts he had been trained well to perform.

"An enigma, Donald, that's what you are," Oumi had croaked. It was on a sunny afternoon, twelve hours after Briggs had killed a Soviet agent. He and Oumi met in Hyde Park, where Briggs had been eating his lunch.

"Are you mourning Comrade Yaschenko's death?" Briggs had asked. He had come to the park because he had not been able to face his own dreams.

Oumi shook his head, turned and walked away. Briggs had wanted to run after him, and explain that it wasn't simple, it was a hell of a lot more complicated than everyone made it out to be. He wanted to tell his mentor that he put up a good front, but that he was almost always frightened, and that he was so terribly lonely.

But Oumi hadn't listened that day, nor had there been anyone else to listen to him; to care about him. And at the end, when the SIS was closing in on them all, making their lives difficult, it wasn't very hard for Briggs to decide to get out. Really, there was nothing or no one to remain behind for.

Briggs stepped out of the woods and started around the pond, but then stopped again, Sir Roger's words coming back to him:

*I wouldn't have come out here, you know, if we didn't need you. I can't give you a past . . . but I can give you a direction.*

The moon was high now, reflecting off the flat water. The falling down picnic bench, and the weed-filled rowboat seemed like works of art.

*You are the man for this assignment. There is no one as uniquely qualified as you.*

Across the pond, the stone bench looked pale, and cold, and very lonely.

*You don't have a home, but we could give you one. You are right for the job. We could drop you in the middle of Moscow tomorrow, and you'd fit right in.*

One of the paths led directly back to the house. The other led farther down the driveway, behind the garage.

*It's terribly important, Donald. Will you help? Will you help?*

It was tempting. He had to admit that. It had all the elements for something that suited him, but instead of playing with small time operations in

91

Soho, he would be doing the real thing; the big time. Moscow itself.

He stood at the side of the pond for a few indecisive moments longer, as he weighed the alternatives.

He could continue . . . go back to the road. Con his way into one profession after the other. In fifteen or twenty years, twenty-five years if he was very lucky, he would be burned out. Probably sitting in a prison somewhere. Safe, in many respects, but locked up nevertheless. Still alone.

On the other hand, if he went along with Sir Roger, what would he have? A bullet in the head this year? Maybe next year or the one after? Or, if he was lucky, he might retire from operations and be given a desk job. In the end he'd be let out to pasture with a pension. Boring. But he wouldn't be alone.

He looked back the way he had come. There was no going back. How many times had he learned that since London?

He looked toward the path that led to the house. He could drop out any time he wanted to. He could have gotten away this time, if he'd wanted to. He shrugged.

But he wasn't going to make it easy, he thought as he headed back up to the house, a half smile on his lips. If he was going to work with Howard as his control, there were going to have to be a number of understandings. Among them the idiots he had working for him. Briggs decided that since it was his life at stake here, he wasn't going to put up with any more crap. If they got in his way, they'd start getting hurt.

# EIGHT

The ground floor of the house was lit up, but there didn't seem to be any activity outside from where Briggs watched at the edge of the woods. The moon was full now, and a cold breeze had sprung up, causing him to shiver. The mist that had hung over the trees earlier had thickened, lending an eerie feeling to the place.

Briggs wondered if any of Howard's men had remained behind to watch the house, but guessed that they wouldn't have thought it necessary. He had taken off in a car, and surely his intentions were not to return here like this.

He made his way back through the woods parallel to the driveway, to a point where the lights from the house did not have an effect. There he crossed the driveway, keeping low, and moving fast. On the opposite side, he made his way to the back of the house, and climbed the back stairs. He paused a

93

moment to listen, then tried the knob. The door was unlocked. He let himself in to a wide vestibule that led straight forward to the front of the house; to the right into the kitchen, and to the left up a flight of stairs to the second floor.

At the corridor door Briggs again listened for sounds from the front of the house. Someone was arguing. He could hear the tone but not the words. It sounded like they were in the study. It was probably Sir Roger and Howard.

He had the urge at that moment, to slip back out of the house, and make his way down to the river. Somewhere along its banks he would find a boat, and he could make his way out of here. It would not be too difficult. And afterwards he could hide himself. He had even toyed once with the idea of going over to Europe. Another challenge.

Instead, he turned and crept up the stairs, along the back hall (which had once served the servants' quarters) then out into the main corridor.

He slipped into his own room, and locked the door. Putting his suitcase down, he went across to the window and looked outside. There was no one there. Howard's people would be at it for the remainder of the morning, and probably for days unless they were stopped. Briggs had to smile. Howard had been so smug.

Someone knocked at his door and he spun around. Who the hell knew he had come back?

He went to the door as someone knocked again. "Yes?" he said, his hand on the latch.

"May I come in?" a woman asked. It was Sylvia. Briggs unlocked the door and she stepped inside.

She was dressed in her night clothes, a robe over her shoulders.

"It was very clever of you," she was saying, as he checked the corridor.

He closed the door and turned to face her. "What are you doing here like this?"

"I came to congratulate you. Everyone's in a tizzy. The only bad part is daddy. He's been up all night."

"I was getting set to go down. He and Howard are in the study together."

Sylvia just looked at him, for several seconds. "It was wonderful," she said at last.

"You watched?"

"Everything. From my window. I thought you might be leaving. Everyone did. That's why the guards were posted."

"You are a spoiled little bitch," Briggs said. "First you insult me, then you come round with a half-baked apology by way of congratulating me on my escape efforts." He shook his head. "Go on back to your room, like a good little girl. I'm sure your teddy bear must miss you something awful."

Sylvia stepped forward and slapped him on the cheek. He slapped her back just hard enough to sting her pride.

"The first time I accepted it . . . I had it coming. But this time I did not."

"You bastard," she cried, her hand to her cheek.

"And I'll tell you another thing," Briggs said menacingly. She stepped back. "If you ever raise your hand or your voice to me again, I'll turn you over my knee and give you the hiding of your life."

She was sniffling, but she did not call out, and Briggs felt a moment of tenderness toward her. He wanted to fold her in his arms, and make love to her.

The moment passed.

"Now get the hell out of here," he opened the door, and she ran, sobbing, across the corridor, and into her room, slamming the door.

Briggs took off his jacket, draped it over his arm, and went out into the corridor, to the main stairs and started down, as Howard and Sir Roger appeared at the bottom.

"What the hell : . ." Howard sputtered.

Sir Roger was smiling and shaking his head.

"Sorry about the door up there. It got away from me," Briggs said.

At the bottom he took out the wallet he had lifted from the agent in the garage and handed it to Howard.

"Belongs to one of your people, I believe. Hope I didn't damage him too badly, but he was in my way, you see."

Howard took the wallet, his control very good, only the set of his jaw and an artery throbbing at his temple giving any indication that he was having a difficult time.

"I think you know why I left," Briggs said, turning to Sir Roger.

"Why did you come back, Donald?"

"I'm tired of running. Besides, Hollywood's a dying town anyway."

Howard had pocketed his agent's wallet, and now he held out his hand. Briggs looked at him, his right eyebrow raised.

"They said you carried a knife. I want it."

Briggs shook his head. "No."

"You will," Howard demanded. "And you'll give up any other little tricks you might be carrying."

"I said I was tired of running. But I won't trade that for jail."

"Donald?" Sir Roger said.

Howard advanced a step, and Briggs sidestepped away from him.

"I won't work for him this way, Sir Roger," Briggs said. He was really feeling cornered now . . . just as much by Sir Roger here and his daughter upstairs, as by Howard.

"And I won't have you unless you give up your little toys," Howard said.

From the time he had been a young man, and he had been taught how to use the stiletto, it had been a part of him. His safety, his security was linked strongly with the blade, that had, on more than one occasion, saved his life. Nor did he want to part with the passports he always arranged to have; they too were a part of his security blanket. Without them he'd feel naked.

"Why *did* you come back, O'Meara?" Howard asked.

"To do as Sir Roger asked. To help my government out."

"You do understand, then, why my government has agreed to help."

Briggs nodded.

"Which means you will be working for me," Howard continued. "Which also means we will play by my rules. You'll be expected to abide by them.

You'll be expected to complete an accelerated training course. Accelerated, I might add, not because you are special, Mr. O'Meara, but because I understand there is a problem here of time."

"Rudyard is correct, Donald," Sir Roger said sympathetically. "Popov will not be able to hold out for long. He will be ready for public use very soon. We simply must get to him before that happens."

"Brezhnev is sick," Briggs said. "Once he dies it won't matter about his illegitimate daughter."

"He's been ill for months. There is no reason to believe he'll die so conveniently soon for us."

"I'll go through the training, and I'll go through with the mission. But I will not give my stiletto to Howard."

"Then give it to me," Sir Roger said, and Howard started to object, but he held him off.

Briggs was indecisive now.

"When this is finished I'll return your things."

A car pulled up in the driveway, and Briggs stepped a little farther back into the shadows. Howard turned on his heel, and went to the door as someone came up on the porch. He opened the door, and went out.

"It's your choice, Donald," Sir Roger said coming closer, and keeping his voice low.

Howard was speaking with someone out on the porch.

"I said I'd do this mission," Briggs repeated.

"Then give me your knife. And your passports."

"You know about them?"

Sir Roger nodded.

Someone out on the porch swore loudly, and Sir

Roger smiled. "The training won't be easy. They all hate you, but there isn't one of them who doesn't respect what you have done and can do."

He was being asked for a committment on a man's word. It was novel, for Briggs, who had lived all of his life by his wits . . . where every person on every street corner, where every phone call, and every letter, meant potential danger.

He reached behind him, beneath his shirt, and pulled out his stiletto in its sheath, and handed it over.

"Wicked looking thing," Sir Roger said pocketing it.

Briggs pulled out the plastic-wrapped package with his money and passports, and handed it over as well. "I'll want the money back . . . the passports will be worthless."

"I won't open this."

"Sure you will, Sir Roger. You'd be a fool not to. But none of the passports are stolen. They're all legitimate."

Howard shut the door and came back to them. "They found the car."

Briggs grinned. "That was quick."

"There are a number of them who'd like to take you apart."

Briggs laughed. "Send them in, I haven't had a good brawl in ages."

"What's it going to be, O'Meara?" Howard said after a moment.

"He's given me his knife, his passports and his money," Sir Roger said.

"Good," Howard said obviously relieved. He held

out his hand. "I'll take them then Sir Roger."

"No. I'll keep them."

Howard was surprised. "We can't allow that, sir."

"Then I've chosen wrong," Sir Roger smiled sadly. "I'll speak with David Stansfield, and see if perhaps the Central Intelligence Agency might wish to handle it after all."

"No, Sir Roger, that won't be necessary," Howard said. He turned back to Briggs. "Do I have your word you will cooperate with my people?"

"As far as it concerns the mission, yes," Briggs said. "Anything else . . . I'll see."

"I was afraid you were going to say something like that."

"When do we start?"

"First thing in the morning . . ." Howard started, but then he glanced at his watch. "In an hour or two, you'll be taken to our training depot. We should be able to get through it all in a few days. Perhaps as long as five or six."

"I'll inform Hope-Turner," Sir Roger said. "I'm sure he's on pins and needles by now."

"How are you going to work Obyedkov," Howard asked. "He was the facility director, from what I understand."

"Yes he was. Hope-Turner will send over several tapes, and a packet of diagrams. If we need more, we can pull him out and bring him over here. But that would be terribly dangerous."

"We'll see then," Howard said. "It depends on how bright boy here turns out."

Briggs laughed. He had gotten exactly what he wanted, and now he was tired. "I'm going back to bed. Don't bother waking me for breakfast."

He stepped around Howard and went up the stairs. Sylvia stood just within the shadows at the head of the stairs, and she drew him down the hall.

"I warned you, I'll hit back, and this time much harder," Briggs said.

"It's not that."

"What then?"

"I wanted to tell you that you can trust my father, implicitly."

"I know that."

"And you can trust Uncle Rudy."

"Uncle Rudy . . ." Briggs started to say, but then he held off. "Rudyard Howard. Your uncle?"

"Not actually, silly. But he is . . . or was, a British citizen. Was naturalized here in America when he was eighteen or nineteen in the service. He's been a great help to my father. We . . . our families have become friends."

"He's not particularly friendly."

"He hates the Irish. His brother was killed by the IRA."

"I've never had a thing to do with them."

"He knows that. And he'll come around, you'll see. You two are so much alike, you'll end up friends."

Briggs glanced over his shoulder toward the stairs. Howard and Sir Roger had been talking, but their voices had faded away. They had probably returned to the study. He turned back.

"What's your part in all this?"

"I don't understand?"

"How much of all this are you privy to? I mean

your father is on the watchdog committee for the secret service. How much of his work are you involved with?''

''None officially. Incidentally I do pick up bits and pieces.''

Briggs shook his head in amazement. ''No wonder the bloody British are always being scandalized.''

''Just what do you mean by that?''

''Nothing, Lady Hume,'' Briggs said, and he started toward his room.

Sylvia came after him. ''I'm not Lady Hume.''

''Princess Hume, then.''

''I'm not a princess, you idiot.''

Briggs stopped at his door. ''Queen Sylvia. Your Royal Highness, then. I don't bloody well care, just leave me alone.''

''I asked you a question, and I demand an answer.''

Briggs laughed. ''You can *demand* all you want, you spoiled little bitch, but it doesn't mean a thing to me.''

''Can't you be a little more inventive with your invective than that?'' she snapped shrilly.

They'd wake up the entire house before long, but Briggs didn't give a damn as he turned to face her. ''Daddy's little girl is afraid of the big bad world . . . she just takes potshots at whoever wanders by?''

''Bloody bore.''

''Shriveled up virgin.''

That one got to her, and she screeched out loud. ''Oh . . . you bastard! You bloody orphan bastard!'' She slapped him in the face, but then pulled her hand back as if she had touched live coals. ''Oh,'' she said in a small voice, and she stepped back.

There were a pair of Louis XIV chairs flanking a high table just down the corridor. Briggs grabbed Sylvia's arm and propelled her, nearly off her feet to them.

"No," she wailed.

He sat down, and forced her down over his knee. "Don't you dare . . . you . . . bastard! You bloody bastard!" Sylvia screamed.

Briggs swatted her three times in quick succession on her backside, then let her stand up. "Now go back to your room . . ." he began, but she slapped him very hard on the face.

He laughed, and grabbed her, pulling her down on his lap again. This time he was not so gentle with his slaps, although he did not use his full force.

When he was finished, he pulled her up to her feet. Tears were streaming down her cheeks, and as he stood up, she tried to slap him again, but he just warded off the blow.

"I was wrong about you," he said sadly. He felt like an asshole for hitting her, and yet she had deserved it. She had hit him first.

"I wasn't about you," she screamed.

"I thought that beneath that bitch exterior of yours, was a caring, understanding, intelligent woman." Briggs shook his head. "Sorry, Miss Hume, my mistake."

He turned and went back to his room, where he locked the door, and lay down on his bed.

Out in the corridor Sylvia stood looking at his door, tears still welling from her eyes. The house was quiet now, although certainly everyone had to have been awakened by all the racket. Sylvia felt very alone; very lost.

She turned finally. Marta Howard stood by her open door, an oddly sad smile on her lips, and she held out her arms. Sylvia ran crying to her.

## NINE

Jeff Dayton, one of the legmen assigned to the mission, drove, while his partner Bruce Palmer sat in the back seat with his eyes closed. The sky was perfectly blue, and the morning was warming up, the clean, fresh smell of the forest lands along the river filling the car. Briggs had decided to go along with whatever Howard wanted, at least for the moment. But the way Dayton and Palmer had talked this morning they were a permanent part of the team. They'd be tagging along to Moscow. That, of course, would be totally impossible. Briggs was essentially a loner . . . he always had been. He saw no reason now for a change. They had picked up the Leesburg Pike near Dranesville and headed north toward the Shenandoah River and Appalachian Trail country; rolling hills and lush green woods. No one had spoken for the last twenty minutes.

"Were you two in on the fun last night?" Briggs

asked. "Or was it just the people at the house."

"We were there," Dayton said.

"Hope I didn't hurt the fellow in the garage . . . at least not too badly."

Dayton laughed. "Bob Chiles. He is pissed off."

"Will he be at the training center?"

"Oh yes, he'll be there," Palmer said from the back seat. "As a matter of fact he may be assigned to the team. Drop man or something like that. Maybe radio watch."

Brigg smiled. Howard was doing Sir Roger's bidding, they were old friends according to Sylvia. But he wasn't going to make it pleasant. If Briggs couldn't handle it, that would be too bad, but not the fault of the service.

"I've heard of the CIA, the military branch intelligence units, and the National Security Agency," Briggs said. "But never the State Department Intelligence Service."

"Oh yes, we do a job," Dayton said.

"How long has this been going on?"

"A while."

"Since just after the second world war," Palmer offered.

"Even before the CIA?" Briggs asked.

"Even before. The handwriting was on the wall as far as the OSS was concerned. We all knew what was coming."

Briggs turned around to look at Palmer. The man was in his thirties. "We?"

He chuckled. "I'm a history buff." He was a short, husky man, with an incredibly ugly nose and mouth. He could have passed anywhere for a wrestler. Dayton, his partner, on the other hand, was tall, suave looking, and had probably passed for a movie star. They were like Mutt and Jeff, or, Abbott and Costello.

"How about the training center . . . what's it all about?"

Dayton glanced at Briggs, a broad grin spreading across his features. "It's called Central School One. Run by Burt Higgins normally, but from time to time Mr. Howard comes up to take over a pet project."

"I take it Howard will be in on this one," Briggs said dryly.

Both Dayton and Palmer laughed.

"You can bet your sweet ass, Irish," Dayton said. "All the way."

The drive up took a couple of hours, and it was warm by the time they arrived. They turned off the highway, drove several miles along a narrow black-topped road, then bumped along an even narrower dirt track that led finally to a very tall gate in a steel mesh fence. DANGER HIGH VOLTAGE signs were posted on the mesh, but there were no guards in sight. Dayton pushed a button on what appeared to be a garage door opener, the gate swung open and he drove through, the gate closed behind them.

"Where the hell are we?" Briggs asked.

"Southeast of Harper's Ferry," Dayton said.

It meant nothing to Briggs, but he would pinpoint his location on the first map he got his hands on.

Another mile farther in, the road came out of the trees into the clearing, at the center of which was an old three-story colonial-styled house. There were several other, smaller buildings to its left and right, and at the far side of the clearing Briggs could see what appeared to be some kind of an obstacle course. A set of railroad tracks led roughly from east to west.

"Looks like a ghost town," Briggs said in amazement as they approached.

There were a number of cars parked in front of the main building, and as they got closer, he could see a group of people on the obstacle course. They were dressed in olive drab.

"Almost," Palmer said from the back seat. He was leaning forward. "About a hundred years ago it was an old terminal station, and the beginnings of a small town."

"Why out here?"

"They thought they had discovered gold, believe it or not. There's a stream that runs into the Potomac not far from here. The town was started, the hotel put up, before anyone realized it was a hoax. The government took it over when the railroad went defunct."

Only in America, Briggs thought, as they pulled up in front of the old hotel, and he got out.

Briggs had signed in with administration on the ground floor, was assigned a room, and brought his things up, where he washed up. Dayton and Palmer came for him fifteen minutes later, and they all went downstairs to a large room that apparently served double duty as a dining hall and meeting room. There were enough long tables and chairs to seat a hundred people at once. To the back was the kitchen and serving counter on either side of a stone fireplace. To the left a recreational library (some of the trainees evidently remained here a long time). To the right was a wet bar and a jukebox, and at the front of the room a lectern, behind which was a projection screen.

Four men were perched on the tables at the head of the room. Three of them younger, and the fourth an older, sparrow of a man with thinning white hair, and a beak-like nose, jutting chin and protruding eyes. He looked like what Briggs envisioned an Ichabod Crane should look like—only older.

The older man put his coffee down and jumped up when they came in. "The infamous Donald Briggs O'Meara, isn't it?" he said. His voice matched his appearance.

"Burt Higgins?" Briggs guessed.

The old man grinned, and nodded. "Welcome to CS-1. If you'll take a seat we'll get started. We've a lot of ground to cover before Rudyard gets here. Coffee?"

"Yes, please," Briggs said, sitting in the proffered seat at the head of the table.

Palmer got him a cup of coffee, and they all sat down. Higgins made the introductions of the other three men, a tape unit was turned on, and a thick batch of forms was passed down to Briggs.

"Now, we'll start on your personal history and evaluation. With luck we'll be finished by two. This afternoon you'll have your physical and psychological workups, and this evening you'll meet with the tailor and your armorer. Tomorrow AM we'll go through the code and radio sequences . . . a thirty day course by the way . . . so that by afternoon you'll be ready for your mission briefing. Questions?''

"Why don't we skip all this, and get right to the mission," Briggs said shoving the papers aside.

Higgins reached across the table with a pointer, and shoved the papers back. "Don't be a difficult little boy. We all have our paperwork to do. It's the bane of modern man's existence, don't you know. We'll all drown in our own paperwork someday. But for now, there's nothing to be done for it, except to do it. Clear?''

Briggs took a deep breath and let it out slowly.

"That takes us through Sunday. Then on Monday, we're going to run you through your paces in the morning . . . test the waters, don't you see, hmm . . . and in the afternoon you can have at it with Rudyard and the Obyedkov tapes. Tuesday ditto. And Wednesday . . .'' Higgins smiled, showing badly nicotine-stained teeth. "And Wednesday will be totally up to you. May be bye-bye time already.''

Briggs' eyes strayed around the room. There were several inane posters stuck up on the walls. One actually said: the walls have ears . . . button your lips. Briggs had heard of things like that, he never imagined they were real.

"All this information you want to gather on me,'' he said. Everyone was looking at him, as if he was an animal in a freakin' zoo. He felt detached. "What are you going to do with it?''

"Stuff it in a file, and leave it there. Until we have to dig it out for the next time.''

Briggs shook his head. "Wrong. There will be no next time."

"Then we'll leave the files in a cabinet to gather dust. I don't care," Higgins said. He was becoming frustrated.

"No way," Briggs said.

"Fill out the goddamned papers! We don't go to the next step, 'til this one is completed."

Briggs didn't really know why he was being stubborn. He guessed it was because he had been so invisible all his life, that to lay it out in black and white now ran contrary to his nature.

"The hell with it," Higgins said, getting to his feet. "I'll have one of the transportation people drive you down to Washington." He turned to one of the other people, "Tell Daggart to have the eval team and archives people stand down."

"I'll do the assignment, but not the paperwork," Briggs said.

"Not one without the other," Higgins said. He came around the table, and looked down at Briggs. "I think you'd make one hell of an operative, son. From what I understand, you've already run circles around my people. We could learn a lot from each other, I figure. And by the time we were finished, we'd both be the better for it."

"Where do you fit into all this, Burt?" Briggs asked. For some reason he liked the man.

Higgins smiled and straightened up. "I'd take care of your physical training, and the implementation of your cover. Rudyard takes mission control. I'm the uncle, he's the old man."

Briggs sighed again, in an effort to clear his chest,

and glanced down at the stack of papers. He shook his head. "Anyone have a pencil?"

The paper work was interminable, amounting to forty sets of questionnaires—one for each year of his life. To the best of his ability he was to fill out each set with his own physical characteristics, his schooling, his play, and most especially his contacts.

A lot of time was saved by allowing him to dictate his answers into the tape machine, but even at that he had to go back repeatedly to correct faulty memories; to make his dates, times and places, match what Higgins had in writing in front of him.

The files had been brought over by Sir Roger, presumably, and Higgins would never let Briggs see them, not even a glance of what they contained. Just, from time to time, Higgins would refer to the documents and correct a date or place that Briggs had given. It was disconcerting at times, to be remembering your own life, and have a perfect stranger correct you.

Lunch of soup and sandwiches and more coffee was served on the run, and it wasn't until nearly four o'clock before they were finished, and Higgins took Briggs down the hall, past administration, to the medical center.

"This Oumi Pavlachek then, was the closest to a father you've ever had?" Higgins asked.

"There were a lot of them. But yes, he was the closest. My mentor. A chief instructor."

"And interrogator."

Briggs nodded, the memories now very fresh for just having gone over them in detail. "My interrogator. After a mission he would sit with me for hours going over in minute detail every single thing that had happened."

"It made you an astute observer."

"I had to be. I lived in mortal fear that Oumi would ask me a question I would have no answer for. The temperature. The color of the grass. The leaves on the trees. These details were as important to that old man as the actual moment of the kill."

"We have a word for people like that."

"I know," Briggs said. "He . . . they all were like voyeurs. I think they could only get their kicks by vicariously living my life."

They stepped into medical center, equipped like any doctor's examination room, Higgins introduced him to the medical staff, then left.

For the remainder of the afternoon, and until shortly before nine o'clock, Briggs was poked and prodded; blood and urine samples were taken; his heart was listened to, electrically monitored, and artificially stimulated to determine how well it dealt with stress. He was X-rayed, and weighed and measured. His eyes and ears were checked. Every square inch of his body, inside and out, was examined.

During all that, a pair of psychiatrists battered him with questions . . . some of them highly penetrating and more personal than Briggs thought any question could be, and others so silly they defied understanding.

"Would you rather attend a scout meeting, remain home and read a good book, or see a Baltimore Colts game?"

"The way the Colts have been playing, I'd just as soon go to a scout meeting."

"How often do you think of your mother?"

"Often."

"Do you ever masturbate when you think of her?"

"What the hell kind of a question is that, you son of a bitch?"

No matter the response, the questions continued, interrupted only when it was physically impossible for Briggs to speak, and ending barely a few minutes before his physical was completed.

Higgins had told him that the training facility operated around the clock, and Briggs could well believe it. He went back up his room with every intention of sleeping for the next twenty-four hours . . . he was totally exhausted . . . but he had company. A tall, burly, dark-skinned man, with a tape measure draped around his neck, had been sitting on the windowseat. When Briggs dragged himself in, he jumped up.

"I thought you'd never get here, Mr. O'Meara," the big man said. He grabbed Briggs, pulled his jacket off, and began measuring him.

"You're the tailor?" Briggs mumbled.

"You got it," the man said measuring Briggs.

"Don't you people ever sleep?"

"Not around here, we don't. No future in it," the tailor said.

Within a couple of minutes the man was done. "Shoe size?"

"Ten, sometimes ten and a half."

"Do you wear gloves?"

"When my hands are cold."

"Belt or suspenders?"

"Belt," Briggs said. "Now get the hell out of here, please."

"Done," the tailor said, closing his book. "See you tomorrow," He went out, and seconds later as Briggs was sitting down on the bed, a very large man, with thick, ponderous features, and dark eyebrows came in. He carried a large, apparently heavy suitcase, which he set down on the table.

"Who are you?" Briggs asked blearily.

"Roger Moulten . . . but everyone around here calls me Wyatt."

Briggs just looked at him.

"Wyatt Earp? The cowboy? The gunslinger?"

"You're the armorer."

"You've got it now," Moulten said. He opened his suitcase, pulled out an automatic and tossed it to Briggs, "How about something like that? Should fit with your cover."

It was a Graz-Buyra, large, very heavy, with tremendous stopping power, great accuracy over a respectable distance, and very reliable. "The weapon of choice for most of the Komitet."

"You recognize it?"

Briggs nodded tiredly. He tossed it back. "It has been known to jam. There's a detent pin . . ."

"One in a million," Moulten said, impressed. He tossed another automatic over.

Briggs tossed it right back. "I don't like Beretta. Not this nine-millimeter, nor the .380." Moulten was reaching in his case. "And don't throw me a Walther PPK, for Christ's sake, this isn't a James

Bond movie."

The armorer seemed hurt. "You apparently have a specific weapon in mind, Mr. O'Meara?"

"Indeed," Briggs said. He got up, went across the room, looked down at the weapons, then closed and latched the suitcase and handed it to the armorer. "Mine never jams, never ever malfunctions."

"No such weapon has been built."

"Oh yes it has. And I've used it for years."

Sudden understanding dawned on the armorer's face. "You mean your knife?"

"My stiletto. It's even quieter than a silenced .38."

"Crude."

"Effective, Wyatt Earp. Very effective."

# TEN

Something slammed into the side of his bed, waking Briggs instantly. He opened his eyes and looked up into the face of a well built, fair skinned man, with light brown hair, and deep blue eyes.

"Let me guess . . . Bob Chiles."

"Bingo," Chiles said coming around from the foot of the bed. He pulled the covers off and stepped back. "Hit the deck, *Wunderkind.*"

"Funny," Briggs grumbled, swinging his legs off the cot, and glancing at his watch. It was barely six o'clock. "I know," he said. "You're getting back at me for what I did to you in Howard's garage."

"An alternator, for Christ's sake. You could've killed me."

"You had a gun, sport."

"And you had a pig sticker."

Briggs got up, and smiled. "Be happy I used the alternator, Bob," he said, and he went in the bathroom, and started the shower. Chiles followed him in. "What's on the agenda this morning?"

"Radio work. Some coding. Simple one time pads."

"I'd rather do a random substitution," Briggs shouted over the running water as he lathered up. "That way if I'm taken, I won't have to explain some code book."

"I've never worked with it."

"I'll show you," Briggs said and he stuck his head out of the shower. "And Bob . . . no radio."

"That'll be up to Mr. Howard . . ." Chiles started to say, but Briggs began singing an old Irish ballad at the top of his lungs, his voice surprisingly good.

When he was finished, he got dressed in clothing the tailor had finished overnight, and that Chiles had brought up with him. Definitely Russian cut. Briggs recognized the style from the Russians he had associated with nearly all his life; at least until fifteen years ago.

The trousers were thick, and on the baggy side. The shirt barrel chested, the sleeves wide, and the jacket, substantial. A jacket to last a lifetime. The socks were wool, and the shoes, surprisingly comfortable slip on half boots.

Chiles had watched him dress. When he was finished and ready to go, the agent looked around the room. "You don't have your pig sticker with you this time?"

Briggs shook his head, disappointed. Chiles had seemed reasonable up to that point, but with that comment, Briggs figured the man held a grudge, and would sooner or later do something about it. He

118

didn't want that kind of trouble, not here with these people, but if it was going to come . . . so be it.

Downstairs, they entered the dining hall, which was filled nearly to capacity with mostly men, but with a good number of women, got their trays, and took a seat at one of the corner tables. A few people looked their way, and a couple waved at Chiles. Other than that no one paid any attention to them.

About halfway through breakfast (which was surprisingly good) Burt Higgins joined them with a cup of coffee.

"Very becoming," he said sitting down.

"The outfit?" Briggs asked. "I. Magnin will never stock them."

Higgins chuckled. "Your physical and psychological profiles all came back positive. You're healthy as a horse, and your head is screwed on reasonably straight."

"Glad to hear it."

"But Wyatt tells me you kicked him out last night, without making a choice."

"I don't like guns."

"You'll have to have one."

"Like hell," Briggs said, pushing his tray aside. He was getting tired of this.

"Bright boy here doesn't want a radio either. Nor will he use a one time pad," Chiles said. "Nothing much for me to do."

"I'm not a bloody Boy Scout," Briggs said. "I'm not going to waltz into Moscow with my backpack loaded with lovely little toys."

"It'll all be sent over in the diplomatic pouch, so

that it'll be there if and when you need any of it."

"I don't need, nor do I want any of it." Briggs shook his head. "I'm just going over there to snatch . . ."

Higgins jumped up. "Not here," he cut Briggs off.

"Sorry," Briggs said, looking around.

"You've got a big mouth, you know that?" Chiles said half under his breath. Briggs looked at him and grinned.

They left the dining hall, and went across to administration section where they entered the conference room, furnished with a long oak table, a dozen chairs, and a sideboard at one end that contained glasses, an ice bucket and several bottles of liquor.

"Have a seat," Higgins said, closing the door.

Briggs went over to the sideboard, and poured himself a healthy measure of brandy, drank it down neat, then shuddering at the impact the alcohol had on his system, came back to the table and sat down across from Higgins and Chiles.

"First of all I won't use a gun. I hate the damned things. They weigh too much, they make too much noise, they're apt to fail you when most need them, and they make for a false sense of security."

"You're going to be another Jack the Ripper?" Chiles asked. "That's real cute."

"I won't fight you on that point for the moment," Higgins said. "I'll let Rudy take it up with you. How about the radio?"

"It's the same as the one time pad; they're both unnecessary burdens. If I'm caught with either, the

120

mission is over. Even if I'm stopped for loitering, for something I could normally talk my way out of, I'd be dead with everything you want me to carry."

"What do you propose?"

"In the event I have to communicate with you people and not in the clear, I'll use a random substitution code."

"Like how?" Higgins said. Chiles was glaring.

"We'll do it in Russian. Take the Moscow Trade Newspaper for that day. Start with the page number that corresponds with the day, the odd numbered columns if it's an odd numbered day, and the odd letters of every odd word as substitution." Briggs grinned. "I can carry a newspaper without suspicion."

"Even numbered columns, even numbered words, even numbered letters, on even numbered days," Higgins said.

"That's right. Then the letters you come up with each will each have a value. One for the first letter in the Russian alphabet, two for the second, et cetera. Subtract that number, from the number value of the letter in the message, and you will come up with the number value of the plain text letter."

Higgins was shaking his head. "Very nice. O'Meara. Simple, a very old variation, but probably workable because of it."

Chiles started to protest, but Higgins held up a hand to silence him. "What about the radio?"

"This will not be a team effort, Burt," Briggs said strongly. "I'm not going to be running around Moscow with your people tailing me. The KGB picks one of them up, and we're all dead. I don't like the odds.''

"You've never been to Moscow," Chiles snapped angrily.

"No," Briggs admitted. "But I know it well enough. All my life I listened to stories about it. I know the city, and the entire country, better than I know my own country."

"You don't have a country," Chiles said.

Briggs' first urge was to lunge across the table at the smug, supercilious bastard, but by dint of great will he held himself in check. "If you ever say that to me again, laddy, I'll kill you."

Chiles stiffened, and started forward, but Higgins' hand shot up and he stopped him. "He will and he can, Bob."

Chiles looked from Briggs to Higgins. He got up. "Then pull me off this assignment, Burt. I can't work with him."

"As you wish," Higgins said.

Chiles glared one last time at Briggs, then left the room.

"You have an enemy there. Watch your step," Higgins said sadly. "He's a good man. A little high strung, that's all."

"No team in Moscow, Burt," Briggs said.

"Nothing I can do about that. You'll have to take it up with Rudy. But I do like your code. We'll use it."

"What's next then? Will Howard be here soon?"

"Not until tomorrow afternoon. But Sir Roger Hume will be here around noon."

"Sir Roger? Here?"

"He wants to personally brief you on Popov, the

122

Savin woman . . . I'm still having a hard time accepting that little twist . . . and of course your own Peter Houten, whom Hope-Turner suspects is a double."

Briggs was happy that he was going to see him again. He wanted to apologize to him for his behavior, and pass along an apology to Sylvia.

"Meanwhile, Wyatt . . . our armorer . . . asked to see you whenever you had the free time."

"No guns."

"Just talk to him, that's all. Maybe you two can work something out. Some compromise. I don't know." Higgins shook his head. "He's in the next building to the east. Wing L. I'll tell him you're on your way over."

"I'll talk to him," Briggs said getting up.

"Come back here when you're finished."


No one paid much attention to Briggs as he went down the corridor, through reception and stepped outside into the bright morning. It was a cool, lovely day, and although it was a Sunday the training camp seemed busy. It was a workday as usual. In the distance, behind the main building, he could hear the rattle of small arms fire, and an occasional light explosion . . . either grenades or perhaps plastique. Briggs had worked with the latter, but just as he disliked firearms, he hated explosives. Too mindlessly violent. If a man was to be killed, Briggs wanted no part of impersonally blowing him to bits, or engaging in a shootout. A man's life was a high personal concept . . . his death even more intensely personal.

There were several jeeps parked outside the smallish building marked WING L, and as Briggs approached, Roger Moulten, the armorer, came out, several men right behind him. His face lit up when he spotted Briggs.

"Ah . . . O'Meara, you've changed your mind after all," he shouted.

"Not at all . . ." Briggs tried to say, but the man ignored it, indicating one of the jeeps.

"We're going out to the range. You can tag along."

Everyone climbed in the three jeeps, Moulten in the lead, and they took off around the building, and straight out across the field along a deeply rutted dirt track, at high speed.

"Do you always drive this fast?" Briggs shouted. He hung on for dear life with both hands.

The driver laughed. "Only when we're chasing after Wyatt. He's a crazy man. Loves speed just as much as he loves guns."

Within a couple of minutes, they pulled up in a cloud of dust at what obviously was the firing range. A half a dozen men and a couple women were firing a variety of weapons, including the Israeli-made Uzi submachinegun, at man-silhouettes down range. A spotter sat on a squat tower above and behind the shooters.

Moulten jumped out of the lead jeep, and for several minutes he was busy with the other people. Setting them up with weapons, discussing their techniques, and their scores. Finally, however, he broke away and came back to where Briggs had remained leaning against the jeep.

"So, you don't like guns, but you know them," he said.

"I've handled them."

"In London?"

Briggs nodded.

"The Graz Buyra?"

"I've taken one or two off dead Russians."

"Russians you've killed with your blade."

Two of Moulten's assistants had come a little closer and were listening to the conversation.

"Yes. And by other methods," Briggs replied.

"With your bare hands?"

Briggs glanced at the other two men. He nodded. Their eyes widened slightly, and they edged back a bit.

"But you do know how to use a hand gun, I'm assuming." Moulten kept after him.

For a moment there the man's questions had been almost hypnotic, but Briggs shook himself out of it. "Like I said, Wyatt, I'm not going to carry a gun."

Moulten smiled. "That's up to you, in the end. I'm certainly not going to supply you with a weapon that you'll just throw away. Nevertheless you're going to have to qualify before you leave here."

Briggs started to object again, but then he shrugged. "Christ-all-mighty," he said, pushing away from the jeep. "If I qualify with your bloody weapons right now, will you detach one of your people to drive me back?"

"Absolutely," Moulten said.

There was a lull in the firing, and Moulten

turned and gestured to the spotter on the tower. Immediately the man's voice blared over the loudspeaker.

"SHOOTERS STAND DOWN. STAND DOWN AND SECURE YOUR WEAPONS."

Moulten and his two assistants accompanied Briggs over to one of the center shooting stands as the other agents using the range stood back and watched curiously.

Laid out on the stand was a variety of weapons, including the Soviet weapon of choice, the Israeli submachinegun, an American military .45 automatic, a couple of Berettas, and a silenced Smith & Wesson .38 Police Special.

"Anything here you're not familiar with?" Moulten asked.

"I've seen them all," Briggs answered. He could feel sweat crawling down his sides and his chest. His stomach felt queasy, and his knees were weak. He didn't want to think about it though. It was buried deep in his past, during the day. Only at night, when he was in the gray world between sleep and consciousness did even part of what had happened come back.

He looked at Moulten and at the others, all staring at him now. Moulten was saying something, but his voice seemed to be in slow motion.

It had been so long ago. He had forgotten. He had tried to forget. Damn!

Down range, three man-sized silhouettes leaped up from the trench and began a macabre dance. Running and jerking back and forth. Running away. Trying to escape. Christ on a cross.

The loudspeaker was blaring. Moulten was saying something and one of his assistants had a smug grin on his face.

Briggs reached down and picked up the Smith & Wesson, crouched in the classic shooter's stance, both hands out, left palm up, elbow down, and fired, each of the six shots hitting the heart outlined in red on the dancing silhouettes.

It hadn't been hot that summer and the fall had been miserable. It had been cold and rainy all week. This evening as he climbed the steps from piano lessons the rain was changing to spits of snow. And he was cold. He was little, his coat threadbare, his shoes thin, and the westend London damp chill permeated his bones.

New silhouettes had popped up, and Briggs had the nine-millimeter Beretta automatic in his hand, the safety off, and he was firing . . . blindly it seemed . . . but each of his shots finding their exact mark. One to the heart, one to the neck, one to the head, then the next silhouette. Instinct, almost. Hate.

The light in the stairhall had been out, and he trudged up the stairs in the dark, his hand scraping along the damp wall, his gut churning for the thought of cockroaches, and spiders or rats somewhere above him. At any moment something was going to drop down on his head, or leap out at him from the dark.

On the first three landings he was able to make out thin slivers of light from underneath doors, but then he was on the narrow stairs leading to the attic apartment he shared with his mother and his Uncle Louis. It was dark up there. Dark, and damp and cold, and far too quiet.

Still another set of the silhouettes popped into place, and Briggs snatched the Graz Buyra, huge and heavy in his hand, and he began firing, the explosions tremendous, yet somehow very far away. Each shot hitting its mark with deadly accuracy.

At the top landing he realized that the door was open, he could see inside the apartment from the small amount of light coming in the windows. The curtains had been pulled away. Something was lying in a heap near the windows. Something else lay in a heap by the open bedroom door.

The Uzi submachinegun was in Briggs' hands now, and he was firing, literally cutting the thick paper targets in half, the bottoms dropping back into the trench.

He flipped on the lights. His mother lay by the window, blood everywhere, her neck ripped apart, the front of her head blown away so badly he could not recognize her.

His Uncle Louis lay by the bedroom door. He too had been blown away brutally. But why? By whom?

"Christ," Briggs said, coming back from the past. He stepped away from the table.

There was no sound now on the firing range. Everyone had gathered around, most with their mouths hanging open. Moulten, the armorer, had a deeply thoughtful look in his eyes. Two or three of the men were frankly frightened.

"I hate these fucking things," Briggs said. He was

drenched in sweat. "Do I qualify?"

Moulten laughed, long and loud. No one else did though, and his laughter suddenly died. "You qualify, O'Meara. God help the man or beast who ever got in your way."

## ELEVEN

When the knock came, Briggs was standing by his window, a brandy in hand, staring out across the field to the north to where the forest began a couple of thousand yards away. He turned toward the door. He had seen something in himself out at the firing range that he hadn't wanted to see. Something he had hoped was buried forever. Seeing the guns. Hearing the noise, and actually firing the bloody things, had brought it all back to him. His mother's death, Oumi and the others convincing him that the Russians had killed them because his uncle had been involved in some intelligence position in West Berlin. And then the relentless training leading to his first missions. All of it . . . every horrible, blood-and-guts moment came back to him out there, and the memories had deeply shaken him. The knock came again.

"It's open," he called out.

The door swung open and Sir Roger, wearing a tweed shooting jacket, tweed trousers and jodhpurs came in. "We waited for you downstairs, but when you didn't show up, we were told you might be here. Anything the matter, Donald?"

"Everything's the matter, Sir Roger. I don't think I'll be able to go through with this."

Sir Roger closed the door, came across the room and perched on the edge of the desk.

"Care for a drink?" Briggs asked, and Sir Rogers nodded. Briggs poured it for him. "I suppose you've been told about the debacle this morning."

"A fellow they call Wyatt Earp, for some obscure reason, is very impressed, as are a number of legmen. But the psychologists are beside themselves. They can't understand how they missed the mark so widely with you."

"Perhaps they'll pronounce me unfit for further duty."

"No such luck, Donald," said Sir Roger sadly. He took a sip of his drink. "I've come to begin your background briefing, but I suppose I've popped in at just the correct time for another attitude, or motivational lecture."

"A half time peptalk?" Briggs said. He almost had to laugh, but it wasn't funny. None of this was funny. If he went through with this, he'd be in Moscow in a week, perhaps sooner, and people could start dying.

Sir Roger bridled. "None of them here, Howard included, know the extent of your background . . . nor shall they. There's no need, unless you want to tell them."

131

"But you do," Briggs said sharply.

Sir Roger nodded.

"And about now you're wishing Sylvia had never come over with you. Wishing she'd never even heard my name mentioned, much less met me."

Sir Roger wanted to lie to him; Briggs could see it in his eyes. But he shook his head instead. A sad gesture. "She's downstairs in Higgins' office."

"She's here? She came with you?" Briggs said brightly.

"Yes."

"I wanted to see her. I need to apologize."

"For what?" Sir Rogers said suddenly alarmed.

Briggs had to laugh. "Nothing like that . . . I assure you. But I was rude. Terribly so. I'd like to make it up to her."

"I'm sure she understands."

"Then why is she here?"

Sir Roger started to open his mouth, but then shut it.

"But that's separate," Briggs said. "Totally separate. We're talking now about this assignment . . . my part in it. What if I decide not to go along? What then? Will I go to jail?"

"We can excuse your crimes at home. You were young, and some of them worked out quite for the best. But not here. Howard would have his way."

"Which means I'd have to go on the run. Back to London."

"We would have to extradite you. We do have the treaty."

"I could always join the IRA."

Sir Roger smiled. "Hardly," he said. "You're not

the fanatical type, Donald. You may have your problems, we all of us do, but you certainly are no terrorist.''

"Thank you for that, at least," Briggs said. He turned suddenly to look out the window. It had turned out to be a lovely day. It was just noon, and he thought about the beach in California. They'd be wondering what the hell happened to him. He'd have to at least telephone. The studio would shut down his office for him. The Guild would find other writers and directors to work on his projects. Within a month the confusion would subside. Within three months the questions would die down. And certainly within a year cocktail conversations might not even include the vaguest of references to him.

He was the invisible man . . . or very nearly so. Here one moment, gone the next, like a magician's rabbit in and out of the hat. He was magical. A magic man. Lonely.

"In the meanwhile, it's this assignment or you will have to go on the run," Sir Roger said.

Briggs turned around.

"I could turn my back . . . if you opt to run . . . but that is the best I could do. You would be on your own.''

"And you would have to return to England to find someone else for this little job . . . a job, by the way, that has never been clearly explained to me.''

"What does that mean, Donald?" Sir Roger said, impatiently. "I don't understand what that means.''

"You came to brief me on the background. Do it, so I can go downstairs and apologize to your daughter.''

"She would be flattered if she knew that affairs of state were being expedited on her behalf," Sir Roger said. The comment was light, his tone was anything but.

"No wrong side of the tracks relationship for your daughter, hmm . . . ?"

"I didn't say that."

"You didn't have to," Briggs said. "Who is Mikhail Vladimir Popov, and where is the Yedanov Rehabilitation Center . . . both new names to me."

"It's a complicated arrangement, Donald," Sir Roger began. "Most of the details are quite unimportant. Suffice it to say we're left with two choices. Either we manage somehow to get Popov out of the Soviet Union, or we eliminate him."

"Hope-Turner wants the man eliminated."

Sir Roger nodded. "It's the safest, most intelligent means to deal with the problem."

"You mentioned something about a woman."

"Lydia Savin. Brezhnev's illegitimate daughter. Her existence is a state secret."

"What's the worry then?"

"Brezhnev's an old man. Ailing from what we can gather. And old men sometimes are wont to go back over their sins, and do something to rectify them. Brezhnev, it is feared, has been in contact with his daughter. They presumably have talked. At length. There's no telling what he may have told her."

"Has that happened? You said Popov and this Savin woman were having an affair."

"There has been some information. But Popov's control officer is a chap named Peter Houten. Hope-Turner believes Houten is a double. So if Popov indeed has been trying to pass along important information, it has been stopped, or at least altered by the man."

There was much more to this, but still Briggs was not quite grasping the entire picture. "Why not just take out Houten?"

"We may eventually, but there is much more at stake here, Donald. Much more," Sir Roger said. "Brezhnev's health is failing . . . we do know that. What very few people know for sure, however, is who his successor is."

"We do?"

Sir Roger nodded. "Yuri Andropov."

"I've heard the rumor. Surely to God it can't be true."

"Yes. The former head of the KGB will become the next Soviet leader."

"Mikhail Popov is . . . or was . . . a British puppet. All that time a British spy was making love to the daughter of the Russian leader."

"It will make things difficult, if not impossible for us," Sir Roger said gravely.

"It could come down to war."

"Yes it could. So you see, Mikhail Popov is, at this moment, an extremely important fellow."

"It *would* be easier to kill him."

"We don't work that way, Donald," Sir Roger said, but then he was embarrassed. "At least we don't like to think we do. We don't do such things unless they are absolutely necessary."

"Besides," Briggs interjected, "if we could have Popov here, if we could talk to him at length, I'm sure he'd be able to give us a wealth of information about Comrade Party Secretary Leonid Brezhnev.''

"An unsavory aspect," Sir Roger said distastefully.

"An important, intriguing one, nevertheless," Briggs said. "Now tell me about Lydia Savin."

"There isn't much to tell for certain. We don't know how much has been altered by Houten."

"Have the Soviet authorities arrested her?"

"From what we gather, no. Besides the fact her father is still too powerful, they may be afraid she would become something of a national embarrassment."

"Come on," Briggs said. "Illegitimacy is no longer grounds for that kind of worry."

"It's not that so much, as the fact the girl has gotten herself involved with the dissidents. Popov was a dissident writer. It's how she met him. She's still active, our sources other than Peter Houten tell us."

Briggs stiffened at that. "I hope to hell, Sir Roger, that Hope-Turner's people haven't been mucking about over there. Because if they have all bets are off. Houten would be tipped that something was going down."

"*Going down?*" asked Sir Roger, his right eyebrow rising.

"Something was about to happen. That somehow you had found out about him. He and his pals would be waiting for some poor slob like me to come along. I'd be a sitting duck."

Sir Roger looked at him with open amazement. "You *have* picked up the American pattern of speech. Colorful."

"Is Lydia Savin approachable?" Briggs asked, ignoring the comment.

"I don't know."

"Who does?"

"Peter Houten, I suppose. We don't have any information we can trust. But your speech pattern is important, Donald. You will be going to the American Embassy in Moscow. As an American. Only one or two people in the embassy will even know that you are British. Your speech pattern is important."

"Ducky, guv'ner," Briggs said in his thickest cockney. "What about this rehabilitation center where Popov is being kept? Can you tell me anything about it?"

"I can do much better than that. We have the center's former administrator."

"Here?"

"In London. He's with the trade mission at the Soviet embassy in London. He's prepared diagrams and several tapes about the center for you. In Russian, I might add, so you can have the practice."

"It may not be enough," Briggs said thoughtfully. "I may have to talk with him."

"That may not be possible, given the time and the circumstances. We're going to have to move fast here, and we don't want Obyedkov compromised from his present position just yet. At least not until after Andropov takes over and the dust settles."

Briggs thought about that for a moment. There were more than one or two ways to skin the cat. "What's his name?"

"Anatoli Fedor Obyedkov. He's got a little place

off St. James Park, believe it or not."

The name meant nothing to Briggs. But he had been away from Oumi and the other emigres for so long it would have been surprising if he had recognized anyone.

"What can you tell me about the center?" Briggs said. "I presume Howard has the tapes and will bring them out tomorrow."

Sir Roger nodded. "He's reviewing them personally. He'll probably get some of his staff in on it. I've left it all up to his discretion." Sir Roger leaned forward. "He is rather good, you know."

"Friends of the family. Yes, I know."

Sir Roger didn't look at all pleased, but he plunged on. "The Center was built even before the Revolution as a sanatorium. One supposes for tuberculosis care. It's to the northeast of Moscow. A few miles. Not far. The unique feature of the place, however, is the lack of roads."

"Sir?"

"There are no roads leading to the place. No way in or out except by train. I suppose in the early days the doctors felt the brief train ride would be less strenuous than an automobile or carriage journey over rutted roads. And since the sanatorium had been converted for other uses, the isolation suited them just fine."

All that was tugging at Briggs' memory. Somewhere at the back of the mind there was something . . . something he strained to remember. He could remember a hot, smoke-filled room. There were a lot of people. Talking. Story telling.

Sir Roger was continuing. "Since the revolution,

but mostly since the middle of Stalin's reign, the place has been used as a sort of a multi-faceted jail."

"Such as Lubyanka. A lockup as well as an interrogation center?"

"It's much more sinister than that, from what Obyedkov tells us. It's a mental institution, primarily, at which dissidents and the like are taken to . . . how shall I put it . . . have their patterns of thinking, their personalities, their memories and likes and dislikes, all of that, altered."

"Good Lord."

"Yes, it is rather gruesome. It still is, of course, a lockup, and an interrogation center. And it is said, that the trip to Yedanov is one-way. There is no coming back . . ."

Suddenly Briggs had it. Suddenly he remembered Oumi and the others talking about the place. They were frightened even to think about it. He remembered clearly now. "The train to nowhere. It's gray. Leaves from the Main Moscow Railway Center downtown. No one ever comes back."

"You've heard of the place."

"It's nearly folklore. All the gremlins and trolls and bad faeries dwell there."

"Quite," Sir Roger said. "Popov has been taken there."

"He'll never come back."

"Not as Popov, but he will come back as someone else. Someone who atones for his sins against the state. Someone who will be perfectly willing to tell his fellow dissidents, tell the entire world that he was sleeping with Brezhnev's daughter at the behest of Her Majesty's government. The British will stop at nothing, they will maintain. When Andropov takes over the harm will be irreparable."

It was all painfully clear to Briggs now. Every bit of it, including the dangerous role he was being asked to play. "I can understand why Hope-Turner opted to kill Popov. It'd be the easiest way out for us?"

"It would."

Briggs took a deep breath, and let it out slowly. He poured himself another drink, and freshened Sir Roger's. Then went back to the window and looked outside for several long seconds.

"Is there some sort of a plan for getting me into the place, then back out?"

"Still vague at this point. But the details are being worked out."

Briggs turned back. "Let me guess. I'll be plunked down in Moscow at the American Embassy. There will be a party, perhaps a dinner party at a hotel, or perhaps even a dacha outside Moscow . . . in the general direction of the Center. Sometime during the party, I'll slip away and make it through the woods to the place, climb over the wall, find Popov, convince him to come along with me—all without alerting the guards—then simply pop back over the fence, and back to the party. Let me see . . . We'll disguise him, and get him back to the American embassy, and from there he'll be smuggled out of the country in a big box."

Sir Roger wasn't smiling.

"Was I close? Do I get an A?"

"Actually it's a drainage tunnel into the place. You'll be given a drug to make Popov more cooperative, and he'll be brought directly to our own embassy, where eventually, after the furor dies down, he'll be sent across at the Finnish border."

"Who besides you will know of the plan. Besides Howard and his staff, that is?"

"Hope-Turner."

"No one else, Sir Roger? No nuts-and-bolts people? No one in the embassy in Moscow?"

"There'll be one or two key people here and there. Liaison. Contact people."

"To smooth the way?"

"Yes."

"Including our embassy in Moscow?"

"Of course, Donald. What do you expect? None of this has the slightest chance of getting to Houten. Not the slightest. On that score you will be perfectly safe."

"I see," Briggs said, but he didn't. Not at all.

## TWELVE

Sylvia Hume was waiting downstairs in Burt Higgins' office, and when Briggs saw her his breath caught in his throat. She was beautiful. Her long black hair shimmered like a waterfall cascading down over her shoulders, and her wide, wonderfully expressive eyes seemed to drink in every move he made.

"Sorry to be so long, darling," Sir Roger said.

"Not to worry, father, Mr. Higgins and I have been having a splendid chat. We've even included Mr. O'Meara, here."

Briggs had to smile. She was doing it again . . . acting out the part of the haughty British bitch-goddess. He wasn't going to succumb to it this time. The more his blood boiled, the more he'd bite his tongue.

"It must have been an amusing discussion then," he said, despite himself.

She laughed. "On the contrary, Mr. O'Meara. It was hilarious."

Higgins was embarrassed. He came around his desk. "If you will excuse me, I have some business to attend to." Sylvia inclined her head. "I'll speak to you before you leave, if you've a chance, Sir Roger," he said.

"I'll tag along with you now," Sir Roger said. He turned back to his daughter. "Whenever you and . . . Mr. O'Meara are finished talking I shall be around the side by the automobile."

"Yes, father," she said, and Sir Roger and Higgins left the office.

They both started to speak at the same moment, then stopped, smiling.

"I'm sorry," Briggs said. "Go ahead."

"No, you go first."

He hesitated for just a moment. "I wanted to speak with you before I left . . ."

"You're leaving soon?" she interrupted him.

"In the next few days. It's why I wanted to see you now. I wanted to apologize."

Her right eyebrow rose. At that moment he could see a lot of Sir Roger in her. But that was good. He respected the man. "For what?" she asked.

"For my behavior the other day. I said and did a lot of things that I'm not particularly proud of. I'm sorry."

She stared at him for a very long time, her eyes wide, her mouth pursed. Then she smiled. "I came for exactly the same purpose, Mr. O'Meara. To apologize."

"My friends call me Briggs," he said.

"Only your friends? No one closer?"

"There is no one closer. But if there was, I'd be Briggs." His heart was hammering, and his mouth dry. This was crazy. It was worse . . . it was stupid.

She said nothing.

"Well . . . I'm glad I got this chance. I didn't want you to think too badly of me," Briggs said. "Have a good trip back." He started to turn.

"Oh, we're not returning until you've finished," she blurted.

"Your father will be liaison between the SIS and Howard's bunch?" Briggs asked, surprised.

"He likes you, you know."

That meant Sir Roger was working directly with Howard. It meant Sir Roger knew all the details of the plan, which wasn't quite the impression he had given just a half hour ago. So why the deception? What was he holding back?

Sylvia was saying something else. He didn't quite catch it.

"Thank you, Miss Hume, perhaps I'll see you again when I return," he said, and he started to turn toward the door, but Sylvia called out his name.

"Briggs?"

He turned and went across the room to where she stood by the desk.

"I did mean it . . . my apology that is," she said.

He took her in his arms and kissed her deeply. At first she struggled, but almost immediately she melted, her body pressed against his.

"Hmm," he said smiling.

"Hmm?"

"I've never kissed gentry before. Not bad."

Sylvia stepped back, the color rising to her cheeks. "You bastard," she said, barely able to control her voice. "You bloody bastard."

"Yes, I am," Briggs said, not quite sure himself why he had done and said what he had. He turned and left Higgins' office, cursing himself across Administration, and out the door.

Sir Roger and Burt Higgins stood talking by a gray Chevrolet with government plates. Briggs stepped off the porch and they looked up, as he strode past.

"Donald?" Sir Roger asked, but Briggs ignored him, continuing around back of the building, and heading out the rutted dirt road toward the firing range and obstacle course.

When he was a young boy, his mother had always been too busy for him. She had worked hard to make a living for them; to provide food on the table and a roof over their heads. After she and his uncle were killed, and he had been taken in by the emigrés, little if anything had changed. He had still existed in a world of emotional nothings. Coldness, sharp words at times, most often indifference. Then as an adult, here in the States, there had been less than that. Americans were bright, vivacious, very open and friendly . . . to a point. After that point, there was nothing for a very long time. The process of making very close personal friends in Europe was almost impossible, and in the States, a long drawn out process. Here he had never spent enough time in one place to make those kinds of lasting relationships.

As he walked, he looked up at the bright blue sky, with its few puffy white summer clouds. He was lonely. That was the short and the long of it. He was damned lonely.

"You want friends? You got friends," Oumi had said to him when he was sixteen. For a month or so after that all the emigres, or at least a good number of them, had tried to entertain Briggs. They had staged parties. They had bought him presents. Had stopped in for chats. Had invited him for cakes and tea. They had been wonderful, insomuch as sixty, seventy and eighty year olds could provide companionship for a teen.

Christ, he thought as he walked. Christ. Where the hell had his life gone to? He was forty goddamn years old, and he had nothing. A car. A few clothes, books, pots and pans. No country estate. No wife and children. No deep friends. Nothing or no one that counted.

Not even a country.

The path branched left toward the firing range, straight ahead to the light explosive testing grounds, and right to the obstacle course that meandered a couple of miles farther back into the woods.

Briggs took the road to the right, as a jeep came from the obstacle course toward him. He stepped off the road to let the vehicle, which was moving at high speed trailing a thick cloud of dust. There was a driver and one passenger and Briggs got a good look at both of them as they passed.

Bob Chiles was driving, and the passenger was Dick White, the agent he had had a run-in with at the studio back in Los Angeles.

Briggs watched the jeep for several long moments. White turned in his seat and looked back. The two of them together meant certain trouble. The only question was when was it going to come.

Whenever, Briggs decided, stepping back onto the road, and continuing over to the obstacle course, he would be ready for them. Maybe they could get this nonsense out of their systems once and for all. They'd all be better off afterwards.

The course master was a youngish man, in his early to mid-thirties, Brigg guessed, who stood well over six-feet but weighed no more than 175 pounds. He looked almost emaciated, but he moved with the smoothness and grace of a predator. His name was Stu Danielson. He had been in Vietnam for two tours, and he was proud of it. His course assistants were Vietnam vets as well.

"Mr. O'Meara. You're not scheduled until tomorrow morning," Danielson said coming out of his office at the base of the observation tower.

Briggs came the rest of the way up the sand and gravel approach ramp. Just beyond the tower was a high log wall.

"I have the afternoon free. Thought maybe I'd take a dash through."

Danielson shook his head smugly. "Doesn't work that way out here, pal. Anyway, you're not dressed for us."

Briggs looked down at his Russian-cut clothing.

"Fatigues or jumpsuits, combat boots and a pot."

"Don't think I'll be running around Moscow in an outfit like that. I'll either be dressed in something like this, or in American civilian clothing."

"Doesn't matter. You *will* run my course in the

147

proper attire.''

Briggs was getting angry. "See here, old chap.''

Danielson came closer. "I suggest, Mr. O'Meara you turn your butt around and shag ass out of here before I call someone.''

Briggs had had his fill, between Sir Roger hiding something from him, to the likelihood of some kind of a confrontation with Chiles and White, and now this tin soldier.

"You'd better call someone then, old top, because I'm going to run your course . . . now.''

A jeep pulled up behind them before Danielson could answer, and Briggs turned around. Chiles and White climbed out of the jeep and started up the ramp. Briggs could feel a looseness coming over his muscles. His heart rate settled down, and began breathing shallowly through his mouth. He was ready.

"Some kind of trouble here, Stu?" Chiles asked.

White just stared at Briggs, who stared back at him. There was a lot of animosity in the man's eyes, and in his stance. But there was a wariness there as well. Both had had run-ins with Briggs. Both remembered.

"He wants to run the course right now, in those clothes. He's not scheduled until tomorrow. I was just about to call Higgins.''

"Don't bother," Chiles said. "Do you want to run the course now, O'Meara?''

Briggs nodded.

"Then let him do it," Chiles said. "We'll stick around in case he gets into any trouble out there. You won't have to send any of your people after him."

"I don't know, Bob . . ." Danielson said.

"Thank you Mr. Chiles," Briggs said. "Perhaps I'll see you two out there."

"I wouldn't be too terribly surprised," Chiles said.

Sudden understanding dawned on Danielson's face, and he smiled and stepped back. "It's all yours, Mr. O'Meara."

Briggs looked up toward the log wall. "What's on the other side?"

"A surprise," the course master said. Several of his assistants had come out of the hut, and the officer on the observation tower was looking down at them. They were all grinning.

Open your big mouth, and back yourself into a corner. It happened every time, Briggs thought. When would he ever learn?

The man on the observation tower would be able to pinpoint his every move, relaying the information to Chiles and White, who would be able to easily intercept him at the point where he was under the maximum stress. At least that would be the way it worked if he remained on the course-lines.

"Gentlemen," he said, nodding. He turned and sprinted easily up the ramp, hit the wall and pulled himself over it. The wall was ten feet high on the outside, but dropped to fifteen feet into a watery mudhole on the other side.

Briggs hit on his left side splashing mud and water back up on the wall, soaking himself to the skin. As he crawled soddenly out of the hole, he looked up over his shoulder at the officer on the tower. The man was studying him through binoculars.

Briggs raised the middle finger of his right hand in a salute, then turned and trotted into the woods along the path that went up a small hill then down the other side to a long horizontal ladder over big rolls of barbed wire.

He hit the ladder running, and worked his way across, hand-over-hand, swinging his lower body in perfect rhythm for momentum.

On the other side, the path curved left then zig-zagged across a narrow field, over unsteady barrels, across a narrow, peeled log, over tires, beneath barbed wire, and over another mudhole on a rope swing.

Briggs had swung into an easy, ground covering lope that felt very natural and rhythmic to him. From time to time he glanced up toward the observation tower, and several times he caught the glint of the afternoon sunlight off the binoculars the officer was using to watch him.

On the far side of the narrow field, the path cut through a dense section of woods, and for a hundred yards he was out of sight of the tower.

He raced to where the path came out of the deep woods, then held up, still out of sight from the tower.

Twenty-five or thirty yards across an open space, the land dropped away, past a jumble of large boulders. There were several sets of heavy timber tripods set up, with rope disappearing over the edge. It was a standard obstacle course set up. There was a cliff there. The next step of the course would be to climb down the ropes, and pick up the path below.

They would be waiting for him down there. At least Chiles and White. Perhaps some of Danielson's men. They'd be hiding. The moment he hit the bottom they'd be on him.

Quickly Briggs took off his boots and his socks, then peeled off his sodden jacket. He laid his things out of sight in the underbrush, then moved away from the path and silently through the woods, parallel to the cliff face, and only a few yards away from the edge of the woods.

He had gone less than a hundred feet when he caught a movement ahead and to the left, a little closer to the edge of the trees, and he ducked down.

Someone was there. Hiding. Watching the cliff, and the tripods. But why?

Briggs crawled a little closer. It was one of Danielson's men, dressed in fatigues. He held a machete.

Suddenly it dawned on Briggs, what they were going to do. The others were hiding below. But as soon as he started down the rope, this character hiding up here would come out brandishing his machete, and start cutting the rope. Briggs didn't think they'd go so far as to actually kill him, but they certainly intended on roughing him up.

He moved up closer so that he was less than ten feet behind the waiting man, when he heard the hiss of a walkie talkie. The assistant course master pulled the radio out of its belt holster and raised it to his lips. "Three here."

"Has he shown up yet, Hap?"

"Not yet."

"Keep your eyes open. He's somewhere between A field and the cliff. I lost him."

"He's probably on his ass taking a breather."

"I don't know, Hap. Just keep your eyes open."

"Roger," the man said, and he holstered his radio.

Briggs hit him then, yanking the machete out of his hands, and tossing it out into the woods.

The man scrambled backwards and started to reach for his radio.

"Touch that radio, my friend, and I'll break both of your arms," Briggs said softly. He was smiling.

The man's eyes were wide, his chest was rising and falling as he tried to catch his breath. But his hand stopped.

"Where are they?"

The man shook his head, and Briggs was on him, his right hand around his throat, his thumb up under the man's chin. He snatched the walkie talkie with his other hand, and stuffed it in his back pocket. Then he eased up slightly on the pressure.

"Where are they?" he asked again.

The man was frightened. "Chiles and White are pissed off about something. I don't know nothing about it."

"I know," Briggs said soothingly. He loosened up a bit more. "Who else is down there?"

"Danielson."

"And where are they?"

"To the east. Down the path. Just beyond the last rope."

Briggs released him and stepped back. "I want you to stay right here for ten minutes, then head back up the course to the start line. I don't want you to make any noise, or in any way try to warn those people down there. Do I make myself perfectly clear?''

The man nodded.

Briggs smiled again. He really felt loose now. ''If you should do anything to displease me, old top, I'll come back and take you apart. I mean that sincerely.''

''I . . .''

''I know,'' Briggs said. ''Ta ta.'' He turned, and headed in a run through the woods, but now angling back toward the path. The terrain sloped toward the east, and within a few hundred yards the cliff had flattened out so that the woods reached the lower level.

Moving much more cautiously now Briggs headed back toward the base of the cliff, spotting Dick White almost immediately, where he hid behind the bole of a large tree.

Briggs pulled the walkie talkie out of his pocket, and raised it to his lips. ''White . . . Your ass is exposed, don't you know, sport.''

White spun around, and when he spotted Briggs standing at the edge of the path, he glanced over toward his left. Chiles and Danielson stepped out of the brush a moment later.

Briggs stepped up on the path, and walked toward them. When he was close enough he tossed the walkie talkie to Danielson.

''You fellows play these little Boy Scout games all the time?''

Danielson said nothing, he seemed almost embarrassed, but White was boiling. He leaped forward, swinging as he came. Briggs easily sidestepped his charge, smashing a fist into the man's solar plexus, which doubled him over, then back-handed him between his shoulder blades, knocking him to the ground.

Chiles was on him in the next instant, but Briggs managed to step back and he connected to the man's chin with a solid right hook that knocked Chiles on his back, and nearly broke Briggs' arm.

"Jesus," Briggs winced, stepping back, when something very hard smashed into the back of his head.

He went down to his knees, his stomach churning, the ground spinning, as someone kicked him in the side. He rolled with the punch, trying to regain his balance, but they were after him, kicking him in the back, then the shoulder.

He rolled over twice more and got back on his feet, as the agent he had taken the walkie talkie from above, came at him with a long, thick piece of tree branch. He swung, and missed, Briggs kicked his elbow, and grabbed the wood.

Danielson who had been right behind him, stopped his charge. Briggs' head was still spinning, as he advanced, "Poor sportsmanship, that's what this is," he said. He poked the tree branch into his adversary's chest, nearly knocking the man back.

"And it pisses me off," Briggs said. He was getting madder by the moment. "I want you to know that."

"What do you think you're going to do?" Danielson shouted, self-righteously.

Briggs just looked at the man, and he shook his head, and tossed the club away. He started to turn, but then shook his head again. "Oh hell," he muttered, and he turned back to the two men, leaping into the air, as he kicked out.

His left foot caught Danielson high in the chest, knocking him on the ground. In the next instant, Briggs snapped off a half a dozen karate chops to the other man's mid-section, chest, neck and head.

Danielson was getting up, as Briggs spun around, catching him neatly in the chin with his heel.

And it was over.

# THIRTEEN

Back at the top of the hill, Briggs retrieved his clothes, then hiked up to the start of the obstacle course where a half a dozen men and women were gathered to begin their run. Several of the assistant course masters were there, and those who knew what was supposed to have happened didn't appear too happy. Everyone was taken aback by his bedraggled appearance, and the wild look in his eye.

He strode barefooted down the gravel ramp, tossed his jacket, socks and boots into the jeep that Chiles and White had driven over, and climbed behind the wheel.

One of the assistant course masters hurried over. "You can't take this vehicle," he shouted.

"Watch me," Briggs said looking up as he started it.

"But Mr. Danielson . . . where is he?"

"He's dead," Briggs shouted perversely, and he

took off.

Twice on the way back, he almost turned around and returned to the obstacle course to get the young kid off the hook, but both times he ignored his own good sense and continued driving. He pulled up in front of the administration entrance, jumped out of the jeep, and with his sodden jacket and boots in hand strode up the steps and inside.

It was just a few minutes before the early dinner hour and there were quite a few people about, all of whom took an amused interest in the barefoot Irishman, obviously mad as hell.

Burt Higgins intercepted him in the corridor between the orderly room and the stairs to the BOQ.

"What the hell happened to you?"

"Nothing to be concerned about," Briggs snapped over his shoulder, sidestepping Higgins and striding down the hall.

Higgins caught up with him. "Nothing, my ass. I want to know what happened? I demand to know what happened to you!"

Briggs paused at the stairs. "Leave it be, Higgins. Forget you ever saw me. Forget you ever heard of me. I'm not accepting this assignment."

"What happened this afternoon . . . Briggs?"

Briggs turned on him. "The name is O'Meara, old top! And all that's happened so far is lies and deceit. And I've had my fill of it. From Sir Roger right on down the line. You can tell Howard to . . . shove this place right up his commodious ass."

Turning back, Briggs headed up the stairs, taking them two at a time.

"You can't quit now!" Higgins shouted up after

him. "Sir Roger's counting on you. Your government is counting on you."

"I have no government . . . don't you know?" Briggs shouted at the first landing. He continued up. Higgins clattered up the stairs after him.

"For Christ's sake, O'Meara, what the hell happened to you?"

"Doesn't matter what happened to me. I'm out," Briggs shouted back.

"Not like this, you're not."

Briggs stopped at the second floor landing, and waited for Higgins, who was out of breath already, to catch up. "Don't fuck with me, Higgins. Don't send your Boy Scouts to fuck with me. The next person that pushes at me will get hurt."

Higgins stood one flight down looking up at Briggs. He shook his head. "A lot of people are depending upon you, Briggs."

"I don't want it! Can't you see, you bastards?"

"Take it easy," Higgins said, starting up.

Briggs backed up. He was feeling trapped. Caged. Like an animal. He wanted to run, or at least to lash out. Goddamnit . . . he did not like this. He had not asked for this. He did not want any part of this.

"I'll telephone Rudy. He can take a chopper and be out here within an hour . . . maybe a little longer. We can get Sir Roger back. Sylvia. Anyone you want. But you can't just walk away."

Someone was coming down the second floor hall, and Briggs backed up, dropping into the classic karate stance, his hands at angles out in front of him. The man, stopped, confused.

Higgins reached the landing. "Get the hell out of

158

here, Stanford! Now! Move it!''

The man spun around and took off down the hall.

"I know the kinds of trouble you've had, Briggs. Not all the details, but certainly the flavor.''

It was stiflingly hot here. Briggs really wanted to open a window. For most of his life he had been in control. At this moment, however, he felt as if his entire life was like a heart palpitation . . . unnecessary, out of sync, and useless.

"I don't want to hurt you, Higgins. I don't want to hurt anyone. If you leave me alone, everything will be fine.''

"I can't do that, Briggs. You know that.''

Briggs was in a dream. He stuck out his hand. "Stay back, Burt. Just stay back. Please.'' He turned and raced up the stairs to his floor, hurried down the corridor and let himself into his room, throwing the bolt when he was safely inside, his heart pounding nearly out of his chest.

He had never felt this way, at least he hadn't since he was a young boy.

He moved to the window and looked out. Stealing a vehicle to get out of here would be no problem. But then what? Where in God's name would he run to? He didn't know anyone he could trust enough to hide him. In fact there weren't many people who knew his real background. A few people here and a few in England. That was it.

All his life he had wanted a place; he had wanted to belong. For that he would have done anything. But it wasn't to be.

At least until now, he thought bitterly, turning around to face the door.

The window at his back was open. He could smell the air, feel the fresh breeze. There was escape that way. Freedom . . . of a sort. While ahead, through the door and downstairs was . . . what? Responsibility? Or manipulation? Duty? Or an attempt to cover up a badly conceived mission?

He went slowly into the bathroom, took off his sodden clothing, and took a hot shower. When he was finished he got dressed in clean clothes, and lit a cigarette.

Stay or go?

If he stayed, Howard would be out here either this evening yet, or at the latest tomorrow afternoon to begin his briefing about the Yedanov Rehabilitation Center. How much of that would be truth, and how much lies was still another question.

If he went, he'd be hunted. There was little doubt that Howard would send someone after him. Perhaps White and Chiles. They now had a score to settle with him.

If he stayed, he'd be manipulated. If he left, he'd be hunted. Two clear choices. Or was there another variation, he asked himself.

Someone knocked at his door, then tried the doorknob. "Briggs? You in there?" Higgins called.

"No. I'm gone."

"I want to talk," Higgins said. "Howard is on his way out with the tapes. At least keep an open mind until he shows up."

Briggs went to the door, unlocked it, then stepped back to the window where he lit another cigarette.

Higgins came in. "The kitchen is holding dinner for you."

"I'm not much hungry."

"They'll hold it anyway. There are still a few others out."

"Such as Chiles and White, and Danielson?"

Higgins shook his head. "Chiles and White showed up just a minute ago. They'll be up here as soon as they clean up."

"Going to trot them by for their dutiful apologies?" Briggs asked. "Is that it, then? Like good little boys?"

"Something like that. Unless you want them, and the rest of the staff as permanent enemies."

Briggs laughed. "That is the situation at hand. One I did not cause, and one I can't do much about."

"On the contrary, you could try a little cooperation."

"With whom? For what? So I can be lied to again?"

"Your disdain is showing," Higgins said heavily. "You're nothing more than a variation of the spoiled, petulant child. Totally unapproachable."

"Certainly not approachable by deceit," Briggs flared.

"You keep saying that. Who's lied to you?"

"Everyone. Sir Roger, for example. He's running this show . . . or at least is acting as liaison. He never told me."

Higgins had to laugh. "The commander tells his troops every move he makes? Come off it, Briggs. Grow up. You're either going to be a part of this, or you're out. At this point, I guess I really don't give a damn except for the fact that Rudyard Howard is one fine man, as is Sir Roger."

"And Chiles and White . . . two more fine men?" Briggs asked. He was confused.

"Yes, they are. Afraid for their jobs probably, and their pensions. They have families to support."

"So they set up an attack on me . . . ?"

"They set out to put down what appeared to them to be some low class English hotshot over here to set the world afire, while ignoring practically every law on the books. They are policemen, you know. And you are an illegal alien."

"Christ," Briggs said turning to look out the window. He was even more confused than before. Higgins was . . . or at least appeared to be . . . a decent sort. But the others seemed to be more concerned about his past than about what he could do for them. And then Sir Roger had lied to him. Or at least held back. Yet what Higgins was saying to him made a certain sense.

"I know that you're thinking about bugging out of here. I read it on your face the moment I walked into this room. And there's not much doubt you could pull it off. Chiles and White and some of the others would be delighted. They'd be able to say, I told you so. But then what, Briggs? From what I've gathered so far, you're sick to death of the running. You wanted to stop. Now's your chance."

"You're going to dangle another carrot under my nose?"

"Yes."

Briggs turned around.

"U.S. citizenship, if you want it. A home. A place."

"In trade for going on this mission?"

Higgins nodded.

"You bastard."

"For giving you what you most want?" Higgins asked.

"For dangling it in front of me like that. When the mission is done, it won't have been quite enough. Oh, the paperwork will have been started. Bit of a delay; you know how these things go, old chap. Just time enough to pop around for another little job. Then another. Prosecution if I don't."

"We don't do things that way over here. You are being offered citizenship and dismissal of all charges pending against you for this mission. Afterwards, depending upon how you do, I have been told you will be offered a job with us."

"You're going through a lot of trouble for Sir Roger and the SIS. Why?"

"We're allies."

"Bull."

"No, it's not bull, but then perhaps you are incapable of understanding," Higgins said. He looked long and hard at Briggs then turned and went to the door. Before he left, however, he looked over his shoulder. "If you want to talk with Rudy he'll be here soon. Just call down to my office. Otherwise, we'll expect you out on the confidence range at oh-eight hundred." He left, closing the door softly behind him.

Briggs stared at the door for a long time, willing it to open; willing Higgins to return so that they could continue the discussion, which had . . . as far as Briggs was concerned . . . gone very badly.

But he did not return and after a couple of minutes, Briggs poured himself a stiff shot of Irish whiskey (Higgins had provided him the bottle), then sat down at the table, and put his feet up.

All his life he wanted to be a part of something, and now that it was finally being offered to him, he did not trust them.

But he was tired of running, without purpose. Lord, how he was tired of it.

He sat way back in the chair and closed his eyes, letting the whiskey he had drunk warm his insides, loosen the knot in his gut.

He had handled everything badly, beginning with White and Byers back in California, to Howard and Sir Roger outside Washington. Most of all he had handled Sylvia very badly. But there was something about her, about the way she talked, the things she said, that made his blood boil. He had even botched his apology to her.

If he stayed he was going to have to make it up to her, somehow. He could see her face in his mind's eye. Her eyes flashing. She was saying something. But he could not quite hear her.

Someone knocked at his door, a half an hour later, and he opened his eyes and sat forward. "It's not locked."

The door swung open and Rudyard Howard stepped in, looking like a particularly mean bulldog, his shirt collar open, his tie loose, the veins bulging at his thick neck.

"You're done, O'Meara," Howard roared.

Briggs got to his feet. "That's fine with me."

"I don't know who the hell you think you are,

164

coming in here, running around the countryside, beating up my people. Sonofabitch . . . one of my people has a broken jaw. He'll be out of action for weeks!"

Briggs had to smile. "Chiles or Danielson?"

Howard reached in his pocket and took out a .38 Police Special, and pointed it at Briggs, who stiffened. "Two U.S. Marshals are on their way out to pick you up. Get your things together, we'll wait in Burt Higgins' office."

No stiletto, no passports, no money. He was stuck here. For the moment.

"Move it," Howard snapped. He was very angry.

Briggs pulled down his bag from the closet shelf, and threw his things inside, including his shaving gear from the bathroom. When he had it latched, Howard kicked the corridor door the rest of the way open and stepped aside.

"Let's go, hot shot."

"What's this all about? Or is it you're mad that I beat up a few of your people who were trying to hurt me?"

"I'm not going to listen to any of your lies, you sonofabitch. Now move it!"

It wasn't fair, but then Briggs hadn't really expected anything else from this man, despite what everyone said about him.

Howard stepped forward, raising the pistol, and Briggs could feel his muscles going loose. He didn't want to do this, but Howard wasn't leaving him much choice. Before he left, though, he was going to make Howard understand what had really happened out there.

Briggs headed for the door, and as he passed Howard, he dropped his suitcase. "Ooops," he said and started to bend down to pick it up. At that moment Howard's concentration wavered for just a split second, and Briggs simply reached out and snatched the pistol out of his hand, and stepped back.

"Oh . . ." Howard started, but the words died in his throat.

Briggs smiled. "We'll wait in Burt's office for the Marshals. But while we're waiting, you're going to listen to what I have to say."

"Don't make this any worse than it already is, O'Meara."

"I don't have much to lose," Briggs smiled. He pocketed the pistol, and picked up his suitcase, with the other hand. "After you Mr. Howard."

Howard hesitated a moment, but then turned and marched out of the room, down the corridor, and took the stairs down, Briggs right behind him.

Burt Higgins was in the first floor corridor talking with Chiles and White when they emerged from the stairwell.

"Ah, Rudy, Briggs . . . everything has worked out?" Higgins asked, but then he saw the look on Howard's face. "Oh Christ," he said.

"He has a gun," Howard said as they approached.

"I don't want to use it," Briggs said, Chiles and White stepped back.

"We'll tell him everything," Chiles said.

"Indeed you will," Briggs said. "We're going to have a long chat . . . a nice long chat."

"Where'd you get the gun, Briggs?" Higgins asked.

"From your boss here. He was pointing it at me, and calling me a sonofabitch and all. You know, I didn't like it."

# FOURTEEN

They were settled in Higgins' office, Briggs leaning against the wall by the window, the others seated, looking up at him. "We don't have very much time, so we'll make this short and sweet. From what I understand I'm to be arrested very soon."

"What?" Higgins said sitting forward.

"I telephoned Billingsly as soon as I found out what was going on out here," Howard said, but he didn't seem quite as sure of himself as he had earlier.

"Pardon me, sir, but I think you've got it wrong," Chiles said.

"What?"

"We . . . that is Dick White and Danielson from the confidence course decided to . . . have a little fun at Mr. O'Meara's expense. It . . . well, it backfired on us."

"What do you know about this, Burt?" Howard asked Higgins.

"Not much, other than what these two just told me. Danielson's jaw was broken. He'll be laid up for a bit. Evidently they tried to waylay Mr. O'Meara on the confidence course, and he found out about it."

"And took them on," Howard said, eyeing Briggs. "No weapons?"

"Mr. O'Meara had no weapons, sir," Chiles said.

"Why did you break his jaw?"

"I was mad," Briggs said. He took the pistol out of his pocket, and laid it down on the desk. Everyone looked at it. "I'm not playing games any longer, Mr. Howard. Anyone, and I do mean anyone, comes after me, and they will get hurt. Badly."

"Are you threatening us?" Howard snapped.

Briggs nodded. "Yes I am." He turned and looked out the window. "But the next step is yours."

There was a silence in the office for several long seconds until a chair scraped and someone got up. The door opened, at least two people, maybe three left the office, and the door was closed again.

"You'll have to make up your mind then, whether you're staying or leaving," Howard said.

Briggs turned back. They were alone in the office. "What about the U.S. Marshals?"

"Burt will be calling them off. It was a mistake. I am sorry."

Stay or leave. This was getting much more complicated than he thought possible.

"If I stay, and go on the mission, then I will become a citizen? No strings attached?"

"No strings attached," Howard said, but there was something in his eyes. Briggs could see it clearly.

"What is it?" Briggs asked. "What the hell is *with* everyone around here?"

"I don't know what you're talking about."

"You're hiding something from me. I can see it in your eyes. So is Sir Roger. And so is Burt. What is it?"

Howard seemed to think about his reply for a long time. He got to his feet, picked up his gun and holstered it beneath his jacket, then pursed his lips. "I have to return to Washington. A chopper will take me back. I'll be here around noon tomorrow with Obyedkov's tapes, and we'll go over the best three scenarios so that you can get a feel for what you'll be up against."

"What about my question?"

"I think it'll be answered sufficiently in the briefing."

It came clear to Briggs. "So that's it," he said. "You think my chances for survival are next to nothing. You can offer me the moon, but chances are I won't be around to collect, so no one is taking any offers seriously."

Howard said nothing.

"Sir Roger knows this . . . he's the one who told you."

"If you succeed you'll get just about anything you want, within reason. There isn't a lot of money in this . . . but then I don't suppose you've ever killed a Russian for money."

"No."

"Which brings us back to my question. Are you

170

staying with us, or are you going on the run again?''

"If I do go on the run?''

"I will come after you, O'Meara . . . and that's not a threat, that's a promise.''

"You'd send White and Chiles after me?''

Howard smiled. "Yes. And five more. Ten more. Two dozen more. A hundred. A thousand. I can field a lot of men, O'Meara. How long can you keep it up? Just how much fight is there in you?''

"A lot,'' Briggs said. "But I wouldn't just run. I'd come after you, first.''

"Maybe my wife, my family?'' Howard said grimly.

"I don't operate that way, and you know it!''

Howard nodded. "Still leaves us my question. Stay or go? I'm not going to waste much more time or effort on you if you're going to bug out on me.''

Stay or go? Which? If he could return to his old life in Hollywood he'd return. Or would he? Was he just kidding himself?

"I'll be here for your briefing tomorrow.''

"Still doesn't answer my question,'' Howard insisted.

"Nor can I at this moment,'' Briggs said. "I want to know exactly what the operational plan is before I make my final decision. I'm not going to do this blindly. I know what I'll be up against if I refuse. I want to know what I'll be up against if I go ahead.''

At the door Howard stopped and looked back. "I'll ship Chiles, White and Danielson out of here so you won't have to contend with them any longer. We'll put someone new on the team.''

"Don't,'' Briggs said, surprised with himself as

much as Howard was. "I mean . . . if I take this assignment, I'd like them to be in on it."

"I don't understand."

"They're just about broken in by now. I wouldn't want to go through that all over again."

Briggs detected a marked new respect after barely one or two minutes on the dirt ramp below the observation tower at the confidence course. Danielson was conspiciously absent, but his assistant course masters scurried about giving instructions to the two dozen men, including Briggs, who'd be running the course this morning. And all of them spoke in somewhat subdued tones around him, as they seemed to go about their business on tip-toes.

Chiles and White showed up in a jeep, and like Briggs and everyone else they were dressed in olive drab coveralls, and flight boots.

"Good morning, Mr. O'Meara," Chiles said, he and White coming up the ramp.

Briggs turned to them, and he could almost hear everyone pulling in a deep breath; everyone waiting for another confrontation. But he smiled. "Good morning, Bob. Dick." They shook hands.

"Look, we're sorry about what happened yesterday," Chiles said.

"It's over now."

White seemed sheepish. "I . . . sort of got off on the wrong foot with you, right from the beginning. Sorry."

"It's all right," Briggs said. At least they were professional enough to offer their apologies.

Chiles nodded toward the log wall. "We'd like to

run the course with you this morning. It's usually a buddy system, but I don't think there'd be any objections to us going as a trio."

One of the course masters, a younger man with blond hair, shook his head. "It's perfectly all right with us, gentlemen. In fact, if you're ready, we'll let you off first."

Briggs smiled. "That'd be fine, just fine," he said. He turned to the course master. "Why don't you have that fellow up there on the tower time us."

"We time everyone, sir."

"Oh, I see," Briggs said, his smile wider. "What's the course record?"

An increase in interest stirred through the group. "Eleven minutes and fifty-six seconds, sir," the young man said without hesitation. "It was set three years ago by Stu Howard."

"Any relation to Rudyard Howard?"

"Yes, sir. His son. He was killed in Santiago that summer."

"I see," Briggs said. He turned to Chiles and White. "You two up to a challenge of the record?"

Chiles shrugged. "Probably not, but it's worth a try."

Briggs turned to White, who also shrugged. "What the hell."

"Let's do it then."

The course master set them on their mark fifteen yards down from the log wall. He had a stop watch in his hand, at the ready. "In addition to actual time, there will be a ten second penalty each time you get wet, five seconds for each bar skipped on any horizontal ladder, or tire or log missed on any coordination exercise, and a full one minute if you leave your buddy behind.''

Chiles and White were looking at Briggs who was beginning to feel loose again. His muscles felt like hydraulic fluid at the slack, but ready to slam pistons home when needed.

"On your mark, gentlemen," the course master said, holding the stop watch up.

Several of the other students had clambered up the observation tower.

Briggs, Chiles and White stood sideways to the wall.

"Get set . . . go!" the course master shouted.

Briggs hit the wall first, the other two a split second behind him, scrambled up to the top, and instead of dropping over the other side, like he had done the first time, he vaulted away from the wall, landing well away from the mud hole.

Chiles and White did the same . . . they had been on this course many times before.

They raced up the hill, and down the other side, Briggs gaining twenty yards by the time he hit the horizontal ladder and started across.

On the other side he started to sprint left down the path, but then stopped and waited for the other two to catch up.

They did, seconds later, and the three of them made it to the narrow coordination field where they dashed through the barrels, peeled log, tires, barbed wire and the rope swing.

Briggs' heart was pounding in a steady rhythm, and he felt good . . . better than he had felt for a long time. But he had gained at least fifty yards on the other two, and at the path that led into the woods, he again stopped to wait for them. Chiles waved him on.

"Come on," Briggs shouted.

"Go on," Chiles shouted. White was waving for him to continue without them.

Briggs glanced up the path. There would be a minute penalty for each man he left behind. Even with two minutes added to his elapsed time, Briggs felt he could match or better the record. He was rested now. He had eaten well. And he was motivated.

He looked back at Chiles and White racing across the field toward him. Who gave a damn about records, anyway? "My grandmum can jog better than that, you bloody sods," Briggs shouted.

"Go on," Chiles shouted as he and White finally reached the spot where Briggs waited. Chiles was well built, but White was carrying a little extra weight around his middle, and he was beginning to have a hard time.

"We're a team," Briggs shouted falling in step with them, as they pounded down the path through the woods.

They made it to the cliff in short order, each of them starting down a different rope.

Again Briggs hit the bottom first, Chiles next. White was still halfway up the cliff which towered at least eighty feet.

"Move it, Dick," Chiles said.

White did not reply, but he kept climbing down, slowly and unsteadily. It was clear that he was moving at a reckless speed for his strength, and he was in danger of losing his grip.

Chiles was going to shout up again, but Briggs held him off. "The hell with the record, it's not worth him killing himself."

Chiles looked at him for a long moment, some confusion on his face. "Why don't you go? You still have a chance at the record. I'll wait for Dick."

"We're a team, remember?"

White was still twenty feet up.

"Howard told us we would have been reassigned except for you."

Briggs shrugged. "I'm a bloody masochist."

Chiles laughed, and at that moment White lost his grip and fell the last fifteen feet, landing on his right leg which buckled under him. He let out a short cry of pain.

"Jesus," Chiles swore. He and Briggs hurried to the fallen man, and gently straightened out his leg. He was in great pain, his complexion pale.

Chiles was examining his leg.

"Is it broken?" Briggs asked.

Chiles shook his head. "Just a bad sprain, I think."

"Sonofabitch . . . sonofabitch . . ." White kept swearing. "I'm sorry, O'Meara. Jesus . . ."

"Get the hell out of here," Chiles said, "while you still have a chance."

Briggs shook his head. "My friends call me Briggs. Now let's get Dick up to the dispensary. You do have a dispensary in this joint?"

"Go on, you stupid bastard, get the hell out here. You're still required to run the course," White shouted in pain.

"They can shove the course," Briggs said as he and Chiles carefully lifted White, and carrying him so that there was no pressure on his sprained ankle, headed back to the starting position.

"They'll send a chopper in here for me," White complained.

"We came in under our own steam, old chap, and we'll go out the same."

White started to protest more, but finally he started to laugh, which caused Chiles and Briggs to laugh.

"Fuck you, Briggs," White said. "My name is Dick, not *old chap.*" He said the last with a bad British accent, which caused them all to laugh even harder.

The zoom lens on the television camera atop the confidence course observation tower gave a very clear image to go with the sound picked up by microphones hidden at various spots along the course.

Howard and Sir Roger were seated in the study at Howard's house, watching and listening.

"More coffee?" Howard asked.

"A bit," Sir Roger replied, holding his cup out.

"I guess I underestimated your boy," Howard said as he poured. "I didn't think he'd ever work as part of a team."

"Don't be fooled, Rudyard, Briggs is still primarily a loner. If someone needs his help, he will help them. But when the crunch comes, when it all starts to close in on him, his natural reaction will be to chuck everything and head out light."

"Can you trust him then with Popov?"

"Completely. If we asked him to bring the man out, he will. I'm just talking about his nature . . . his tendencies, if you will."

"We'll have to watch that closely."

"Channel it, I think would be more appropriate."

"Just like his dislike of guns?"

"Your people certainly missed that on their psychological profiles," Sir Roger said with some amusement.

"There were some certain unclear indications, from what I've been told," Howard said. "But no one was quite sure what they meant. It really doesn't matter, though, he *does* know how to handle a gun."

"I think it would be a mistake to force the issue with him, however."

"Leave him go with that . . . toy?" Howard asked incredulously.

A faint smile crossed Sir Roger's lips. He sipped at the very bad coffee. "That *toy,* as you call it, has killed its share of men, beginning before the Russian revolution."

Howard glanced at the television receiver. Briggs, Chiles and White were headed up the shortcut path that led directly back to the start point. They were joking and laughing.

"His stiletto has a history?" he asked, turning back.

"Quite a colorful and bloody history, most of which Briggs is not aware of. It was commissioned by the King of Denmark in the late eighteen hundreds. Made by a Swedish sword maker. Finest steel. Very strong, and all that. The hilt was jeweled

178

in France, and the thing was presented as a sort of peace offering to the Czar of all the Russias. After the revolution, the jewels were taken off the handle, and sold, and the blade was locked away in a museum."

"How did Briggs come to have it?"

"His adopted guardian, Vasili Oumiatin Pavlachek . . . whom he has always called Oumi . . . was head of our VST network operating in and around Moscow before and during the Second World War. There was a raid, and Pavlachek lifted the stiletto, fixed the handle, and used it to kill Germans, then Russians. When Briggs took over from where he and the others had left off, they gave him the blade and taught him how to use it."

"I see," Howard said, glancing again at the television. Briggs and the others were almost up to the observation tower. "I suppose he's good with it."

"Very," Sir Roger said. "A nasty skill, actually, but for someone like Donald O'Meara, who probably won't live to see his next birthday, it may not be nasty enough."

## FIFTEEN

Briggs had not felt as much a part of something for a very long time . . . since Soho and his emigre family there . . . as he did at this moment. They had gathered in the conference room in the administration wing, to listen to and attempt to pick apart Howard's best three scenarios for the mission.

There had been a lot of congratulations at lunch, and good natured kidding of Dick White, whose ankle was bandaged. He'd be hobbling around on a cane for a few days, but he'd be all right.

Afterwards, Higgins had called them into the conference room where Howard had been waiting. A screen had been set up at one end of the room, the projector at the far end of the conference table. A tape recorder was laid out and ready beside Howard, a blackboard behind him.

When they were settled, Briggs, Chiles and White on one side, Howard on the other, Higgins locked the door and flipped on the light switch which activated a tape recorder as well as electronic eavesdropping jammers. The room was safe.

"We have a lot of ground to cover, gentlemen, so I'll be very much to the point this afternoon," Howard began without preamble.

Briggs had half expected Sir Roger to show up for this little tea party. He had to admit he was somewhat disappointed the old man had not. Perhaps Sylvia would have come with him again.

"All of you have been briefed on the situation as it exists, and the request by our British counterparts for help. Mr. O'Meara here will be the star, so to speak, of our operation."

"It's not clear to me about this Peter Houten," Chiles spoke up.

"We're to leave him strictly alone. He's off limits."

"Unless he gets in my way," Briggs said softly.

"Yes . . . well, you're to avoid any such confrontation if at all possible," Howard said. "From what I have been told, this Houten character is well placed in Moscow, not only with the KGB, but with the civil authorities as well. Mess with him, on his own turf, and we'll find this entire operation blown up in our faces."

"But he suspects someone will try for Popov," Chiles said.

"The SIS believes that to be the case. But Houten will expect that someone to be a British citizen . . . therefore operating out of the British embassy. And further, he will believe that Popov will be assassinated, not rescued."

"If I can't get him out, then what?" Briggs asked.

"In that event, you will have to kill him. He is entirely too dangerous not only to your government, but to ours, to remain in Soviet hands." Howard had taken off his jacket. He loosened his tie and undid the collar button. Briggs figured his neck size to be at least 21 inches. The man was built like a battering ram—thick in the middle, blunt on top.

"So the operation is easy. We need merely to get me to Moscow, then into the lockup where I either snatch our man or kill him, then get me back to Moscow and finally out of the bloody country."

A faint smile crossed Howard's lips. Chiles and White did not seem too happy. Higgins merely waited by the projector.

"The operation is easy, the execution is difficult," Howard said.

Briggs winced. "Bad word in front of the condemned man."

The quip momentarily broke the tension. They all chuckled.

"We'll get to the Rehabilitation Center . . . by way, it's a psychiatric hospital, not simply a lockup . . . a little later. First we'll run through the steps. We've come up with three scenarios, each with its own difficulties, and its own probability for success."

"Or failure," Briggs said softly.

"Yes, or failure," Howard agreed.

"Getting me to Moscow, I suspect, will pose no particular difficulties," Briggs said after a moment or two.

"None. You will be there as a State Department

employee. We thought as a cook. You'll be less likely to come under any suspicion that way, and no one will pay much attention to you, inside or outside the embassy. We can get you out the same way when it's over. Popov would remain there until the dust settled, so to speak, and we could fetch him back in disguise.''

The room got quiet then, except for the slight hum of the fluorescent lights.

"You've three plans," Briggs said. "Run them by me, one at a time. Just the highlights."

"You can pass as a Russian, I'm told."

Briggs nodded.

"Your informant, Obyedkov in London now, tells us that the hospital, being so old, has almost constant maintenance problems. It is not unusual for several maintenance people to come out each day by train. Our intelligence will pick one out for you, whose place you will take. Once inside the hospital, you'd have to find out where Popov is being kept . . . and Obyedkov has some very definite ideas about that on tape . . . and take him back with you, dressed as your assistant."

Briggs shook his head. "What probability for success did you assign to that one?"

"Forty-sixty. But we're here to pick these apart. Come up with something viable."

Briggs didn't have to ask which way the split went. "In the first place, Popov will probably be drugged."

"We can supply you with counteracting drugs. Like uppers."

"Second of all, if Popov is such a hot political

183

prisoner he'd be watched more closely."

"That may not be the case. It may well be that only a handful of people know that he had been . . . involved with Brezhnev's daughter. Could be they'd keep a low profile while they worked on him, so as not to call any undue attention to the situation."

"We're guessing at that point?" White asked.

Howard nodded. "We're guessing."

At the first sign of trouble, they'd shut down the trains, the only way in or out of the place, according to Sir Roger. The idea was gutsy, though, and even though it had its difficulties, there was a certain appeal to it, in Briggs' mind.

"That's the side door approach," Howard continued. "Obyedkov thought it possible to come in the front door."

"Let me guess," Briggs said sitting forward. "As a KGB officer. Probably a colonel. With proper orders and codes. There to pick up political prisoner Popov, Mikhail Vladimir, for transportation to Lubyanka."

"Something like that," Howard said. "In this case you'd be there to transport Popov to a place of execution."

Briggs smiled. "That has a nice flair. But I'll do you one better. Why not identify me as a personal aide to Brezhnev himself? That would carry more weight."

"Yes," Chiles popped up.

"No, to both," Briggs said, thumping his fist on the table. "One simple telephone call would queer the entire deal."

"Obyedkov bets that with the proper bluster no

one would make that call."

"Obyedkov is a betting man," Briggs said. "That's fine, but not with my life."

Howard was doing a good job holding himself in check, Briggs thought they all were. But his life would depend on this. If he had to be a bastard to work it all out, then so be it.

"Which leaves us the back door. We can get you within three miles of the place. From there you could go on foot, and Obyedkov thinks it's possible for the right man to go through the fence, a drainage tunnel. Once inside you'd become a hospital orderly. Snatch Popov, and take him out the same way you got in."

This one struck a nerve, in Briggs. "Transportation would be waiting for us at the other end to get us back to Moscow?"

"Yes."

There were flaws in even this plan, though. Serious flaws. As soon as he breached the security of the hospital perimeter, the clock would begin ticking on his discovery. If there was trouble inside. Difficulty in finding Popov, or releasing him. Or getting him ready to travel. Any delay would astronomically raise their chances of exposure. But the elements were there.

"Someone would have to keep an eye on Houten all the while. Make sure he didn't make any sudden moves."

"That would be no real problem. Jeff Dayton and Bruce Palmer are two of the best legmen in the business. They're on their way to our embassy over there now. They'd be put on Houten."

"The train itself would have to be watched.

Closely."

"That's already being done."

Briggs got up absently, walked around the table and sat back down. He was deep in thought. They were right at the edge. It was so close he could taste it.

"What is it?" Howard asked. The others in the room had picked up Briggs' intensity as well.

"The last bit . . . sneaking in the back door. That's close."

"But?"

"But not quite," Briggs said. "If I go over the wall or through the fence, the penetration could be discovered at any moment. The plan hinges on my being able to get Popov away to our transportation before that occurs. There has to be some way of circumventing their security alarm system. Or their guards. Something."

"All right," Howard said. "We'll put the other two scenarios on the back burner, and concentrate on this one. We can work out something."

"The trouble is time," Higgins said. "This all has to be in operation within days."

"We'll have to figure it out on the run then," Briggs said. "But, damnit, I know it's there. Something. I can feel it."

"What have we got and what do we need?" Howard asked rhetorically. He ticked the points off on his fingers. "We have Houten taken care of. If he so much as blinks we'll know it. We have activity around the train covered. It moves we know it. Anyone unusual gets aboard . . . any muscle . . . we also know it." He paused to gather his thoughts.

"We've got Briggs' entry to the Soviet Union covered, and I don't foresee any trouble with his leaving the embassy grounds any time he wants to, without causing undue notice by the opposition. We can get him to within a couple miles or so of the hospital. Which leaves us the physical plant of the hospital and its security measures . . . which Obyedkov has supplied for us on tape and in diagrams. It leaves us Popov's actual location within the hospital . . . for which Obyedkov has also provided clues. And finally his physical and mental condition."

"Stubin has a medical kit for Briggs, containing a number of concoctions," Higgins said. "Unless Popov is physically injured, he'll come around."

"Will he be willing to cooperate?" Chiles asked.

Howard was about to say something, but then checked it.

"Of course he'll cooperate," Briggs said. "Russian prisons are hell holes. Their psychiatric hospitals worse . . . much worse."

Again there was a pregnant silence in the conference room as everyone searched their experiences for objections. None were forthcoming.

"That it then?" Howard asked at last. "No objections?"

"No," Briggs mumbled, already the first faint glimmerings of an idea beginning to form in his mind. An idea that at once frightened him deeply, and yet intrigued him. Not possible, he kept telling himself. But another part of him felt it was the only way.

Chiles and White left to work on the preliminaries, leaving Briggs alone with Howard and Burt Higgins, and Obyedkov's dark, slavic features on the screen, his thickly Russian-accented English over the speakers.

The Yedanov Rehabilitation Center, named after some obscure court physician of a Czarina, was connected to Moscow only by train tracks with an ancient but efficient switching yard at the hospital so that the trains could be turned around for the return trip.

In the old days, the hospital treated consumptive patients of well-to-do and royal families, who needed the rest and clean air away from the city. At one time, in the hospital's heyday, there were six hundred patients being served, with a staff of more than one hundred-fifty.

After the revolution, of course, the hospital was closed and lay dormant for sixteen months, until it was re-opened as a prison for men and women condemned to be executed. It was away from Moscow, and yet easily serviced.

The hospital was again closed, in the early twenties, but was once again re-opened in the early thirites as one of the *gulags* of the famous archipelago.

Stalin used it extensively for political prisoners, and during the war captured Nazi officers were interned there, prior to their execution.

The KGB took it over in 1954, turning it into what they called a psychiatric care and rehabilitation hospital. In effect it became the most horrible of the brain washing clinics. Being sent to the Yedanov

Rehabilitation Center was a thousand times worse than a lifetime sentence to Siberia. There was no return. No one who rode the dull gray train, returned. No one; or so it was said. Thus the name, *train to nowhere*.

None of the dissidents, who coined the phrase, ever stopped to think that if no one got away from the center, then how did anyone know conditions there?

Simple, Obyedkov explained in his heavy voice, it was nothing more than a propaganda campaign.

"Oh, the YRC is a terrible place, make no mistake of that my friends. But the monsters who dwell there do not have forked tails, nor scaly hides. Instead they are reasonable, bespectacled ladies and gentlemen who dress in long white coats, and speak in incomprehensible jargons which only the devil understands."

Obyedkov's voice paused on the tape for a long moment. "Oh, but they are experts, and they produce results. When they are finished with a . . . patient, there is little to recognize of the original. No one ever returns from the center? That is true only in the sense that the people who came to us were so drastically altered that by the time they were sent far west, they were totally different human beings. Broken of will and spirit. Totally different."

"Lovely concept," Briggs replied.

"Yes, isn't it?" Briggs replied.

Obyedkov's voice continued with the narrative of how he rose in ranks first within the KGB, then with the diplomatic corps, then a two year stint (a reward supposedly for work well done) as chief administrative official at the hospital. It was a post that was entirely unsuitable to Obyedkov's nature, and by common agreement he was removed from the job, and posted to London.

Next, the Russian double-agent delved into the physical layout of the hospital, his comments keyed to several diagrams and sketches he had drawn himself.

The grounds, which covered nearly sixty acres, were completely enclosed by tall wire mesh fence, electrified, with coils of barbed wire at the top. Only one gate opened through the fence, and it was to admit the daily trains. Tall guard towers, manned 24-hours per day, flanked the gate, and in addition were located every hundred yards or so around the perimeter.

The gate, switching yard, and turntable as well as a maintenance shop were located in the southeast corner of the compound. In the northeast corner was an old horse stable and other buildings, now no longer in use. The heating plant was located in the northwest corner.

On the west side of the center of the compound was the main hall, as it was called; a four story brick building, bristling with chimneys, dormers and windows. Here were the main treatment rooms, the dining halls and kitchen for staff and some patients, doctors' offices, and other hospital functions. Some patients were kept here on a short term basis.

Directly behind the main hall was the research center, a building nearly as large as the main hall; to the north of it was the records keeping section and computer, and to the south, administration.

Along the south fence were four long, one story brick barracks. A and B housed routine internees awaiting treatment. Patients who were not considered dangerous, politically or physically, were placed here. Buildings C and D, however, formed what was known as the *majors compound*. These two buildings housed the really dangerous political dissidents, the buildings enclosed within their own separate fence . . . twelve feet tall, and electrified with 5,000 volts. Guard towers rose above each corner, and at the single gate.

Dogs roamed throughout the compound, as did randomly scheduled patrols.

"A difficult place, my friends," Obyedkov said. "A very difficult place, indeed."

Popov, he guessed, depending upon what was being done to him, would be housed either in the majors compound, or in the main hall.

"Either way, it will take a magician to get in there and rescue our poor friend. But I wish you much luck," Obyedkov said, and the tape ended.

"Any photographs of the place?" Briggs asked, his mind working.

"None that we know about," Higgins said.

"Plans, blueprints . . . anything in addition to what Obyedkov drew for us?"

"Nothing. You're looking at our available information," Higgins said.

"All right. How about a survey map of that area."

Higgins shook his head.

"Christ, what the hell do you have?"

"You saw it."

"And that from a fucking Russian."

"He's an ally. A friend," Howard said.

"No such animal, not wearing the coats he's worn."

## SIXTEEN

It was before 10 P.M., when Burt Higgins came back to the conference room. Howard had left hours ago, and Chiles and White had returned to listen to the Obyedkov tapes. They had gone to research about an hour ago to do their homework, leaving Briggs alone to replay Obyedkov's information once again.

The lights in the room were out, only the image on the projection screen providing any illumination. Obyedkov was going over the treatment of the inmates at the center; how they were altered. His voice sounded like a parody of a Russian accent it was so thick.

Higgins pulled up a chair and sat down next to Briggs, who had his feet up. For a time both men listened to the tape.

"What's troubling you, Briggs?" Higgins finally broke the silence between them.

Briggs looked away from the screen at the older man. Higgins looked worn out, his thinning white hair mussed up, his normally protruding eyes red-rimmed and puffy.

"You look like hell, Burt."

"Didn't answer my question. Something's eating you, what is it?"

Briggs glanced back up at the screen on which one of Obyedkov's sketches was projected. "There's something missing, Burt." He could feel it around the edges.

"The tapes are incomplete, we all know that. We'll pick that information up on the fly."

"I don't know if we can. It's something Obyedkov would have to tell us. Or perhaps a former inmate . . . is it all possible to locate one?"

"Not likely. You've listened to the tapes. The lucky bastards who get out of there alive are in no shape to tell us anything."

Briggs reached behind him, on the table, and switched the tape recorder off. Higgins got up, switched on the lights, and then turned off the projector.

"What is it you need, Briggs? What's missing?"

Briggs yawned. "Everything and nothing. Impressions, I guess." He got up and smiled tiredly. "It's something I'm going to have to work out."

Higgins seemed unconvinced. "We're here to help. Anything . . . anything at all."

"I understand that."

"How about the plan? Maybe we should scrap it. Start over again. We're short on time, but damnit, we're talking about lives here."

"My life," Briggs said. "The plan is all right, almost."

At the door, before they went out into the corridor, Higgins stopped him and looked up. "I wouldn't want you to do anything foolish, Briggs."

"What do you mean?"

"I don't know. Maybe try to back out. Take off after all."

"Am I locked into this mission then?"

"Not actually. But if you're not going to accept the assignment, we'd like to know. We'd have to inform Sir Roger, and find someone else to do the job."

Briggs looked into the man's eyes for a long time. Higgins was very bright, and a shrewd observer of human nature. He liked the man. "I'm not going to back out. I promise you. I *will* get Popov out of there. Or at least give it a romping good try."

"But?"

"There are a number of things I have to work out in my own mind, first. And I do need more information."

"We're running out of time."

"I know that," Briggs said. "I want you to know that no matter what happens over the next forty-eight hours or so, I will not back out. I will take this assignment."

"What the hell does that mean, O'Meara?" Higgins asked.

"It means not to worry. I may be a rascal, or a bastard . . . and I've been called much worse, deservedly so . . . but I never go back on my word. Never."

Higgins shook his head. "Goddamnit," he said, his Adam's apple bobbing. "I'm believing a con man. I can't believe it."

Briggs patted him on the shoulder. "Good night, Burt," he said, and he went out into the corridor, through administration and trudged upstairs to his room.

He took a quick shower, then dressed in light slacks, an open collar shirt and a sports jacket, taking care to make as little noise as possible. He repacked his overnight bag with a few items, including his toilet kit, then switched off his lights and looked out the window.

There wasn't much going on this evening, although the lights were still on across at the firing range. He could hear the faint popping of small arms fire across the field.

At the corridor door, he listened for several seconds, and hearing nothing, slipped out of his room, and hurried downstairs.

There was no one in administration to challenge him, as he strode across the entry hall, out the front door, and around the side of the building where the vehicles were parked.

There were a half dozen jeeps lined alongside three trucks, a van and four civilian cars. The keys were in the ignition of all the jeeps. He tossed his bag in the back seat of one of them, climbed behind the wheel, and within a few minutes he arrived unchallenged at the main gate. The headlights illuminated the tall wire mesh fence and the bulky mechanism for opening the gate. Briggs had taken a quick peek at it when they had come in, so that now he was able to

196

go immediately to the control housing at the side of the road.

The system had been built to keep people out, not hold them in, and within seconds Briggs had located the override, and the gate swung open.

He drove the jeep through the gate, then ran back inside, hit the close button, and as the gate ponderously began to close, ran through, jumped in the jeep and took off.

The night was absolutely clear, the weather perfect, and he made good time, encountering no traffic until he reached the main highway near Leesburg. Then, what traffic there was, consisted mostly of trucks.

An odd sense of freedom came over him, as he drove.

For awhile back there, he had felt a very strong sense of belonging. But now, looking back on it, the feeling was what Briggs imagined prison would be like. Confining, regimented. He didn't know if he liked it. The countryside was hilly and forested, the easternmost ramparts of the Blue Ridge Mountains, not too far behind him. As he did with every other place he had ever been to, or traveled through, he tried to imagine himself living here. Being a part of the area. Knowing the backroads. Knowing the gravel pits where the kids parked. Knowing the hunting areas. The little country taverns. The places for bargains. All that information normally taken for granted that indicates long term residence, was not his except for Soho, and to a much lesser extent Los Angeles.

Driving, alone with his thoughts, he wondered just

how much London had changed in the years since he had left. How many of his old friends were still there alive? Any of them?

Oumi had been a very large, nearly obese man, with long fingers that looked like sausages, a swarthy complexion, and eyes that never seemed to rest on any one spot. He had been prone to high blood pressure and was constantly forgetting to take his medicine. He had gout too, Briggs thought, and the chances that he would still be alive had to be very slim.

The trip up had taken nearly two hours because of the traffic, but this evening, he made it past Sterling to the turn-off that led up to Howard's house in less than an hour. It was barely 11:15 P.M., when he shut off his headlights, and went the last mile and a half slowly in the dark.

A few hundred yards from the house, Briggs pulled the jeep off the road, and made his way deep into the woods, maneuvering around trees and stumps and deadfalls, finally stopping deep within a thick area of brush.

He switched off the jeep, grabbed his overnight bag and hurried around in a wide arc to the northwest, coming out finally on the far side of the garage.

There were lights on upstairs in the house, but other than that the place could have been deserted.

Briggs scooted across the road, and at the rear of the garage ducked inside. The Ford he had taken two days ago had not been brought back. The Lincoln was gone as well, which possibly meant that at least Howard was gone somewhere. He hoped Sylvia and Sir Roger hadn't left yet. If they had, it was going to make things deucedly difficult.

The half-stripped Edsel was still there, as was the MG. Briggs crossed to the sportscar and tossed his bag inside. They keys were not in the ignition, but after a moment's study, he decided that breaking the steering wheel lock, and hot-wiring the car would present no problem.

He unlatched the main service door and swung it open, then stepped outside, and hurried around to the back of the house, where he tried the back door. It was not locked. Evidently Howard and his wife did not feel the need for the security of a locked door this far out in the country.

Inside the wide vestibule, Briggs held his breath listening for sounds from the house. He thought he could hear music playing faintly somewhere upstairs, but then it faded, and he wasn't sure he had heard it at all. He felt like a housebreaker . . . like a common burglar being here, and yet he felt a keen anticipation for seeing Sylvia Hume once again.

The front hall was empty and the kitchen was dark. He went up the stairs, taking them on the balls of his feet, two at a time, where he stopped again in the back servant's hall. Here he could definitely hear music playing somewhere on this floor. It sounded like a radio or a record player.

Out in the main corridor, he moved silently down to Sylvia's room. The music was coming from the other side of her door. Light spilled from beneath the crack of the door at the far end of the hall. Briggs supposed it was the Howard's room. He would have to be very quiet now.

He tapped softly at Sylvia's door. There was no

response. He tapped a little more forcefully, and almost immediately the radio was turned down.

"Yes?" Sylvia called. "Marta?"

Briggs opened the door. "Don't cry out."

Sylvia was in bed, the pillows propped up behind her, several magazine on her lap. Her eyes went wide when she saw who it was, but she did not say a thing.

Briggs came in, and softly closed the door. He stood there a moment listening for sounds from the corridor, but there was nothing.

"No one's here except for Marta and me. Daddy and Uncle Rudy went into Washington," Sylvia said softly. "But what do you want here?"

She was beautiful. Achingly beautiful, Briggs thought. Her long dark hair cascaded down around her milk-white shoulders, and when she spoke her lips moved as if they had a separate wonderful life of their own.

"What's wrong with you, man?"

Briggs shook himself out of his daze. "I've come for a package I left with your father."

"I told you, daddy is gone with Uncle Rudy to Washington. They won't be back until sometime late tomorrow."

"Then we'll just get the things out of his room."

Sylvia shoved the magazines aside, flipped the covers back and got out of bed. Her nightgown, although cut off the shoulders, was very long so that only her tiny feet showed.

Briggs found them faintly sensuous.

"What are you doing here? You are supposed to be at the training center. What's the matter, did they kick you out already?" Her voice had steadily risen through all that.

Briggs quickly stepped forward and clamped his hand over her mouth. She struggled for just a moment, then settled down.

"I've come for my things. Items that belong to me. That I gave to your father for safe keeping until I needed them," Briggs said.

She looked at him.

He took his hand away from her mouth. "I don't want to wake up Mrs. Howard. But I need my things."

"Are you on the run?"

"No," Briggs said.

"What do you need passports, money and a knife for, then?"

"Does your father tell you everything, then?"

"Nearly. But you haven't answered my question."

Briggs stepped around her, went to the window, and looked outside. There was no movement there. From here he could just see the front of the garage at an extreme angle. The door was still open. No one was there investigating. No one had closed it.

He turned back. "How much has your father told you about my reasons for being here?"

"Not much," she admitted. "From what I've pieced together, though, there is some Russian friend in a hospital somewhere near Moscow. You've been hired to go rescue him." She paused.

"And?"

She held her silence a moment longer. "Your chances aren't awfully good."

"No," Briggs said, coming closer to her. "So I need all the help I can get."

"With your things?"

Trust her or not? It was a hell of a question. Her conscious loyalties were to her father. But what of her own feelings.

"Look, if you tell me the truth I might be able to help," she said before he had a chance to speak.

"I can't," he said. "It's classified."

"Then there's the door," she said, pointing toward the door.

God, she was beautiful, Briggs thought. His heart ached for the thought of her.

"There is a Russian with the Soviet embassy in London who has information."

"Obyedkov," Sylvia said. "I've met him."

Briggs was genuinely surprised.

"He was at the house with that silly faggot, Hope-Turner."

Briggs was more than surprised, he was amazed. "Hope-Turner, the head of British Secret Intelligence Service is a fairy?"

"Oh silly," Sylvia said. "What the hell difference does it make in the scheme of things? And who knows. What do you want with Obyedkov?"

"Information," Briggs said. "I've got to get to London to speak with him."

"Daddy can . . ."

"Without your father. Without Howard or Hope-Turner. Without the establishment. My way. I want to talk to him on my own terms. I need information."

"Of what sort?" Sylvia asked.

"Of the sort to protect my life, which is as far as I go with you."

Again Sylvia stared at him for several long seconds. "Wait here," she said at length.

"What are you going to do, call the cops?"

"Hardly," Sylvia said disdainfully, and she left the room, closing the door softly behind her.

Three minutes, Briggs told himself. He would give her that much time before he'd get the hell out of here. It would take a while before the state police could get out this far. Time enough for him to get away. But what then?

Goddamnit, he thought. He hated being this dependent on anyone.

Sylvia was back in two minutes. Breathlessly, she handed Briggs his stiletto still in its leather case, and the plastic bag containing his passports and money.

"I almost left the knife," she said, looking into his eyes as he strapped the stiletto at his back, and stuffed the package in his jacket pocket.

"Stiletto," he said.

"Stiletto," she repeated, her voice very soft now.

It was warm in the room, suddenly. Briggs could feel his heartbeat throbbing at the side of his neck just below his ear.

"I'm glad you didn't."

"Are you going to kill someone with it?"

"Only the villains."

Her breath caught in her throat. "What?" she squeaked.

"I'll only kill the bad guys," he said.

"Villains. You said villains," she said, and she started to laugh. "Oh . . . God . . . villains."

She was making too much noise. "Quiet. For Christ's sake, shut up."

She held her hands over her mouth as she tried to stifle her laughter.

If Howard's wife woke up and sounded the alarm, he'd be on the run again. He did not want that. But he was going to have to make sure Sylvia was calmed down before he left.

"Oh . . . Briggs . . ." she laughed.

He came to her and grabbed her by the shoulders. "You'll wake up Mrs. Howard."

"Briggs . . ." she laughed.

And then she was in his arms, her body pressed against his, and they were kissing deeply, her lips wonderful, her body beneath the thin robe, incredible.

# SEVENTEEN

It was well after teatime when the BOAC 747 landed at London's Heathrow Airport. Briggs sat by a window looking out over the expanse of the great city that had been home to him. It felt very odd now to be coming back like this. Odd, and strange; exciting and sad; comforting yet nerve-racking . . . all that at the same time.

His emotions were further confused by the thought of Sir Roger's daughter: she wasn't yet thirty, she certainly wasn't a virgin, and she was very beautiful. He thought he was in love with her.

She had brought him his things from her father's room, and then had willingly took him to her bed. They had made love with great passion, while at the same time trying not to make so much noise they'd wake Mrs. Howard.

When they were finished, and Briggs was smoking a cigarette, she lay against his chest, her breasts crushed against him, her fingers caressing his cheek.

"Truly, are you coming back, Briggs?" she asked languourously.

He kissed the top of her head. "Yes," he said. She looked up, and he kissed her lips. "On Wednesday sometime."

"Do they know at the school that you've gone?"

"No. No one knows. There'll be a lot of noise when they find out." He looked deeply into her eyes. "I want you to promise me something, Sylvia."

"Anything," she said, "as long as it brings no harm to my father."

"I don't want you telling anyone, except your father, that I'm going to London to speak with Obyedkov."

"Uncle Rudy will be hopping mad."

Briggs had to smile. "Tell your father it will be up to his discretion whether or not he tells Howard. But I just want to talk with Obyedkov. I need some information that only he can provide. And I have to know that it's the truth. That it isn't lies. I don't want anyone breathing down my neck. I want a clear field."

She had been concentrating on the movement of his lips.

"Are you listening to me?" he asked.

She kicked the sheet completely off, and she kissed his chest now, and then his flat stomach, her lips and tongue working lower, until she took him in her mouth, and they were lost again in their lovemaking.

They had stopped at the terminal, and Briggs looked up out of his thoughts as the other passengers all got up, retrieved their carry on luggage and other things, and shuffled toward the doors.

He unstrapped, and got up. Sylvia had driven him down to Dulles International first thing in the morning, and he had caught the early flight out. She was going on into the city to do some shopping and would meet her father and Howard for lunch. They'd suspect nothing. Before he left, they had kissed deeply. "I love you, Briggs O'Meara," she said with much feeling. And now it bothered him. For once in his life he didn't know if he wanted to continue with a relationship. He did not want to hurt her.

He was passed through customs under the name Lawrence Woodworth with absolutely no trouble. In the men's room, he switched passports again, then out in the main terminal, he changed some of his American money into British pounds, and rented a Ford Cortina from the Hertz counter under the new name Claude Yates.

Driving into the city, traffic was heavier than Briggs had remembered it. But the air was much cleaner. In the old days there was a constant haze hanging over the city. But now the air seemed, if not sparkling clean, at least clear. In town, many of the buildings had changed, new faces on some of them, others torn down to be replaced by new ones. But basically it was the same London he had been raised in. But although he wanted very much to feel as though he had come home at last, the emotion never surfaced. This was merely London. Not home. He knew the city. He had memories of its streets and back alleys. But it simply was not home to him.

He parked the car in a garage up near Regents Park, took a cab back down to Piccadilly Circus, and headed the rest of the way on foot, the crowds of young, mostly unwashed people, thick.

As he walked, it all began to come back at him, in waves; memory after memory flooded into his consciousness from the deep well he thought he had covered over. Most of his recollections were of night time. Darkness inside and out. Misty, foggy nights when he stalked his victim who had been set up by the networks. The kills . . . sometimes very clean, but often (especially in the beginning) very sloppy, very noisy and messy. Then other dark nights, inside dimly lit, smokey rooms where arguments in a half dozen different languages flowed hypnotically back and forth, like a king cobra coming out of its basket. Then the street-corner whores where he lost his virginity. All of it, every stinking bit of it came back on him, causing his step to falter at every corner.

He passed the small, grimy porn shop on Excelsior and was twenty yards beyond it, before he realized exactly where he was. He went back and looked in the window at the magazines, very badly done photographs and jars of ointments and creams. This had been the Indian herbal shop. He was certain of it.

He stepped back to the curb and looked up. There were curtains on the windows above. The stairs, however, were inside, at the back of the shop.

He went inside. Instead of spices and incense the place now smelled of newsprint, and smoke and sweat. An incredibly grimy little man, with jowls sat on a high stool behind a glass counter. There were several old men in the shop, one of them at the side looking into one of the movie projectors.

"May I be of assistance, sir?" the clerk asked, not bothering to get up.

Briggs approached the counter. "I'm looking for someone," he said, keeping his voice low.

"Oh no you don't," the clerk protested. "I don't run that kind of a place here. Just books and pictures and the flicks, you know."

"Not that," Briggs said. "There are people living upstairs in the apartment."

Understanding dawned on the man's face. "The crazy lady," he said. "She's back on her rent. You here to take her away?"

"Is her name Moinezti?"

"Crazy Romaine, is all I know. Her and her samovar of tea."

"What's she owe you in rent?" Briggs asked. He pulled out fifty pounds, and laid it on the counter, without waiting for an answer. "Whatever . . . this should take care of it."

"Handsomely, sir, quite handsomely. Would you be going up?"

"Right," Briggs said.

"Stairs to the left at the back . . ." the clerk was saying, but Briggs was already starting back.

His memories were ever more acute as he went up the narrow, very dirty stairs to the second floor, to the boarded over glass door. The etched glass had at one time been Romaine's pride and joy.

He knocked, and after a moment or two he heard someone stirring inside. He knocked again.

"Go away you fucking sonofabitch," an old lady cackled. "You prick! You bastard!"

Briggs opened the door and stepped inside. An incredibly old woman in a black dress and black shawl stood at the end of the short hallway that led to the kitchen straight back, to the reading room on the left, and the bedroom to the right. It took several seconds for Briggs to recognize her, she had aged so badly.

"Romaine?" he said, closing the door behind him, and stepping a little closer.

"Don't you come in here, you . . ." she cried, her accent still very thick.

"It's me, Romaine. It's Briggs. I've come back to see you and Vatra and Thomas and Sitía and the others."

The old woman worked her toothless gums, and stamped her foot in frustration.

Briggs came a little closer. "It's me, Romaine. Donald O'Meara. Briggs."

"Oumi's little boy?" she asked.

Briggs smiled and nodded. "From Oumi."

She allowed him to kiss her on the cheek, then shaking her head and muttering something, led him back into the reading room. There were two tables, covered with heavy brocade tablecloths, chairs around them, a cutglass lamp on each. There were books and magazines everywhere, just as in the old days. But the magazines, Briggs noticed were all from at least ten years ago. There was nothing new here.

"Vatra is dead," Romaine said after they were settled, and she had poured him a very small cognac, and herself a glass of tea.

"When?"

"When?" she shrugged. "When. A month ago. A year ago. I don't know. There were some of the old ones there. Only a few. So many are gone." She looked up defiantly. "But the work continues. The printing still goes on. There will come the day I will be able to move dear Vatra's bones home at last."

"How about Oumi?" Briggs asked softly. He was afraid to raise his voice, for fear the sound waves themselves would disintegrate everything in the room.

"He is still there, Briggs. The work continues, I tell you. We still have our network." She leaned forward to the edge of her chair, and tapped the table top. "Just last . . . last . . . week, Anton Pavolich found our revenge. His car exploded."

Pavolich. Briggs tried to search his memory. He vaguely remembered seeing something about it in the newspapers. "The under secretary to the Soviet ambassador?"

Romaine smiled and laughed. "That's the one. The dirty whore, bastard never knew what hit him. Just last week."

It had been two or three years ago, maybe longer, and Briggs' heart sank. He did not think he would get the help he needed here.

"But you came to see Oumi, didn't you?" Romaine said. "He is still at the same place."

"The coal merchants. Edwards?"

"No longer a coal merchant. The boys all left. The place is closed and very run down, Briggs. But your father still lives there in the back. We go to him from time to time to see what he needs. But he seems self-sufficient."

211

Briggs finished his drink, got up and went around the table, where he kissed Romaine on the cheek again. "I'm going to see him," he said. He took a hundred pounds out of his pocket and pressed it into her hand. She didn't want it at first.

"I don't want the fucking charity," she cackled.

"It's not charity," Briggs said firmly. "It's for the cause. For paper and ink, and for bullets."

"The cause," she said.

Briggs nodded, and she put the money down the front of her dress. Briggs kissed her again. "I'll see Oumi now."

"Tell him we need some more excitement around here. I haven't seen a good pamphlet in ages."

"I'll tell him," Briggs said, and he left her apartment, went back downstairs and out on the street again, walked slowly down the block and around the corner to a ramshackle old building, the front of which was nearly caved in. Over the doorway, was the faded old sign: EDWARDS & SONS COAL MERCHANTS.

Inside, he went up the rickety old stairs, and knocked at the door. His heart was hammering, his mouth was dry. It had been so terribly long. It was almost inconceivable that Oumi could still be alive. He'd have to be in his late eighties; more likely in his mid-nineties.

The latch clicked from inside, and the door swung open. A tiny, frail old man in slippers, gray trousers held up by suspenders, and a fairly clean white shirt, stood there. For a long time they just stared at each other, until Briggs finally recognized him. It was Oumi, who at one time had been nearly obese. Briggs finally knew him because of his eyes.

"Oumi?" he said.

"I was wondering if you'd come back to work for us," the old man said emotionlessly. He turned and shuffled back into the apartment. Briggs followed him inside.

Oumi's appearance had changed drastically, but the apartment had not. It still was lined with books, and yet it was still very neat. Despite his age, he had kept up the place. It looked absolutely no different than when Briggs had been a young boy growing up here.

The old man sat down in his favorite easy chair by the window, and waved Briggs to the couch.

"We'll go out for a bite to eat a little later," Oumi said. "But first we must talk."

Briggs just nodded. He did not trust himself to speak just yet. There was a terrible lump in his throat. Who had said: You can never go back? It was true. Or at least going back was impossible without a great deal of pain.

"You've come for another assignment, no doubt. Bored with your life in the United States." Oumi shook his head sadly. "It is not for the likes of us, Briggs my boy, to enjoy the fruits of our labor . . . to enjoy the freedoms of America. It is for us to make sure others are safe, by crushing the ugly Red Tide."

It was the same old Oumi. Nothing had changed here, except his appearance.

"I've come for some help," Briggs said at last.

"You were at Romaine's. I know. It must have been a blow to learn of Vatra's death. But Romaine is now in her own world. She is better for it . . .

believe me."

Briggs had to smile. How the hell had he known about the visit to Romaine.

"You laugh? You think that just because you have left that we no longer function?" Oumi said, raising his voice. "The network still lives."

"Romaine mentioned Pavolich . . ."

Oumi cut him off. "That was nearly five years ago, Briggs. Nearly five years. The old woman is senile. We are not. We have done many things since that time." He wagged his finger. "And watch the name Prime. Cheltenham. Just watch. We are working on that. It will be a great victory."

Briggs did not know what he was talking about, but it all sounded like the old Oumi, and he began to hold some hope again, that they might be able to help . . . although his heart was breaking that Oumi's reception had not been warmer.

They were silent for a moment or two. Oumi sat back.

"You've come for help. What kind of help?"

"Does the name Obyedkov mean anything to you?"

Oumi stared at him. "What do you want with him?"

"I need some information."

"About what?"

"I can't tell you that, Oumi. Not yet."

"Let him alone," the old man said. "He is a friend of ours. Leave him be."

"I know he's a friend. That's why I'm going to him for information."

Oumi got up from his chair, went across the room

to a cabinet and when he turned around he was holding a pistol in his hand, pointed at Briggs. He came back across the room.

"Now tell me why you have suddenly become friends with the Russians? What have you been taught in America?"

"You said . . ."

"I said nothing," Oumi snapped. "What is this Obyedkov to you?"

"He is a double agent. He is working for us."

"No he is not. And I know that for a fact."

"Sir Roger . . ."

"Sir Roger Hume is a doddering old fool. He and his pansy Hope-Turner have run the SIS nearly into bankruptcy. Now, what do you want with Obyedkov?"

"If what you say is true, I will kill him," Briggs said. He didn't know what to believe at the moment. Sir Roger, the man he most admired and respected, was possibly foolishly mistaken. And Oumi, a man who had been like a father, was holding a gun on him.

"It is true. I can prove it. One of the cooks and a janitor at the Soviet embassy are our people. We know."

"Then you had better sit down, Oumi, and I will tell you what must be done, and what information I must have before I kill the man."

Oumi stood a moment longer, but then he sat back down. He kept the gun pointed at Briggs though.

"The train to nowhere, you remember telling me of it?"

Oumi's hand shook. He nodded.

"It goes to a psychiatric hospital."

"We know," Oumi croaked.

"Obyedkov once was its chief administrator. There is a prisoner there that must be gotten out."

"Impossible."

"Nearly. I need information from Obyedkov. I will kill him when I have it . . . providing you can prove to me he is what you say he is."

Oumi lowered the gun, then placed it on the table. "I will help you . . . son."

## EIGHTEEN

Briggs followed Oumi's directions to the letter, just as he had in the old days. It was late. A light mist had formed from the river, and there wasn't much traffic out and about. He stood in the darker shadows beside Apsley House near the Hyde Park Corner underground station, waiting for Obyedkov to come, on foot from Kensington. Everything was set. He was booked on the early morning return flight to Washington, under the name Webster Ambler. Oumi had taken his money and had sent someone out to pre-pay his ticket, so that there would not be much of a delay in the morning. The rental car would be returned on Friday, and Woodworth and Yates were checked in to two different hotels. Ambler was coming up from Croydon.

Incredibly, all this had been set up by the old Balkan network . . . or what was left of it . . . in just a few hours, from the Slânic House, a Rumanian cafe in the heart of Soho. That part hadn't changed either. It was the same restaurant Briggs remembered from his youth. Upstairs was a large meeting hall for rallies, and dances. But downstairs, and sometimes outside at the tables on the sidewalk, the real business was conducted.

Oumi had put on a tie, painfully pulled on his jacket (among other maladies he had developed arthritis) and they had walked to the restaurant.

Bouska Slânic, the aging owner, seated them at Oumi's corner table, the same as ever, and even before their drinks had come, old people began dropping by the table to offer their respectful greetings, and inquire after Oumi's health.

Some of them remembered Briggs, although he remembered only one or two, but all of them treated him warmly. He was, at the least, a friend of Oumi Pavlachek, he was to be treated with dignity and respect.

Through the first half hour, Oumi had written notes on a small pad, giving them to various people who stopped by. He was dispensing his orders, setting up a deal; that hadn't changed in the past twenty years or so, either.

"We will eat now," Oumi said, at length, putting away his notebook.

On cue their supper was brought out to them, consisting of thin slices of veal, lentil soup, thick black bread with unsalted butter, and a very distinctively flavored white wine, that Briggs remembered well. He smiled.

"Ah, you do remember then," Oumi said.

Briggs nodded. "There cannot be many bottles of

this remaining?"

"No. It is sad but true. Since the war there has been no more wine from Walachia. But when we return . . ." Oumi let it trail off, his eyes glistening.

They ate their meal in silence, Slânic himself, making sure their wine glasses were never empty. When they were finished, and the table cleared, he brought them strong black coffee and a good cognac.

Immediately people began streaming into the restaurant, to their table, where they either handed Oumi a note, or bent over to whisper something in his ear. Each time, Oumi smiled, shook their hand and sent them on their way.

Around nine o'clock, the restaurant full, a short, dark, very intense man, with thick black hair came in, and sat down with them.

He and Oumi stared at each other a long time, until he turned to Briggs.

"This is Jani Lugoj, Donald. He is the pastry chef at the Soviet embassy."

Lugoj appeared to be in his mid to late forties, with a haunted expression on his face. He must have been under a great deal of pressure. He and Briggs shook hands.

"So you are the one who Sir Roger has picked to go after Popov," Lugoj said.

Briggs was stunned. How the hell much was known? And exactly what kind of a set up was it?

"Where did you get your information?" he asked.

Lugoj laughed, the sound almost sinister. Slânic brought him a vodka. "From Obyedkov himself. He has been bragging about this."

"He knows my name?"

Lugoj waved his finger and shook his head. "No, not that. He knows that Sir Roger will send someone to rescue Popov. It is a laugh. It is a very big joke. As soon as you contact Peter Houten you will be very closely watched."

"And if I don't contact Houten?" Then what?"

The little man glanced over his shoulder before he sat forward, and lowered his voice. "Listen to me, my friend. Popov is only secondary. They will use him if they can, against us. But the real reason is to find out for certain if you suspect Houten of being a double. They think it is possible, but they cannot be sure."

"Houten is the real key, then," Briggs said. That opened another wide range of possibilities that Sir Roger or Howard had not mentioned. He could take Houten out, or he could totally leave him be; leave him in place, so that no matter how the Popov thing turned out, they could continue to use Houten to feed disinformation back to the Russians.

"Do they know that Sir Roger has gone outside the SIS for help?"

Lugoj looked at Oumi. "What is he saying?"

"It is all right, Jani. He is one of us. He is to be trusted without question."

"No," Lugoj said. "They do not even suspect such a thing. Is it true? You do not work for Hope-Turner?"

It was Briggs' turn to hesitate, but Oumi nodded sagely. "No, I do not work for the SIS," Briggs said, and Lugoj started to speak, but he held him off. "And that's as far as this will go. You are a gatherer of information, Mr. Lugoj. I understand and respect that. So too must you understand that my life very much depends upon this conversation."

Lugoj nodded. "I understand, and we will go no further."

"I need proof . . . to take to my people . . . that Obyedkov is a traitor to us," Briggs said.

"You meet with him tonight?"

"It is being arranged," Oumi said.

"Good. Then ask Comrade Obyedkov about a conversation he had two evenings ago with Yevgenni Voronin at the Café Le Bistro."

"It is a tourist spot," Oumi offered. Briggs knew it.

"Watch his eyes. You will know if what he tells you is the truth. It will be your proof."

"What was said at this meeting? Who is this Voronin?" Briggs asked.

"They discussed Peter Houten and Popov," Lugoj said. "And Voronin . . ." He and Oumi both smiled. Oumi answered.

"Yevgenni Voronin is the new chief of London station for KGB operations. Offer that to Sir Roger for proof. There aren't many who have that information yet."

Oumi motioned for Slânic who hurried over with more coffee and cognac. Lugoj declined more vodka.

"I must return before I am missed." He stood up and shook hands with Oumi, then with Briggs. "I wish you very much luck, mister. I think you will be a very lucky man to come out of this alive, so do as much damage as you can, as early as you can.

Perhaps your fool's errand won't be a complete waste.''

He turned, hurried across the street, then disappeared around the corner.

Oumi looked at the large clock on the iron post at the curb. "It is nearly time for your meeting with Obyedkov. You have what you need?"

Briggs nodded.

"When it is finished, return to Romaine's. She is expecting you. Someone will be there very early to drive you to the airport. There should be no troubles.''

Again Briggs nodded. "Thank you, Oumi.''

They stared at each other for a very long time, until Briggs finally understood that Oumi was waiting for him to leave. There was no warmth here. No humanity of any sort, just a very ancient operative in the last days of his life, playing out the role that had been thrust upon him three-quarters of a century ago.

But then, Briggs thought as he turned and left the restaurant, Oumi had never been the wellspring of human warmth. None of them had. He didn't know why he had come here expecting anything different.

The set-up for the meeting with Obyedkov had been simple to arrange. A telephone call had been placed to his house, in which Hope-Turner's name had been mentioned . . . in a roundabout way . . . along with a certain gentleman of Tunbridge-Wells. There was no mistake that the reference was not only to Sir Roger Hume, but to the meeting between Hope-Turner, Sir Roger and Obyedkov.

The Russian had wasted no time leaving his house near St. James Park on foot, passing Buckingham Palace all the way down to Victoria Coach Station, then taking a cab up into Kensington, somewhere around the Royal College of Art. From there he had come on foot again, his instructions to take the underground from the Hyde Park Corner station (where Briggs was waiting) across town to the Old Street station. If the meeting was on, it would happen somewhere between his house and Old Street. If something was wrong, he was to exactly retrace his steps.

Obyedkov came from out of the park, behind Briggs and headed immediately down the stairs to the underground. Briggs recognized him immediately from the photographs, hurried around the building he had been hiding behind and followed the Russian down.

He caught up with him at the first level, and was right behind him through the turnstyle.

"Sir Roger sends his greetings, Anatoli Fedor," Briggs said in King's English.

Obyedkov jerked as if he had been shot.

"Easy now, sir. No one has followed you. No one knows we're together."

At the bottom, there were only a few passengers on the train when they got on. Moments later the doors shut and they were off.

"Is there trouble?" Obyedkov asked under his breath. "Who are you?"

"In a bit, sir," Briggs said. Oumi would have someone watching at the Old Street Station, he thought as they stopped at Green Park a minute later. There was no one behind the Russian, and Briggs did not want anyone in front of them.

Piccadilly Circus was next, and then Tottenham Court Road, where Briggs suddenly jumped up, pulling Obyedkov after him, and they managed to get off the train just before the doors slid shut, and the train took off.

There was no one on the platform to watch as Briggs led the unresisting Obyedkov past the stairs, and into the men's room. Inside he leaned against the door, not only so he could stop anyone from walking in on them, but also so he could hear if someone came.

"Now what is there?" Obyedkov asked. "This is very dangerous to meet like this."

"I am the one Sir Roger has picked to go after Popov," Briggs said carefully.

The Russian's expression and manner changed dramatically from one of petulant annoyance to one of anticipation.

"When do you leave? It will have to be very soon."

"Very soon. Within the next day or so," Briggs said. "But I need more information."

"Of what sort? I have given Hope-Turner everything you will need."

"I will need more."

"What plan will you be using? Are you going in as a maintenance man?"

"I want to get in as a patient," Briggs said, watching the man's face.

Obyedkov's eyes widened, his lower lip quivered. "Impossible. Totally impossible . . . how?"

"You are going to tell me that. It is why I have come here like this to see you."

"You must be insane," Obyedkov said. He turned away, and walked down the line of stalls to one side and sinks with mirrors behind them on the other. His voice echoed off the tiles. "In the first place, when you show up in Moscow, you would be shot."

"Why is that, Anatoli Fedor?"

The use of his patronym seemed to irritate him. "Foreigners are not sent to Soviet psychiatric hospitals."

"No outsiders into the archipelago?"

"I am leaving," Obyedkov snapped, coming toward Briggs purposefully.

"*Nyet,*" Briggs shouted harshly. "Not yet, Comrade," he continued in the perfect gutter Russian of a Muscovite.

Obyedkov was stunned. The color left his face.

"I have come to you for information," Briggs hammered in Russian. "And information is what I shall receive. I will be in Moscow within hours. I will, in a fashion you shall instruct me in, become a prisoner in the gulag they call the Yedanov Rehabilitation Center. I will take the train to nowhere."

Obyedkov was speechless.

A train rumbled up the tunnel, and came to a stop outside. Briggs and Obyedkov both listened as someone shouted something . . . it sounded like a kid. The train rumbled away, there was more shouting, that finally faded, then silence.

"Who are you?" Obyedkov asked.

"It doesn't matter," Briggs said switching back to English. "Sir Roger has hired me to bring Popov out of the Soviet Union. It is a job I will do. But I need your help."

Obyedkov looked at him as if what he was saying was totally incomprehensible.

"My language is good. I understand the people. What must I do to assure I will be sent to the same place as Popov."

"There is no way."

"There must be," Briggs insisted. "Something I could do, or say. Someone I could offend. Something."

"And if it were so? If indeed you are sent to the center? Then what?" Obyedkov asked. "Then we not only have Mikhail Vladimir in that place . . . but we have you as well. What good would that do us?"

"You haven't answered my question."

"Nor have you answered mine. And how did you come from Moscow, to be here in London? Is your face known by the Komitet?"

Obyedkov had begun pacing again, but again he stopped to face Briggs. He was beginning to sweat heavily. He looked like an irritated bear, ready to lash out at any moment.

"If I can get into the center, I will find Popov, and together we will escape into the woods from the southwest. A car will be waiting for us. From there we go back to Moscow to the embassy (Obyedkov thought Briggs meant the British embassy, which is what Briggs wanted) where we wait for everything to cool down. Afterwards . . . months if need be, we can figure out how to smuggle Popov and myself out of there."

"Foolishness."

"First I must know how to become an inmate. What must I do?"

"I don't know."

"You were the administrator there. If you don't know, who would? Where could we get that information?"

Obyedkov paced to the far end of the room as another subway train rumbled into the station. There were the sounds of passengers getting off, then the train departed, and silence fell again.

"You would have to be a dissident," Obyedkov said. "You would have to be an enemy of the state. A hooligan."

"How about my records? My fingerprints?"

"If you are caught, it is of no consequence. It would not be checked . . . you are who you say you are. Who would be so foolish as to impersonate a man certain to be sentenced to rehabilitation?"

"How do I insure I am not treated as a common criminal?" Briggs insisted. "How can I be certain I will be sentenced to rehabilitation? I must get to Popov."

Obyedkov laughed. "Tell them Popov is your god. Tell them he is your morning light. Your reason for existence. Your being."

Briggs too had to smile. He should have known. "Tell them I think he is god."

"Yes," Obyedkov said. "And they will sentence you to hell with him."

Obyedkov had paced closer, and he suddenly thrust his right hand in his coat pocket, and pulled out a large handgun: a Graz Buyra.

Briggs stiffened.

"Who are you? Exactly," Obyedkov demanded.

"Why have you pulled a gun on me? What have I done? I am just working for Sir Roger and for Hope-Turner. I have studied your tapes and your diagrams. What is it you want from me? I am only trying to do as you wish?"

"Shut up," Obyedkov shouted. He came closer. Briggs could feel his muscles loosening. He felt very smooth, as if every muscle, every bone, every joint had all melded into one single unit.

"This is a trick," Obyedkov said. "We will see."

Briggs leaned back against the door, shifting all of his weight to his left foot. "How long have you and Peter Houten worked together?"

Obyedkov's mouth came open, and at that moment Briggs kicked out with his right foot, the toe of his boot catching the barrel of the gun, shoving it aside.

An instant later, as the big Russian scrambled back and to the side in an attempt to regain his balance, Briggs danced left, as he pulled out his stiletto. He was on Obyedkov the split second later, his left hand on the man's back between his shoulder blades, the stiletto up under his chin, ready to drive up.

"No!" Obyedkov screamed. He tried to twist around while at the same moment he brought the big handgun around, pulling himself off balance. He stumbled forward, the stiletto driving up through the back of his throat, deeply into his brain.

Briggs jumped back so that he would not be splattered by the blood, as Obyedkov shuddered powerfully, then fell to the floor, his legs jerking spasmodically; blood everywhere.

For a moment Briggs was seeing his mother's shot-away body lying in a pool of blood. But then he wiped his stiletto on Obyedkov's shirt sleeve, sheated it, and left the bathroom. He was nearly all the way up the stairs, when he heard the train rumbling into the station, and he quickened his step.

# NINETEEN

The plane from London landed at Dulles International Airport around noon, but it wasn't until nearly 12:30 p.m. that Briggs had cleared customs and he stopped for a drink in the main terminal. The airport was very busy. Briggs sat with his back to the bar, gazing across the terminal toward the main doors, his overnight bag, which contained his stiletto, spare passports and money, beside him. There were two police officers at the center doors, and after a time their presence began to grate on Briggs' nerves. What the hell were cops doing here? Waiting for someone?

He got up and with his drink in hand, went to the wide door from the cocktail bar, and looked out. There were pairs of uniformed cops at all but one set of doors.

It was a funnel. Someone would see the uniformed policemen, and naturally head to the apparently unguarded doors. Very amateur, but typical of what he had seen of Howard's people so far.

Briggs finished his drink, grabbed his overnight bag, and started away from the doors, when he spotted Bob Chiles leaning against the information counter in the center of the main floor. He was watching the approaches to the main exits.

There was no one else waiting for him that he could see, and as nonchalantly as possible he worked his way around the information counter, coming up behind Chiles.

"Waiting for someone, Bob?" Briggs asked.

Chiles spun around, his right hand going instinctively for his shoulder holster beneath his jacket. But then he stopped.

"Jesus H. Christ. Where the hell have you been?"

Briggs smiled. "Gathering information for the mission. Can I bum a ride out to the school?"

Chiles had to laugh. "Christ," he said again, shaking his head. He turned, picked up the phone on the counter, and dialed three numbers. "He's here," he said. "No. He got me. Have everyone stand down, I'll take him back. And, thank Smitty and the others. We'll definitely remember them when we're done with this one."

"Howard is mad?" Briggs asked when Chiles hung up the phone.

"Surprisingly, no," Chiles said. They headed across the terminal. "Where've you been?"

"London."

"We figured as much."

They went outside, and took the ramp across to the parking garage, where on the third level they climbed into a gray Chevrolet sedan with government plates.

"Obyedkov is dead," Briggs said, before Chiles pulled out of his parking slot.

"What?"

"He's dead."

"What the hell happened? I mean, Christ . . . what the hell is going on?"

"I killed him. He was a traitor. He was setting this entire thing up with Houten."

Chiles' face was red. He was not understanding what the hell was happening.

"Let's go out to the camp. I'll explain everything when we get there."

"Obyedkov is dead?"

"That's right."

"Christ. Jesus H. Christ."

"Let's go, Bob," Briggs said after a moment. Chiles pulled out of the parking slot and within a few minutes they were heading north toward Sterling on Highway 28.

For a long time Chiles concentrated on his driving, and would not look over at Briggs. The day was lovely, the sky clear, the temperature warm. There was quite a bit of traffic, a lot of it out of state, and it took more than an hour before they had passed Leesburg, had picked up Highway 9, and had turned into the dirt road that led to the school. It seemed like old home week to Briggs, he had been here so many times before.

"Is Howard here?" Briggs asked.

"If he isn't now, he will be soon."

"Sir Roger?"

"I expect he'll be here as well. There are a number of people who would very much like to speak with you."

They came to the main gate. Chiles pushed the control button, the gate opened and they drove through, continuing up to the main building, where they parked around the side.

Together they went inside and through administration, where everyone stopped what they were doing to look up at Briggs, then into Burt Higgins' office.

The little sparrow of a man was on the telephone when they came in, and he just waved them to have a seat. Briggs set his overnight bag down in the corner, then sat down next to Chiles.

"We're just going to have to stonewall it, until Sir Roger gets out here. It's his decision," Higgins said. He did not seem particularly happy. "Absolutely not, Stewart. No. He's right here. Just came in." Higgins rolled his eyes, then nodded. "Right. We'll let you know. Bye." He hung up.

"You've heard?" Briggs asked.

Higgins looked across his desk for several seconds, then he nodded. "We received the first indications late last night. This morning this place has been like a madhouse." He looked at his watch. "Rudy and Sir Roger should be here any minute now. They've taken a chopper up from the city."

"What are the Russians saying?" Briggs asked.

"Plenty, but nothing implicating us."

Higgins was holding something back. Briggs could suddenly see it in the man's eyes. "What is it?" he asked.

"This morning, a group calling itself the Balkan

States Alliance phoned the BBC and claimed responsibility for Obyedkov's death. They said he was working for the KGB in London, that he was a dangerous man, that he was responsible for countless deaths, and had to be eliminated."

Oumi, Briggs thought. "Christ."

"It's your friends, isn't it?" Higgins said.

Briggs nodded. "I killed Obyedkov. There is proof that he was a double, that in fact he was working for the KGB."

"That sounds like more of your paranoia, Briggs . . . pardon me for saying so. But not every Russian is an insane monster bent on destroying the western world."

"Obyedkov and his people have set this entire thing up in order to find out if the SIS suspect Peter Houten of being a double. They don't really give a damn about Popov."

The phone rang, and Higgins picked it up. "Higgins," he said. "Good. We're in my office. He and Bob just showed up." Higgins replaced the phone. "Rudy and Sir Roger are here. They'll be right in."

"This was a set-up from step one," Briggs said.

"And you have the proof of it?"

"I wouldn't have killed him otherwise."

"Did you go over there planning on killing him?" Higgins asked. "Because if you did, I just don't understand any of this."

Briggs shook his head. "I went over there to speak with him. I needed some information straight from the horse's mouth."

"On what?"

"On the center."

"And did you get the information you so desperately needed?"

Briggs nodded.

"Yet you killed him. Brings up two interesting questions, Briggs. If he gave you information you needed, why did you kill him? Or, if you felt you had to kill him, is the information he gave you any good?"

"I got the information I needed from him before he suspected I knew what he was really all about. And later when I told him I knew, he pulled a gun on me. There wasn't much I could do at that point."

Higgins said nothing.

"I don't go around killing in cold blood!"

Higgins' intercom buzzed, then his office door opened and Howard came in, Sir Roger right behind him. Briggs got to his feet.

"Did you have a hand in Obyedkov's death?" Howard asked, without preamble.

"I killed him," Briggs said.

"I see."

"Not without good reason, I suspect, Donald?" Sir Roger asked, closing the office door. "Everything is in a bit of an uproar at home. Hope-Turner is beside himself."

"Obyedkov was a double. Had been all along, from what I gather."

"A double?" Howard asked. "You can prove that?"

"Yes I can."

"Oumi's group took credit for the kill," Sir Roger said. "They're looking for him now."

"The SIS?"

"Scotland Yard too."

"And the Russians?"

"If what you say is true . . . then the Russians," Sir Roger agreed. He took the last available chair, Howard perched on the edge of the desk, and when they were all seated, Howard began.

"I've crossed swords with you before, O'Meara, and ended up on the bottom, so I'm giving you the benefit of the doubt for the moment. But I'm telling you that right now, here in this office, the five of us are going to come up with a decision, and it'll be final." He turned to Sir Roger. "Sorry, but I got that from David Stansfield himself."

"I understand Rudyard, and I am in full accordance. But I believe Donald may have something of significance. The Balkan network people under Pavlachek may have been fanciful dreamers, but they never were fools."

"From the top," Howard said. "Why'd you feel the need to hightail it over to London in the first place?"

"I needed more information from Obyedkov."

"We could have arranged that for you. Hope-Turner has easy access . . . or did have, from what I understand," Howard said. "Or did you already suspect the man of being a double?"

"A triple," Briggs corrected. "But no, I had no inkling. I truly went there to speak with him. I needed to find out something from him—directly from him."

"What was this information you so desperately needed?"

Briggs figured all his other choices were easy. This one however, which involved his own plan, was a bit more difficult. He did not believe for one minute that Howard or Higgins or anyone else in this room was a traitor. But mistakes could be made. The fewer people who knew about the plan, the fewer chances for a slip-up there'd be.

"I needed information about the hospital."

"Something Hope-Turner couldn't have secured for you?" Sir Roger asked.

"Something only a person who understood the Russian mentality could get."

"Bullshit, O'Meara," Howard snapped.

Briggs had to laugh. "As much as I hate to admit it, you're absolutely correct, Howard."

Sir Roger was smiling, Howard was not.

"The truth of the matter is, none of your plans works for me. So I came up with my own."

"For which you needed information from Obyedkov?"

Briggs nodded.

"Still doesn't answer my question: Why didn't you speak to us about it? We could have got the information for you."

"As it turns out it's fortunate I did not do just that. I would have been a dead man once I set foot in Moscow."

Howard and Sir Roger looked at each other. Through all this Higgins and Chiles had held their silence.

Higgins spoke up now. "You mentioned earlier that Obyedkov was a triple. You said you had proof."

237

Briggs nodded. "Pavlachek and his people provided it."

"The person you call Oumi?"

"Yes. I went to see him, and he told me that Obyedkov was a KGB agent, and that he wasn't really working for us."

"Why did you go to him?" Howard interjected.

"I needed his help to approach Obyedkov without tipping off the Soviet embassy."

"How did Pavlachek know about Obyedkov? Where's the connection," Higgins asked.

"Oumi still runs the old Balkan independence network. One of his people works in the Soviet embassy."

Sir Roger was surprised. "Who is it?" he asked.

"I'm sorry, Sir Roger, I can't . . ."

"Sorry? Good God man, do you know what you're saying?" Sir Roger exploded. It was the first time Briggs had ever seen Sir Roger lose his composure. "The network . . . Oumi and all the others are done. They're half dead."

Briggs said nothing. He felt very bad about this.

"You have to make up your mind, Donald. And very quickly. You are either working for us, or you are against us. There is no middle ground."

Briggs nodded. "You want me to give you the name of the person in the Soviet Embassy that Oumi and his network have been using for information? So that Hope-Turner can put someone on it? A control officer?"

"Exactly."

"Such as Peter Houten, perhaps?" Briggs snapped. "Or, perhaps Obyedkov's control officer would be the fitting one to take over.''

"There have been mistakes, although you have not as yet proved that Obyedkov is a triple. And we are not absolutely certain that Houten is a traitor.''

"Come off it, Sir Roger,'' Briggs said. "I'll give you another tip. Maybe Hope-Turner won't screw this one up. Find out about a man named Prime. Chap works at or for a place called Cheltenham.''

"Good Lord,'' Sir Roger said. "Cheltenham. It's our radio-codes facility.''

Briggs laughed. "I'll give you a third tip, courtesy of the washed-up Balkan network. Yevgenni Voronin. He's the new chief of London station for KGB activities. Did you know that?''

Sir Roger was deeply shaken. Howard and Higgins both were openly amazed.

"Now that we've established some bona fides, let's get to the heart of the matter, shall we?''

He had their attention. No one moved a muscle.

"Three evenings ago a meeting took place at the Café Le Bistro. It's a tourist restaurant on Brompton Road. The subject was Peter Houten, Mikhail Vladimir Popov and you, Sir Roger.''

Sir Roger said nothing.

"Present at this little tête-à-tête were Anatoli Fedor Obyedkov, and none other than Yevgenni Voronin. Curious.''

"That tears it, then,'' Sir Roger said heavily. "They'll be expecting us, especially now that Obyedkov has been murdered.''

"Not necessarily,'' Briggs said. Oumi's source . . . and I spoke with the person . . . says Popov is merely secondary. He apparently isn't the threat we take him to be."

"What then?"

"Houten. They're not yet sure that we suspect the man of being a double. They think it's possible, but they're not sure."

"Then they can't be sure that we had any hand in killing Obyedkov," Higgins put in. "They might guess, but they can't be sure. They'll have to believe that it was just a plain coincidence."

"The Balkan network hasn't been totally dormant all these years. They still are a thorn, albeit a minor one, in the side of KGB London operations," Sir Roger said.

"Then nothing changes," Briggs said. "I still go. Only the plan is somewhat different."

"I don't know, Donald," Sir Roger said.

"We still want Popov. If we can get him out of there, it'd be a blow. We could even set Houten up to take the fall for his escape. Of, if you'd rather, we could feed the man disinformation. Let him unwittingly work for us."

Higgins caught Briggs' use of the word *us* and he nodded. "What's your new plan for getting in, then, Briggs?"

"It's fairly simple, actually, and quite foolproof. I'll be in there legitimately."

"I don't understand."

"It's the Russian sense of grim humor," Briggs said. "We'll get me over to Moscow. I'll drop out of sight from the embassy, and when I turn up, I'll be a Russian dissident spouting Popov's virtues. He is my god incarnate."

"I still don't see," Higgins said.

"Don't you understand, Burt? I'll shout it on street corners. I'll go to Red Square and hang up posters. I'll write pamphlets if need be. And I will be arrested. I will be tried and I will be sentenced. To the Yedanov Rehabilitation Center."

"My God," Sir Roger said softly.

"How can you be sure you'll be sent there?" Higgins asked.

"Obyedkov supplied me with that assurance. If Popov is my god, they will be more than happy to send me to hell with him. They'll be delighted."

"Impossible," Higgins said.

Chiles was shaking his head. Sir Roger was speechless. But Howard nodded.

"It may work," he said.

"You're damned right it will," Briggs said. "Just keep Houten out of my way."

# TWENTY

It was just past 3:00 P.M., and Briggs was dead tired. He stopped his packing for a moment, poured himself an Irish whiskey and went to the window. Dick White was just climbing into a car, his bags in the back. He'd be in Paris very late tonight, then Helsinki by tomorrow, from where he'd take the express train to Moscow.

The team was gathering, Briggs thought as the car pulled away from the building and headed out to the gate.

White would be in charge of setting up the escape . . . that is if Briggs got out alive with Popov.

He shook his head. He wasn't nervous, now that it was coming to a head, rather he was anxious. He wanted to get it started. He wanted to be doing it. Not sitting around waiting.

The pace in the last twenty-four hours since he had returned from London had been nothing short of frantic. No one had slept, nor would they until Briggs and the last of the crew had gone.

Jeff Dayton and Bruce Palmer, who, as it was decided, would be watching Peter Houten, had left days earlier. Tom Byers, who would be in charge of the surveillance teams watching the train, along with Clifford Wells who'd act as liaison between the American and British embassies, had left this morning.

Chiles, who would be Briggs' only contact man in Moscow had left a little after noon. Which left only Burt Higgins, who would be in charge of operations from the U.S. Embassy. He was flying out to Vienna tonight. From there he'd take the Aeroflot flight to Moscow tomorrow.

Someone knocked at his open door, and he turned around. It was Higgins.

"You about ready?" the older man said, coming in.

"Just about," Briggs said. "Care for a drink?"

"Why not."

Briggs poured him one, then perched on the wide windowsill, while Higgins leaned against the desk.

"Butterflies, Briggs?"

"Not really. Just anxious to get it started."

"This is always the worse part. The waiting." Higgins lowered his eyes and looked into his whiskey glass. He sighed. "They found Pavlachek this morning."

Something clutched at Briggs' heart. "Who found him?"

"Scotland Yard."

"He's all right then? They have him in custody

. . . ?" The words died on Briggs' lips, as he saw the expression of sadness come over Higgins' face.

"He's dead."

"Was . . . it an accident, Burt?" Briggs asked. He could hear how foolish the question was, but he had not been able to help himself from asking it.

Higgins shook his head. "A standard Moscow Center assassination."

Briggs felt his entire body go weak. He was back again as a kid, climbing the dark stairs to the apartment. He was cold, frightened and very much alone.

Higgins was saying something, but he wasn't really hearing it. The door was coming open, and in the darkness he was seeing his mother lying in a pool of blood. His uncle's body wasn't too far away. *A standard Moscow Center assassination. A mokrie dela. Blood will be shed by* . . .

"Are you all right?" Higgins' voice seemed to come back into focus.

Briggs nodded.

"There was no indication that he talked. He was shot from behind at close range in a crowded subway. He couldn't have known it would happen."

"He knew, Burt. He knew damned well what he was doing, and what was going to happen because of it."

"I don't follow you."

"I told him what we were going to do, Burt. I told him about Popov, and about the hospital, and about how I needed information from Obyedkov. He set Obyedkov up for me, and when I killed him, Oumi set himself up for the fall. He wanted to make sure that there would be absolutely no suspicion on me.

The Russians don't know that we're sending someone."

Briggs stood up and looked out the window at the lovely day outside. Training was going on as normal. There was laughter out there. Life. Obyedkov and now Oumi. He thought of another thing.

He turned back. "Have someone check the personnel roster at the Soviet Embassy in London. There'll be someone else turning up dead. Probably a car accident."

Higgins looked at him wonderingly. "The contact Pavlachek arranged for you to meet?"

Briggs nodded.

"A pastry chef. Jani Lugoj."

"When did it happen?"

"Last night. In Soho. He was run over by a bus. Crushed his skull."

Oumi had arranged that as well. There was no one who knew now. There were plenty of people who had seen Briggs talking with Oumi and with Lugoj. But a lot of other people were there too. It had been routine. No one who knew the entire story was left alive.

"He was the contact?"

"Yes," Briggs said tiredly. "There's no one left now who knows the entire story. We're perfectly safe."

Sir Roger appeared in the doorway. "Is there a third glass for that whiskey?"

Higgins turned around, and Briggs looked up.

"You were right," Higgins said.

"About what, pray tell?" Sir Roger said, remaining where he stood just within the doorway.

"Pavlachek, and Lugoj."

Sir Roger was wearing a blue blazer, club tie and smartly tailored slacks. He seemed to sink into his clothing. "I see," he said.

Higgins put his glass down, and turned to Briggs. "I'll see you in Moscow, then."

Briggs came across and they shook hands. "We'll make the sonsabitches pay, Burt."

"You're damned right we will, kid," Higgins said. At the door he shook hands with Sir Roger.

"Good luck."

"Thank you, sir," Higgins said and then he was gone.

Sir Roger closed the door, as Briggs got a clean glass from the bathroom, poured him a stiff shot of the Irish whiskey, and another for himself.

They stood facing each other.

"You were wrong about Oumi, it appears."

"Wrong about what?"

"His concern for you," Sir Roger said softly.

Briggs was choked up. He could not talk. He had always thought it was so lonely. But the loneliness of his past was nothing compared to what it was now. Oumi may have been a cold fish, but at least he had always been there. He was gone now. And the emptiness seemed terribly immense.

"You do understand what took place."

Briggs nodded. "He called me son."

Sir Roger put a hand on Briggs' shoulder. "He was a soldier, and he'll be given a soldier's funeral. He did a lot of fine work."

Again Briggs could not speak. He just nodded.

After a bit, Sir Roger took his drink to the

window, and looked outside as he thoughtfully sipped it. When he turned back he seemed resolute, as if he had gathered himself up by his mental bootstraps. "Are you going to be all right for this operation, Donald?"

"I'll be fine."

"It won't work if you become reckless."

"I've heard the lecture before, Sir Roger. I've been along this path."

"In London. When you were a kid. Your own back yard. Moscow is quite a bit different. You won't have a nearby bobby to run to for help, don't you know. Romaine and the others won't be there to hide you, and feed you, and bandage your wounds."

"I'll be fine. It's a job that has to be done, and I'll do it."

"Not with vengeance, Donald, that's what I'm trying to get across to you."

"That's asking too much, Sir Roger. Far too much."

Again Sir Roger fell silent. "I suppose there's no helping that, then. We picked you in the first place because you were right for the job. Despite the unfortunate complications which have arisen, you are still right for it."

"Then wish me luck and see me off," Briggs said.

"I wish it was that simple," Sir Roger said. "There is another complication."

"No one else in London knows the full story."

"It's not London, and it's not the assignment. It's my daughter. She is downstairs at this moment, wishing to come up to speak with you."

"What do you want me to say?"

247

"She's in love with you, I think," Sir Roger said. He was having difficulty with this. "Are you with her?"

"I have no intention of hurting Sylvia."

"I asked you a question, Donald."

"For which I shall give you no answer. It simply is none of your business, sir."

"Damnation," Sir Roger said in frustration. He put his drink down, and went to the door. "I'll send her up." he said.

"If it's any consolation, Sir Roger, I did not start it, but I will end it now."

Sir Roger looked back. "I don't know if that's possible, Donald. The damage may have been done." He shook his head. "In any event, good luck over there. I'm sure you'll do a splendid job. When it's over I'm sure you will make a fine American." Then he was gone.

Briggs didn't know how he should take the last remark. Sir Roger had said it with a touch of sarcasm. He hurried to the door but Sir Roger was already gone.

Sylvia was coming up here. What the hell was he going to say to her?

He downed his drink, then poured himself another and drank it straight, the whiskey hammering his insides. He poured himself a third.

Making love was one thing, being in love was an entirely different cricket match. Christ, the committment alone was enough to choke a horse.

He was looking at his reflection in the mirror on the open bathroom door. He was dressed in fatigue trousers and an olive drab T-shirt, nothing on his

248

feet. His hair was mussed, he was in bad need of a shave, and his eyes, he could see even from where he stood, were terribly bloodshot. He looked like hell. And tomorrow he'd be in the Soviet Union. His life in danger.

"Feeling sorry for yourself?" Sylvia asked from the doorway.

He turned around. "Do you want to come along to Moscow with me?"

"I'd love to. But I'm afraid daddy would take a dim view of it."

"He already does," Briggs said.

She came the rest of the way in and closed the door, then leaned up against it. She was wearing a white sun dress, a bow in her hair, sandals on her feet, but no nylons on her legs. She looked incredibly inviting.

"It's not lady-like to be in a man's room with the door closed."

"I'm not a lady," she said breathlessly.

"I'm leaving first thing in the morning," Briggs said.

"I know."

"I'm glad you came to say goodbye. I wanted to thank you . . . and to apologize."

"Apologize for what?"

"For what happened the other night when I came to get my things."

"There is nothing to apologize for . . ." she started, but then she paused. "Unless . . . you mean . . ."

Briggs couldn't face her any longer, so he turned away. "I took advantage of you. I'm sorry." He felt like an asshole. He was screwing this all up.

"You took advantage of me?" she said. "Is that what you're saying?"

He didn't know what the hell to say to her. Christ, he didn't even know how he felt about her.

"Turn around and looked at me, you bloody bastard," she shrieked.

He did. Her face was mottled, and tears streamed down her cheeks.

"We slept together and now you're sorry?" she cried.

Briggs was really feeling cornered now. Down deep he knew damned well what his trouble was. Or at least he thought he did. He just didn't know a way out of it at the moment, because his feelings were getting in the way.

"Talk to me," she said.

"I don't know what to say, Sylvia," he blurted.

"What was I then, just a . . . a piece of nookie, or whatever you call it when you're with a prostitute?"

"No," he shouted back at her, his anger suddenly rising. "Don't say that."

"What then?" She shook her head, trying to search for the right words. "A one night stand? A lay? A piece of ass? A good fuck?"

Briggs went to her, grabbed her by the shoulders and shook her so hard she had to gasp for air. "Don't ever say that," he shouted. "Don't ever think it. You're a lady."

"No!" she wailed.

"Yes. And I love you!" Briggs said. He stopped shaking her.

She hiccoughed and looked up at him, her eyes

wide, her lips half parted. "Briggs?"

"Oh Christ," he said, and he gathered her in his arms and held her close as she cried in earnest. Her heart was hammering, he could feel it through the thin material of her dress. She was shaking too.

"I love you," she said. "Briggs . . . I love you."

"Don't say that."

"I'm saying it. I love you!"

"No, Sylvia, you may not say that. It's not possible . . . not for you and me."

She pulled away and looked up. "What are you telling me?"

"You're Sir Roger's daughter."

"So what?"

"You're Sylvia Hume. Daughter of a Member of Parliment. Daughter of a man who has been knighted, for Christ's sake!"

"What the hell does that have to do with what two people feel for each other?"

"I never knew my father. My mother was killed when I was a little boy. I have no sisters or brothers, no aunts or uncles. Nothing like that."

"So what?"

"I have no background. I'm a misfit. I've killed people. I . . ."

"I love you Donald O'Meara," Sylvia said. She reached behind her and turned the latch on his door, then put her arms around his neck, and drew him down to her.

Despite himself, Briggs responded. He did not want this . . . or at least the saner more sensible section of his brain said that what was happening between them was no good . . . although deep inside he felt so damned good.

"Briggs," she moaned, and her hands were up under his T-shirt caressing his back and then his chest.

"We can't do this, Sylvia," he said. He was so goddamned confused.

"I love you."

Somehow they were on the bed together, and her dress was off. She wore no panties or bra. And he was nude. They were making love, her body incredible against his; her breasts firm, her muscles lithe.

"Don't leave!" she cried at one point, but it was lost in the passion of the moment.


It was early in the morning and still dark when the car bearing Briggs passed Sterling, Virginia, then the cut-off north to Howard's home, where Sylvia and her father were staying, and finally Highway 28 south to Dulles.

The morning was chilly; there was a slight mistiness to the air in the distance, yet overhead the stars were crisply bright.

To the east, the horizon was beginning to lighten, and as they drove, Briggs had to wonder about everything that had happened over the past few days.

He had telephoned his secretary back in Hollywood, and she had assured him that everything was going smoothly.

That had depressed him. He wasn't really being missed. Although he had known what to expect, it had nevertheless bothered him.

The eastern horizon was definitely light when they reached the airport. The roadway lights were a harsh blue-white, when they came around to the unloading zone in front of the terminal.

Briggs jumped out and grabbed his bags.

Sylvia had wanted to come out with him, but he had put his foot down. They were going to make it a clean break . . . for his sanity, he had finally convinced her. When, *if,* he returned, they would see if they should take up where they had left off.

"Good luck, Mr. O'Meara," his driver said respectfully.

"Yeah, thanks."

"Wish I was going with you."

Briggs smiled, and shook his head. "No you don't." He turned and went into the terminal to the TWA counter.

"Three-seven-eight to Paris, then Moscow?"

"Yes sir. Your name?" the clerk asked.

"Wheeler, Tom Wheeler," Briggs said pulling out his passport.

# TWENTY-ONE

It was very early in the morning and still dark when the plane carrying Briggs landed at Frunze Central Airport just outside Moscow. They were made to wait for more than a half an hour way out on one of the taxiways, before they were allowed the rest of the way to the terminal. Then two uniformed soldiers came aboard, and collected all the passports and customs declarations, before the plane was unloaded and everyone herded across to customs.

The morning was very cold, the wind brisk, and a great many of the passengers were tired and cranky. But no one said a word above a whisper, and absolutely no one complained.

This was the Soviet Union. Briggs' skin crawled, the hair at the nape of his neck on end. He was neither sleepy nor cranky. He was, he had to admit, somewhat awed. He had killed a great many Russians, and now he had voluntarily walked into the heart of the enemy camp. If Howard had guessed wrong, and the KGB did know his face, he would be a dead man before very long.

Inside the terminal building they were marched down a long, featureless corridor, and into a huge room with soldiers and uniformed customs agents at each of five long counters, soldiers and baggage handlers at swinging doors through which hand-trucks came with their suitcases; and soldiers and four civilians at four desks, where their passports were stacked.

"Anderson, Aberg, Beardsly, Dane," a young woman wearing the Intourist pin on her lapel shouted. Those four broke from the others, and approached the desks, where they were quickly processed and four more were called.

Nearly an hour passed before Briggs' cover name of Thomas Wheeler was called, and he went to one of the desks. The official there looked from his pass-port photo, up to his face and back, stamped something in the booklet, wrote something on a sheet, then looked up again.

"Your purpose of visit to the Soviet Union, Mr. Wheeler?"

"I am a cook. With the American Embassy."

The official consulted a list. "Yes," he said. "Mr. Vincent Fullmer is here to meet you." He handed over Briggs' passport. Wilson," he said to the Intourist girl.

Briggs retrieved his two suitcases, and brought them over to one of the customs counters, where his passport was checked again, and his bags thoroughly searched, then electronically scanned, and finally he was directed to a door at the far side of the room. There were very few people from the flight left to be processed.

Through the door, Briggs found himself in a wide waiting room, one wall of which was glass, overlooking the terminal beyond. A guard was posted at the door. Briggs gave him his name, the man consulted a list then phoned for Fullmer, a tall, rotund man, who came to the door. The guard nodded, and Briggs stepped out.

"Tom Wheeler?" the large man asked.

"None other," Briggs said.

"I've got a car outside," Fullmer said, and he turned and headed across the busy terminal toward the main doors, leaving Briggs to catch up.

Outside the sky was starting to get light as Briggs tossed his bags in the back seat of a battered Chevy sedan, then climbed in the passenger side.

Fullmer pulled away from the curb, but did not say a word until they had been passed through the airport security post on the exit road, and were heading into the city on the main highway.

"Name's Fullmer. I'm chief of embassy staff and maintenance. You have any problems . . . and believe me you will . . . come to me first, and I'll see if I can't help you. Clear?"

"Perfectly. Where will I be staying?"

"In the embassy, at first, until we can find you quarters. Shouldn't be more than a week." Fullmer looked over. "Let me tell you, Wheeler, that week in the embassy will be your best here."

"I take it you don't like living on the economy."

Fullmer laughed derisively. "It sucks. Let me

tell you."

They came into the city on Leningradskoye Road, past the huge Hippodrome, then onto Gorkogo Street, and finally south toward the river.

Although Briggs had never been here before, it was all startlingly familiar to him. Years of stories by Oumi and Vatra and Romaine and all the others, had imprinted the roads and back streets, the buildings and monuments, the squares and walls on his memory so deeply, it was almost like coming home now. And their information had not been old either. They had kept up with events in the Soviet Union, especially in Moscow, just as he continued the same thing when he had moved to the United States.

He knew Moscow . . . if not its exact smell or flavor, certainly its geography, and its language. Coming here like this now, he felt a sense of *deja vu,* while simultaneously he could feel the first pangs of claustrophobia clamping over his heart.

The American Embassy was housed in what appeared to be an old yellow stucco slum building on Tchaikovsky Street, just a block or so up from the Moscow River. The Marine guards on the gate passed them through into the compound without question, and Fullmer drove around behind the main building, to a small parking lot.

He took one of Briggs' suitcases, and they went inside, where they signed in with a Marine guard sitting at a desk. From there they went back along a very narrow, very dark corridor, then up a flight of rickety stairs to the second floor.

"Staff dining room is to the front," Fullmer said,

as they turned the corner and headed down another corridor, this one wider and much better lit, off which were offices. There weren't many people up or about yet, because it was so early in the morning. But Briggs could smell breakfast cooking.

"Upstairs and across in the ambassador's wing is the executive dining room. There's a separate staff for it. For now you'll be down here with us peons."

"Sounds good to me," Briggs said.

"Doesn't matter how it sounds, son, it's the way it'll be," Fullmer said sharply.

They crossed an enclosed skywalk over a driveway to a smaller building, down still another winding corridor, and finally to an open door.

"This is it, Wheeler. Your home-sweet-home for just a week," Fullmer said. He dropped Briggs' suitcase on the bed. "Enjoy it while you can."

Briggs put his suitcase down. "When do I start?"

"Today's off . . . jet lag. Saturday you'll have your briefing. Sunday's off. You start 0400 Monday. What's your breakfast specialty? I haven't had a chance to study your jacket."

"Eggs Benedict."

"That's for upstairs. I'll put you on the French toast, pancake line. And let's not be too fancy. We don't have the budget for it."

"Right," Briggs said.

"Okay. Need anything give me a shout," Fullmer said at the door. "I'm in the directory," he said, pointing vaguely toward the telephone hanging on the wall, and then he was gone, closing the door behind him.

Briggs went across to the window and looked

down at a narrow courtyard below. Two black Cadillac limousines were parked in front of a garage. A man in dungarees and tall boots was washing one of them.

The telephone rang, startling Briggs out of his thoughts. He answered it. "Tom Wheeler."

"Bob Chiles. Are you alone or is this a wrong number?"

"I'm alone."

"Be right there," Chiles said and he hung up.

Briggs looked at his watch. It was 6:30. Early enough where they could move around, at least within the embassy, without attracting too much attention.

He took off his jacket, and laid it over a chair, then lit a cigarette. Chiles knocked at the door moments later, then came in. He seemed tired, and very harried.

"Burt is waiting downstairs. We have to talk right now."

"Troubles?" Briggs asked.

"Plenty," Chiles said. He opened the door and looked back out into the corridor. "What'd Fullmer give you for today?"

"I have today and Sunday off. Tomorrow I'm to be briefed."

"That'll be staff. Gives us three days," Chiles said. "We'll need it." He slipped out into the corridor, Briggs right behind him.

They went directly downstairs, passing the first floor to the basement, along a narrow corridor, and through a thick, sliding steel door, into a large room containing a dozen men and women at desks.

Without a word, Chiles led Briggs to another door at the back of the large room, where he knocked once, then went in. Burt Higgins sat on a couch along one wall. An intense looking white-haired man sat behind a desk. They both looked up. Then Higgins jumped up.

"Am I glad to see you, Briggs," he said.

He and Briggs shook hands, and Higgins introduced the other man who had gotten to his feet. This was his office.

"Rob McCann, Briggs O'Meara."

They shook hands.

"I've heard a bit about you," McCann said.

"I'm at the disadvantage," Briggs said. "But I can guess." McCann was probably CIA.

"Don't," the man said pleasantly. He motioned for them to take a seat.

"We have a bit of a problem, Briggs," Higgins began.

"Anything serious?"

"I don't know. That's why I came to Rob here, and it's why I've called you out. Peter Houten has disappeared."

"Disappeared?"

"Just like that. Yesterday. Clifford Wells, our liaison man with the Brits is over at their embassy now trying to figure out what the hell happened."

Briggs tried to think this all out. Peter Houten was supposedly a double. He had evidently been turned some time ago. But he had also been Popov's control officer. Within a week or so of Popov's arrest, Houten disappeared. Another way of looking at it, however, was that at the very same moment an

260

operation to rescue Popov was being mounted, Houten turned up missing.

"How about Lydia Savin?" he asked.

McCann seemed startled. "What about her?"

"Has anyone been keeping a watch on her, and Popov's group?"

"We thought it best we stay away from her. After all she was Popov's girl, and Houten was suspect."

"Well, there are no answers then," Briggs said. "Unless you have some good ideas."

"What the hell are you talking about?" McCann asked.

"You've been briefed on all the relationships we're dealing with here?"

"Yes."

"Fine, then we have to know about Lydia Savin."

"What are you getting at, Briggs?" Higgins asked.

"Bloody hell, Burt. Houten has disappeared. Does it mean they know about our little tea party? Or is it because he fingered Popov? Finding out where Lydia Savin and her crowd are, and what they're up to, will go a long way in telling us which."

"You think it's possible that they figured Houten was a double, and killed him?" McCann asked.

"The thought crossed my mind."

"We can't get close to that. It's not for us."

"Then I'll find out."

Higgins sat forward. "You'll jeopardize the entire mission."

"And what's the situation right now?" Briggs asked. "Are you going to send me out into the street with Houten possibly on the loose out there somewhere?" He shook his head. "No thanks. I'm not going anywhere near the operational plan until I find out what happened to that sonofabitch."

"How?" Chiles asked.

Briggs looked at him. "I'm getting out of here. I'll hit the streets. I'll find Lydia Savin and her bunch. That won't be difficult."

"You'd be missed."

Briggs thought about that a moment, something Oumi had once told him coming back.

"Apparently I'm not scheduled to begin work until Monday morning at 0400. Can you cover my absence until then?"

McCann nodded slowly. "I suppose we could manage that without too much fuss."

"Good. Now, is there any way for me to get in and out of this place, short of using the front door?"

McCann hesitated.

"I can have the President on the encrypted line within five minutes," Higgins said.

"There are a number of ways, depending upon your destination, to get you out. Coming back in is a bit more difficult."

"They count heads on the way out, don't they?"

"Across the street. Fourth story apartment. Permanent team," McCann said. "But we can get you out in the trunk of a car, in a delivery van."

"Are your vehicles searched coming in?"

"Sometimes. One in three, perhaps."

"The driver and his helper questioned? Their papers checked?"

McCann's eyes narrowed. "Almost never. They make a head count on the way out. If it agrees on the way in they don't give a damn. They look in the back to see if we've brought anyone in.''

Briggs' mind was racing. He knew exactly what he wanted to do; the question was, could he get away with it? So far it seemed feasible.

"Is there any other way for me to get back in? At night, so I wouldn't be seen?"

McCann hesitated for just a second, but then he nodded. "They closed our tunnel down several years ago, but they haven't found our sewer route."

"Where is it picked up?"

"That's the beauty of it. You can go damned near anywhere you want throughout the city. Provided it isn't raining, and providing you don't mind what you smell like at the other end."

"Do you have a map?"

"The system is numbered. We're easy to get to."

"Fine," Briggs said. "I'll want you to show me." He looked at his watch. It was still early. "I want to get out of here by noon as Lopatin."

McCann nodded again. "We'll put you in the trunk of one of the staff cars."

"I want the most beat up vehicle you have that still runs."

"I don't understand."

"Doesn't matter. Just pick a vehicle you wouldn't mind losing."

McCann started to protest, but Higgins held him off. "You can't be going off on your own like this Briggs. You have to tell us what you'll be doing. If something should go wrong, we'd never be able to get to you, unless we know what the hell you were doing. Where you were."

This trusting business was becoming even harder

than Briggs had imagined it would be. Yet what Higgins was saying did make sense. On this one, it would be next to impossible for him to work alone.

"I need some time to work this all out, without attracting the wrong kind of attention."

"What do you mean the wrong kind of attention?" McCann asked.

"If Tom Wheeler disappears from time to time, we're going to attract the wrong kind of attention. So we shift gears and point a big finger at him instead."

Higgins wasn't understanding this. It was clear on his face.

"It's simple, really. Tom Wheeler is going to die, and Ilya Petrovich Lopatin will be born," Briggs said getting to his feet. "It will be an unfortunate accident that the Soviet civil police themselves will investigate."

Everyone was looking at him, and Briggs had to smile.

"The head counters out front will have watched poor Tom Wheeler and his driver leave the embassy in the old vehicle. A few hours later, while on the way back, the vehicle will catch fire and burn. Only the driver will manage to escape."

"You'd need a body for that," McCann said.

"Yes," Briggs said.

"Good Lord, you're not planning on . . ." Higgins started.

"No, Burt, I'm not planning on going out and killing someone, even if he might be a KGB operative. I'm not that crude."

McCann was smiling. "You want to get out of

264

here by noon?''

"Yes," Briggs said.

"All right. It gives us a few hours to work out the details. We'd better get started."

## TWENTY-TWO

The beatup vehicle turned out to be a Ford
Econoline van, and Bob Chiles drove, while Briggs
changed into his Russian-styled clothes in the back,
once they had cleared the embassy gates. The day
was still cool, but the sky was clear. Briggs felt a
great sense of anticipation. Finally he was going to
be doing something with meaning. How it would
turn out, or what would happen later, as a consequence, didn't really matter now. Merely to be *doing*
was the important thing.

The clothing tailored for him had been made from
used cloth that was threadbare in some places. He
pulled the soft, cloth cap down over his eyes, and
eased himself into thinking in Russian; pulling his
mouth down, his lips forward so that he could form
the vowels; his eyes slightly downcast, his back bent
(the heritage of hundreds of years of oppression,
Oumi had said); his shoulders sagging and his hands

shaking slightly, as if from a palsy caused by lack of proper nutrition.

He smiled, but without humor. *"Eh, Comrade Chiles, how do you think I look now?"* he said, in gutter Russian.

Chiles glanced in the rearview mirror, then turned to look over his shoulder. "Holy shit!"

Briggs laughed. It took a moment for him to switch mental gears into English. "Watch where you're driving. All we need is an accident."

They were past the Lenin Library, Red Square just ahead, when Briggs directed Chiles to turn and cross the river. The traffic here was very light, nevertheless a uniformed civil police officer stood on a raised platform waving his arms and blowing his whistle as if he were in downtown Tokyo.

Crossing the river, Briggs looked out the rear window. From here the seventy-foot-high walls of the Kremlin were visible as were most of the nineteen towers, and the mammoth Great Kremlin Palace within. The area was very green, with trees growing thick on both sides of the walls. Below, on the water, were several barges, and one large passenger vessel. It all seemed to be so peaceful; so free of oppression. But that was only an illusion.

The river looped south toward the east and the west from this point. To the west were Gorky Park and Lenin Park. Briggs directed Chiles in the opposite direction.

As they neared the eastern loop of the river, the buildings became more and more run down, rickety old commercial buildings, and rat-infested warehouses intermingled with incredibly ancient wooden houses and apartment buildings.

This was a Moscow tourists would never see, Briggs thought as he continued to watch out the rear window.

"Turn down one of the side streets then slow down," he told Chiles.

"We're coming up on the river."

"I know. As soon as I'm off, you can get back to Sadovaya and cross the river on the Krasnokholmskiy Bridge. It's just ahead. You won't be able to miss it."

"What about you?" Chiles said. He turned off the main street and down a narrow avenue barely wider than an alleyway.

No one was following them.

"I'll be back in the embassy sometime after dark tonight," Briggs said. He unlatched the back door, opened it and jumped out on the run, slamming it shut before the van got away from him.

Stuffing his hands deeply into the pockets of his tattered jacket he walked quickly away in the opposite direction without looking back, the odors of cooking cabbage, wood smoke and open sewers mixing with the rich odors of the river less than a block away.

At the corner he turned down another very narrow street, that seemed to run more or less parallel to the river, and within a block and a half he came to a very rough-looking riverside café, across the street. The windows were very dirty, almost opaque; and from the open front door, a thin blue haze of smoke swirled with the breeze.

Oumi and Vatra and the others had trained him

well . . . or had they, he wondered. It was a test he was needing. And the grimy little place across the street was certainly going to provide it. If he could pass here, he could pass anywhere in the city.

He let himself slip firmly into the Russian peasant mentality, his thoughts twisting to conform with the language, and he went across the street.

The place was crowded, mostly with men, eating their lunch and drinking either vodka or kvass from one liter jugs. Almost everyone was either smoking, or had a lit cigarette in a shallow plate in front of them.

Briggs lit one of the CCCP cigarettes McCann had supplied him with, then found an empty table off to one corner, and sat down. No one paid him the slightest attention, and within a couple of minutes a filthy young man, wearing a long gray apron came to him.

"What will it be?" he asked wearily.

Briggs looked up at him. "Soup. Bread. Vodka. Some cheese."

There was a lot of noise in the place, but the four men seated at the next table over, looked around. One of them, an old man with a face that seemed as if it had been chiseled from rock, and hands that seemed to have been cold molded from black iron, laughed.

"Cheese," he bellowed. "This one wants cheese."

Half the men in the place looked over at the commotion.

The old man shoved his chair back and got up. Alarm bells were ringing along Briggs' nerves. He had wanted a test, but not like this.

"And what do you expect for cheese, young fellow?" the old man asked rhetorically. "That the great red god of St. Basil's environs will come down off his perch and shit it for you? Shit it right on your plate?"

There were a lot of guffaws. The young waiter was terrified.

"Is that your game then? Suck the shit out of the great red asshole across the whore's river?"

One of the old man's friends got up and left. One of the others shook his head.

If it was going to come this way, then so be it, Briggs thought, the loose feeling coming over him. He looked up at the waiter.

"If there is no cheese, then at least bring me my bread and soup and my drink."

The young man backed up, then scrambled to the back room.

Briggs shoved his chair back, and got to his feet. There was dead silence in the room. The old man had a bemused expression on his face. Briggs stuck out his hand.

"Lopatin," he said. "You may call me Ilya Petrovich."

The old man batted his hand away. Briggs laughed out loud.

"So, old fool, maybe it is you who are sucking the other end of the great red bastards across the river. Tell me. I will stand in your line."

The young waiter had appeared in the doorway from the kitchen with a full liter of vodka. He dropped it on the floor, the glass shattering. Someone got up and shut the front door, bolting it.

"Who are you, Lopatin?" the old man growled.

"A man just as yourself, comrade. I have come here for a meal. Nothing more. I was told there might be cheese here."

"Who told you?"

"A friend."

"What friend?"

Briggs said nothing, one part of his mind exulting that his veracity as a Russian was not being questioned, another part wondering just how the hell he was going to get out of here with the minimum of fuss.

The old man lunged forward, but Briggs sidestepped around the table, keeping it between them.

"I don't want to fight you, old man. I have had enough fighting to last a lifetime," Briggs said. Most of the men had gotten up and spread out along the walls. An old woman, wearing a long apron, stood in the doorway from the kitchen. She did not look too happy. Yet Briggs did not think the civil police were called down here too often.

The old man slammed the table aside, and started forward, his hands out in front of him like a clumsy wrestler's.

Briggs danced back and to the left. "I don't want to do this with you, old man, but if you persist I will break your left arm."

The old man stopped, threw his head back and roared. Everyone else in the room laughed. Even the proprietress smiled.

"My goatherd who loves cheese promises to break a limb," the old man snickered, and he charged.

Briggs had seen it coming from the look in the old

man's eyes. He stepped aside at the last moment, grabbed the man's left wrist with one hand, and his underarm just above his elbow with the other, and swung inward, bringing the arm down, and his own knee up. The bone snapped with a loud pop, and Briggs leaped aside.

The old man was stunned into silence, as were the others in the room, but then pandemonium broke out.

Briggs hurriedly backed himself against the wall near the door, and pulled out his stiletto as a half a dozen burly men turned on him. They all pulled up short when they saw the blade.

"I came in here for a drink and a meal. I did not come in here to start a fight. But comrades, believe me, if you want to continue this, by the time it is finished several of you will be lying dead on the floor."

"Who are you, Lopatin?" the old man asked, grimacing.

"Merely a man who wanted a meal."

"Stay and have it."

"No thank you, Comrade," Briggs said. He edged over to the door, unbolted it then slipped outside, concealing the stiletto out of view at his side, until he was around the corner, and could re-sheath it.

Although he had gotten himself into immediate trouble, back there he had passed his first test. None of them gave the slightest indication they didn't believe he was a Russian. He had passed. He had actually passed.

It was mid-afternoon by the time he had worked

his way south along the river front, to the commercial district, where large ships were tied up at the docks. There was a lot of activity down here, and Briggs, just one more face in the crowd, was not noticed.

Oumi had told him about this place, along the river. It was a world unto itself. The government seldom made itself felt down here, except for customs and tariffs on a few restricted outgoing cargos, so that people came and went as they pleased, without restrictions, and a free enterprise black market flourished.

The buildings were all very old, most of them stone, some of them unpainted wood. There were a maze of alleys and tunnels, and back courtyards and paths throughout the district. There were a lot of underpasses, and storm drains, and piles of brick and old garbage: A million places for a man to hide, and to die, Oumi had said. Although this was not a residential area, tattered laundry hung from many second and third story windows, and the ever present odor of cooked cabbage seemed to hang in the air. It was very depressing here to Briggs; depressing and confining. But it was exactly what he had expected to find from the stories Oumi and the others had hammered into his head. Although he did not like it here, it did feel familiar. He wanted now only to find what he had come looking for, then get back to the embassy. The sooner this part of the operation was over with, the sooner he could begin agitating his way into jail.

He walked along the crowded wharves to the south, the central city behind him, until the people and the ships became fewer and shabbier. Garbage lay in heaps seemingly everywhere, and there was a miasma of undefinable odors now hanging over the quay. He came to a narrow path between two warehouses. The way back was partially blocked by a tangle of tree branches, which seemed oddly out of place here, bricks and other junk. But people had gone this way before. He could see a path clearly defined over and then through the tangle. A half a block back he had wondered if he had set himself on a fool's mission; now he knew differently.

He ducked down the path, and scrambled over and through the thick pile of debris that was at least twenty feet high and perhaps a hundred feet deep. On the other side was a rabbit-warren maze of greasy packing crates that appeared to have once contained very large pieces of industrial equipment. Briggs was mildly surprised that the crates hadn't been dismantled and carted off for firewood, but immediately the strong smell that assailed his nostrils told him why the wood had not been disturbed. It had probably been here for years. No one would touch it. Not the local people, and certainly not the authorities.

He ducked down one of the jumbled tunnels, the daylight instantly gone, the smell of death much stronger now. Twenty feet in, he stopped.

"Vatra," he called the first name that came to his mind. He stopped to listen, but there was no answer. "Vatra," he called louder. "It is your brother, Vatra."

Someone or something moaned from deeper within the maze.

"Vatra?" Briggs called, cocking his head.

The moaning came again, loudly enough this time so that he could get the general direction, and he worked toward the sound, calling out as he went, stopping frequently to listen.

He came upon the old man lying inside one of the crates, his clothing sodden with his own excrement. He looked up, his eyes running, open sores everywhere, even inside his mouth and on his tongue.

"Vatra?" the old man moaned.

This was the place Oumi had described. *There is a river of darkness, a trash yard for poor lost souls too weak even to fight for their own survival. The river styx, beside the Muscova River. They will crawl there, then lie down to die. Women. Old men. Children. Entire families. It is a human junk yard. No one cares.*

That story had made a powerful impression on Briggs, but nowhere near as powerful an image as what he was seeing at this moment.

"Vatra?" the old man croaked again.

Briggs wanted to do something for the old man, but there was simply nothing he could do. He had come here for a specific purpose, and he hardened his heart for it.

"I am looking for my brother. A man my age. He is here. Do you know where?"

"Vatra?"

"He is a man my age."

"So many," the old man croaked. He waved a boney hand off to the left. "So many."

"Vatra is there?" Briggs asked looking to the left. The smell was very bad now. Nearly overpowering.

"They are all there," the old man whispered. "They fought. They are in there. Last night." The old man's eyes closed, and for a moment Briggs thought he was dead. But then he realized that the man had just fallen asleep.

Last night they had fought. Briggs looked that way. What had the old man meant? There was death and dying here. People came to die. Within days, a week at the most, the rats took care of the remains. Very efficient. The lowest end of the Russian sewage system.

Briggs left the crate containing the old man and peered down one of the tunnels beneath the boxes to the left. The hairs at the nape of his neck stood on end. He could smell blood. A lot of it. Very strong.

He reached behind his back and slipped out his stiletto. This place was bad. Very bad, the odor of evil even stronger in the air then the smells of death.

Carefully Briggs started down the tunnel, and ten or fifteen feet in, turned a corner where he was stopped in his tracks.

Three men lay dead in a wide, thick pool of blood. Two of them had evidently chased the third man who had turned on them in here. The face of one of them was torn up, as if by an animal. One of the others lay with his guts spilling out between his fingers clenched to his stomach. And the third man, the one who had been chased, lay on his side, his eyes open, a knife jutting from his chest. He was a younger man . . . all of them were . . . about Briggs' age and general build. He would do. He would do just fine, Briggs thought, slipping his stiletto back in his sheath, and getting out of there.

Briggs spent the remainder of the afternoon at several waterfront dives, eating soup, and drinking kvass, which was a very poor substitute for American beer or British ale.

Just after dark, he took a subway across town to the area of the State Conservatory of Music, then walked to within a block of the embassy, where on a quiet street, he slipped down into the sewers, and quickly made his way back.

They were waiting for him there.

# TWENTY-THREE

The storm sewer opened into a small room off the embassy's boiler room in a sub-basement. Water pipes and gauges adorned the walls and ceiling. Circling the manhole were six Marines, their automatic weapons at the ready. Burt Higgins stood in the doorway, Rob McCann directly behind him.

"Greetings, Comrades," Briggs said in Russian.

Higgins laughed in relief. "You may stand down. He's one of ours."

A Marine sergeant glanced from Briggs, half in and half out of the floor, to Higgins, then relaxed and stepped back, bringing his weapon up. "You heard the man," he snapped.

The other Marines stood back slowly, as if from a trance, clicked their weapons to safety, then crowded out of the tiny room.

Higgins and McCann came in, and helped Briggs climb the rest of the way out of the sewer. He had gotten soaked to the knees, and he did not smell very pretty.

"Any trouble?" the CIA man asked.

"With the authorities, no."

"Did you find what you were looking for?" Higgins asked.

Briggs nodded. It was going to be a long time before he would be able to clear his memory of the image of the old man lying in the wooden crate. Lying there waiting to die.

"We're going to have to do it tonight. Has Chiles got the van ready?"

"He's working on it now," Higgins said, but McCann interjected.

"This is going too fast. I'd like to wait until tomorrow night. Until we've had a better chance to study this."

"It's not possible. We go tonight," Briggs said. "Now I need a bath, and a change of clothes."

"This is my territory," McCann snapped. "We'll do as I say."

Briggs looked into his eyes, a retort on his lips. But he held his temper in check. "In a couple of hours I'll be out of here. Out of your hair, and then you won't have to worry about me for a bit."

McCann started to protest, but Higgins held him off. "Can you find your way up, Briggs?"

Briggs nodded. "Give me an hour. I'll meet you back in McCann's office. Have Bob there too, ready to go." He turned to McCann at the door. "I really don't want to give you a hard time, Mr. McCann. But this has all been worked out. My life is on the line, so I'll be calling the shots. I'll be out of here in a couple of hours, and Tom Wheeler will be officially dead. You may have to fend off some heat from the Soviet civil authorities for a day or two, but I shouldn't imagine that will cause you much trouble."

"Off you go, then," Higgins said.

"Right," Briggs replied, and he went out the door, and across the boiler room. McCann said something to Higgins, but Briggs didn't quite catch it. Then he was out of earshot, and starting up the stairs.

Back in his room, he stripped off his filthy clothes, put on a bathrobe and went down the hall to the bathroom where he took a long, hot shower. Once again in his room, he lit an American cigarette, and poured himself a drink of Irish whiskey. He hated vodka and kvass . . . he had even in the old days when that was all the old Balkans drank. Even more, he despised Russian-made cigarettes. For the next few days, though, he would have put up with those inconveniences, and in fact appear to those around him that he relished such things.

He got dressed in his American-cut clothing, including a very loudly-patterned sportcoat, stuffed his Russian things in a battered old Russian Army issue duffle bag, and went back downstairs to McCann's office.

He was stopped at the outer door by a pair of Marine guards, and held there until Higgins came to escort him in.

McCann and Chiles were already inside, along with another, tall, very thin man.

"You know Cliff Wells, our liaison man with the British Embassy?" Higgins said.

He and Briggs shook hands. "We met," Briggs said. "Anything new on Peter Houten?"

They all sat down.

"It appears as if he's gone back to London," Wells said.

"Sir Roger has been informed?" Briggs asked Higgins, who nodded. Wells went on.

"From what I can gather, his trip back was routine. Been on the roster for months. No one stopped to think he'd actually go back now."

"How the hell does a senior SIS officer return to London without his own embassy knowing about it?" Briggs asked astounded.

"Good question. He apparently works with a degree of autonomy. He comes and goes as he pleases."

"No wonder we damned near lost the war. Good Lord," Briggs said disgusted. "What's he done in London?"

"He's only just arrived, from what I understood," Wells said. "It's possible he's returned in response to Obyedkov's death. Could be he's testing the waters. Trying to find out just what his own people know."

"If that's true, the man has got balls down to his knees," Briggs said. But at least with Houten out of the way it would make his job here somewhat less complicated.

He turned to Chiles. "Is the van ready?"

Chiles nodded. "The fuel pump is set to spray gasoline over everything."

"We can get at it from the inside?"

"That's the beauty of it. Raw gasoline will be sprayed all over . . . ah . . . the body, which will ignite. Within seconds the inside of the van will be a blast furnace."

"I don't want you getting caught."

"I won't," Chiles said. "Did you find what you were looking for?"

Briggs nodded. He turned back to the others, and quickly explained where he had gone, why he had gone there and what he had found. When he was finished McCann looked a little queasy.

"I've been here for the better part of four years, and I never heard about that place," he said.

"You don't get out enough," Briggs quipped. He turned back to Higgins. "How about the others. Everything set up?"

"So far so good," Higgins replied. "Dayton and Palmer, who were supposed to be watching Houten, have been rotated over to Byers' team watching the train."

"What's it like?"

"In a word . . . grim. There are a lot of pople going out there. The train always comes back empty."

"Have we figured how the so-called rehabilitated ones are gotten out of there?"

"Not for sure, Briggs, at least not yet. Byers has a couple of his people working on it. Our best guess is that there is a station somewhere between Moscow and the Center. From there they could be taken by truck almost anywhere. No one would know."

"It's a secret even to the dissidents, then," Briggs said. "So wherever the train stops, it must be disguised as something else. Probably a fuel bunker, or perhaps a maintenance depot. Something like that. They could get the poor bastards out of there without anyone knowing. The prisoners probably don't even know what's happening to them, so that later they could not talk about it.''

"Are you thinking about using that way out?''

"No. We'll stick with the original plan. Has Dick White shown up yet?''

"He's not due until tomorrow. He made contact with our people in Paris, and then Helsinki. Everything is fine. He's clean.''

"Have him at the rendezvous then from midnight to 0400 beginning the first night after my trial.''

Higgins nodded, but it was very clear that McCann wasn't liking any of this.

"What happens if this all blows up in your face?'' he asked.

"Then I lose, and the others return home,'' Briggs said.

"It'd push back our work here by years.''

"That won't happen.''

"Won't happen?'' McCann exploded. "You stupid son of a bitch, what you're proposing is impossible. You have some flimsy Russian identification that the British arranged for you through our old Balkan network, from what I understand. And on that basis, you're going to get yourself sent to a specific prison? Do you realize what you're trying to tell me?'' McCann stopped only long enough to catch his breath. "That'd be like going to Kansas City figuring to commit just the right crime so that you'd land in Leavenworth. And that's the easy part.

283

From there you'd plan on busting out of the place with one of the prisoners."

"That's what I like about this man, Burt," Briggs said lightly. "He is succinct. He came right to the point."

"He is right, you know."

"Leavenworth would be a snap," Briggs said, getting to his feet. "Let's do it, Bob. I'm tired, I need to get someplace to sleep."

McCann jumped up, sputtering for a moment, but then he looked at the three of them standing there, and he finally shook his head. "You're all crazy," he said. "You do know that." He stuck out his hand to Briggs who took it. "Good luck to you, O'Meara, or Wheeler, or Lopatin, or whoever the hell you really are."

"Thanks. I think I might need a wee bit of the magic."

"If you get in too deeply . . ." Higgins started, but then he backed off. He and Briggs shook hands. "Luck."

"Sure," Briggs said, and he and Chiles left McCann's office. They went up to the ground floor the back way.

Chiles went outside first, to make sure everything was clear, and bring the van around to the rear door. The fewer people who saw the cook Tom Wheeler climbing into a van with an old duffel bag, the better off they'd be.

Briggs tossed the bag in the back, and Chiles drove around to the front where the Marine guards let them out. Briggs deliberately looked up at the fourth floor windows of the building across the street so that the Russian observers would be sure to see him. Then they were past and heading once again across town.

"Did they get a good look at you?" Chiles asked.

"I think so. They shouldn't have any trouble identifying this sportcoat."

"I was going to talk to you about that. Where in the hell did you get it?"

"You don't like my fashion-sense?"

Chiles laughed. "Haven't seen any yet."


Although they were not followed, Chiles took a circuitous route to the riverfront warehouse area where Briggs had found the body. They were running just a bit low on time. This would all have to be completed before midnight. Too many questions would be asked by the Soviet authorities if the time got any later than that. It just didn't do for foreigners . . . especially Americans . . . to be out and around after midnight.

They found the place with no problem, and Chiles parked the van in the deeper shadows several yards away from the path between the buildings. Briggs had already changed back into his Russian-cut clothing.

"Wait here," he told Chiles, and he slipped out of the vehicle and hurried back to the path.

There was some activity farther north on the docks. They had passed the brightly area where a large boat was being loaded. But here, everything was dark and quiet.

He ducked down the path, over the pile of debris, and then into the odiferous jumble of packing crates.

There was a noise to his right, and Briggs stopped, his hand instinctively reaching for his stiletto as he held his breath and listened. The noise came a moment later. It was a soft, scratching sound. As of little, clawed feet running over . . .

It was rats, Briggs realized. He shuddered. They were feeding now.

He hesitated just a second near the crate in which he had seen the old man, but then decided he did not want to know what had happened. He had come here to do something. He just wanted to get it over with.

To the left, he ducked down one of the tunnels, and in the very dim light filtering in through the jumbled pile of crates he was able to make out the three bodies lying there. A very large rat, with eyes that glinted in a stray bit of light, was perched on the shoulder of one of the dead men. Briggs started to reach for his stiletto, but the creature, sensing danger, skittered away. To wait, either for the stranger to lie down and die, or to leave.

He pushed the rest of the way into the narrow opening between the crates, and careful not to get any of the blood on himself, he pulled the knife out of the chest of one of the bodies, then pulled the poor creature over to the opening, where he hurriedly undressed it, tossing the clothing away.

Briggs felt like a ghoul. By the time he was finished he was sweating, and his stomach was churning. The smells were beginning to get to him. This man had probably been dead for more than twenty-four hours, and already there was a powerful odor coming off his body. The rats had not gotten to this one yet, and the chest wound was only a puckered mark, red with a blue tinge under the beam of Briggs' penlight. His hair was the wrong color, and so were his eyes. That would be taken care of in the fire, so it didn't matter.

With care then, so as not to mark up the body any more than need be, Briggs dragged it back through the maze of crates, the skittering of the rats all around him, then over the pile of debris and finally to the end of the buildings.

Leaving the body there, he hurried around the corner to the van, where he opened the back doors.

Chiles was looking back at him. "You find it?"

"Right," Briggs said. "Anyone come by?"

Chiles shook his head. He was nervous.

Briggs went back to the path and quickly dragged the body back to the van, where he heaved it inside, climbed in with it and latched the door.

"Let's get the hell out of here."

Chiles' eyes were wide. "It stinks . . . goddamnit, it's already started to rot."

"This was one of the better ones."

"One of the . . ." Chiles let it trail off. He started the van, and headed away from the warehouses.

Briggs dressed the corpse in the American clothing he had worn from the embassy. It was not an easy task, but everything fit, more or less, except for the shoes which were several sizes too large.

In fifteen minutes he was finished, and he directed Chiles to drive down another dark, narrow avenue, and park.

Between the two of them (Chiles gagging through

it all) they managed to horse the body into the front passenger seat. They strapped it in with the seatbelt and shoulder harness.

"I can't believe this," Chiles kept saying.

"Neither can I," Briggs said. "How did you rig the fuel pump?"

For a moment Chiles just stared at the body dressed in Briggs' loud sports jacket. But then he shook himself out of it, and lifted the engine cowling between the seats. "A clamp under here, on the fuel line," he said reaching in. "It's on the verge of coming off. I just have to give it a little tug."

"All right," Briggs said. This was it. Shortly he was going to be out on his own. No longer officially alive as Tom Wheeler. "We'll drive back across the river within a few blocks of the embassy. Up on Arbat Street somewhere. Maybe Smolenskaya Plaza."

"What if we're stopped?"

"Don't get stopped," Briggs said.

They made it across the river once again, and to within a few blocks of the American Embassy, where Chiles opened the cowling, and with the engine still running, loosened the fuel line clamp. Instantly, gasoline began spraying out, all over the corpse.

"Watch the three letter drops," Briggs said. "If anything comes up I'll leave something." They had slowed to a bare crawl, and Briggs slipped out the back doors, and headed up the street, to the shadows of an apartment building entrance.

The van stopped at the end of the block, Chiles leaped out and a couple of seconds later, a bright flash illuminated the interior of the vehicle, and flames shot out from the open door.

Tom Wheeler was officially dead, Briggs thought as he pulled his cap low, stuffed his hands deeply into his pockets and headed away. Long live Ilya Petrovich Lopatin.

## TWENTY-FOUR

Briggs arrived cross town, once again on the south side of the river, a few minutes after midnight, stopping at a boarding hotel off Pyatnitskaya Street. He had to ring the bell for more than ten minutes before the old woman dressed in a thick housecoat and felt boots answered the door. At first she was very cross, her tongue sharp, thinking that Briggs was a friend of one of her tenants. When she realized he wanted a room, and had money to pay for it her manner became effusive. By 12:30 he had inspected his room at the rear in the basement, with its own private entrance, had paid for two weeks in advance, and the old landlady had shuffled back to her own apartment. By one o'clock, her light was out, and the house had settled down. Briggs slipped noiselessly out the back door, crossed the courtyard, and hurried up the next block. The quietness and darkness of the city struck him then. It was a very lonely feeling. Yet, despite that, and despite the extreme danger all around him, Moscow was like home to Briggs. He knew its streets, its music and its people. Most of all he understood what it was to be a Muscovite; it was an attitude at once scornful of the Soviet Central government, and of the shortages of consumer products, while at the same time prideful of the fact that the city was *the* mecca of Soviet life. Automobiles, refrigerators, shoes, television sets, and steak. If any of it was available, it was available first here in Moscow.

Added to that swagger Briggs had adopted the attitude of belligerence common to most dissidents. He was on a cause; it shone in his eyes like a light, and rode on his shoulders like a suit of armor. He was invincible, he seemed to say.

At the corner, he turned away from the river, deeper into the heart of the city. Here there were more lights, but still no traffic. To be caught here at this time of the night, would invite questions that he was not quite prepared to answer, so he quickened his step, as he let his mind range ahead to the tasks still to come.

The Metropole Hotel and the Crystal Café were the two hot spots of Moscow night life for the upper strata; for the foreign journalists, and the Soviet officers and government ministers. Popov and men of his ilk were at the opposite end of the scale, or very nearly so. Their hangouts were places like Porfiri's (where Briggs was heading) and the Café Samizdat, a writers' haunt that poked fun at government regulations of the arts.

Peter Houten's reports, at least in these sorts of

details about Popov's life, were thought to be accurate. "No reason for the bugger to lie about something like that," Sir Roger had assured them.

Briggs had gone over in detail the typical itineraries the dissident had followed (the man's days usually began in mid-afternoon, ending around dawn), his habits, his likes and dislikes, his friends, including Lydia Savin, and in some ways even more important, Popov's writing—political tracts mostly, but some very good, if obscure, poetry.

Popov was a complex man, but like so many men of his ilk, his life was routine, very predictable. He had been in trouble with the Soviet authorities from his early college days. Always the agitator, he had been in and out of scrapes for such things as artistic freedom, human rights, the Jewish Freedom League. Any cause that might attract a crowd in Gorky Park was of interest to Popov who had written, in the early seventies, that life is nothing more than a series of battles for human rights and dignity. The early cavemen had no "rights" to a good education, or even to proper shelter and food. He fought for what he could get. "These days," Popov wrote, "we are fighting for our right of free thought."

If Lydia Savin were to be found, Porfiri's was as good a place as any to begin the search.

Two burly men, dressed in baggy gray suits, leaned against an automobile across the street from the club. They exuded officialdom. As Briggs approached, one of them pushed away from the car and ambled across the street. He was not smiling.

"Let's see some identification, Comrade," he

said harshly.

Briggs grinned. "Would you care to step inside . . ."

The burly official grabbed Briggs by the front of his jacket. Out of the corner of his eye Briggs could see the other one across the street step away from the car, his hand reaching beneath his coat.

"I'm sorry, Comrade. Truly sorry," Briggs said. "I did not mean any disrespect." He pulled out his internal passport which limited his travel between Moscow and his home in Leningrad.

The official closely scrutinized the well-worn document, looking from the photograph to Briggs' face. "Let's have your work card."

"I don't have a work card. I am a writer."

"The Writer's Union card, then."

"I am samizdat."

The official's lip curled up in a sneer. "You self-publish. Perhaps you are a capitalist then? You have money? You are independently wealthy? Perhaps there is a western patron."

"I am sorry, comrade, but I have money sufficient to my needs."

The other official had come across the street. "What have we got here, Vasili, another parasite?"

His partner laughed. "He says not. Perhaps he is a criminal. Where do you get your money, sufficient to your needs, Lopatin, can you tell us that?"

"By working where I can."

The second man had taken Briggs' internal passport, and was copying the information into his notebook. When he was finished he handed it back to Briggs.

"I advise you to return to Leningrad, Lopatin. In the morning. Take the first train."

The other one poked a finger into Briggs' chest. "Moscow does not want more of your kind. There are enough parasites and hooligans as there is."

They both stared at Briggs for several long seconds, then they turned and slowly went back across the street where they again took up their positions against the parked car.

Briggs turned and went into the smoky, crowded club. There had been some music playing, he had heard it out on the street. Now the place was quiet. Everyone looking his way. He stopped just inside.

An old woman, a dirty white apron over her long dress, a brightly colored babushka on her head came from the back.

"You are alone this evening? You wish for a table?"

Briggs could almost feel Popov's presence here. There were many posters on the wall depicting everything from the war in Afghanistan, to Polish Solidarity. Very dangerous to display here. He glanced over his shoulder at the door, and shook his head.

"The filthy pigs," he said with much feeling.

There were a few in the crowd who nodded, but the old woman just clucked and led him to a small table near the back.

"Are you hungry? Do you want to eat?"

"That would be nice. And some vodka."

"Of course, vodka," the woman said, and she shuffled back to the kitchen.

Gradually the hum of conversation rose to its

earlier level. By the time the old woman had brought Briggs a glass and a carafe of vodka, everything had gone back to normal.

A very large man, dark-skinned, with thick, greasy-black hair, threaded his way across the room and sat down at Brigg's table. He stuck out his hand. "You have the honor to meet Yuri Dmitri Myakov."

Briggs shook his hand. "I am Ilya Petrovich Lopatin."

"A solid name. But what brings you to Porfiri's? I have not seen your face here before. And believe me, I know everyone."

"I have come from Leningrad in search of an old friend," Briggs said. He pulled out one of Popov's political tracts and laid it on the table.

Myakov blanched. "You are a friend of Mikhail Vladimir's?"

"Not actually. But I feel as if I know Popov from his writings." The people at the tables around them stopped what they were doing and looked over.

"He is gone."

"I can see he is not here. I will wait for him."

"You don't understand my friend. He is gone . . . permanently."

Briggs grabbed the tract, stuffed it in his pocket, and got to his feet. "Tell me where Popov has gone. I will follow him. I will bring him back."

"No . . . No, my friend," Myakov said. He reached out and pulled Briggs back down. The old woman, and a couple of men from another table came over and introduced themselves. The one called Stepanovich, an older firebrand who reminded Briggs of Vatra, was clucking like an old woman at the various explanations. He finally cut through the others.

"The train to nowhere, Ilyasha . . . perhaps you have heard it mentioned."

"It is a fairy tale," Briggs said looking up.

Stepanovich shook his head.

"He tells the truth," the old woman said. "Vladi was tried for parasitism three weeks ago now, and afterwards . . . ten days ago perhaps . . . he was seen boarding the gray train. He is truly gone."

"He will be back."

"No," the woman said.

"He will be back and I will wait for him."

"You will wait in hell for him," Stepanovich said sadly.

"Then so be it. But I will see the great man. We will talk. We will be together. There is so much to say. So much for me to share with him."

Several others had gathered around the table, and still others were moving over.

Briggs looked up and smiled inwardly. This was working even better than he thought it would. If there was one thing the Russians loved to do more than drink vodka, it was to talk and drink vodka.

"The Soviet Union will become a free state within twenty years," Briggs began. "But only after an economic revolution sweeps this land."

"Revolution," someone in the back shouted. "That's all you young people talk about. Guns and killing. Next will come the tanks."

"No, my old friend," Briggs said. "I am not talking about that kind of revolution. I am speaking here of much different kinds of pressures. The great human tide." Briggs sat forward and tapped his finger on the table top for emphasis. "In 1961 there was a great need for boots. All up and down the land, the people screamed for boots. Soon there was an upwelling of voices . . . a choir of cries . . . give us boots. Give us boots!"

Stepanovich's eyes were bright.

"And what happened? I will tell you my friends . . . we were given boots! Oh yes. From Minsk and Donetsk and even from Kiev the factories poured forth boots! That kind of a revolution my friend." Briggs laughed, and thumped the table. "Listen. The people wanted boots. The people cried for boots. The people got boots."

"What do we cry for now?" a short, somewhat stockily built, but nevertheless attractive woman said from beside Briggs.

He turned and looked up into her eyes, his heart skipping a beat. It was Lydia Savin. Popov's lover. Brezhnev's illegitimate daughter.

"Something much simpler than boots," Briggs said.

"But more expensive?"

Briggs shrugged. "The freedom to say what we are saying right this moment."

"You are speaking."

"Not without a certain fear of retaliation."

"No one has come in here to arrest you."

"They wait outside," Briggs said. "They have questioned me. They know my name. They have advised that I return to Leningrad on the first train in the morning."

"Then go home, Lopatin. Return to your wife

297

and children.''

"I have no wife or children. And I will not return home. My work is here. I know it now." Briggs looked at the others standing around. Some of them seemed expectant. Others seemed fearful. They all looked tired.

But Lydia Savin was the key, for the moment. She had dropped out of sight, but now she was back. Where had she been? If the authorities had had her . . . if her father had convinced her to work for them . . . then at this moment she'd be the most dangerous person in Russia as far as Briggs was concerned.

"Won't you join me? Or perhaps you don't believe in what Popov had to say," Briggs said to her.

Something flashed in the woman's eyes. She reached back to slap him, but then decided against it. "You don't know, do you?"

"Know what?" Briggs asked. "I only know that Mikhail Vladimir Popov is a great man. If he is gone, his teachings must not go as well. I will bring his message. I will talk for him. I will stand on Red Square and shout it from the ramparts."

Myakov shoved one of the other men out of his chair, and pulled it out so Lydia could sit down. Looking at her, Briggs could see some slight resemblance to her father, the Soviet leader. The high cheekbones, the dark eyebrows.

"You say you know Vladi's works. And you are willing to carry on?" she said.

Briggs nodded.

"It will be very dangerous," she said.

"She is right, Ilya," Stepanovich said. "You

should do well to listen to her."

"Very dangerous," she said. "You will most likely be arrested."

"Let it be," Briggs shouted, his face contorting into a mask of hate and fury. "Let it be! Then they can send me to be with him. It would be fitting."

The woman reached out and placed her hands over his on the table, so that he could not pound again. She had a wan smile on her lips. "No. That would do you no good. Nor would it do Vladi any good."

"I am not afraid of martyrdom."

"No one says you are, Ilya," she said. "And there are times when that course may be the best for the people. But not now. No one knows of Vladi, where he has gone, what has happened to him. It is a crime, in fact, merely to mention his name."

"I don't care. I know his name," Briggs said. He was really getting into it. He *felt* like a Russian dissident now.

"If they had searched you out front, and had found Vladi's pamphlet, you would have been taken to the Lubyanka. Perhaps you would have been tortured. If you were lucky you would have been sent to Siberia. If you were really lucky you would have been shot. Don't you see? What good would you have done?"

"But I wasn't searched. I am here now. And tomorrow I will stand in front of St. Basil and talk with anyone who cares to listen. Peasant and western journalist alike."

Lydia got up. "You are a disgusting man," she spat.

"Because I love Popov and what he taught?"

"I loved Vladi," she said leaning down. "But you are disgusting because you are so ready to throw your life away. At least Vladi had the sense to temper his work with some caution."

"And look what it got him." Stepanovich said from the other side of the table.

Briggs looked around, a bewildered expression on his face, deep in his eyes. "What then? What can I do?"

"If you want to help, then you may help," Stepanovich said.

Lydia Savin shook her head, but Myaka spoke up. "I agree with Alexandr. We should allow Lopatin to help. He seems to know what he is talking about."

"He is either a fool, or he is a spy from the komitet," Lydia hissed. "Either way he will bring death to us."

She turned and pushed through the crowd. Briggs jumped up, upsetting his chair, and pushed after her. He caught her at the back door, grabbed her by the elbow and spun her around.

"You say you love Popov. Then how can you walk away like this."

"You are a *spion!*" she screeched, and she tried to scratch his eyes.

He grabbed her wrists, and for several intense moments they struggled. But then she relaxed and he pulled her closer so that he could whisper into her ear.

"You are wrong, lovely lady. I am not a spy for the komitet. I am a man who knows and loves Mikhail Vladimir. I have come here to help his cause."

## TWENTY-FIVE

Briggs followed Lydia Savin from Porfiri's, five blocks to her apartment in an extremely rundown building across the river from Taganskaya Prison. She had pulled out of his grasp at the restaurant, had slipped out the door into the night, and had given no sign that she knew she was being followed until she mounted the steps to her building. Then she turned around and waited for Briggs to catch up.

"You are trouble, Lopatin," she said.

"My name is Ilya. My friends call me Lasha."

"It is a silly, inconsequential name."

"Perhaps," Briggs shrugged. "But I am neither silly nor inconsequential."

"Perhaps not. But you are dangerous," she said. She turned and went into the building, leaving the door open behind her. Briggs looked both ways along the dark street. No one had followed them from the club. Then he bounded up the four steps, and slipped inside, closing the door softly.

Lydia paused at the first floor landing, above him, and their eyes met when he looked up. There was a single small lightbulb shining another flight up. She continued up and he followed, taking care not to make any noise.

The building was very old, the stairway littered with trash. There was the ever-present stench of cooked cabbage, as well as other smells . . . garbage, urine. Yet a lightbulb was burning above. That did not make much sense to Briggs' way of thinking. If the people who lived in this building were poor, they certainly would not be able to afford a lightbulb, let alone the electricity to burn it.

At the second floor, Lydia unlocked her apartment door, which was directly beneath the light, and when she had it open she reached inside and flipped on a light.

"Shut off the corridor light, please," she said as Briggs came the rest of the way up.

There was a switch at her landing. He flipped it off, plunging the corridor into darkness except for the light spilling from Lydia's open apartment door.

After all, she was Brezhnev's daughter. It was not inconceivable that she was being supported. But, if that was so, how did she reconcile her work with Popov and others like him, with her government support, unless she was a komitet agent.

She was just stepping into the bathroom, when Briggs came into the apartment and closed and latched the door.

"Fix yourself a drink, if you wish," she said, and she closed the door.

The apartment was small, but very well furnished, and neat, belying the appearance of the building and the hallway. Lydia Savin definitely had money (at least by Soviet standards) and she had made no effort to conceal the fact. There were a lot of books and periodicals throughout the apartment, nice furniture, a telephone, and in one corner even a television set.

Briggs found the liquor in the kitchen, and poured a glass of brandy. He drank it neat, shuddering at the impact, then poured vodka, and went back into the living room.

Lydia came out of the bathroom a couple of minutes later. Briggs had been standing next to the bookcase looking at some of the titles (many of them in English or French). He turned around. She had changed out of her street clothes, and was clad now in a thick, terrycloth bathrobe, nothing on her feet.

"You may stay here this evening, but in the morning you are returning to Leningrad, Lasha," she said.

Briggs set his glass down. "I've come to Moscow to follow in Mikhail Vladimir's footsteps."

"He is gone, you stupid peasant! Can't you get that through your thick skull?" Lydia cried.

"Then I will do his work."

"You will be arrested."

"You will protect me," Briggs said, smiling.

Her eyes widened. "What? What are you saying, you crazy man? How can I protect you?"

Briggs waved his hand to indicate the apartment. "Look at all this. You must be very well connected to be able to afford this."

"You're crazy. This isn't even my apartment. It is Vladi's. He bought all these things. He sold his writing. His poetry made good money, especially after he began getting into trouble." She shook her head. "I have nothing. I don't even have an apartment any longer." Tears were beginning to well up in her eyes.

Peter Houten had pumped Popov money all along. In addition to the dissident's writings, he had probably been making an excellent living for a Muscovite who was not a government official.

So, what about Lydia Savin? Was it possible, he wondered, that she didn't know who her real father was? Was it possible that Hope-Turner and his analysts had been wrong, and Brezhnev had not yet made any contact with her?

"What about your brothers and sisters? Your parents? Can't they help you?"

"I have no one," she cried, hanging her head.

She was either a consummate actor, or Hope-Turner and the others were mistaken.

"Where will you go when this is all gone?" he asked.

"By that time it will not matter, I will probably already be in the Lubyanka awaiting sentencing."

"On what charges?" Briggs asked. "What have you done?"

"You had one of Vladi's pamphlets back at the club?" she said. Briggs nodded. "I put it together for him. I got the type set and I ran the copies off. I even helped distribute the things. When they came for him, I was sure they'd take me too. But they did not. They will come, however. I know it." She turned her head away as she ran a hand nervously through her hair. It was obvious she was barely hanging on. Briggs felt very sorry for her.

"I will not return to Leningrad, but I will go away from you and your friends. I do not wish to contaminate anyone, making their troubles worse."

"No . . ." Lydia cried, holding her hand out.

Briggs said nothing, and a moment later Lydia came across the room to him, and threw herself in his arms.

"Don't leave me, Lasha. Not this night." She began to cry, her shoulders heaving, her entire body shaking.

It had been less than a month since Popov had been taken, but those days must have been pure hell for her. Not only had she lost her lover, she lived in constant fear that she would be taken next. There was nothing she could do about it. There was nowhere she could run to. She was a prisoner in her own city. And very frightened.

Briggs was convinced . . . or very nearly convinced . . . that she was not guilty of any duplicity in this affair. Whether or not she knew who her real father was, made no difference. She appeared to be exactly who she represented herself to be; a frightened young woman who had lost her lover, and who knew her arrest was imminent.

She looked up from his shoulder, their eyes met for a long moment, and then she kissed him, deeply, her body pressing even more tightly against his. For a tender moment Briggs thought about Sylvia Hume back in Virginia, how they had fought, and how she had helped him, and finally how they had made love.

But then he was here, and now, on a very difficult assignment that had every chance of failure, which would certainly end in his death.

They parted and he followed her across the room where he helped her take the back cushions off the large, flat couch, making it into a bed. From a closet, she brought out sheets and blankets, and within a minute or two she had made up the bed. She turned to him, undid the tie at her waist, and let the robe slip off her shoulders to the floor. Her breasts were small, her stomach and hips rounded. She was a lovely Russian woman. Safe, and very comfortable, Briggs found himself thinking as he got undressed. She would be loyal once she fell in love with you. She would follow you to the ends of the earth, even give up her life if need be.

They kissed again, her body smooth and very warm against his, and then they got into the bed, and Briggs was completely lost in the moment, as she kissed his neck, his chest, his flat stomach, then took him in her mouth.

The sun shone in the windows when Briggs woke up. He could hear Lydia singing in the kitchen. It was a tune vaguely familiar to Briggs from his own past in London. Light, lilting, but with faintly sad undertones, as all Russian peasant songs were.

He got up and strapped on his cheap East German-made watch which showed it was a few minutes before noon, then went across to the front windows, where he parted the curtains and looked carefully down at the street. A small black car was parked across the street, two men inside. They were smoking and talking. One of them looked up, and Briggs eased away from the window.

Lydia had come to the kitchen doorway. She wore only an apron. "They were there when I got up," she said.

"Could someone from the club have told them you and I came here together?"

"Yes, it is possible. There are informers wherever one goes. Even among friends."

"I'm sorry. I did not want to get you in trouble."

She laughed bitterly. "I am already in trouble. I told you that last night, Lasha. But now, as you can see, it would be better if you caught the next train to Leningrad. It would not guarantee your safety, but it certainly would help."

"I really don't want to leave you here, like this. Is there anything I can do for you?"

She shook her head. "Not beyond what you . . . what we did for each other in the night. You were wonderful."

"And so were you." Briggs started forward, but she backed off.

"No," she said. "It is over. I have loved Vladi, and now I will have to live with my unfaithfulness to him. It is a burden I will have to carry. But I will not compound my crime."

The Russians were worse than the Jews when it came to carrying self-imposed burdens. But Briggs said nothing.

"There is hot water now, if you wish to take a bath," she said.

"Thank you," Briggs said. "Then I will leave."

"Yes. Then you will leave." She turned and went

back into the kitchen.

Briggs took his bath, got dressed then ate the breakfast she had prepared for him; an egg, some dark bread and real coffee. Finally it was time for him to go. As he looked into her eyes, he wondered for a last time whether or not she had been lying to him. Perhaps this all was a set-up. It was possible that Peter Houten had been waiting for someone to show up, Lydia Savin being part of the plan.

"Goodbye, Lasha," she said.

He focused on her. "What will you do?"

"Wait," she said simply.

Briggs wanted to take her away now. He knew he could get her into the American Embassy. But she was being watched. If she disappeared from the two goons downstairs, suspicions would be raised which would jeopardize the entire mission.

"Goodbye Lydia."

He kissed her, then left the apartment. Outside, one of the men in the black car took Briggs' photograph with what appeared to be a 35 mm camera. He stared defiantly into the lens aimed at him from across the street, then turned and strode off down the block, his hands thrust deeply into his pockets.

On very short notice, Howard and his people over here, had managed to come up with a background for Lopatin which included a home but no relatives in Leningrad. The fabrication would not stand up to intense scrutiny, but a routine request for information on a dissident standing trial for hooliganism (which was the Soviet term for agitation) would not elicit a deep search. Or so they all hoped.

As he crossed the street at the end of the block, he

noticed out of the corner of his eye that the black car had turned around and was following him. They may have been there to watch Lydia, but now they were after him. Perhaps they checked out everyone who had contact with the woman.

Briggs quickened his pace, turning the corner at the next block then crossing the street to a subway entrance.

The black car pulled up behind him, as he started down the steps, and he could hear the car doors opening and someone coming up the sidewalk.

At the first landing, Briggs turned and looked up the stairs, stopping in apparent surprise when he saw the two burly men coming down.

"Wait up there," one of them said.

Briggs stepped back a pace. "I . . ."

There were a lot of people on the landing, and more below on the stairs. They all looked around, at first in curiosity, but then in fear.

"Halt!" one of the men shouted. He reached inside his coat.

Briggs raised his hands high over his head. "Do not shoot!" he cried. "I have done nothing! Do not shoot!"

A woman cried out, and the crowd scattered as the two men spun Briggs around, and shoved him up against the tiled wall, his arms and legs spread.

One of them quickly searched him coming up with his wallet, his internal passport and several of the Popov political tracts. He thanked his lucky stars he had decided to leave his stiletto, his extra money and spare identification papers behind at the room he had rented. He had not planned on dumping them until sometime later today, after he had begun his work. But last night, before he had gone out, he had decided to leave them behind. It was fortunate he had.

They spun him around. "Lopatin," one of them said. "We have heard of you." He was about the same height as Briggs but at least fifty pounds heavier. His partner was a bit shorter and lighter, but his head seemed out of proportion to the rest of his body. It was very large, and almost square; his features cut from rock. Neither of them smiled.

"What have I done, Comrade . . ."

The short one held up the pamphlets. "This is very dangerous material to be carrying around, Lopatin."

"I want to know why you did not take the friendly advice given to you last night . . . run back to Leningrad?" the taller one said.

"And money, Lopatin. Twenty-five rubles is certainly not enough to live on," the square faced man said. "Where did you intend on spending this night . . . in the bed of another whore?"

His partner shot him a dirty look, and the short one backed off.

"At any rate, I think you'd better come along nicely with us. There are a number of things we would like to know about you."

The short one laughed. "Yes, Comrade, we would very much like to hear your political views."

"Popov, your mentor, sang like a broken record when he was picked up. We want to hear what you have to say."

"Fuck your mother," Briggs said in gutter Russian, and he tensed his stomach muscles.

The taller one hit him, a short, hard jab high in the stomach, driving the air out of Briggs' lungs, and slamming him back against the tiled wall. The short one had to hold his partner back from doing any more.

Briggs smiled through the haze of pain. He had gotten their attention. Good, cooperative dissidents were treated civilly by comparison to the hard-liners. Burt Higgins and the others had drummed into his head that only the hard-liners made it to the Yedanov Rehabilitation Center.

"Fascist pig," Briggs muttered.

They took him under the arms and dragged him across the landing and up the stairs. Other people coming down flattened against the walls, their eyes averted. They knew better than to look, let alone do anything about the arrest.

"Arise, and fight for your freedom," Briggs shouted as they reached the street.

The tall one gave him another shot to the ribs, causing him to double over in pain, his legs giving out beneath him.

The officers half carried him over to their car, where they shoved him into the back seat, and slammed the door.

"It's nothing, everyone go about your business," one of them was saying to the people by the subway entrance.

"He's nothing but a dirty hooligan," the other one said, and they both got into the car.

"You have caused us a lot of trouble, Lopatin," the big one said, a sneer on his face. "I for one do not like trouble. You will see."

## TWENTY-SIX

The Lubyanka Prison was an awesome structure to anyone who saw it for the first time, and especially someone such as Briggs who had been raised on horror stories about the place. A part of him had wanted to rebel in terror when they had first driven through the gates, but the stronger, more rational part of his being had held back. This was exactly what he had worked for. Lubyanka was the first, most important step toward Yedanov and Popov's rescue. And it had come for him much faster than he had hoped for.

They had all figured he'd probably be in and out of jails for up to three weeks, before he'd be brought to Lubyanka, then the center. Yet on his first day as Lopatin he was here. The speed frightened him. He had no control.

The building was divided into two sections—the smaller hidden behind a bricked-in courtyard, was

312

the actual prison, while the adjacent, much larger building housed a number of major departments of the KGB.

It was a bright, sunny afternoon when the car containing Briggs was cleared through the tall gates, and as they went in he caught a glimpse of the black statue of Felix Dzerzhinsky, the founder of the Cheka which was the forerunner of the KGB. The figure seemed ominous, as if it had been deliberately placed there to warn all who entered the gates, that hope was gone. Briggs shivered.

They pulled up at a wide, steel door, and the big officer who had given Briggs so much trouble jumped out and yanked open the rear car door on Briggs' side.

"Out of there, you little bastard," the man bellowed. He was very angry.

Briggs made a motion as if he was masturbating, which further enraged the big man who reached in, grabbed Briggs by the shirt front and pulled him out of the car, sending him sprawling to his knees. When Briggs was down, the officer kicked him in the side with a hard-toe shoe.

He rolled with the blow, so that his ribs would not break, but even so the wind was knocked out of him again as he flipped over on his back, groaning.

"This one's a glutton for punishment," the smaller official said coming around the car.

"They all are, Yurianovich. And I tell you I am getting sick of it. Very soon, unless something changes, I'm going to kill one of these bastards. Maybe even this one."

Briggs looked up, his face contorted in pain.

The smaller man shook his head. "It would not be worth it. Think of the mark on your records. Not worth the trouble."

They both reached down and dragged Briggs to his feet, then inside the building which smelled, for some reason, like a combination of printer's ink and urine.

Down a flight of stairs, they went into the first office off a busy corridor. Clerks, uniformed officials and other men like the two who had picked up Briggs, hurried back and forth. There was a buzz of conversations, telephones ringing, typewriters clattering, that died only slightly when the office door was closed, but was cut off completely when Briggs was led into a small, soundproofed room, and that door was closed.

There were a couple of desks and a few file cabinets in the outer office, but in this room there was no furniture, only a bare tile floor with a bucket in the corner, and a single light behind a cage recessed in the ceiling.

The big man left, and the shorter man leaning nonchalantly against the wall near the door, smiled.

"Tell me Lopatin," he began, "how long it has been since you first fell in with Mikhail Popov and his band of trouble makers."

Briggs had paced the room, examining the walls, as if he was looking for a means to escape. In the corner near the bucket, there were several ominous looking stains on the dirty white acoustical surface of the wall. Blood, Briggs figured, reaching out to touch it.

"You know people like us really have very little patience with people like you," the officer said, still

314

in a reasonable tone of voice.

Briggs turned around. He could be across the small room in a split second, and an instant later the man would be dead. The urge was there all right.

"You're all fascist pigs. Mikhail Vladimir Popov was one of the few true patriots Moscow has produced. It is to men like him we must look for our salvation from the doddering old fools of the Kremlin."

The official laughed. "So you and Popov were friends."

"How can you be friends with a god?" Briggs shouted. "The man is our salvation, I tell you." Briggs took a step forward, his hands outstretched. The official straightened up. "Look, you can join us. It would be easy. Say a mistake had been made on my part. Let me go. We can meet later somewhere. You will be welcomed. We can join Popov."

The official laughed again, as if Briggs had told him an amusing story. "How long have you known Lydia, then?"

"I don't know her."

"You slept with her last night."

Briggs shook his head. "No, not with Popov's woman. But she may be a traitor. It was she who turned me in, wasn't it."

"What I really want to know, Ilya Petrovich you rascal, is where the two of you disappeared to over the weekend. Do you two have a secret dacha out in the country? Or perhaps a pleasant inn by a lake somewhere?"

Briggs just stared at the man. Had they really lost

track of Lydia, or were they merely testing him? She was Brezhnev's daughter. If they had actually lost track of her for the weekend there would have been an uproar. It was the reason Briggs had been arrested, then. The brochures from Popov were only a slight bonus. If that was the case, he was going to have to give them a reason to keep him, and to press serious charges against him.

"Don't be shy, I have heard these stories before. I will not be embarrassed, or shocked."

But not too easily, he cautioned himself. He was going to have to pick his way through this with great care.

"What has happened to Mikhail Vladimir?" he asked. "Where has he gone?"

"Forget him for the moment. Remember, I asked you a question first."

"Forget him hell, you faggot, he is everything!"

The official moved away from the wall with lightning speed, and Briggs had to control his instinct to protect himself as a rock-hard fist slammed into his collar bone, driving him back against the wall, pain exploding in his skull.

"I asked you a question, Lopatin," the man's voice came to Briggs through the pain.

"Popov is our savior . . ." Briggs grunted.

The official raked his shoe down Briggs' right shin, and instantly Briggs could feel blood running down into his shoe.

"Our hope is Popov . . . he knows . . ."

The official did the same thing to Briggs' left shin, the pain causing his stomach to turn over.

"Is it worth all this, Ilya Petrovich? Do not be a

316

fool. Don't you know Popov is never coming back?''

"Then I will do his work. I will stand at his side," Briggs gasped. He spit into the man's face.

"Bastard!" the official swore. He stepped back and slammed his cupped palms against the side of Briggs head.

The pain was unbelievable. Briggs was reasonably sure his ear drums had been burst by the pressure. He shoved the man bodily aside, and crouched to the left as he whimpered.

The man's taller partner was at the open door, a smirk on his face.

Briggs looked from one to the other. "You bastards," he gasped. "You don't give a damn about Popov, or about the people. All you want to know about, is what's it like to fuck Brezhnev's daughter."

The effect of his words was galvanizing. It was as if a high voltage charge had been released in the room. The taller man, at the door, straightened up, stepped the rest of the way into the room, and shut the door. The other grabbed Briggs by his collar and hauled him upright, slamming him into the corner. His partner joined them. Neither of them was smiling, nor did they seem angry. It was more like they were frightened.

"What did you say, you slimy little toad?" the big one hissed.

"Please . . ." Briggs whimpered.

The little man kneed Briggs in the crotch, the pain hammering up to his armpits, taking his breath away, but they held him upright.

"I asked you a question, you scum."

Briggs was in pain, but he was beginning to feel loose. This was going to have to end very soon or he was going to take these two out.

"What gave you the idea that Lydia Savin was Comrade Brezhnev's daughter?"

"I know," Briggs mumbled.

The big one slammed his fist into Briggs' nose, blood instantly gushing down his chin and shirt front.

"Mikhail Vladimir said so," Briggs cried. "He knew. I believed him. I trust him. He is the savior of our people."

"When did that traitor tell you that?"

"Last month, maybe a little longer. He told me."

"Here in Moscow?"

They had said Popov was in Leningrad seven weeks ago. But that information, Higgins had warned, was the iffy sort of thing that could either guarantee his credibility, or kill him. If Popov had not been in Leningrad (if for some reason Houten had lied about that) or if his every move had been watched, then Briggs was going to be in big trouble now.

He shook his head. "No, in Leningrad. Five, maybe six weeks ago. I don't remember."

The two interrogators stepped back and looked at each other. "Get him secured," the tall one said. "I'll go up to see the chief prosecutor. He has to be informed about this."

They had dumped him on the cold cement floor, and it took him twenty minutes to crawl over to the narrow cot, with its filthy bare mattress and climb up on it. He fell asleep for a long time, although he had no way of knowing for how long. There was no window in his cell, and the overhead light never went out. They had taken everything from him, including his watch, and had dressed him in light, cotton pajamas. The tiny cell was very damp, and cool.

Briggs awoke with a start, his body a mass of aches and pains. They had worked him over pretty good. Although he was in pain, nothing had been broken, or damaged permanently, except, perhaps, his eardrums.

He had been lying on his side, facing the wall so that the light did not shine directly into his eyes. He turned over, careful not to hurt anything. Someone had brought in a table and chair. An older man was sitting there. He had thinning white hair, and wore steel rimmed glasses. He did not look unkind. With his rumpled gray suit, and loosened tie, he gave the appearance of being someone's favorite uncle.

"Ah, Lasha, I am glad to see you are finally awake," the man said, his Russian very Muscovite . . . very European and cultured. He came across the room, helped Briggs to sit up, then brought him a glass of tea with lemon, and a lot of sugar. There might have been something else in it as well—perhaps rum.

Briggs drank some of the delicious brew, watching the man over the rim of the glass.

"Quite a story you told Balan and Yurianovich upstairs . . . quite a story indeed."

Briggs maintained his silence, studying the man. The two cops who had picked him up were rough-necks. But this one was much more refined.

Infinitely more dangerous.

"But let me introduce myself. I am Andrei Yanovich Zhuravlev, from the State Prosecutor's office."

Briggs was not surprised.

"I came down to hear with my own ears the nonsense you supposedly spouted upstairs."

Briggs managed to laugh. "You do not have the courage, Comrade State Prosecutor, to place me in the dock in a public trial. You want a story? You would hear a story."

Zhuravlev sat forward. "Tell me, Lopatin, why does a man such as yourself want so desperately to go to jail?"

"Jail?" Briggs shouted. He snapped his fingers with some difficulty. "That is what I think of your jails. I tell you Comrade Popov had the right idea. Write it all down, publish it, and let the people know what they are missing. In 1961 the people needed boots, and the people cried for . . ."

"Yes, yes, I've heard that tedious story before, you little bug. But where did you hear this fabrication, this fairy tale about Lydia Savin?"

"It is no fairy tale. Mikhail Vladimir told me."

"Yes," the prosecutor said. "In Leningrad."

"That is correct. He would not lie."

"But you do. Comrade Popov has not been in Leningrad for at least a year and a half."

If that was truly the case, Briggs figured he had bought the farm. But he had told the same story twice now. He was committed. "I did not fly to Moscow to see him. He came to see me. Unless Comrade Brezhnev changed the name of my city by decree."

"And what did Comrade Popov tell you, during this supposed meeting in Leningrad last week."

"Five or six weeks ago," Briggs corrected. To say exactly seven weeks or give the exact day, would tip his hand. Most people did not remember such things with that accuracy unless they were lying.

"A month or two ago," the prosecutor conceded.

"The revolution is coming. But he worried about Lydia. He thought she might be telling his plans."

"To whom?"

"To her father. Comrade President, Comrade Party Secretary."

"Rubbish," Zhuravlev said getting up again. He went to the door and banged on it. "You want a trial, Lopatin? You shall have your trial. Swift and very very just. You will see."

The door was opened and the prosecutor was gone. Briggs hurled his nearly full glass of tea after him, then laid back down and began to cry for the benefit of anyone watching.

He was going to have to conserve his strength as best he could. Very quickly, he suspected, he was going to be in the middle of it, either trying to get Popov out of the Yedanov Rehabilitation Center, or getting himself out of some other prison. He hoped that Burt Higgins was on the ball. This had gone so fast that there hadn't been time to send out the message. There hadn't been time for much of anything, as a matter of fact.

They came for him two meals and a sleep period later, which turned out to be early the next morning.

The pair who had picked him up drove him northeast past Sokolniki Park to a small courthouse in a very quiet neighborhood along the Yauza River. There were no spectators, and the only persons in the courtroom besides the panel of three judges, were the recorder, the clerk and, curiously, the chief administrator for the Park—which was not really a park, but was a residential area.

The trial was a casual affair. He was charged with hooliganism against the state, as well as the somewhat more minor charge of parasitism, but unlike western courts he was not immediately asked how he wanted to plead. Nor, in this instance was he permitted the luxury of an attorney.

As evidence the state produced the Popov pamphlets he had been carrying, and the expert testimony of his arresting officers and of the prosecutor all of whom had personally conducted interviews with the subject.

On the lesser crime, the state produced as evidence two facts: the first was that he had only 25 rubles when he was picked up (certainly not enough to support himself), and secondly, he had no work card. He was samizdat. Terrible.

No mention was made of Lydia Savin, nor was he allowed to make any remarks on her, although he wanted to.

In the end he was sentenced to life imprisonment, or until such time as it could be proved that he would be a useful citizen to society.

His place of incarceration: The Yedanov Rehabilitation Center.

## TWENTY-SEVEN

Briggs was held in isolation in a small room in the courthouse until a few minutes after two in the afternoon when the officers who had arrested him came to pick him up. The small one whose name was Yurianovich, and the taller one whom the State Prosecutor had identified simply as Balan, were both in good spirits, laughing and joking with each other, as they handcuffed Briggs' hands behind his back, and shackled his legs.

They ignored him, talking around him, and when they finally led him out of the room, across the courtroom, and outside into the warm afternoon sun, there was no one to see them. The building, the streets and the park across the avenue all seemed deserted. There wasn't a single person, or moving automobile in sight in any direction. It was spooky.

He was shoved in the back seat of the same black automobile that had brought him out here, the rear doors were locked, and in minutes they were heading at a leisurely pace back into the city.

Balan was driving. Yurianovich turned around "You know, Lopatin, if you hadn't given us such trouble, and if you had kept a civil tongue in you head in front of the State Prosecutor, you might only have been sentenced to five or six years on a farm Before long you would have been a free man in Yakutsk or perhaps even Khabarovsk. Certainly no Moscow, but then again you'd be free."

Briggs turned and looked out the window at the passing scenery. Yurianovich reached back and cuffed Briggs on the side of the head.

"Look at me when I talk to you, parasite!"

Briggs glared defiantly at him.

Balan glanced at him in the rearview mirror "Shall we stop somewhere and teach this one another lesson?"

"I don't think it's worth the effort," Yurianovich said. "I think we have an incorrigible on our hands here."

Balan laughed out loud. "That will be cured sooner or later, so maybe you are right. Maybe it is not worth our effort . . . although it would be fun."

They rode a while in silence, until Yurianovich turned back to look at Briggs. He had an odd pensive expression. "There is something about you Lopatin, that does not ring quite true. Something . . ."

"Don't get like that," Balan said to his partner.

"I tell you there is something about this one that bothers me. It's too easy. He wanted to be a

324

Popov's side, and he's gotten exactly what he wants."

"Don't, Yuri . . . the last time you got this way, we spent three months running down a collection of insignificant facts."

"And got our man, never forget that," he said without taking his eyes off Briggs. "But this one will be easier. We'll know exactly where to find him whenever we need him."

Briggs stared at the man. All he would need were a couple of days. Forty-eight hours . . seventy-two hours at the most, and he and Popov would be out of there, and on their way west. It was Thursday. The weekend was coming up. Perhaps Yurianovich would not be so over-zealous until Monday.

"I think I will begin in Leningrad, Lopatin. What do you say to that? This afternoon."

They ran down through Sokolniki Park then west to Yaroslavskoye Road, pulling up at length to a side entrance to the Main Moscow Railway Center, a huge, ornate building.

Inside the building, they led Briggs along a wide corridor, then down a flight of stairs to the far end of the boarding platform, separated from the main section by a tall iron fence with canvas draped over it. Briggs could hear the sounds of hundreds of people coming and going, of whistles blowing, and trains arriving and departing. Overall was the pervasive odor of sulphur mixed with diesel fumes.

Parked directly across from where they stood was a small, old fashioned steam locomotive. Three cars were attached to it. Everything on the entire train was painted a dull gray. There were no markings, no insignia, no flags. Nothing but dull gray metal, except the pushrods for the great wheels which were grease-covered polished steel.

Briggs stopped in his tracks. It was just as he had heard it would be. The train to nowhere. What he was seeing represented a one-way trip for tens of thousands of men and women over several decades. What unspeakable horrors he would find at the other end of the line could only be guessed at.

"He knows," Balan laughed.

"Don't give us trouble now, Lopatin," Yurianovich whispered in his ear. "It makes no difference if we put you on the train awake or sleeping. It is your choice."

Briggs screwed his face up in an expression of terror. "No . . ." he whimpered. "Not this . . ."

Yurianovich took one arm, Balan the other, and together they started across the platform toward the first car of the train, dragging Briggs between them.

A door popped open, and two armed guards jumped down to the platform. A third handed down a step.

"No . . ." Briggs continued to whimper, until they were across and he was handed over to the personnel from the train.

Balan passed up a thick file to the guard on the train, and without warning doubled up his fist and smashed Briggs in the face, splitting his already battered nose.

Briggs had seen the blow coming, by the way the man had shifted his weight, and had bunched up his muscles. But he had willed himself to take it without making a move to defend himself.

When Balan stepped back, Briggs felt the same loose feeling coming all over him, as before, but he held himself in check, forcing himself to continue his whimpering. Soon, he told himself, very soon.

"A trouble maker, is he?" one of the train guards who had a tight grip on Briggs' arm asked.

"Of the worst kind," Balan said, a self-satisfied smirk on his face.

"Well, we know how to handle people like this."

"Don't bang him up too badly for a week or so. I may need to ask him a few questions," Yurianovich said.

"Then why bring him to us? Why not hold him at Lubyanka?" the train guard asked harshly.

"The prosecutor said the Rehabilitation Center, and the Center it is."

"Then don't try to tell us our business, Comrade detective," the guard said. He and his partner hustled Briggs up into the train, down a short corridor, and into a large, featureless cage, where he was locked in alone.

Within a few minutes the train lurched, and they were heading out of the station, slowly picking up speed as they bumped and jerked over the switches in the main yard.

Within ten minutes they were out of the downtown area, and within fifteen minutes the screaming had begun; first a sharp, piercing scream, followed by moaning, then a second scream, and a third and a fourth. There was a pause, and a second man screamed, then moaned, then screamed again, the pattern the same as the first.

One by one the screams came closer to the cage in

327

which Briggs had been locked, until at last his door was thrown open and three burly guards, including the one from the platform who had told Yurianovich off, came in. One of them carried a rubber truncheon.

"This is the trouble maker," the guard said.

Before Briggs could move, the other two had grabbed him, pulled his prison pajamas down, spread his legs and bent him over.

The man with the truncheon came up behind Briggs, and swung the rubber hose with all him might, slamming the end of it into Briggs's anus and testicles from behind.

The pain was awesome, and Briggs let himself scream as he had heard the others do, his scream turning to a low animal-like moan. A second blow came, causing him to bite his tongue as he screamed. A third and fourth blow came, and Briggs' entire groin seemed to be on fire, and still they continued to hit him, until his legs finally gave way, and they let him slump to the filthy floor. He involuntarily voided himself as the guards left his cage, laughing.

"No more trouble from Lopatin, I'd guess," the guard carrying the truncheon said at the doorway.

Briggs managed to look up at the man and their eyes met as Briggs concentrated on his face. He definitely wanted to remember the man.

The guard started to say something, but then Briggs' eyes fluttered and he gradually slipped into unconsciousness, totally unable to bring his legs together.

Except for the tall fences and the guard towers, the

Yedanov Rehabilitation Center could have been exactly what it purported to be—a research and treatment facility for psychiatric illnesses. In reality it was a rehabilitation and mental conditioning center right out of George Orwell's *1984*.

Briggs had regained consciousness as they pulled through the gate at the center, and he had cleaned himself off as best he could, and had pulled up his trousers. He was standing, braced against the outer wall, his legs spread as he tried to fight back the pain, when the door to his cell was flung open.

"All right, out of there, Lopatin," the guard who had wielded the truncheon bellowed.

"I cannot walk," Briggs whimpered, which was partly true—he could not move very well, yet.

The large man came in, looked at the mess on the floor, then up at Briggs. "Well, I am not going to carry you, you're a filthy mess." He slapped the rubber truncheon against his open palm.

"I . . ." Briggs whimpered, but he managed to take a couple of steps forward, before he lost his balance, tottered, then fell at the guard's feet.

The guard kicked Briggs in the side, then went back out into the corridor bellowing for someone to come fetch the prisoner in four.

Two prisoners, wearing the typical thin gray cotton pajamas with only slippers on their feet, came into the cell, and picked Briggs up off the floor. Evidently they were trustees, and they were none too gentle.

"He smells terrible. I may throw up," one of them complained as they dragged Briggs out into the corridor and to the door at the end of the car.

"If they wouldn't beat them so hard on the way up, they wouldn't soil themselves," the other one said.

"Watch your tongue, man, do you want us both sent to Section One?"

Outside, a half a dozen half-dazed prisoners were sitting or lying on a flat bed truck. The trustees dragged Briggs over to it, and lifted him up. No one reached out to help.

The weather was sharply colder now, and lying on his back, looking up, Briggs could see that the sky was becoming overcast. This had been an unusually mild fall for the region around Moscow. Often, by this time of the year, there was snow in the air, and cold winds down from the arctic. Only a few more days, Briggs thought. It wasn't asking too much.

There was a lot of commotion by the train. Briggs turned his head in time to see one of the other prisoners being kicked off the boarding step down to the gravel road. He fell badly, probably breaking an arm, but the other guards waiting for him began kicking him in the side, and in the head. Over and over again they kicked the poor man around the road with their heavy boots, blood everywhere.

When they were done, it was obvious the prisoner was dead.

Two trustees wheeled up with a hand cart, hoisted the body into it, and headed up a path to the right. Toward the graveyard, Briggs thought, remembering Obyedkov's diagrams and his briefing.

"That one was an incorrigible," one of the guards said.

The truck pulled out and headed up toward the group of large buildings on a slight rise. Briggs had been called *incorrigible*. He was going to have to watch himself so that he did not end up like the poor devil on the way to the mass burial yard. Chiles and White would know by now that he had stood trial and had been sentenced. Or at least he hoped the combination of the CIA and SIS efforts here, under the direction of Burt Higgins had been sharp enough to catch it. If they had, beginning tomorrow night, Dick White would be waiting for him and Popov at the rendezvous point not too far outside the fence. But if he was beaten much more, Briggs knew that he would not be physically able to travel, much less anything else, for several days—if ever.

They lumbered up the gravel road where the truck pulled behind the main hall where it stopped in front of the northernmost building which housed the records section.

A dozen trustees were waiting for them, and they helped the prisoners down from the truck and inside, to a large incoming reception room.

They were made to strip, their soiled clothing taken away. Nude, they were slowly paraded through a cattle chute, above which stood a barber with hair clippers. In less than ten seconds, he shaved each man's head to the skin, the hair falling through a grate in the floor.

Next, they were led into the showers where they washed the blood and filth from their bodies with luke-warm water and very harsh, gritty, foul-smelling soap.

The water felt very good to Briggs who could only shuffle bow-legged. They had hurt him on the train even more than he wanted to admit at the moment, and besides the deep anger that had built up inside of him, there was the nagging fear that he'd remain in this condition—or even get worse—and escape would become impossible.

After their shower they were issued clean pajamas, and very cheap cardboard slippers, which they were not allowed immediately to put on. First they were weighed, measured, their photograph taken, and a nine digit number was painfully tattooed in their left armpit.

Clean and clothed finally, they were led to a large office at the back of the building, where a dozen men and women waited at desks. There were eight prisoners. Briggs was led to the desk of a stocky woman of perhaps fifty, who had a very stern expression on her face, and cold, fish eyes.

"So, Lopatin the trouble maker," the woman said looking at him like an undertaker might look at a corpse. She opened a file folder in front of her and began scanning its contents.

"Born in Leningrad, although there still is some question about that," she mumbled. She looked up. "There is a police detective in Moscow . . . a very good one from what I hear . . . who has his suspicions about you. What are you hiding from us, Lopatin? A family, perhaps? A wife and children tainted by your wisdom?"

Briggs said nothing. He could hear similar conversations going on at the other desks. First the arrest and trial, then the horrors of the train, followed by the processing. And now the browbeating continued, never to be let up for a moment until the man or woman was either broken, or was dead.

His interrogator continued to badger him. He could see her mouth opening and closing, her nostrils flaring, her eyes flashing, but he wasn't really hearing the words. They were the same as he had heard from Oumi and Vatra and the others whenever they'd talk about the system.

*There have been a million interrogations, let me tell you boy. And there will be a million more. And they are like a vast broken record . . . everyone of them. It was a vast joke. The record played and we all sang the same song, over and over and over . . .*

Briggs sat beside the desk, his left hand resting on top of it. The woman interrogator casually reached over for a large, metal paperweight, and just as casually brought it down on Briggs' fingers.

He pulled them back, the pain bringing him back in focus.

"You will keep your hands off my desk, and you will pay attention, Lopatin, or you will end up as someone's plaything in Section One."

Briggs blinked rapidly as he held his throbbing fingers. None of them were broken, luckily, but his entire hand was numb.

"I am very sorry, Comrade," he said. "It will not happen again."

The woman looked at him for a long time, then glanced down at his file. "It says here that you are a lover of Mikhail Popov."

"Vladi . . . he is here?" Briggs said excitedly. He sat forward.

"You like that?" she asked sitting back.

"Yes. Vladi is my friend."

"So it says in your records. Would you like to see him? Right away?"

This was much better than he had hoped for. Briggs nodded.

The woman laughed out loud, the sound terrible. "Then you shall, my little toad, you shall." She selected a rubber stamp from a rack, inked it and stamped something on his file, inside, and then outside on the jacket. Then she passed it up to one of the guards, who dragged Briggs out of his chair.

In that brief moment, however, when she was handing the file up, he managed to catch a glimpse of what she had stamped.

ISOLATION

120 DAYS

# TWENTY-EIGHT

Everyone was laughing, and at the doorway the guard shoved Briggs causing him to stumble outside, and fall on the gravel walkway, skinning his hands and tearing his pajama trousers at the knees. The laughter from inside intensified as the guard kicked out, catching Briggs in the buttocks, slamming him over on his side, and causing the pain to course through his body. Never before in his life had Briggs wanted revenge as badly as he did at this moment; never before in his life had he held back like this for any reason. In the old days there would have been a lot of dead people around him by now, including the smug guard who stood over him, gesturing for him to get up.

Briggs got unsteadily to his feet, and the guard feinted to the left as if he was going to kick out again, causing Briggs to stumble and nearly fall again. There were several other guards and three prisoners coming up the walk, they all were laughing. At the doorway several interviewers were lined up to watch the show.

They too were laughing.

A moment that in actuality only lasted for a second or two, but to Briggs seemed to stretch for hours, passed over him. During this time he could see everything and everyone around him with an amazing clarity. He could see the vulnerable position his guard was in. He could envision the steps he would need to take the rifle away from the guard coming up the walkway. He could see himself at the train, through the gate. He could see it all . . . including his own death sooner or later. No finesse. But while it lasted the revenge would be sweet . . . St. Patrick above, and the devil below, it would be sweet.

He shuddered, once more regaining control of himself, and docilely allowed the guard to manhandle him to the left down the walk toward the research building next door.

Isolation was in the basement of the research center, the material Obyedkov had sent over revealed. And Research was where Obyedkov's best guess placed Popov. It was possible the woman interviewer had dealt him a straight shot. It was conceivable that Popov was still in Isolation, and she was sending his professed admirer to join him.

It was sharply colder than it had been this morning, and Briggs shivered involuntarily as he stopped at a rear door into the building, to look up at the gray sky. A front was on the way. They were in for some worsening weather.

His guard laughed. "Take a long hard look, Lopatin. It'll be the last of the sky you'll be seeing for a long time."

Briggs didn't look at the slightly-built man, instead

he hung his head in dejection, and allowed himself to be pushed inside. He had to maintain the image of the beaten, cowed prisoner so that their vigil would be comparatively lax.

Just inside, to the right, a corridor ran the length of the building, while to the left, wide concrete stairs led down, to a thick steel door. A guard was seated at a desk.

At the bottom his guard signed in, but exchanged no words with the man stationed at the door, who slowly got up, unlocked the steel door and opened it.

Inside, was another flight of stairs leading down, these narrower, and darker than the first set. At the bottom another guard sat watching a long narrow corridor, from an office behind a glass partition. He came out when he saw them.

"What have we here?" he asked, his voice very soft, barely above a whisper.

"Lopatin."

"A trouble maker?"

"He has given everyone trouble, from what I've been told. A friend of Popov's."

"I see . . ." the downstairs guard said thoughtfully.

Briggs raised his head. "Mikhail is here?" he asked.

The downstairs guard slammed his fist into Briggs' stomach, knocking him across the corridor, and into the concrete wall.

For several, frightening seconds the corridor went dark, and there was an intense ringing in Briggs' ears. He could not seem to make his arms or legs do what he wanted. But then the downstairs guard had him by the lapels of his pajamas.

"Down here, scum, no one speaks unless spoken to,

and then we do not raise our voice."

It felt as if his brain was loose in his skull, it was very hard to come back into focus.

"We're going to be together for a long time," the guard continued as Briggs' head cleared.

"One hundred and twenty days," the other guard prompted.

"One hundred and twenty days during which there will not be so much as a sound from you. Not a word, not even a whimper."

The guard's eyes were bloodshot, his breath foul, greasy sweat on his brow, and staining his khaki uniform shirt below his armpits.

"If you will sign for him, Arkadi, I will get back," the guard who had brought Briggs down said, handing over the file.

"Remain where you are, toad," the downstairs guard told Briggs. "Do not move so much as a muscle."

He turned and went into his office with the other guard, where he signed something. They came back out, the first guard turning to the stairs and heading up.

The downstairs guard came back to where Briggs stood, but said nothing for several long seconds. From above came the sound of someone banging on the steel door, which opened, and closed. Then a deep, heavy silence descended on the dim, narrow corridor. Only one small light shone from the low ceiling fifty feet down the corridor, and some dim red light shone from the guard's office.

"On your knees you little bastard," the man whispered.

Briggs' legs were weak, yet he could feel an easy

338

gracefulness, almost liquid in its smoothness coming over him. How much of this could he take?

Slowly he sank to his knees. It was still daylight outside. He was going to have to wait until night to make his move. Midnight, or perhaps a little later. But not now. It was still only late afternoon.

The guard unzipped his trousers and pulled out his penis, a huge grin on his face.

No, Briggs thought in horror, this much he could not do. Even if it meant his life.

But it wasn't what he thought it was going to be. The guard began to urinate on him, his stream hot and strong, as all the while he laughed, the sound low, and very soft.

Briggs hung his head in shame, and in the most intense anger he had ever felt in his life, as the stream soaked him from head to foot. His anger frightened even him, it was so intense. It was like the heavy bass notes of an electric guitar at full volume, pounding in his head, thrumming dangerously down his already overloaded nerves.

Gradually the man's stream weakened, then stopped. Briggs looked up as the guard delicately shook his penis and put it back in his trousers.

"Welcome to hell, Ilya Petrovich Lopatin," the guard said. "If you make any sound over the next one hundred and twenty days, many things very much worse than what has just happened, will be inflicted on you. I am *the* master at this game."

What depths could a human being sink to, Briggs thought looking up at the insane monster.

"Now get to your feet, it is time to put you away for the night."

Slowly, painfully Briggs got to his feet, and apparently totally broken in spirit, beaten and weak, he meekly followed his captor down the dim corridor to a door no more than four feet tall, near the end.

The guard unlocked the unadorned, windowless metal door, opened it and stepped aside.

Without looking up Briggs ducked inside, catching only a momentary glimpse of his cell before the door was closed, and locked, plunging him into total darkness.

For several seconds he stood, hunched over, but then he tried to straighten up, his head coming in contact with the rough concrete ceiling almost immediately. There was no standing headroom.

He reached out left and right, his fingertips brushing the walls on both sides, then groped forward, coming into contact with the rear wall after two steps.

His cell then was a little more than four feet high, six feet wide and perhaps six feet long. And after a minute or two of explorations by feel, he found out that the walls and ceiling were totally featureless, that the back left corner had a drain hole in it, and that there were no bucket, blanket, or anything else in the tiny space. It was very cold.

After awhile, Briggs crawled to the corner opposite the drain, and sat down, his back against the wall, his knees hunched carefully to his chest to give him a little extra warmth without causing him too much pain from his bruised legs and testicles. He began to shiver.

He remembered once, when he was just a young lad, and Oumi was trying to teach him patience. He had been set out in some bushes in Hyde Park during a late fall drizzle. The weather was very cold, just a degree or two above freezing, Briggs had on only a light jacket over a thin shirt, and his instructions were to hold there supposedly waiting for a rendezvous for as long as he could.

The cruelty of the assignment was not the thin clothing he had been given to wear, or the lateness of the season, or the icy cold rain. The real cruelty was the ambigousness of his instruction: wait for as long as he could.

All that night he waited, and all the next day into the second evening, supposing that Oumi was home talking and drinking and eating with Vatra and the others. Still, he remained.

It was four in the morning of that second night, that a soaked, bedraggled Oumi appeared out of the bushes not fifteen feet from where Briggs huddled and took him home.

"You have the patience it takes to fight our enemy," Oumi said. He had been there the entire time.

They both were sick for two weeks. Sitting here now in his cell he remembered, and could recall the feeling with great accuracy, of how cold and miserable he was. But later he had felt such a huge sense of accomplishment.

Shortly afterwards he had killed his first man.

Maybe it was six o'clock by now. He did not think he was more than an hour off either way. In another six hours it would be midnight—plus or minus. In six hours he would go. This night, because there was no way in hell he would be in any better condition by tomorrow. Each day here, he was sure, would mean escape was that much more impossible. Tonight, he told himself, a thin smile coming to his lips.

341

He laid his head back against the cold concrete and closed his eyes as he hugged himself in an effort to conserve his body heat.

Sylvia Hume and Lydia Savin. Images of both women swam into his mind's eye. They were so totally different, they came from such diametrically opposite worlds, and yet he had made love to both of them. He tried to tell himself that with Sir Roger's daughter it had been nothing more than lust for a beautiful, available woman, and that for Lydia Savin it had been nothing more than pity for a lost, lonely soul, but neither was the entire truth. He *had* taken pity on Lydia Savin, and yet he had needed the comfort as much as she had, and he had found her desirable. In her case he had given as much as he had taken. And with Sylvia Hume there certainly *was* lust, yet there had been and still was more. Love?

He opened his eyes. He had asked himself that question many times before, but only once—back in Montana—had he had difficulty in coming up with the answer. His memories of Montana had faded with time, but at first he had had trouble dealing with it. And that was when he had been young, more resilient. Now that he was older, and had begun to question his motivations, such things were no longer so easy to shove aside.

Sylvia Hume. Did he love her, or didn't he? Christ, what was happening?

He closed his eyes again, and slowly let his muscles relax, the sharp localized pains of his injuries gradually melting into one gray ache through his body that was somehow more endurable.

Sylvia had been soft and lovely. Although she was a

sharp tongued, spoiled bitch, she was a lovely woman, and Briggs thought he *was* falling in love with her.

Damn, he thought softly, and he drifted, half in and half out of sleep—aware of the passage of time and of his surroundings, but resting just the same.

From time to time, he straightened out his legs and stretched, so that he would not get cramps. Gradually, despite the damp chill of the basement cell, his body heat dried his wet clothing, although the stench of the strong urine remained sharp.

For a while he let his mind drift from one unconnected thought or image to another. To the days in Soho. To his first, pleasant memories of his mother, and of his uncle. To Montana, and Denver, and Hollywood the land of flim flam.

Then for a time he set himself to listening for a sound, any kind of a sound . . . someone coughing, a shoe scraping against concrete, water running in the pipes. But his own sounds became too magnified in his ringing ears for him to detect a thing.

Much later he gingerly explored his injuries, probing with his fingers here and there, trying to gauge the extent of the damage that had been done to him. Mostly his wounds were superficial. His only concerns were for his eardrums, which he thought may have been permanently damaged, and his testicles, of which he had a vague fear that he would be impotent. His bones were intact and his muscles were sore, but working.

Finally, as it approached midnight, in his estimation, he spread out diagonally across the tiny cell and did one hundred situps in rapid succession, then turned over and did one hundred pushups, sweat breaking out over his body, his heart pounding, his muscles loose. Ready.

"No!" he screamed, letting the single word stretch like a howl. "Oh . . . God . . ." he moaned. And he began to sob, loudly at first, but then softer and softer, all the while muttering to himself, as he waited, hunched up in the far corner.

There was a sudden noise at his door, and Briggs moaned louder, his entire body shaking as if he was having a seizure.

The door was flung open, the light nearly blinding for several moments, despite the fact Briggs' eyes were hidden behind his hands.

He cried again, much louder. There was no one behind the guard.

"Shut up in there you motherless whore bastard," the guard whispered. It was a different one from before.

Briggs moaned louder. "No . . ." he howled.

The guard's hands were on his shoulder, Briggs' muscles were loose, and he looked up, a grin on his face.

"Surprise, you son of a bitch," he growled softly, grabbing the guard by the throat and pulling him down.

The man struggled wildly for several intense seconds, but the more he thrashed, the more pressure Briggs put on his throat, nearly crushing his windpipe.

"You will die here in this filthy cell, unless you calm down, comrade," Briggs whispered.

The guard finally settled down, and Briggs eased up on the pressure.

"I will crush your neck if you make so much as the tiniest of twitches, for you see I'm not what I appear to be."

In the very dim light spilling in from the corridor Briggs could see the fear on the man's wide eyes. His mouth was open, and flecks of saliva were on his lips.

"I need two answers. Do not lie to me. Where is the guard who was here earlier this afternoon? The one called Arkadi."

The guard started to shake his head, but Briggs applied a little more pressure to his tender throat.

"He is off duty . . . please do not kill me."

Briggs knew what he was going to do, and he knew how foolish and dangerous it was. But it did not matter. First, though, was Popov.

"There is another prisoner here I must see. His name is Mikhail Vladimir Popov. Where is he?"

"I don't know . . ."

Again Briggs applied the pressure to the man's throat, only this time, with his free hand, he reached down and grabbed the man's testicles and squeezed, once very hard.

"Here," the guard squeaked when Briggs released the pressure on his adam's apple. "He is here. At the end of the cell block."

"Any other guards here tonight?" The man was going to lie, Briggs could see it in his eyes. He reached down again.

"No," the man hurriedly said. "I am alone tonight."

"Good," Briggs said, shoving the guard forward, out the tiny door, and following him.

He was going home now, and God help the man who stood in his way.

## TWENTY-NINE

The single small lightbulb in the corridor seemed like a huge spotlight to Briggs, and it took several seconds before he could see much of anything other than dim blurs. The guard half crouched in front of him, tears beginning to well up in his eyes.

"You are going to kill me," he whimpered.

"Not unless you lie to me," Briggs said. "Get Popov out of his cell."

"I . . ." the guard stammered.

Briggs was out of patience. He stepped forward and slammed the guard against the far wall. "The next time, Comrade, I have to tell you something twice, I *will* kill you. In a most hideous manner!"

Tears streaming down the guard's cheeks now, he skittered down the corridor, Briggs right behind him. At the farthest door from the stairwell, he produced a key, and unlocked the door. He pulled it open, and stepped aside. "He is here."

"Get him out," Briggs ordered, glancing over his

shoulder at the stairwell. If someone came down now the game would be over.

Briggs turned back, and the guard nearly jumped out of his skin in his haste to go into the cell. A second later there was some mumbling from inside, and then the guard's bent back appeared as he dragged a filthy, inert form from the cell.

Mikhail Vladimir Popov was a physical wreck. It was obvious he had been beaten, starved and psychologically abused. In the ten or fifteen days he had been here there didn't seem to be much left of him except a bag of bones covered mostly with his own excrement.

Christ, Briggs thought. He would have trouble getting himself the hell out of here, let alone rescuing this poor wretch. Yet looking at the guard, and remembering what they had done to him in the short time he had been a captive, he knew that he could not simply leave this man here. The crime of it all was that knowing what he knew now, he was unable to release all the prisoners. But that was something he could not dwell on . . . for the moment.

"Where is your weapon?" Briggs hissed.

"I have no weapon . . . there are no weapons allowed down here."

"No one who comes down here carries a weapon?"

"It is against regulations."

"How about the guard at the desk just by the door upstairs?"

The guard's eyes automatically strayed toward the stairwell. "He is armed."

"Pistol? Rifle?" Briggs asked. He had not seen any weapons when they had come in. But then at the time he was being careful to seem as beaten as possible.

"An automatic rifle. A Kalashnikov."

Briggs nodded. He had Popov, he had his means of getting out of at least the basement, and he would have a Soviet assault rifle in a few minutes. Now all he needed was revenge.

"Close and lock this door," Briggs said. The guard complied immediately. Briggs gestured for him to help drag Popov back up the corridor to the glassed in office, where they propped him up in a chair, and fed him some tea. He came around slowly.

"Vladi," Briggs said close to his ear, while keeping one eye on the guard who sat at the desk, his mouth open in fear.

Popov mumbled something as he tried to focus on Briggs.

"Lydia sends her greetings. I have come to take you out of here. Will you help me?" Briggs said that low enough so the guard could not hear him.

"Lydia?" Popov mumbled his first coherent word. He blinked rapidly, his eyes tearing from the light. "Lydia?" he asked again.

"Yes, my old friend. Lydia is waiting. We are leaving here. Can you help me?"

Finally, Popov nodded. He was understanding. It was obvious he did not know who Briggs was, but he seemed convinced that a friend of Lydia's had actually come for him.

"Do you think you can walk, and perhaps even run with help when the time comes?"

"We are actually leaving this place?" Popov asked, his voice low, ragged, his words halting. He was a very weak, sick man.

"Yes, we are. There may be shooting. But we are

348

leaving here in a very few minutes."

"Oh . . . God . . . is it possible . . ."

Briggs turned his attention back to the guard. Straightening up, he went over to the desk, and perched on the edge. "Now you are going to telephone Arkadi. Wake him up. Tell him there is trouble here. With me. You need him immediately."

"I . . ."

Briggs shook his head. "You are doing fine so far, Comrade, do not disappoint me now." He picked up the telephone and handed the instrument to the man. "Don't make a mistake. It could be fatal."

The guard hesitated just a second, but then dialed three numbers. He waited for what seemed like hours, and was just about to say something to Briggs when he stiffened.

"Arkadi," he said.

Briggs gestured at him, his finger across his own throat, and the guard nervously nodded.

"Yes, Arkadi, I know what time it is. But . . . there is trouble with the new patient. He is moaning, and . . . calling your name. He won't shut up. The other prisoners will soon be getting out of hand. I do not know what to do."

The man was doing just fine, but Briggs was ready to silence him at the slightest sign he was cracking.

"Yes, Arkadi," he said. "Yes, I know. Thank you." The guard hung up the phone, and nearly collapsed.

"He is coming? He believed you?" Briggs asked.

The guard nodded. "He is coming. But please, comrade, do not kill me. It is not I who did the terrible things to you."

"He told you?" Briggs asked, his jaw tightening.

The guard shook his head. "He did not have to. I know Arkadi, he is a mean one. He has the reputation."

"And how about you, comrade? Do you never abuse your . . . patients?"

"I do my job, comrade, nothing more. Just my job," the guard said.

"I recognize him," Popov spoke up.

Briggs turned to him.

"You are the one they call Yevgenni?" Popov asked, his voice still ragged, but gaining strength.

The guard nodded.

"He is not as bad as many," Popov said.

There was hope in the guard's eyes.

"Your life will be spared, comrade, if you continue to cooperate," Briggs said.

"Yes . . . yes, anything."

"Take off your uniform then. I will be needing it."

With no further hesitation, the man jumped up, peeled off his tunic, his boots and his trousers. He was wearing long underwear, which he also started to pull off.

Briggs shook his head. "It is not necessary. But I want you to go across the corridor now, and get into my cell."

The guard seemed frightened.

"You will be out of harm's way, comrade. It is for the best."

Slowly the guard complied, looking at Popov as he passed. Once he was in the cell, Briggs looked in. "No noise now until morning. When they come for feeding time you will be discovered. I sincerely do not want to come back here and kill you because you called out."

The guard nodded his fearful agreement, and Briggs closed and locked the door.

Hurrying now, he went back into the office, stripped off his filthy pajamas, and pulled on the guard's uniform. It smelled of stale sweat, and was too small, but it was certainly better than what he had been wearing.

"How are we going to get out of the compound, and then where will we go? They will never stop searching for us."

"Through the drainage culvert near the tracks," Briggs said, listening for the door upstairs. "A car will be waiting to take us into Moscow."

"From there?"

"To the west."

Popov sucked his breath. "You may have wasted your time, Comrade. I do not know if I am ready to leave my country."

"Don't be a fool, Popov, if you are re-captured they will kill you."

"Then perhaps my martyrdom will serve some useful purpose."

"None," Briggs argued. "No one would ever know what happened to you. Your name might be on everyone's lips for a month or two . . . perhaps even a year. But then surely the memories will fade, and it will be as if you had never existed."

"And the alternative, like Solzhenitsyn? Publish my attacks from the west?"

"Why not?" Briggs snapped.

"It is not my . . ." Popov began, but the door upstairs opened, the noise reverberating through the corridor, and he clamped it off.

Briggs motioned for Popov to get up and move away from the open doorway, into the shadows beside a file cabinet, as he grabbed the guard's cap from the shelf.

Arkadi came into view and Briggs turned his face away from the window.

"What is going on, you stupid fool, that you had to wake me in the middle of the night," the man whispered loudly as he barged into the office.

At the same moment Briggs turned around, the man spotted Popov hiding in the corner, and he started to back off. Briggs was on him before he had the chance to cry out, stiff-arming him on the chin, and as his head snapped back, hammering a short, very sharp jab to the solar plexus.

Arkadi fell out into the corridor, his head bouncing off the concrete floor, and his face rapidly turning blue as he tried ineffectually to breathe, his heart stopped by the blow to his chest.

Watching the man die, Briggs had only one regret . . . that he was not able to prolong the man's death, and make it more agonizing.

Popov came to the doorway. "He was a very cruel man."

Arkadi's breathing stopped, and his body lay still. Never would the bastard abuse a prisoner.

As quickly as he could, Briggs dragged the man's body down the corridor to Popov's old cell, where he opened the door, and rolled the body inside, closed the door and re-locked it.

Back in front of the office, Popov was staring at the locked doors. "What about the others?" he asked.

"It is not possible to do anything for them. We must

save ourselves."

Popov stepped closer and looked into Briggs' eyes, sudden understanding dawning on his face. "You were . . . sent here."

"Yes," Briggs said. "But not by whom you think. Peter Houten is a traitor. It was he who turned you in."

"Why?"

"Because of Lydia. They think you were using her to get information about her father. They were afraid."

"Why not just shoot me then?"

"They were going to use you to prove to the world what the British are capable of. Using a daughter against a father."

"It was not my writing . . . not my . . ."

"No, it was not," Briggs said as gently as he could. "But we can talk about that later, we must leave now."

"Escape from this place is impossible, didn't you know?" Popov said pathetically.

"Not any more," Briggs said. "Just stick close to me. And no matter what happens, don't say a word. Don't make a sound. No matter what."

"I can't . . ."

"It's either that or remain here, go back into your cell and close the door on yourself. Have you given up?"

Popov raised his head defiantly. "If we get out of here we will take Lydia to the west with us."

"She will not go, she is Brezhnev's daughter," Briggs said. "No more talk now," he said, glancing up the stairs. "Follow me."

Briggs turned without another word, and hurried up the stairs, taking them as fast as he could despite his injuries which were causing him a lot of pain. At the top he listened but could hear nothing. He waiting until Popov reached him, motioned for the man to flatten himself against the wall, out of the way, then banged hard on the steel door with the heel of his hand.

The bolt was thrown back, and the door came open. Briggs reached up, caught the surprised guard by the front of his tunic and dragged him through the doorway, kneeing him in the stomach as he fell, and slamming the side of his hand into the man's neck sending him tumbling down the stairs.

Checking to make sure no one was out in the corridor, Briggs and Popov slipped out, and closed and locked the heavy steel door.

The guard's Kalashnikov was leaning up against the wall behind his table. Briggs grabbed it, and dragged Popov down the short corridor to the rear door. He looked outside.

It was dark and very cold now. In the distance, toward the south, beyond the administration building, Briggs could see the lights atop the guard towers over the compound housing the dangerous internees, as well as the taller guard towers over the main fence beyond which was a wide birch forest.

For now there was no one in sight, but getting out wasn't going to be particularly easy. The drainage ditch Obyedkov had spoken about was behind the internees maximum security compound, in full sight of the guard tower in the main fence near the railroad gate. Guards from the train, from the internees compound and from the main tower would be able to see them.

Unless there was a diversion, and they all were looking someplace else.

"Are you ready?" Briggs asked turning back.

Popov's nostrils were flared. It seemed as if he was having a little difficulty breathing, but he nodded. "I'm following my fate."

"Shit," Briggs said. "Stay close. You're my prisoner." Briggs made sure a live round was in the rifle's firing chamber, then he opened the door, and led Popov out into the cold night.

They had come out the rear of the research building, opposite one of the guard towers in the west fence. Briggs shoved Popov ahead of him, nearly knocking the man off his feet for the benefit of anyone in the tower watching, and in a few seconds they were around the corner, out of sight from the tower, without an alarm being raised.

That was their first hurdle, Briggs thought, breathing a bit easier for the moment.

At the front of the building, but still within the deeper shadows, Briggs held up. Across the walk was the rear south corner of the main hall. According to Obyedkov's notes, the large building housed the staff quarters, as well as the staff dining rooms, some of the labs and medical facilities, as well as equipment and supplies in the basement. There were no prisoners housed in this building, he had been assured.

Obyedkov had been playing games with them, but so far as Briggs had seen his information was as good as gold. He had not lied about the physical details.

"Stay here," Briggs whispered urgently.

"Are you going to leave me?"

"Just for a couple of minutes."

"What if someone comes?" Popov protested, grabbing Briggs' arm.

Briggs pushed him down on his haunches close to the building. "Stay down and don't make a sound. You'll be all right."

Before Popov could voice another objection, Briggs stepped out onto the walkway, and boldly marched to one of the rear entrances of the main hall, and went inside.

Wide cement stairs led down into the basement. The building was warm, and smelled of kerosene. Somewhere from within the basement he could hear the sound of running machinery.

He hurried down the stairs. To the left was a steel door on slides, and straight ahead was a counter. It looked like a supply depot.

He looked over the counter. Curled up in a deep, overstuffed chair, was a slovenly looking soldier. His eyes blinked, and he looked up, then jumped up, his mouth opening to shout.

Briggs brought the butt of the Kalashnikov around, slamming it into the soldier's chin. The supply man went down like a felled ox, and Briggs was over the counter.

Through a door, Briggs found himself in a large warehouse-like space, filled with rows and aisles of clothing and equipment to the left, and canned goods to the right.

Farther back, through a set of double doors, Briggs came into a much larger room, this one cold, and smelling very strongly of kerosene. The machinery noise came from a pair of generators on the far side.

Keeping low, Briggs worked his way in and amongst

356

the 55-gallon drums of kerosene to the maintenance office where another slovenly looking soldier was sleeping. He never woke up, as Briggs clipped him on the side of the head.

It was war, he thought coming back out into the generator room. The poor bastards in the other buildings . . . the tens of thousands of them over the years . . . had had absolutely no chance for survival.

In ten minutes, Briggs had opened five barrels of kerosene, and had managed to dump them over, the fuel spreading itself out over the floor as he worked his way back toward the supply section.

At the doors, he realized he had no matches. He raced up to the supply counter, immediately finding cigarettes and matches on the desk. Once again back in the generator room, the kerosene fumes thick in the air, Briggs lit four matches before he could get the edge of, what was now a lake of kerosene, to catch fire. When it did, the flames spread slowly across the floor, branching off here and there, as they accelerated, and began to build higher and higher.

They had their diversion now, he thought smiling.

# THIRTY

Popov was crouched, shivering, where Briggs had left him. He could not stand up without help. He was angry and frightened.

"You said you would be back in a minute or two. I was getting ready to run."

"That's exactly what we're going to do. Any minute all hell is going to break loose," Briggs said. A curl of smoke came from the doorway across the walk. "Mean-while I'm taking you back to the internees compound."

Briggs pulled him away from the building, out to the walkway, and they headed away from the main hall, past administration toward the barracks compound, beyond which was the fence and freedom.

There were trees alongside the path, and patches of lawn here and there, but no real attempts had been made to make the place pleasant. As they walked down the hill toward the lights of the barracks, Briggs kept thinking about all the prisoners he was leaving behind. He also thought about all the poor wretches who had already lost their lives or their minds here in the years this place had been operating. Again he had to wonder what kind of monsters there were in the world. What in God's name motivated some of these people? Anger at an enemy was one thing that Briggs could understand. But cruelty on some poor wretch totally unable to defend himself, was totally incomprehensible.

The farther they walked, the madder Briggs became. The anger was building in him, just as he knew the fire in the basement of the main hall was building toward a cataclysm.

He looked back over his shoulder toward the research building, but his eyes were drawn back to the main hall. Smoke was pouring out of the building from the first floor doors and windows. Any moment someone would be sounding the alarm.

Briggs quickened his step, as he tried to envision what it must be like in the basement now. The generators which supplied electricity for the Center were down there. How long before their fuel tanks exploded and the flow of electricity was interrupted?

A siren started on a guard tower somewhere down toward the railroad gate, and a split second later a tremendous explosion lit up the night sky, glass, burning wood and bricks spewing out from the furiously burning building.

Popov was knocked to his knees, more sirens started up, and then the perimeter lights, as well as the lights over the internees compound flickered, dimmed, and then totally died, plunging the camp into darkness except for the flames from the building behind them.

"Now," Briggs whispered urgently, as he hauled Popov to his feet.

They half ran, half stumbled at an angle away from the burning building, toward the fence, midway between the railroad gate and the farthest building in the row of maximum security barracks.

Someone began cranking a hand siren, and soon a second one began to wail. There were soldiers running everywhere, many of them carrying flashlights, the beams of which bounced and jerked up the paths toward the main hall. Commands were being shouted up toward administration, and dogs were barking furiously somewhere in the distance.

There was mass confusion in the compound . . . exactly what Briggs had hoped to accomplish.

A dozen soldiers raced up the hill past them, intent on the fire, as Briggs and Popov continued down the hill, around the compound fence, and then keeping low across a wide field to the shallow little creek that ran under the main fence.

Fifty feet from the fence, Briggs stopped to listen. There was a lot of activity up at the main hall. Everyone was up there fighting the fire . . . or nearly everyone. Briggs did not think everyone would have left their posts. They were not that undisciplined.

With the tower lights out, they would be sending patrols along the fence. It was the only way in which to make sure the fire wasn't a diversion, during which an escape could be made.

Briggs spotted the lone guard, moving as nothing more than a darker shadow against the vague outlines of the fence. He was coming this way.

"Stay here," Briggs whispered in Popov's ear.

"Make no sound."

Before the other man could say anything Briggs had silently climbed up out of the creek bed, and crawling on his stomach approached a spot just ahead of where the guard would pass in a half a minute or so.

Reaching his position Briggs watched the guard coming. The man had his rifle slung over his shoulder, and from time to time watched where he was going. But for the most part his eyes were turned up toward the burning building. Flames were shooting now out of the second and top floor windows.

The guard came opposite Briggs, then stopped and scratched himself as he looked down into the creek bed, and then underneath at the screened-over drainage ditch.

Briggs held his breath as the man scanned the field and the approaches to the fence, then continued along the fence-line.

Leaving his rifle behind, Briggs got up and ran, crouching, to the guard who at the last moment, hearing something, started to turn. But it was too late. Briggs jammed his knee forcefully into the guard's back, while at the same time he pulled the man's head back and sharply to the right.

The guard's spine snapped first, and then his neck broke. Briggs eased his body down to the ground, and laid there with it for several moments, as he waited for an alarm to come. But none was sounded.

A jeep raced by, up on the road, and then a couple of trucks lumbered past from the railway maintenance shed.

Briggs crawled down into the creek bed, dragging the dead guard with him.

He left the body lying near the drainage culvert, and hurried back to where Popov huddled shivering in water up to his knees.

"Is it all right?" Popov asked fearfully.

"We're getting out of here now." Briggs took his arm and dragged him the rest of the way down the creek back to the culvert.

Popov recoiled at the sight of the dead guard. "It is murder now. We will be killed."

"If they catch us," Briggs said. The guard had a bayonet at his belt, which Briggs took, and began working at the grating blocking the drainage pipe. The thick fencing material was intact, but several of the bolts holding it in place had rusted badly, and came loose easily.

As soon as he had a section of the fence peeled back, Briggs stuffed the knife in his tunic-belt, then urged Popov into the low pipe that was about three and a half feet in diameter. At first the man balked, but Briggs bodily shoved him through.

"It is our way out."

Once Popov was inside, Briggs dragged the guard's body through the opening with him, then reached back and pulled the fencing back in place, straightening it out as best he could.

The culvert was only twenty or thirty feet long, and Briggs could see the gray patch of sky at the other end. But the creek was flowing much faster here in the narrower confines of the pipe, and from the other side Briggs thought he could hear the sound of splashing water. It would not do for the guard's body to wash out the other side, and be spotted first thing in the morning.

Using the guard's belt, and the strap from his rifle, Briggs quickly fashioned a sling, which he tied under the body's armpits, and attached the buckle to the fencing below the water. The body would not be washed out the other side, and would not be discovered unless someone actually came down to the culvert and looked inside.

Popov was half lying in water up to his waist two-thirds of the way to the other side. He did not move when Briggs prodded him.

"Popov?" Briggs whispered urgently. "Vladi! We have to keep moving."

"Lydia?" Popov mumbled.

Briggs put his ear to the man's chest. Popov's breathing was fast and shallow, and his heartbeat seemed to have a ragged flutter in it. Christ. After all this the man couldn't die. Briggs wouldn't allow it.

"Lydia is waiting for you," Briggs said, crawling past the man. "We're going to her now. I'll take you."

"Lydia?" Popov moaned.

Briggs eased around, and gently dragged him the rest of the way through the culvert, which opened on the side of a small hill overlooking a thick birch forest. To the south a couple of miles was a road, where Chiles and White would be waiting . . . if they realized that he had been arrested, and already tried and sentenced.

Briggs swung out of the culvert first, and looked back up toward the fence. The guard tower, which was about fifty yards away, was lit up in red from the flames of the burning building. He could see the silhouette of at least one guard up there. If he turned around and looked down he'd spot them.

Briggs eased Popov's frail body out of the culvert, and heaving him up over his shoulder, started to pick his way down the slippery hillside to the protection of the woods. At any moment, he expected to hear a siren, a shouted command to halt, and then gunfire.

His entire body ached from the beating he had received, and with every step he took his legs threatened to give out on him.

About halfway down the hill, Popov moaned something, but then was still again. For several agonizingly long seconds Briggs was certain someone had to have heard it, and he waited for the alarm to come. But there was nothing, and after a bit he continued down the hill, coming at length to the protection of the forest.

Briggs did not stop. He was afraid that if he laid Popov down, he would never be able to get the man up on his shoulders again. The going was much easier here than on the hillside, yet he frequently had to dodge low branches, and pick his way around large tangles of deadfalls.

It was very dark in the woods, the stark white bark of the birch standing out almost with its own luminosity, everything else inky black by comparison.

The weather had turned very cold as well, and soaking wet as they both were, Briggs did not believe they would last very long out here. Certainly not until morning. By then they'd both be dead of exposure.

For a while, as he trudged through the woods, one step after the other, Briggs thought about Arkadi, the cruel isolation guard he had killed. According to Oumi, and to everything Briggs had been taught, the man was merely typical of Soviet officialdom. Places like Lubyanka and the Yedanov Rehabilitation Center, were typical of Soviet justice. But Briggs was beginning not to believe it. Or at least he was beginning to have doubts.

It was crazy, he thought. He had been arrested, beaten and sentenced to hell, and yet he could still entertain some feeling for the Russian people.

He thought of Popov here with him now. He thought of the people he had spoken with at Porfiri's. And of Lydia Savin, with her tragic guilt. Finally he thought of Oumi and Vatra and so many others in exile in Soho. They were Russian, or near Russian heritage. They were odd by British or American standards . . . but they were not evil.

Briggs had no idea how long he had been carrying Popov when he came to the hill that dipped down to a flat spot, then climbed sharply up the other side. He was very tired now, barely able to keep on his feet. And yet he knew he had to keep going. To stop now was to die, he kept telling himself.

He stumbled down the hill, then up on a small bump, and halfway across a flat stretch of gravel before he realized that he had reached the road. He had made it!

A flashlight shone to his left, and Briggs crouched instinctively as he turned to face it. Someone was running up the gravel road toward him.

"It is him!" someone shouted.

Briggs backed up a step.

"Briggs! It's me! Chiles!"

The flashlight was flicked off, and strong hands were on him, Popov's weight suddenly gone from his back, and he would have fallen down except someone had hold of him.

"Holy shit, what the hell did they do to you," Chiles said.

Dick White had Popov and they all hurried back to a beat up old embassy car, where they propped the unconscious dissident in the back, and Briggs crawled in with him.

White was driving, and as soon as they had turned around on the road, and were heading away, Chiles poured him a stiff shot of Irish whiskey.

Briggs drank it, the liquor hammering at his stomach, and he was instantly dizzy and nauseous for just a second or two, but then the feeling passed. Chiles lit him a cigarette and passed it back.

"We just found out about the trial this afternoon," Chiles said. The cigarette tasted wonderful. "The Brits picked it up, and Clifford brought it over around five."

"We just got out here," Dick White said glancing nervously over his shoulder. "I'd just parked the car, and you came stumbling out of the woods. Scared the hell out of us."

"What time is it?" Briggs asked. The cigarette too was making him light-headed.

"Just a few minutes after midnight," Chiles said. "Damn, we didn't think you'd be moving so soon, and certainly not this early in the evening."

There was a silence for a minute or two.

"Was it as bad as Obyedkov's notes made it seem?" White asked.

"Worse," Briggs said. He checked Popov, who seemed to be breathing all right now. His color did not

366

seem too good, but Briggs did not think the man was in any immediate danger . . . at least not from his own health.

"How did you manage to get out?" Chiles asked.

Briggs looked up. There was something in Chiles' voice. Something in his and Dick White's manner that didn't quite sit right.

"What is it?" Briggs asked. "What's happened."

Chiles and White glanced at each other.

"What the hell is going on?"

"We've got some bad news for you," Chiles said.

For some reason Briggs immediately thought of Sylvia Hume, and he sat forward.

"There's no way in hell we're going to be able to get you into the embassy. At least not this morning. They've blocked off our sewer route."

It was almost a relief. "It's all right," Briggs said. "I had decided not to return in any event."

"We have a safehouse . . ." White started.

"That no doubt is being watched," Briggs said. "This is their country, remember?"

"What then?"

"I have a room at a boardinghouse on the south side of the river, just off Pyatnitskaya Street. You're going to drop Popov and me off there."

"We can't just leave you," Chiles protested.

"It's all right, Bob, it's better this way," Briggs said, his mind ranging ahead, a plan already forming. "But I'm going to need a number of things by tomorrow. We'll have to meet someplace."

"What are you going to do?" White asked.

"Go home," Briggs said.

# THIRTY-ONE

They arrived a block from the boardinghouse a few minutes before two, without incident. The street was very dark, and there was absolutely no traffic—automobiles or pedestrians. They might just as well have been back out in the forests for all the activity here. Yet Briggs knew it was an illusion. Every window possibly had a pair of eyes, every rooftop a camera, every door a pair of ears.

On the way into the city, Briggs had changed back into the civilian clothes Chiles and White had brought for him, and took White's jacket to throw over Popov's shoulders.

For the rest of this night, Briggs would sleep. Tomorrow he would go out, with one of his spare passports which showed he was a visiting East German businessman, and then in the evening, sometime between 8 and 10 P.M., he would meet with them at the Metropole Hotel Bar.

"It's short notice," Briggs said. "Only eighteen or

twenty hours. Can you do it?"

"Don't worry about it," Chiles said. "We'll be there. You just take care of yourself. If you're picked up now, you're a dead man."

"Right," Briggs said. He took the insignia off the guard's cap he had worn from the center, and put the cap back on to hide the fact his head was shaved.

He got out of the car, came around to Popov's side, opened the door, and helped the semi-conscious man out. Still there was no traffic.

"Good luck," White said, his window cranked down.

"See you two in a bit," Briggs said, and with Popov's arm over his shoulder, he started down the street and around the corner to the back entrance to his boardinghouse, his muscles screaming in protest, but a fresh package of cigarettes, and the rest of the bottle of whiskey in his pocket.

A police car, its blue lights flashing, but its siren silent, screamed up the street just as Briggs and Popov ducked into the filthy courtyard littered with trash, mounds of dirt and broken bricks and glass. He could hear the car screech around the corner, then accelerate off into the night.

It was a four-story building, all the dark windows looking down at him, as if to say: we see you, we know that you are up to something.

He picked his way across the basement entrance which was always left open, and let himself in to his spartan room, throwing the latch. The curtains were drawn, but he made sure they were tight before he turned on the small table lamp.

Someone had been here. The bedspread had been

slightly crooked when he had left. It was straight now. Carefully he eased Popov down on the narrow bed. The chair by the window had just touched the curtains. It was a fraction of an inch out now. The framed photograph of Lenin on the wall, had been slightly askew, it was askew the other way now. Small signs. But someone had been here. The landlady?

Briggs picked up the table lamp, turned it upside-down, and pried the thin paper bottom off with his thumbnail. Still wedged up inside the base were his money, his extra papers and his stiletto. He breathed a sigh of relief. It probably had been his landlady who had come in and searched the room. A real professional would not have missed this.

He took off his jacket, tossed it aside, then checked out in the basement. No one was up, no lights burned.

He took his wash basin and pitcher across the basement to the sink where he filled them both, then went back into his room and locked the door.

Rolling up his sleeves, he stripped the filthy clothes from the barely coherent Popov, and washed his pitifully frail body. They had beaten him, had pinched and cut him, and had burned him everywhere; under his arms, on his penis, between his toes, and even on his tongue. Dirt was crusted on him, and when Briggs was finished the water in the wash basin was filthy, as was the wash cloth.

Briggs had read and heard stories about the atrocities the Nazis had perpetrated on their victims, and about the terrible things the Russians had done under Stalin . . . but this was the modern world. Brezhnev was supposedly a reasonable man.

When he had Popov covered up, he tied his filthy

rags in a bundle, then stepped just outside, and buried them under some rubble right next to the building so that no one from upstairs could see that anyone was down here.

Back inside, with the door once again securely locked, Briggs eased himself into his chair, pulled the jacket over himself and closed his eyes. He was asleep instantly, although he was plagued by bad dreams in which he was back at the Yedanov Rehabilitation Center and Arkadi had come back from the grave to urinate on him.

A gray light filtered through the curtains, and the wind howled outside as someone knocked on the inside door, pulling Briggs out of his deep sleep.

Popov was sitting up in the bed, a wild, desperate look on his face when Briggs opened his eyes and sat up with a start.

"Lopatin . . . Lopatin, are you in there? What is going on? I demand to know!" The landlady's voice was strident on the other side of the door.

Briggs motioned for Popov to remain silent and to get down under the covers.

"Coming," he called out, getting up from the chair. He took off his shoes and socks, and his shirt, grabbed the cap and pulled it on, then went to the door and unlocked it. He opened it just a crack.

The landlady stood out there, and she craned her neck in an effort to see more of what was going on inside.

"Where have you been?" she demanded.

"Out," Briggs said gruffly. "What's the matter old woman, my money wasn't good enough for you? Perhaps you wish to give me a refund and I can move out?"

"You have someone in there with you!" she shouted.

"Yes . . . my friend!"

"What kind of a friend?"

"A very good kind of a friend," Briggs shouted back.

"There will be no ladies in this house . . ." the landlady started, but Briggs reached in his pocket and pulled out a hundred ruble note. He held it up so she could see it.

"We are both very hungry. The passion, you know. How about tea, and bread and perhaps a little jam. But most of all, peace and quiet."

The old woman's eyes shone, as she reached for the money through the crack in the door. He let her grab it, but before she could take her hand away, he closed the door gently on her hand, trapping her.

"Here, what are you trying to do?" she squealed.

"First I need a promise from you, old lady."

"What kind of a promise?"

"I have paid for my room, fair and square. And now with this money, I've paid even more. Not only do I desire quiet, I desire privacy as well."

"This is a quiet house."

"You will promise never to come into my room without first asking again. Never."

"I have never . . ." she started to protest, so he grabbed the money from her clutching fingers.

"Never," he insisted. "In Leningrad there are ladies and gentlemen. Not like here."

"Oh yes," she wailed. "I will never come into your room, Lopatin. Never. I promise."

"Very well," Briggs said, releasing the pressure on the door. He gave her the money. "Be quick about our breakfast."

She scurried away, and Briggs re-locked the door.

"She is a nosy old woman," Popov said. His voice was cracked and very weak.

"How do you feel?"

"Not very well. I don't know if I can go on."

"Yes you can. You're going to stay here today and tonight. Tomorrow morning we are taking the train."

"To where?"

"Yalta," Briggs said. Popov's eyes lit up.

"The Black Sea. It is still warm there this time of the year."

"But you are going to have to stay here alone today. I must go out for awhile."

"Then you will leave me," Popov said, the bright look fading.

"I will not. I did not come out to the center to get you, just to leave you in some room in Moscow. But while you are here alone, you must let no one in. The landlady will probably be back. You must keep the doors locked no matter what she says or does. And you must make absolutely no noise."

Popov nodded. "What will you do today?"

"Arrange for our travel out of here."

"I have no papers."

"I will arrange the papers."

"Can I return to my apartment . . . to see Lydia . . . to get a few things."

Briggs shook his head. "She is Brezhnev's daughter. When it is known that you are gone, they may come to her to try to make her talk. If she knows nothing it will be better for her as well as for us."

"I understand," Popov said.

The landlady came back a few minutes later with a large pot of hot, sweet tea, several thick slices of bread, and a small bowl of butter. All of that was on a tray, along with two napkins.

"For your friend," she explained about the napkins at the door.

"Just leave the tray, thank you," Briggs said.

"But I would like to come in and set it up for you. Perhaps meet your friend. Sometimes women like to talk together."

"Not now," Briggs said. "She is not feeling well, please leave us."

"Is there anything I can do?"

"Yes, old woman, leave, before I lose all of my patience!" Briggs roared.

The landlady backed off, and Briggs watched as she scurried across the basement, and disappeared around the corner, before he opened the door, and brought the tray in. She was going to be trouble. He could feel it. They were going to have to be very careful around her.

Briggs left most of the money and all of his extra papers behind, but took with him a couple of thousand rubles, his East German identification, and his stiletto at the small of his back.

It was shortly after noon when he stepped across the littered courtyard, went down to Pyatnitskaya Street (which was one of the busiest thoroughfares in the section of Moscow), and blended in with the crowds of pedestrians.

He worked his way back and forth past the Tretyakov Art Gallery, south past Krimskiy Bridge all the way into Gorky Park, where he wandered in and amongst the trees along the river walk.

At odd times during his trek, he would stop and suddenly turn around as if he had just remembered something—always looking for a stumble from someone behind him. Or he would glance in shop windows looking for the telltale signs of interest from passersby across the street. Combined with those bits of tradecraft, he also kept a very close eye on those in front of him. Advance or forward tailing was a difficult art, but the ranks of the komitet were filled with its practitioners. So, from time to time, when the pedestrians in front of him had cleared an intersection that Briggs was halfway through, he would suddenly turn, and head off in a different direction, coming around the block eventually to the same spot—always looking for that same face, for the quickly averted eye, the newspaper under the arm.

But there was none of that. He was clean.

It was very cold by comparison to two days ago. The temperature hovered near freezing for a high, with brisk northwesterly winds off the Ural Mountains beyond the Arctic Circle. It would be a very cold winter. Briggs could feel it in the air, and see it in the resigned expressions of the people he passed on the street; on the faces of the lovers strolling hand-in-hand in the park who knew that mild days for such things were gone until spring.

By four he stopped in a small restaurant for some bread, some borscht and some imported Czechoslovakian beer (which he enjoyed immensely), and by five he was on his way back past Oktyabrskaya Place, Dobryninskaya Place and finally past the Kras-nokholmskiy Bridge, across the river from which brooded the Taganskaya Prison.

This again was the poorer section of the city, and there were a lot of people out and about . . . especially a lot of women with shopping baskets. Today was Saturday, market day for the small independent farmers the state had recently authorized.

No one paid the slightest attention to Briggs as he circled the block around Popov's apartment building twice, before ducking inside and hurrying up to the second floor.

He was about to knock on the door, but some inner warning made him hold up. Instead he put his ear to the wood. At first he heard nothing, but then there was the sound of something breaking in the kitchen, and a man's voice said something Briggs was unable to catch.

There was some music playing from somewhere downstairs. Other than that the building was quiet.

Briggs reached behind him and pulled out his stiletto, then carefully tried the door. It was not locked. Holding the blade in his left hand, behind his leg, he knocked once on the door and pushed it open.

"Lydia?" he called out as he stepped inside, but her name died on his lips. The place was in a shambles. Lydia was lying on the floor in a pool of blood, her eyes open.

Balan, one of the men who had arrested Briggs came out of the kitchen. His eyes went wide when he recognized who it was, and he started to reach inside his coat pocket.

In one smooth motion, Briggs threw the stiletto, underhand, the blade burying itself in Balan's chest. The officer grunted, and stepped back into the kitchen.

Briggs leaped across the room as the shorter one, Yurianovich, shoved his partner aside and burst out of the kitchen, raising his gun to fire.

Briggs batted the gun aside, then hammered the man three quick jabs to the chest, the throat and the face, holding back with each blow. He did not want to kill him . . . just yet.

The heavy gun clattered to the floor as Yurianovich crumpled next to his dead partner.

Briggs spun around and hurried to where Lydia was lying. She had been dead for at least an hour, an ugly, dark hole in her chest, just above her heart, from a large caliber bullet. Probably from the Graz Buyra that Yurianovich carried.

She was Brezhnev's daughter. Why kill her? It did not make any sense.

Back in the kitchen, Briggs pulled his stiletto from Balan's chest, wiped it on the man's jacket, and then pulled Yurianovich into the living room. The man was just starting to come around.

Briggs knelt beside him, and brought the tip of the stiletto to within a half an inch from Yurianovich's left eye.

Yurianovich came fully awake, started to struggle, but then realized what was happening. His body went rigid, his nostrils flared, his lips pursed.

Briggs nodded. "It is good that you understand so quickly. Now you must answer my questions. Why did you kill the girl?"

Yurianovich squeaked something, but Briggs could make no sense of it.

"You will lose your eye unless you answer me. Why did you kill Lydia?"

"She . . . attacked me," the agent stammered. "With a knife."

"So you killed Brezhnev's daughter."

"She is not Comrade Brezhnev's daughter. That was a lie."

"A lie?" Briggs asked.

"Your god, Popov is a traitor. He was working for the British. We decided to give them something to think about."

"So you were done with her, and then you killed her," Briggs said taking the knife-point away from Yurianovich's eye and sitting back on his haunches.

"She was nothing but a whore," the agent said, starting to sit up.

"*You son of a bitch*," Briggs swore in English.

Yurianovich's eyes went wide, and he tried to roll to the left, but Briggs slashed out with the blade, opening his throat. He leaped back, away from the splash of blood, as Yurianovich thrashed around for a full minute, before sinking down on his side, his hands falling limp, the choking sounds ending.

Briggs never felt good about killing. But as he stood up, and looked from Lydia Savin, then Balan and Yurianovich, he did not feel the slightest remorse.

"*Bastards*," he said in English, and he went into the bathroom to make sure he had not been splattered with blood.

# THIRTY-TWO

The Metropole was a large old hotel that the Soviets were constantly re-building, and re-modernizing, but never to any great effect. The rooms were shabby, the plumbing terrible, the wiring dangerous and the fixtures badly worn. But it was *the* place to go in Moscow, and the Grille Room was packed and noisy when Briggs showed up a little past 8:30.

He spotted Chiles and White seated at the long, mahogany bar across the big room, and he went over to them and ordered a kvass.

"How can you stand that stuff?" Chiles asked, glancing over at Briggs.

"I can't. Did you bring the things?"

"In the coat room off the lobby. Brown suitcase. Checked in the name of Karl Oberst."

Briggs drink came and he paid for it.

"How is our friend doing?" White asked.

"He's fine, but the girl is dead."

"What?" Chiles sputtered. He looked around to

make sure no one was listening to them. "What the hell did you say?"

"She's dead. The same pair who arrested me were at Vladi's apartment. I jumped them there. They had killed her."

"You got out before they saw you," Chiles said. "Tell me you didn't hang around."

"I killed them both."

"Jesus Christ," Chiles swore. "All hell is going to break loose. You'll never get out of here. They know by now that Lopatin is missing along with his friend. They'll seal this city tighter than a drum."

"Lydia was not Leonid's daughter."

For several long seconds Chiles and White just stared at him, letting what he had just said sink in.

"You sure of your information?" Chiles finally spoke up.

Briggs nodded. "Reasonably. This was nothing but a set up from the start."

"Houten," White said.

"He and I are going to have a little talk very soon," Briggs said. He finished his drink. "We're leaving first thing in the morning. By train. Once we're gone, tell Burt you can dismantle the operation from this end. But we're going to need a reception committee to help us across."

"Where?"

"We'll try to make Sinop."

"Where the hell is that?" Chiles asked.

"Turkey. On the coast. Black Sea."

"When?"

"Tell Burt to have the patrols out starting three days from now, just outside Soviet territorial waters. But

380

don't worry if we're a few days late, I'll be playing this by ear."

Briggs turned away from the bar, strode across the room without looking back, and instead of going outside, turned left up the stairs and across the lobby to the coat room.

An old woman was at the counter. She looked up and smiled.

"I would like my case now," Briggs said.

"Yes comrade. Your name please?"

"It is a brown suitcase," Briggs said pulling out his wallet, and opening it to his East German driver's license. "The name is Oberst."

"Of course," the old woman said. She disappeared back into the coat room for a moment, and when she reappeared she was lugging a large, brown leather suitcase which she set up on the counter with some difficulty.

"Yes," Briggs said. "That is it. Thank you." He pressed a five ruble note on the old woman, then left the hotel. By ten he had stopped to buy some food for the trip (Soviet trains had no dining cars), had made sure again that he was not being followed, and made his way back to his room, after checking the train schedules.

Popov let him in. He was obviously relieved.

"How did it go?" Briggs asked, once the door was closed and re-locked.

"The old woman came back and tried to get in. She screamed she was going to call the police."

"Did you say anything?"

Popov shook his head. "I did as you told me, and after awhile she went away." He eyed the packages and the suitcase Briggs had brought in with him. "Did you bring some food?"

"Yes, and some wine. We leave in the morning." Briggs opened the packages. He would not tell Popov about Lydia. At least not now. Not until they were safely out of the country. There was no telling what the man might do when he found out.

It was very cold when Briggs woke Popov around four in the morning. Outside, the wind rattled the windows and it was snowing.

"This will never work," Popov kept saying as Briggs started his preparations.

"Sure it will, Vladi. I've seen it done a thousand times."

"I mean, I don't think I can leave Moscow. Not now. Not leave Lydia here alone. My people . . ."

Briggs had opened the suitcase, and had taken out the things Chiles and White had supplied him on such short notice. He turned around to Popov who was seated on the chair in the middle of the room. He had a towel draped around his bare shoulders. He looked very frail; a tiny, insignificant-looking man who had fought the system and lost, and now wanted to try again.

"You know that you'd be taken back out to the center. They'd probably shoot you."

Popov shrugged. "Maybe it would be better. Maybe I don't want to go on living. Not like this."

"It doesn't have to be this way . . . can't you understand that?"

"The others . . . the ones who have gone to America. I have heard that none of them are truly happy."

"They are alive," Briggs countered.

"Are they?"

"You're damned right they are, Vladi," Briggs said, crossing the room to him, and laying some of the things on the bed.

Popov started to protest, but Briggs held him off.

"A lot of people have risked their lives for you. But if you want to stay, then fine. But I have to know immediately. I am a wanted man now. If you are going with me, we have to get ready now. If you are not coming, then I'll have to make different preparations."

"I want to see Lydia."

"You cannot."

"Why?" Popov said sharply.

"She's dead."

The sleep had helped Briggs' mind, but the rest had not been enough yet to do much but slightly dull the pain from the battering he had received. He sat down on the bed, and told Popov what had happened yesterday. When he was finished Popov was crying.

"She wasn't Brezhnev's daughter, so they didn't really give a damn about her," Briggs said. "And they certainly don't give a damn about you now. You are a dangerous thorn in their side. They will have to kill you if you are caught."

"They could have sent her out east. Banished her from Moscow."

"I think she fought them," Briggs said as gently as he could, getting up. He began applying the makeup to Popov's face and neck.

"She shouldn't have."

"She knew she was going to be arrested."

"You spoke with her at length?" Popov said looking up.

"We met at Porfiri's. And then we went up to your apartment and talked. She said she knew she was going to be arrested. It's why I went to see her yesterday. I thought I might be able to take her with us."

"But not now."

"No," Briggs said, and they both fell silent as he worked quickly with an expertise learned on the run and honed to a fine art in Hollywood. Outside, the wind continued to blow, and the snow increased in intensity and some of it began to stick, piling up against the buildings and curbs.

By six Briggs was finished with Popov, and by 6:30, working from a tiny, cracked mirror, he was finished with himself.

The change was startling. Briggs had become a sixty-five year old minor party official from Leningrad, while Popov with a gray wig and a black dress had become his wife. Together they were off to Yalta for a much needed holiday in the sun. There they would hire a boat to take them out into the Black Sea where they would be set adrift at night. Higgins had given him the name of a man and his brother who would do it for them, for a price.

Not foolproof by any means, but it could be made to succeed . . . if they could reach Yalta without attracting any attention.

They left the roominghouse a couple of minutes before 7:00 A.M., picking their way carefully across to the courtyard, around the corner, and up two blocks to the subway. Briggs carried the suitcase in his right hand, and held Popov's arm with his left.

"I feel foolish," Popov said.

"Don't," Briggs replied. "Think of yourself as an

actor. This is nothing more than a drama."

They reached the Central Railway Station well before eight, leaving themselves plenty of time to have their travel plans approved and their internal passports stamped.

The little official at the travel desk did not question the papers, but just beamed effusively and kept nodding his head as he signed the orders, and put his stamp in their passports.

"I hope that you and your wife have had a pleasant stay in Moscow, Comrade Shestakov."

"We have indeed," Briggs boomed in his best, most cultured Russian. Popov was playing his part well. He kept blinking his eyes, smiling and nodding, although it was obvious he was under strain. It would be a long time before his body completely healed, if it ever did, from the effects of his beatings at the Yedanov Rehabilitation Center. "If there is anything we can do for you in return."

"Oh . . . that is not necessary, Comrade."

"Perhaps if you give me your name, and your supervisor's name, I will place a call tomorrow. Tell them what fine service you have given us."

The official's smile widened, as he gave Briggs his name and his supervisor's name. Briggs wrote it down in his notebook, shook the man's hand, then he and Popov went across the depot to the ticket counter, where they purchased tickets to Yalta, with a return to Leningrad in two weeks.

The train did not leave until 9:00 A.M., but by the time they had finished with their passports and tickets, and had made their way down to the trains, it was past 8:30, and they were allowed to board immediately.

They had been assigned one of the few private compartments in the train, with upper and lower pull down bunks, and a tiny cubicle with a fold up wash basin, a mirror and a light. Their window slid up and down, and they had a shade they could lower or raise.

It was very cold inside the train, Briggs could see his own breath in the corridor. When he asked the conductor about it, the man shrugged.

"It will be better once we leave the city," the man said. He was short, very thin, and exceedingly stern looking. "Besides, we are heading south to warmer climates. It's best we leave our heating fuel in Moscow where the people really need it."

The conductor punched their tickets. "There will be a fine for excessive use of water," he said, and he left them.

Briggs closed and locked the compartment door, and Popov released a deep sigh he had evidently been holding, and sat gratefully down on one of the fold down seats. His complexion was pale and his breathing was rapid.

"Are you going to be all right?"

Popov looked up, and managed a weak smile. "It will take us nearly two days to get to Dnepropetrovsk where we transfer to the Peninsula Railway. In that time I will rest. By then I will be able. You will see."

Briggs pulled the lower bunk down, and Popov was asleep even before the train pulled out of the depot. Once they had cleared the downtown area, Briggs slid down the shade, and sat looking out the window as he smoked the terrible Russian cigarettes that were mostly cardboard filter, and drank the whiskey that Chiles had given him.

They were on their way out, and he had done what had been asked of him. Yet he was vaguely dissatisfied. He had made a terrible mistake with Lydia Savin. He knew that now. When he had the chance he should have taken her into the Embassy. They could have figured some way of getting her out of the country. But he had hesitated. It cost Lydia her life.

By late afternoon they had finally passed out of the huge industrial area surrounding Moscow, and finally into the rolling hills of potato farms and sugar beet fields.

Popov awoke briefly, and sat up long enough for Briggs to feed him some cheese, bread and wine, then he laid back again.

Afterwards Briggs had some of the food and then around eight or nine, he pulled down the top bunk and crawled up under the blankets.

He had a troubled sleep, his dreams flitting vividly back and forth between Arkadi urinating on him, to Lydia's body lying in a pool of blood. Over all of that was the nagging fear that they would never get out of the Soviet Union alive.

By the next morning they had come far enough south and west so that the snow of Moscow had changed to a cold drizzle. Even with daylight there was little to see out the windows, other than the misty, waterlogged fields.

They ate more of the bread and cheese, and a small portion of the sausage, Popov relieved himself in a small chamber pot in the tiny cubicle, and Briggs emptied it out the window.

Afterwards they settled down to watch the countryside slowly roll by.

In the afternoon, Popov spent a couple of hours writing poetry, the drizzle changed to a very hard rainfall and Briggs decided to leave the car and look around the train.

Popov was busy again with his poetry, so he barely looked up as Briggs unlocked the door, and looked out into the corridor. There was no one there at the moment.

"Lock this as soon as I'm gone. Don't open it for anyone," Briggs said.

Popov sat with his feet up, his dress half open and his wig lying on the floor. He looked up and nodded. "Sure," he said.

Briggs slipped out into the corridor, and went down to the end of the car where he stepped out onto the connecting platform. It was sharply colder outside, but the air smelled freshly scrubbed. He lit himself a cigarette, glad for the moment to be out of the stuffy compartment.

Early tomorrow morning they would reach Dnepropetrovsk where they would transfer to the Yalta train. That night they would be there.

He had the nagging premonition of doom, though, that grew as he remained on the platform, smoking his cigarette.

Once in Yalta they would go immediately to the shipyard where Higgins' contact was located. They would not risk checking into a hotel. Their passports would be turned over to the local police, and it would not take very long for it to be discovered that they were fakes. If anything happened to delay their departure they could be in big trouble.

Briggs glanced at the door back into his car. His

stomach was churning. There was something wrong. He could almost taste it, the feeling was so strong.

He threw his cigarette down, ground it out, then went into his car, and around the corner, holding up there.

The conductor was standing at the open door to his compartment. He was saying something. Christ!

Briggs pulled out his stiletto, and keeping it hidden at his side, stepped around the corner, and hurried down to where the conductor was standing.

The man turned as Briggs came up. He seemed smugly self-satisfied. "Here he is now," he said to someone in the compartment.

"What is going on here?" Briggs blustered. The train lurched, and he used the motion to fall against the conductor knocking him into the compartment.

Briggs followed, kicking the door closed just as a large man, dressed in a baggy gray suit looked up, and then started around, an automatic in his hand.

The conductor was in the way. Briggs shoved him aside, to the left, as he swung around to the right with the stiletto, catching the armed man in the chest just below his left breast. His gun was pointed downward, and spasmodically he jerked the trigger as he died, the weapon firing harmlessly into the floor. But the noise was very loud, and the conductor began to shout for help.

## THIRTY-THREE

Briggs yanked the stiletto from the dead man's chest, and with his free hand slammed the conductor against the wall, bringing the blade to within a fraction of an inch of his throat.

The man shut up instantly.

"Who was he?" Briggs snapped, motioning toward the dead man.

"KGB," the frightened conductor squeaked.

"What was he doing here?"

The conductor balked. Briggs nicked his neck with the tip of the blade.

"Looking for two escaped mental patients," he stammered.

"Was he alone?"

"There is one other. A policeman from Moscow."

Damn, Briggs thought. They had just run out of time. If they were on this train, then they must have guessed that he and Popov would also be on it. No matter what happened now Yalta was out.

Goddamnit. They were on their own.

"We have to get to Yalta . . . no matter what," Briggs said to the bewildered Popov. Then he stepped back, sheathed his stiletto and clipped the conductor on the jaw. The man went down hard, his head bouncing off the edge of the lower bunk.

Briggs quickly locked the door, then lowered the shade, and the window and looked outside.

It was getting dark out, but he could see that they were not moving too fast. Probably less than twenty miles per hour. It was farm country out there; very few houses or any other buildings, and only an occasional patch of trees. It reminded Briggs a lot of Kansas or western Nebraska.

He turned back, and quickly threw their things back in the suitcase.

"What is it . . . what are we going to do?" Popov asked. He was shaking now. Not only had his treatment at the center weakened his body, it had already begun to seriously affect his mind.

"We're getting off the train," Briggs said. He tossed the suitcase out the window, and with no ceremony or warning, bodily lifted Popov and shoved him out the window, feet first. "Roll with it when you hit the ground," Briggs shouted.

"No . . ." Popov wailed, but Briggs let him go.

Someone banged at the door as Briggs climbed out the window, and dropped, pushing himself away from the train. He hit on the edge of the ditch, tumbling end over end down into the water at the bottom, the train flashing by overhead.

He waited there in the bottom of the ditch for the train to pass, then he jumped up and ran back up the ditch. Popov was just picking himself up.

"Are you all right?" Briggs shouted.

Popov looked up. He was dazed, but seemed not to be too seriously banged up. He nodded uncertainly. "You killed that man."

"It was him or us," Briggs said.

It took him nearly five minutes to find the suitcase, and then he led Popov up the other side of the ditch and they started across the muddy field toward the southeast, as the dusk deepened and night came.

By now they had probably stopped the train and were heading back along the tracks on foot. Either that or they had telegraphed ahead.

But Yalta was to the southwest. If the conductor had believed him, the search would be concentrated in that direction. At least initially.

As they trudged through the early evening, Briggs bone weary and still sore from his beating, and Popov all but dead on his feet, Briggs tried to remember as much of his geography as he could. The Black Sea was about seven hundred miles east to west and a couple of hundred miles wide. To the north and east was the Soviet Union. To the west was Rumania and Bulgaria, and to the south, over the entire length of the sea was Turkey . . . from Istanbul and the Bosporus that led toward the Mediterranean all the way east to the border with Georgia.

If the search was to be concentrated toward Yalta to the southwest, then Briggs would take Popov to the southeast, they'd get across to Turkey themselves.

It took them two hours before they came to the paved highway raised above the general level of the

392

fields. They scrambled up to it, and Briggs looked both ways down the road. There was nothing. No lights. No buildings. No movements, no silhouettes against the overcast night sky. Nothing but darkness in every direction.

The wind was blowing, it was cold (although it had stopped raining) and they were wet from where they had tumbled into the water at the bottom of the ditch beside the tracks. It seemed not only lonely out here, to Briggs, the countryside seemed alien. This was a different Russia than he had been brought up on. These were the plains of suffering. This was where the peasants, exploited by the czars and the revolution, lived. No one understood these people . . . except themselves.

"I must rest," Popov croaked. He would not be able to go on much longer.

Briggs laid the suitcase on the pavement, opened it and pulled out men's clothing for Popov, who got dressed as quickly as he could. When he was finished, he pulled a knit cap over his shaved head.

There was no one out here. They could have been on another planet, or in the middle of some wilderness. And yet they were standing on a paved highway in the middle of a vast area of cultivated fields.

Briggs closed the suitcase and up-ended it so that Popov could sit down.

They could not wait out here, exposed like this, for too long. The search would by now be widening. First to the southwest, but then to the southeast and all around the compass.

A light flashed way off to the west, then was gone. Briggs had caught it just in the corner of his eye. He turned to look that way now.

"What is it?" Popov asked.

"I saw a light. I think someone is coming." Briggs continued to stare toward the west, and he saw it again. Gradually it divided into a pair of lights . . . headlights, that came steadily closer.

"What if it's the authorities," Popov said, getting to his feet.

"Could be," Briggs said absently as he watched the progress of the lights. But he did not think so. Whatever was coming toward them was moving too slowly for that. Besides, he didn't think they'd be looking in this direction yet. They'd still be on the other side of the tracks.

They stepped off the side of the road as the lights finally materialized into an ancient Ford flatbed truck loaded with cages of chickens. It slowed down and stopped.

Briggs hurried around to the driver's side. "Good evening, Comrade, I will need to borrow your truck." He jumped up on the running board.

"What is this?" the driver, a burly man with a barrel chest and gray hair, shouted. "Are you a highway robber?"

"We mean you no harm. But we must use your truck."

The driver looked over as Popov struggled up to the road with the suitcase, then he looked back at Briggs, and he seemed to come to some decision. "You are running from the authorities."

Briggs nodded after a moment. "Yes, comrade. From Moscow. My friend and I were in . . ."

"I do not want to hear it. I will take you wherever

394

you wish to go. But you will drive. You have kidnapped me. It was terrible. There was nothing I could do about it.''

The man slid over, away from the wheel. Briggs looked at the man. With this kind of a Russian, or American or Brit, he had no argument.

He jumped down, and hurried around to the other side of the truck, where he helped Popov. The driver jumped down, and between him and Briggs they got Popov and the suitcase up to the cab. The driver took the window and Briggs went around and climbed up behind the wheel. He had to double clutch to get the truck in gear, but then they were heading smoothly down the road, the engine roaring and the chickens cackling.

Popov was worn out, and his head sagged forward, his chin on his chest.

They drove like that for a half an hour or more before the burly man sat forward and looked over at Briggs. ''Where do you go?''

''To the west.''

''Turkey?''

''Yes,'' Briggs said. ''We thought maybe we could get a boat at Rostov.''

The farmer shook his head. ''You'd have to get out of the Sea of Azov through the straits by the military base at Kerch'.''

''Then where?''

''Kobuleti or Batumi. There are a lot of military there, from what I hear, but you could get a boat and get through. At night. If you were careful.''

Briggs drove a while longer in silence. The countryside was virtually unchanged, the road nearly straight.

395

They had passed no traffic.

"Why do you tell this to me?"

The farmer said nothing.

"My friend and I . . . we could be desperate criminals."

"I think not."

They drove awhile again in silence, until the farmer pulled out a bottle of wine from beneath the seat, took a deep drink, and passed it over to Briggs.

It was sweet but very good, tasting like rhubarb, but with a powerful kick. It had been fortified with grain alcohol.

"It's very good," Briggs said, taking a second drink and passing the bottle back.

The farmer laughed. "It is a long trip to Batumi. All of this night and all of tomorrow. If we are lucky."

"And what of you when we get there?"

"That depends upon the authorities," the farmer laughed even louder.

"I will pay you for your truck and your petrol and your time."

"Oh yes you will," the farmer said. "I am too poor to help, so you will help me. It will be a good exchange."

The farmer's cynicism reminded Briggs of the cavalier attitude Americans had about their own government . . . especially their taxes. Here in the fields of the Ukraine, it was no different than around Des Moines, or Lincoln or St. Joseph. . . . or for that matter some parts of Norfolk to the northeast of London.

Around midnight, when their fuel was low, they

stopped, and the farmer went around back where he pulled out two large carboys of gasoline, which Briggs emptied into the tank, and they continued.

Around six in the morning they crossed the border back into what was known as European Russia, and by eight, they were in the middle of the morning traffic rush of Rostov . . . a city of three-quarters of a million people. There was a lot of hustle-bustle in the city. They crossed the Don River at 8:30 and by 9:00 A.M., they were back in the open countryside to the south, heading straight down to Krasnodar, in swamp country.

Mile by mile they headed south. They had stopped around three in the morning and again around 10:00 A.M., so that they could all get out, stretch their legs, and relieve themselves at the side of the road.

Popov was not doing well, and at times Briggs was concerned that he would die before they got out and he could be hospitalized.

The farmer held the same concern.

"I am afraid for your friend."

"I am too. But we must not stop."

"I understand. It is better to die on the run, then live in burden."

"It sounds like you keep oxen," Briggs said, remembering the things he had been taught.

The farmer laughed again. "No. But in the old days we did. My grandparents lived along the river. They were bargment. They all had oxen to do the work."

Briggs was tired, and battered and a bit frightened. He had been through a lot. Not just here on this assignment, but he had been through more than a lifetime of hell. From his days as a child when his mother struggled to support him and her brother, to his harsh days as a young man with the emigrés in London's difficult Soho district, to what he considered his "gray" period, in which he wandered the United States impersonating one man after the other.

It had been lonely. And now, rushing through a totally alien countryside, Briggs had to wonder what he was rushing toward.

Rudyard Howard, Sir Roger's friend, and the head of this entire operation, had assured him that once it was all over, Briggs would automatically become a U.S. citizen. No longer would he be on the run. No longer would he always have to be looking over his shoulder, always leaving himself a bolt hole, always keeping papers and currency available in case he had to run.

He would belong. Christ, what a concept. He would actually belong somewhere for the very first time in his life.

But did he believe it? Could he believe it? This was a strange business he was in, where lies were an operational necessity, and the truth oftentimes was fatal.

Was the carrot Howard and Sir Roger had dangled in front of him an operational necessity? Or was it the truth? A truth he could live with.

They came into Sochi, a town of a quarter of a million people on the coast a little before six, where they stopped for dinner at a small café on the outskirts of town.

By 7:30 they were back on the road, and Briggs was beginning to get the feeling that he had always been on the road, and would always be.

Popov came awake from time to time, would

mumble something indistinct about Lydia, and then would lapse into unconsciousness again. The farmer had a bottle of water in the back, and from time to time they stopped to give Popov a drink. Briggs did not want the man to dehydrate. In his condition that would be fatal.

And still they drove on. The country seemingly going on forever. The Black Sea to their right, the farmland and the swamps to their left.

Batumi was dark, except for the docks, when they arrived sometime around midnight. There were two large ships in port, evidently with orders to load around the clock. Crews were busy at the ships which were lit up with spotlights like a broadway production, and a steady stream of trucks kept the thoroughfare to the quay very busy.

Briggs gave the farmer a thousand rubles, which the man held in his hands for a very long time. He looked up, finally, an odd expression in his eyes, and handed seven hundred back.

"A thousand rubles are trouble," he said. "Three hundred, and I will be blessed for my good fortune. God go with you."

He and Briggs shook hands, and the farmer climbed up in the cab of his truck, with the promise that he would drive back up to Krasnodar before contacting the police, and then he was gone.

Batumi was like any waterfront city the world round. Money was king. No questions were ever asked. For someone like Briggs, who had lived and operated in a rough neighborhood for all of his youth, finding his way around this town was simple.

By two in the morning he and Popov were aboard a very small fishing-sailboat, two large tins of water and a loaf of bread along with a hand-bearing compass for ten thousand rubles—the last of Briggs' cash, and they were heading out to sea, the waves short and choppy with the brisk winds from the northeast.

Twice, as they headed the twenty-five miles or so to the southwest, Soviet patrol boats passed within a couple of hundred yards of them. But their boat was very small, their sail black, and the night very dark, and they escaped notice.

The rest was a blur. What was actually hours, seemed like days to Briggs who was cold, tired, sore and hungry. Popov remained unconscious in the bottom of the boat, and had absolutely no idea of what they were going through or what could possibly have happened to them.

Dawn broke gray, on a mountainous looking terrain for miles away.

The wind had all but died, but the currents took the small sailboat gradually ashore around noon, where they were met by a half a dozen Turkish soldiers, their rifles at their shoulders.

"American," Briggs kept saying. "I am an American. My people are waiting for me at Sinop."

## EPILOGUE

The BOAC 707 touched down at London's Heathrow Airport a little after four in the afternoon. Briggs was processed through customs with no hitch, and within a half an hour he was riding in a cab into the city. The weather was overcast and rainy.

"Been like this for long?" Briggs asked, the English sounding oddly flat to his tongue.

"It's been bleeding hell for the past week," the cabby complained. "I mean, I don't mind a little rain, but this is too much, if you catch my drift."

Briggs smiled and sat back with a cigarette. Popov would be all right . . . physically. They had brought him to a hospital outside Paris where the doctors said he would have to remain for at least a week. The plan was to eventually move him to the states for a very long series of de-briefings. He had worked with the British for a number of years, including the traitor Peter Houten, but it had been the Americans who had put up the rescue operation.

Briggs had not been back to the States yet. He had some unfinished business here in London first, and then down at Tunbridge-Wells.

Sir Roger and Rudyard Howard were waiting back in Washington, along with Burt Higgins, Chiles and White and the rest of the crew. They'd spend the next few weeks out at the school, hashing through the entire assignment.

Higgins had been fascinated by what he called: "End runs, played by ear." Whatever the hell that meant.

There were a number of other things that would have to be cleared up in the coming weeks—"administrative details," Higgins called them.

All hell was breaking loose at the moment in Moscow over the escape of two of their prisoners. The involvement of the American Embassy had to be covered as much as possible so that a full-blown international incident did not arise.

Besides that, and of course Popov's treatment and de-briefing, there was, of course, the matter of Peter Houten.

For a moment absolutely nothing was supposed to happen to the man. The British wanted to study the situation a bit longer, to see if Houten was of any possible use.

Of course if he tried to jump, they'd stop him. But so far he seemed content to work at one of the SIS annexes off Victoria Street across from St. James Park.

He was working as an analyst on the Soviet desk, and from everything Higgins had heard, the man was doing an outstanding job, although no one seemed able to answer the inquiries as to how he had managed to move from Moscow with absolutely no notice, directly into a desk job in London.

This afternoon in Paris, before Briggs had left for the airport, Higgins had taken him aside.

"Go to London, if you want, Briggs. See Oumi and your old friends. But the word has come down that you are to stay strictly away from Peter Houten.''

Briggs smiled. "Whatever gave anyone the idea I was going to London to see Houten?"

"Don't try to con me, Briggs. I know you better. Houten is a son of a bitch. No one argues the point with you, but the British have other plans in mind for him.''

"The son of a bitch, as you call him, Burt, not only sucked Popov down the tubes, he was responsible for the death of a very nice lady.''

"Lydia Savin.''

Briggs nodded.

"I'm sorry about that. We all are . . .''

"Bullshit," Briggs said interrupting. "You didn't know the woman. None of you did. She was a fucking sacrificial lamb . . . Peter Houten's.''

Higgins shook his head in frustration. "I can only repeat what I've already told you, Briggs. Stay the hell away from Peter Houten. If he turns up dead, and you were anywhere near him at the time, you'll take the fall and there won't be a damn thing I can do to help you . . . despite the fact the bastard deserves to be taken out.''

Briggs smiled. "See you in Washington.''

"By the way, Sylvia Hume is no longer in the States.''

"Did she go back home?''

Higgins nodded. "Sir Roger said she could not take the suspense any longer. It was worrying her too badly.''

"Thanks," Briggs said, and he had left. At Orly Field, outside Paris, he had telephoned a number Oumi had given him, had left a message and a request, and now riding into London he hoped there had been time enough to set everything up.

The cabby dropped him off at Victoria Station, where Briggs went into one of the men's rooms, took his stiletto out of his suitcase, strapped it on, then went back upstairs where he checked his bag in a locker.

Outside, he hunched his coat collar up, bought a London Times from a kiosk, put it under his left arm (a bit melodramatic, he thought) and headed up toward Victoria Palace and the Royal Mews.

He was joined almost immediately, by an incredibly old man in a dark raincoat, a bowler and an umbrella.

"It's all set up," the man said, walking slightly behind and to the right of Briggs. No one would guess that they were talking.

"Where do I pick him up?"

"Outside his office in the next block. He gets out in another ten minutes, and walks two blocks up to where he keeps his automobile in the government car park. You must leave him at the last intersection. Is it clear?"

"Yes," Briggs said without moving his lips.

"Do you know what he looks like?"

"I've seen photographs."

"He'll be wearing exactly the same thing I am right now."

Briggs glanced over at the man, smiled, then turned right, crossed the street and hurried down to St. James Park, where again he crossed the street, and then waited.

Peter Houten came out of the SIS Annex building right on schedule. He was alone, and Briggs came smoothly up behind him.

"Greetings, Mr. Houten, from Vladi and Lydia and

everyone at Porfiri's.''

Houten stumbled, and almost fell, but he did not turn around, or stop. "Who the hell are you?" he said when he had recovered. "What do you want?"

"Nothing except the answer to why Lydia was murdered.''

"I don't know what . . ."

Briggs cut him off. "Why was she murdered, you bastard?"

"I have absolutely no idea what you are talking about, old chap.''

"The game is over, Houten. I just wanted you to know that. I wanted to watch you squirm.''

Houten stopped short, and turned to face Briggs. "See here fellow, I don't know what your game is, but if you don't get away from me I shall call a policeman and have you arrested.''

Briggs smiled. *"Goodbye, Comrade,"* he said in Russian, and he turned and walked away.

At the end of the block, Briggs stopped and looked back. Houten was hurrying down the street.

Briggs turned back, crossed the street, and followed the man.

Just before Westminster Abbey, Houten turned left, and started across the busy street. Briggs spotted the delivery truck just approaching the intersection, and he stopped to watch, with grim satisfaction.

The truck bore down on Houten, who at the last minute looked up, realized what was happening, and threw his hands out as if to protect himself.

The impact threw him fifty feet up the street into the path of an on-coming truck that ran over his body. Women were screaming, and a horn was blaring, as

Briggs stuffed his hands in his pockets and headed back to Victoria Station to retrieve his suitcase, and catch a train.

It was raining furiously and pitch dark when Briggs got off the train at Tunbridge-Wells and hired the lone cab sitting at the station.

"Sir Roger Humes' place. South out of town, I believe," Briggs told the driver.

"You expected, sir?" the driver asked suspiciously.

"No. But I am an old friend of the family's. Sir Roger is still in the States. I've come out to see Sylvia."

"Right," the driver said, smiling. He started the cab, and they pulled away from the station. "Known them long, you say?"

"Yes," Briggs said. "Sir Roger is what you might call my employer."

"You work for the old gentleman, then?"

"After a fashion," Briggs said. His heart was hammering, his mouth was dry and his stomach was churning.

"I'm sure I don't quite understand that, sir," the driver mumbled, and then fell silent as they headed out of town, down a narrow, very dark country lane.

It was possible that she would not be home. It was also possible that she resented the hell out of him for what happened at Howard's house before he had left.

Christ, he was acting like a schoolboy now, he told himself. He could not get involved with a woman. Not now. Not yet. Not until he had his own life straightened out.

He had no real idea what was going to happen to

him over the next months. It was very possible that Howard would renege on his promise, and Briggs would be on the run again. Or it was possible that his involvement with Houten's death would be discovered, and he would be prosecuted for that. Burt Higgins had warned him to stay away. And it was very possible that Sir Roger himself would forbid any relationship with Sylvia.

The cabby turned off the road and headed slowly up a bumpy gravel driveway. In the dark Briggs could just make out a white fence on both sides of the driveway. And in the distance ahead, he could see the lights of the house.

He took a deep breath, held it a moment in an effort to relieve the tightness in his chest, then let it out.

They pulled up at the front door. "Will you be wanting me to wait for you, sir?" the cabby asked.

"No. If I need you I'll telephone," Briggs said, paying the man.

"Just tell the operator. She'll find me."

"Thanks," Briggs said. He climbed out of the cab, and bag in hand went up on the porch, and rang the bell.

He could hear music from within the house, and he could smell wood smoke coming from the chimney.

The cab headed away, its taillights lost in the distance as Briggs reached out to ring the bell again. But the door opened and Sylvia was standing there, in bluejeans and a tattered sweatshirt, her long dark hair hanging loose.

"Hello," Briggs said softly.

"Oh . . . God," she cried, and Briggs dropped his suitcase as she came into his arms, everything at long last, wonderful.

407

# PROLOGUE OF THE NEXT MAGIC MAN ADVENTURE

## THE GAMOV FACTOR

The bulky, black limousine purred up the long, curving drive toward the imposing building that sprawled between two small birch forests outside Moscow. Built before the Revolution as a refuge for aristocracy from the heat and smells of the capital city in summer, ravaged by war then neglect, it had been restored to its former splendor and presented to Ilya Alexandrovich Gamov as a reward for his loyalty and service, and as a mark of his high rank. To call it simply a dacha was gross understatement, and in fact, few did. It was Ilya's Palace, to even the common man; everyone knew who Gamov was, the number three man at the Kremlin, with aspirations for first place, and the trust of the ailing Leonid Brezhnev.

The limousine pulled up near a side entrance, under what had formerly been a protective arch between the main house and a small, subsidiary carriage house. The driver jumped gingerly from the car. He carried no passenger, but brought from the rear seat a small package wrapped in brown paper, that was sealed with red wax, an ornate G design pressed into it.

The driver found no need to knock; the door was

opened to him before he had made the steps, and he was greeted by a dark haired young man, no more than twenty-six or twenty-seven, who had obviously been waiting for him.

"This is the delivery from Marakov, then?" the young man inquired, holding out his hand to accept the package. There was a tired resignation in his voice, rather than the elation the driver would have expected.

"It is," the driver said. He placed the package in the young man's hand. "He said to tell you it's the best quality yet for sound and clarity." He waited for some reaction, perhaps a question, or even the courtesy of a thank you, then turned to leave when none was forthcoming.

As he opened the limousine door he called back to the young man, who was re-entering the dacha: "Marakov will want to know what he thinks when he's finished with it."

The young man nodded and went inside. The driver shrugged, climbed back into the limousine and left.

Inside, the young man walked quietly along one of the two central halls on the first floor that crosscut the building, coming at length to the massive, central foyer. Shaped like an inverted bowl, ornately decorated with murals, gold etchings and hard carved woodwork, it seemed more a museum than a residence. The presence of a small desk next to the wide, marble stairs that swept down from the second floor in an arc, was jarring and out of place, but necessary. Three shifts of security people were required to protect the master of this house each day, whether he was in residence or working in Moscow. The captain of each shift directed his men from this vantage point, making full use of radio communications with each, and monitoring the corridors and grounds via a bank of small television screens.

The captain of this evening's shift, Yuri Provnenko, a bluntly built man of forty-five, looked up as the young man approached. The motion flipped his unruly brown hair up at the crown, and when he moved again, his hair maintained the same stance in spite of the lanoline creme he had layered into it.

"We have another bit of entertainment, Reza?" he asked. The young man nodded. Not very talkative tonight, Provnenko thought. He did not care whether Reza was an aide to Gamov or not; he didn't like Muslims, didn't trust them, and didn't think they belonged in sensitive positions.

"Will you be taking it up to him?" Provnenko prodded.

"I suppose so," Reza replied flatly. "We will need the video equipment."

"It's still there from the last time. In the study antechamber." Those dark eyes, he thought, impossible to read. No way to tell what's going on behind them. No way to know what he thinks, or what he might be planning.

Reza walked slowly, resignedly up the staircase, looking straight ahead all the way, then turned to the right when he reached the top. The second floor corridor, running across the house, was more subdued in decoration than the first floor, but plush and formal nevertheless. Oak chair rails dissected the walls between floor and ceiling, with gold-swirled paper on the top and polished oak on the bottom. Heavy wooden doors broke the pattern of the hall in both directions, and at intervals there were chairs for security persons on watch.

These extreme precautions were not usually required. It was normally sufficient to maintain the monitors and roving patrols of both house and grounds, but on some occasions, Gamov had felt the need of armed men just outside his door. For special interviews with special Politburo members and other high ranking citizens.

Reza stopped at the second to the last door on the left, hesitated, then rapped sharply three times.

"Enter," Gamov said from within. He was not a man to waste words.

"Marakov's video cassette is here," Reza told Gamov, or rather his back, as he entered the man's private study. Gamov was seated behind a large walnut desk, his leather-upholstered chair swiveled around toward the wall.

"Excellent," Gamov said, swinging around to face Reza. He placed his elbows on the desk, and leaned forward, his gray eyes coming to life. Reza had noticed that about his superior early on, that those gray eyes seemed dead until the scent of prey—skewered, helpless—sparked life into them. It was a sick and twisted life; Reza preferred the flat, slate-colored stare of the ranking bureaucrat.

"I'll just go into the antechamber, then," Reza told him, crossing the room. The study had at one time in the distant, Czarist past been the quarters of a doubtless devoted nanny, and the antechamber nursery for her small charge. The only entry and exit to that room was through the study; Gamov's main reason for choosing this as his primary work room at the dacha.

411

Gamov followed his aide, stretching as he stood to his full height, just a shade over six-feet-four. Slender, muscular, with thick but perfectly groomed silver hair, Gamov could incite fear in the broadest, most hardened men. It was not so much his physical presence, for at fifty-four some stooping of the shoulders could be detected. No, he seemed instead to give off a not quite definable aura of impending devastation. He was lean and hungry . . . a dangerous man.

Reza switched on a table lamp adjacent to two comfortable chairs, which were arranged before a small television set. Nearby, with leads attached to the monitor, was a video recorder/player, one of the newer advances in Soviet technology not yet available to the masses. Gamov seated himself as Reza slipped the cassette into place and started the tape. The image of a small bedroom came onto the screen, and Gamov reached for the lamp, turning it off.

"I want to miss nothing, not one detail," he said, as if the lack of light would have enhanced the screen image. Reza silently seated himself next to Gamov.

"Look," Gamov tapped Reza's knee, but kept his eyes on the screen.

Reza saw a plain room, probably in a hotel or nondescript apartment in Moscow, with a double bed in central position, a nightstand nearby, and a door on the far side of the bed. The door opened, slowly, and a man and a woman came into view. Both were nude. The man was behind the woman with one hand on her breast.

"Chernyev," Reza whispered, shocked, though he should not have been. He had seen enough films and videos, and still shots, in this room, to make the most

412

naive person turn sarcastic. But he had never expected to see Ivan Cherynev in any of them. He had been Brezhnev's first appointment to the Politburo. A shining example of the best of the Revolution could produce, beyond reproach, immune to blackmail by virtue of his dedication and morality.

"There is more," Gamov said pointing to the television, redirecting Reza's attention.

As Chernyev sprawled across the bed, the woman took the aggressive role, licking and biting her way down his chest to his groin. A movement off to the side of the screen caught Reza's eye, and he watched as another woman, blonde and slender and good looking just like the first, joined the pair on the bed, straddling Chernyev's face, then running her hands through the politician's hair to direct his movements.

"This is hardly in keeping with Chernyev's solid, grand-fatherly image," snickered Gamov. The figures shifted position, and Gamov remarked in delight, "See the belly? He's soft . . . soft and fat and off guard." He tapped Reza rapidly on the arm. "The sound. Turn it louder."

Reza obeyed, and the moaning of the people on the screen filled the room. Chernyev reached orgasm, the proof of which showed around the mouth of the first woman they had seen. The other woman—they were so alike, they could be twins—would not let Chernyev go, just yet, not until she too had been satisfied.

"Virna," they heard the first woman whisper, pulling at her accomplice and flopping next to Chernyev on her back. "Do not forget me," She parted her legs and held out her arms. The second woman pulled herself off and kissed her deeply while

413

Chernyev directed himself to her satisfaction.

"Does this excite you . . . just a little?" Gamov asked Reza, looking at him peripherally, but missing nothing on the screen.

"Not particularly." Reza did not turn toward his superior to answer, yet he replied honestly. He had seen too much of this kind of thing to be titillated by it.

"Women," Gamov said with disgust. "Breeding stock, that is their purpose. They cannot offer the things a man needs. They cannot understand a man." He stood abruptly, turned off the video and rewound the tape, then handed it to Reza. "Add this to our collection," he instructed.

Reza strode back into the study and stepped behind Gamov's desk. Only he and Gamov knew the combination to the safe secreted behind the wall there; a safe so large that it could constitute a small room in its own right. It had been built at Gamov's direction, to his specifications, and would only open when the correct codes had been punched into a numbered electronic device mounted under the desk.

Reza pushed the series and stood back as the wall slid to one side, then he stepped into the vault.

It was fireproof, bombproof, watertight, perfect for preserving Gamov's most valued documents, tapes, films and photographs for centuries—though far less time would elapse before the contents would be put to use.

Everything was labeled with subject, date and summary of contents stacked in alphabetical order on steel shelves.

Reza pulled a pen from his vest pocket and marked the date and Chernyev's name on the cassette. He paused and added: *ménage a trois*. It sounded less vulgar in French, somehow, than it wculd have in Russian. He felt ill. Chernyev had been his personal hero from the time he was a youngster, though he had never had an opportunity to know the man personally. This was a man above corruption, and ideal to be emulated. Reza sighed. Another fallible, aging, overweight fool trying to live out his fantasies while he was able. And playing right into Gamov's hands. He wondered how long it would take Gamov to arrange a private conference here with Chernyev, and whether he would feel the need of guards at the door when they met.

"I have them all, now." Gamov's voice behind him made Reza jump; he hadn't heard him approach, had been too involved in his own thoughts.

"All?" he echoed. He placed the cassette on the appropriate shelf, then turned toward Gamov.

"The Politburo," Gamov replied. Five seats vacant, and I have all the opposition now with Chernyev. It will be mine."

"But the military . . ." Reza reminded him.

"Enough. I have enough of them one way or the other," he nodded toward the shelves lining the vault. He looked intently at Reza, straight through him, it seemed. "And you are disturbed about this?"

"Disappointed." Reza chose his words carefully. "I admired Chernyev. So did my father. I thought he was above such behavior."

"There may have been a certain amount of, shall we say, cooperation, from the women we saw tonight," Gamov admitted. "How else could we have convinced Chernyev to assist us with recording our

415

entertainment? But no one forced him into anything, and one must wonder how many such instances have occurred over the years, perhaps on a regular basis." He let Reza digest this, then put an arm around the young man's shoulder, nudging him out of the vault.

"The root of Chernyev's problem is obvious." Gamov continued as they stepped back into the study. "Women." He pushed a series of numbered buttons under the desk and the wall slid back into place. "That is one area where your traditions are well founded. Keep them apart, cover them up, don't be distracted by them." He smiled suddenly, sending a chill down Reza's spine.

"It's getting late, sir . . ." Reza began, but was cut off.

"You are correct. We shall retire, then?" He strode to the door, opened it, then turned back to his aide. "Turn off the light. I will wait for you."